Maria Louise Pool

The Red-Bridge Neighborhood

Maria Louise Pool

The Red-Bridge Neighborhood

ISBN/EAN: 9783337047931

Printed in Europe, USA, Canada, Australia, Japan

Cover: Foto ©Andreas Hilbeck / pixelio.de

More available books at **www.hansebooks.com**

THE

RED-BRIDGE NEIGHBORHOOD

𝔄 Novel

BY

MARIA LOUISE POOL

AUTHOR OF "THE TWO SALOMES"
"MRS. GERALD" ETC.

ILLUSTRATED BY

CLIFFORD CARLETON

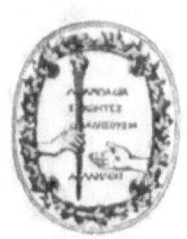

NEW YORK AND LONDON
HARPER & BROTHERS PUBLISHERS
1899

CONTENTS

CHAPTER		PAGE
I.	THE FATHER	1
II.	THE TWO	9
III.	ISABEL	16
IV.	THE MOTHER	23
V.	OLIVE'S CALL	31
VI.	MR. NAWN'S PROPOSITION	37
VII.	ALL OVER	44
VIII.	A LITTLE BALM	54
IX.	LISTENING	61
X.	MR. NAWN AND ROBERT	69
XI.	MRS. NEWCOMB INTERFERES	76
XII.	FORGIVENESS	83
XIII.	MISS RICE AS A WITNESS	90
XIV.	"BRING HER HERE"	97
XV.	MEETING ISABEL	105
XVI.	ENCOURAGING	110
XVII.	THE BUTTER-MOULD	118
XVIII.	INSUBORDINATION	126
XIX.	GOLD	130
XX.	A GIRL IN A SLEIGH	137
XXI.	MONEY LOST	144
XXII.	A STORM	153
XXIII.	AFTER GOLD	158
XXIV.	THE MINISTER CALLS	165
XXV.	ON THE BRIDGE	172
XXVI.	HER BOY	179
XXVII.	A BUNCH OF ROSES	187
XXVIII.	VICTOR	194

CHAPTER		PAGE
XXIX.	COMING COURAGE	200
XXX.	GOSSIP	209
XXXI.	A FIT OF ANGER	215
XXXII.	A FINE FELLOW	223
XXXIII.	THE TWO	230
XXXIV.	WITH ISABEL	240
XXXV.	WITH VICTOR	247
XXXVI.	"I CAME AFTER YOU"	255
XXXVII.	AUNT RUTH	261
XXXVIII.	ROBERT GOES	268
XXXIX.	"YOU'RE A GOOD GIRL."	275
XL.	LOCKING UP	282
XLI.	THE BELL RINGS	289
XLII.	THE ALPHABET	297
XLIII.	"PROMISE"	305
XLIV.	DEATH	313
XLV.	WHERE IS THE NEW MASTER?	318
XLVI.	MR. NAWN'S LETTER	326
XLVII.	ROBERT'S SURPRISE	336
XLVIII.	"IT'S NOT VICTOR"	344
XLIX.	BY THE ROADSIDE	350
L.	A NEW CARE	358
LI.	PEACE	363

ILLUSTRATIONS

"THERE FORMED THE BROAD, HEAVY FACE AT WHICH
    SHE HAD JUST BEEN LOOKING" . . . . *Frontispiece*

"HE TOOK THE HAND THAT WAS SHYLY EXTENDED
    TO HIM" . . . . *Facing p.* 6

"OLIVE WAS LYING ON THE BED WITH HER FACE TOW-
    ARDS THE DOOR" . . . . " 64

"OLIVE'S HEAD WAS UPON ROBERT'S SHOULDER" . . " 98

"SHE DIPPED UP A SMALL MEASURE OF INDIAN MEAL". " 118

"SHE NODDED CARELESSLY TO ROBERT'S 'I'M MUCH
    OBLIGED TO YOU, ISABEL,' AND BEGAN TO TALK
    WITH THIS STRANGER" . . . . " 148

"'PRAY SO THAT GOD WILL HAVE TO HEAR YOU AND
    ANSWER!'" . . . . " 174

"'BOB, WHAT ARE YOU UP TO IN THESE DAYS?'", . " 206

"'OH, ISABEL, WHAT IS IT? HAVE I HURT YOU?'" . " 244

"SHE WENT WITH NOISELESS QUICKNESS TO THE LOUNGE
    AND KNELT BESIDE IT" . . . . " 268

'SHE WALKED TO THE BED AND TOOK THE INERT HAND
    IN HER WARM CLASP" . . . . " 302

"'CAN YOU TELL ME WHERE THE OLD NAWN PLACE IS?'" " 322

"'WHY, IT'S ROBERT!'" . . . . " 360

THE RED-BRIDGE NEIGHBORHOOD

CHAPTER I

THE FATHER

IT was young **Nawn** who was pounding; he was driving tacks into a carpet on the floor of his best room. The hammer, owing to the stillness of the country at this early hour, resounded far over the fields and down the road. It came to the ears of a man who was driving along this road, and who pulled in his horse to listen.

He was an old man, but he looked strong, and good for many years to come. He had a brown face, with straight features and high, narrow forehead. He was not bald, but still retained thick, picturesque gray hair that stood out like a kind of frame. His eyes, when he looked at you, made you, if you were sensitive or had "nerves," wince and wish to turn away.

If you showed this desire on your part, Mr. Nawn senior would smile slightly and make his glance sharper still. But, for all this sharpness, the old gentleman had a great liking for a pretty woman, and a gallant way with one even yet; a pretty woman was made to excite a man's admiration, but a man was a fool who became serious over even the most beautiful of all feminine creations.

1

Mr. Nawn's buggy was very old and shaky; his horse was old too, and the harness was mended with leather strings; but there was a kind of dignity pertaining to the equipage.

This gentleman having stopped his steed, and the steed having immediately fallen to eating the rank grass by the road - side, the sound of pounding was more audible.

"Of course it's Bob," said Mr. Nawn, aloud; "of course he's got up by daylight and come over here to work. I wonder if I was ever like that. I declare, I'm afraid I wasn't. Great thing to be young and in love; only a man doesn't know how great it all is till he gets beyond it." Here the soliloquist reached forward and put a hand on the dasher and a hand on the wheel, and carefully let himself to the ground. "It's a cuss to have to grow old—a regular cuss," he muttered, as he tried to straighten himself after he had planted his feet firmly.

He succeeded so far as to make his tall, bulky form show a sort of impressiveness.

He walked deliberately along by the fence, until he came to a place where the bars had been taken out. He entered this opening, and went on over the rough cart path that led around a hill. Presently he came in sight of a small house, whose doors and windows stood wide open, showing plainly that the building held no furniture.

Through one of these open windows the old gentleman saw the figure of a man in his shirt-sleeves crouching on the floor as he wielded his hammer.

This figure now rose and came forward quickly, with an eagerness of movement that showed expectancy. But this eagerness changed visibly to disappointment, and Robert Nawn said :

"That you, father ? Ain't you out early ?"

Mr. Nawn looked amused at his son's disappointment.

" It seems to me I ain't out so early 's you are, Bob,"
he answered. " Are you looking for Her?—capital H,
you know." Here the speaker chuckled.

Robert frowned, hesitated, then replied that " She
had said she'd come over early if she could get away ;
but it wasn't certain." He added, " She 'ain't seen this
carpet yet, and I wanted to know what she thought
of it."

This young fellow was singularly handsome ; he had
a face almost faultlessly formed, with a sort of Apollo
mouth, which was unobscured by a mustache ; a nose
going in a fine line up to the brows, which were
dark, and arched over blue eyes. You could not find
a fault in the face, save that perhaps the eyes were
too near together. Possibly you would wonder what
would be written on such a countenance, for it was
still too young for much to have been inscribed there.
If you could guess—but no, you wouldn't hazard a
guess.

Mr. Nawn leaned his arms heavily on the window-
casing and gazed about the little room ; and it was a
very little room indeed. There were three pictures on
the walls, chromos of " Life " in three different stages,
illustrated by a person starting out in a bright-blue
boat and meeting some difficulties ; but the difficulties
would probably be surmounted, for in each picture an
angel on a cloud was watching the proceedings of the
human being, with the evident intention of lending a
helping hand now and then.

" I got the carpet over to the Falls Village," said
Robert, with some pride.

" What 'd you pay ?" asked his father.

" Ninety - five cents a yard. It's Brussels, marked
down."

" Too much ; ninety's enough. But you're launch-
ing out tremendous, I should say. Ingrain ought to
be good enough — or plain, painted boards, as to that.

I s'pose you're going to live on love, eh? You know, you ain't going to live on me."

The young man drew himself up, and frowned again. "I'm going to live on my wages," he answered.

"Oh, all right; then I think you were a fool to get a Brussels carpet. You're a fool anyway, Bob, and that's a fact."

Robert Nawn's face flushed. He swung his hammer back and forth in silence for a moment; then he said, "You think everybody who isn't like you, father, is a fool. That ain't fair."

"Ain't it?"

There was something very irritating in the old man's laugh after he had put this question.

Robert's face grew yet more red. He seemed to swallow something before he remarked, mildly, but still with satisfaction in his voice, "They flung in those pictures." He glanced at the things that adorned the walls.

But his father did not glance at them. He was still leaning on the window-shelf and looking at his son. "I don't know nor care about other folks, Bob," he now remarked; "but you *are* like me."

"Am I?"

"Yes; with just a few streaks of your mother, but not enough to amount to anything, I hope. That's why I'm all struck of a heap at your taking that girl, when you might have the other one, that's han'somer, and got some money besides, and that's in love with you into the bargain. Now, you see, I'd take the girl with the money every time. You 'ain't got a penny, and I'm going to live this twenty year; and I may use up all my money, or I may leave it to found an asylum;" here the old man chuckled again. "Hard-hearted fathers leave their money to asylums, don't they?"

"I don't know"—sullenly, from Robert.

"Yes; I've read novels enough to know that. Prime

thing to do, too. Yes, you ought to go to house-keeping on painted floors. Brussels! How much wages do you get ?"

"Eight dollars and a half a week; you know well enough what I get, father."

Robert turned his back, walked to another window, and gazed out of it.

"Didn't know but you'd had a rise, seeing you'd decided to marry, and not marry the right girl, either."

The son flung himself about quickly. He opened his lips as if some hot words had leaped to be spoken. He gasped, but did not speak until he could say in a steady voice: "I saved up a hundred and fifty dollars last year, besides paying my board to you; and if I can do that I can support my wife on my wages. Anyway, I don't mean to apply to you."

"Glad to hear it, 'cause I ain't going to help you. I s'pose you've had to give a mortgage on this little property ?"

"Yes; but I sh'll pay it off."

Mr. Nawn laughed. He drew a quill toothpick from one pocket and a jack-knife from the other. With this latter implement he proceeded to put a finer point on the toothpick, and then to use it on some still sound-looking teeth.

Robert knelt down again on the gay-colored carpet and resumed his work with hammer and tacks. His cheeks were still hot, and his mouth was shut tightly. He was thinking very irreverent things of his father. He drove in a few tacks with vicious emphasis. Then he paused and looked over his shoulder at the man in the window.

"Did you care anything for my mother ?" he asked, suddenly.

Mr. Nawn shut his teeth down on the quill. The next instant he opened his mouth to say, harshly:

"You mind your business, Bob." He turned and

walked towards the rear of the house. He threw his
toothpick away, and went to look at the garden spot,
which was ready to plant.

"That boy must have worked morning and night
over here," he was thinking. "I s'pose he expects to
be happy. That's a kind of thing we mortals seem to
have to go through—to expect to be happy. I went
through it. But the best time I ever had was when I
was piling up dollars. There's some fun in that—
seeing your bank account grow. Yes, some sense in
that."

The man stood, tall and ponderous, with his thumbs
thrust into the armholes of his waistcoat, gazing at the
bit of ploughed land.

In spite of the cynicism in his voice and words, there
was something melancholy in his big face as he looked.

After a moment he moved and grasped the rails in
front of him. He gave his derisive chuckle, and then
he muttered:

"Thinks he's going to be happy, does he? It's
enough to make a horse laugh to see the way a man
tries to be happy."

Though Mr. Nawn was old, he was not deaf, and he
now heard a slight sound in a clump of birches at his
left, a place where Robert had set a hen-coop, and
where already the thrifty young man had induced a
hen to sit on a nest full of eggs.

Mr. Nawn faced about as quickly as he could, and
saw a young woman bending over and looking into the
coop. The man did not move, but stood sharply scrutinizing this figure, which had, seen even in this way, a
grace and attractiveness that were not lost upon the
elderly eyes watching.

"So—so," he murmured under his breath, and he
smiled more softly than he had yet done—so softly, indeed, that his face seemed to lose a great many years
from it, and grow all at once more like that of his son,

" HE TOOK THE HAND THAT WAS SHYLY EXTENDED TO HIM"

whose busy hammer had resumed its steady blows in the house.

"Hullo!" said Mr. Nawn, after he had sufficiently contemplated the girl, who was still peering into the hen-coop.

The girl started erect with the alert motion of a wild animal.

"You needn't be afraid," remarked the man. "It's only the old fellow instead of the young one. Let us shake hands"—walking towards the girl. "I s'pose you're going to marry Bob. He's in there laying a Brussels carpet marked down to ninety-five cents; never was worth more'n ninety, anyway. My sakes!" Here he took the hand that was shyly extended to him, and covered it closely with his other hand. "I declare! Are you little Olive Newcomb that I used to see playing 'round? I 'ain't noticed you since you were grown up."

Olive Newcomb blushed with vivid pleasure because Robert's father was so kind. Robert had been all wrong, then, in thinking that his father did not approve of his son's choice. How could he have been so mistaken?

"I've been living over at the Falls Village with gran'-pa until a little while ago," she now said. "I took care of gran'pa as long as he lived after I was grown up."

Mr. Nawn was gazing delightedly at the face before him. He showed his delight so unmistakably that Olive's heart beat with exquisite gratitude. How very stupid Rob had been! She would tell him. At this thought she blushed still more deeply. Why, she had never met such an agreeable old man! Her grandfather had been deaf and altogether uninteresting.

"Bob's a sly young fox," exclaimed Mr. Nawn. "Why didn't he tell me how Israel Newcomb's daughter had blossomed? I don't see any reason why I shouldn't kiss you, Olive."

So Mr. Nawn bent down and kissed his companion, first on one cheek and then on the other.

Just as he drew back, the girl, with a quick movement, flung her arms about his neck, and for the space of an instant pressed her burning face against his breast.

The old man's eyes sparkled with gratification.

Olive drew back with as quick a motion as she had used in approaching, her face suffused with a beautiful light.

"Oh," she breathed, softly, " you are Rob's father, you know.   I do hope you won't think I'm bold."

" Bold ?"   Mr. Nawn smiled indulgently.   " I think you're the sweetest piece of womankind I've seen in many a weary year."

Olive did not know why she felt like shrinking as she heard these words.   It was as if some unseen hand pressed its fingers on her bosom and pushed her back. She stood still, however.

She was deeply interested in this interview.   She had never seen Roberts's father save as she had seen him drive or walk by her house ; and nobody spoke well of him.   " As tight as old Nawn," " As mean as old Nawn," were phrases she had heard ever since she could remember.

But of course everybody had made a mistake about him.   He was certainly very agreeable.   She had had no idea that an old man could be pleasing.   She thought old men did little but potter about, chewing tobacco and letting the yellow saliva run down the deep wrinkles at the corners of the mouth.

CHAPTER II

MEANTIME the sound of the hammering had stopped in the little house.

Robert Nawn had grown impatient. He dropped his tool and rose to his feet, looked at his watch, and then walked to the window that opened towards the west. It was from that direction that Olive would come if, as she had said, she "could get away." He worked so hard now in the long mornings before his day's labor began, and in the hours of daylight after that labor was done, that he could see Olive but briefly, and this fact was a constant irritation to him. He chafed and felt defrauded when twenty-four hours passed without a moment's interview. He could not go late to Olive's home, for her mother was an invalid, or thought she was, and the elder woman's conviction was that she didn't get sleep enough ; consequently the moment it was really dark the doors were locked, the curtains drawn, and Mrs. Newcomb was in bed.

"I sh'll jest as surely lay awake all night as you go out to walk with Robert," she used to say to Olive, "for I sh'll listen to hear you come in, 'n' then I sh'll be all upset."

So Olive did not go to walk with her lover, and the occasions when she could see him seemed painfully few.

"I won't bear it !" the young man used to say, savagely. Then he would repent, and snatch Olive into his arms as if some one were trying to take her from him. "If I ever do have you for all mine "—tenderly.

She would draw a little away and laugh, but with a blessed light in her eyes. "Then you'll get tired of me, and wish you'd married that Keating girl," she would say. "You know Isabel Keating is said to be dying for you." And Olive laughed again.

Of course it is just a little pleasant for a young man to know that a girl is dying for him, and perhaps Robert looked somewhat complacent, though he hastened to deny the assertion.

"I saw her going by the shop on horseback yesterday," he responded, "and she didn't look at all near to dying. She looked fine, in fact."

"Did she?"

As she asked this question Olive contemplated Robert with an inquiring, persistent gaze. Her face paled a trifle.

"Oh, you dear darling!" he exclaimed, in a whisper, drawing her again to him. "It ain't possible you're foolish enough to be jealous! Are you, sweetheart—are you?"

"Just the smallest particle of a grain," Olive had confessed, recovering her spirits immediately as she felt her lover's arm about her and looked into his eyes. "You know," she added, "Isabel is handsome, she has money, and, best of all, she likes you—that is, they say she does."

"Then I should think," reasoned Robert, triumphantly, "that if I choose to marry you instead of her it is proof enough that I love you."

And so the two liked to talk, as lovers always have talked, and always will while lovers live in this world.

Now this morning Robert found that the time was getting on, and if Olive did not come very soon he would have to go to work in the factory without seeing her. He set his lips together in a fashion he had, and which gave rather a hard look to his face.

"I should think she might try a little more to come,"

he said, aloud, in a bitter voice. He was still bitter from his interview with his father. "And I want her to see this carpet." He glanced down as he spoke. "I do hope she'll like it"—gently. "I think the pink roses spread over the green are real pretty. But she'll know whether it's pretty or not, she has such good taste." He looked about him. "I don't s'pose any two people were ever quite so happy as we're going to be. Father don't understand anything—only dollars."

Remember that this man was not yet twenty-three years old, and at that age it is easy for a lover to believe that no one ever loved as he loves. And when does he not believe so?

He left the house and went to a point where he could see still more plainly along the path which Olive would take if she came. But the bright, dew-wet field with its scattering birches was empty—only birds were flying over it and singing, singing as birds sing of a spring morning when love is new and nests are building.

Robert's heart sank. It was too bad—too bad!

"Now perhaps I sha'n't see her to-night, either. I won't stan' it! I declare I won't stan' it!"

As these words passed through his mind he heard indistinctly the sound of voices at the rear of the house. Had she come and had not hurried to him?

He strode quickly towards the sound. Within sight of his father and Olive he paused to watch them. But unaccountably his face hardened instead of softening.

Olive, without seeing him, yet knew that he had come. She turned away from her companion, and her eyes sought Robert's.

Mr. Nawn laughed a little. "Oh, I'll go instantly," he said. "I won't stay, now She has come—capital S, you know. You haven't much time, Bob. Look out you don't get docked for being late at the factory.

You can't afford to lose ten cents now. Ten cents will buy a loaf of bread."

Mr. Nawn walked as quickly as he could towards the place where his horse was drawing the buggy here and there by the road-side in search of grass.

Robert stood gazing at him until he was out of sight. Then he turned towards the girl, who had come nearer, and whose face was tenderly radiant. She appeared as if she were a part of the bright, joyous morning. An idea that she was a part of it came even to the rather practical mind of the young man.

"You're just lovely!" he exclaimed, in a low voice, gazing raptly at her. "You're like that aurora I was reading about once—only lovelier."

Olive smiled. She dropped a courtesy.

"Thank you, sir," she said. Perhaps she spoke lightly that she might refrain from revealing the emotion that ruled her.

"Only lovelier," he repeated.

"Oh, Robert," she said, just above a whisper, "I'm not, really; but I'm glad you think I am."

"Think so? I know so."

The young man glanced over his shoulder. His father was out of sight. The two were alone in the world in this new day. He made a quick step forward and took Olive in his arms.

"I was so afraid you were not coming," he said. "It did seem as if I couldn't bear it if you didn't come this morning. And yesterday I only saw you at the window. And now I must go in ten minutes. Oh, I hate to go! Sometimes I think I can't leave you. Olive"—with quick change in his manner—"what was father saying to you?"

The girl withdrew herself a little, but took hold of the lapels of Robert's coat. She shook him slightly; she laughed joyously.

"Rob, what a stupid creature you are! Are all men

as stupid as you are? Is it just because you are a man? What made you talk so about your father? He was lovely to me. We shall be the best of friends. Why, I feel quite attached to him already!"

"Do you? That's odd. I s'pose he was sweet to you, wasn't he?"

"Yes. Haven't I just said so? What makes you look like that?"

Olive reached up her hand and drew the tip of her finger down the vertical line that had come between her lover's brows. Then she stepped back, and her face became more sober. "Is your father a deceitful man?" she asked, anxiously.

Robert made an impatient movement. "Father is always horribly nice to a pretty girl," he answered, sharply.

"What!"—with horror—"you don't mean that he is a flirt?"

Robert burst into a loud laugh. "I guess that's what I mean. But I can't stop to explain." He hurriedly looked at his watch. "Come and see the carpet, and tell me what you think of it. It was marked down to ninety-five cents. I was extravagant to get it, but I wanted to please you."

"Dear Rob!"

The half-articulate murmur was rendered still more inarticulate by reason of the girl's being suddenly drawn again into the young man's arms and held tightly there.

It began to seem almost as if the two would not go back to look at the carpet, but Olive disengaged herself and ran forward towards the house. She paused at the door, and glanced in at the gorgeous colors spread out within the room. The carpet was sumptuous, magnificent to her.

"Oh," she cried, "it's fit for a palace!" She turned her glowing eyes towards the eyes that were continually seeking hers. "Dear Rob!" she whispered again. "I'm so happy! It makes me so happy to think you love me."

The two were silent a moment, not looking at the carpet. Robert roused himself.

"I must go. But how can I go? I do wish you could have come earlier! Well, good-bye — good-bye." He stooped and kissed her, kissed her again, then turned abruptly and ran to the fence, vaulted over it, hesitated to call back, "Lock the house and put the key in its place."

"Yes, I will," she answered.

Then Robert ran at the top of his speed through the wet grass, the color rising redly to his face, his blue eyes more deeply blue than ever. In a moment the sound of a town clock, mellow and deliberate, could be heard striking seven, and instantly a sharp steam-whistle sounded some half a mile away. Robert saw the thin stream of vapor rising straight from the pipe into the still blue air.

"Confound it!" he thought, "I sh'll be docked. I do wish she could have come earlier!"

He had dropped into a walk as he had listened, and now he began to run again. Before he reached the factory he saw, off to his right, on the other side of the narrow river, on the road that led to the bridge, an old sorrel horse slowly dragging an old buggy towards the bridge.

"There's father," he thought, with a scowl. "I s'pose he's worth fifty thousand dollars at least, and here I am going to be docked for being a bit late to my work—and paying him board, too. But I'd better pay him board than give him everything I earn, as I did 'fore I was twenty-one. And Olive thinks him lovely!"

He dashed up the steps of the factory, and the next moment had thrown off his coat and put on his thick apron.

As he was buckling the strap about him the foreman came along.

" Late, Robert."

" I know it "—sullenly.

" You see we have to be strict, or nobody 'd be prompt."

The young man answered nothing. His heart burned rebelliously as he began to work.

Away across the fields, at the little house he had left, Olive was standing alone in the carpeted room. Her hands were clasped and hanging down in front of her.

She was gazing at the carpet and smiling vaguely as one smiles whose heart is overflowing with happiness. Her lips were parted, her eyelids drooped.

The sweet air of late May was blowing through the room. Did she hear the birds singing outside, or was the singing of her own heart all that she heard?

A sound of horse's feet cantering in the distance roused her somewhat, though she was not aware that she noticed the sound.

She raised her head, still smiling. She was looking at the carpet.

" The roses are immense—immense," she said, aloud. " But I love them. If we should ever have a mansion, and a hundred carpets, I should love this one best."

The horse's cantering feet came nearer.

CHAPTER III

ISABEL

OLIVE stepped softly across the carpet ; it was as if every step were a caress. She had an inclination to get down on her knees and kiss one of those enormous pink roses, and at the same time she smiled at their incongruity in the bit of a room.

"I suppose a man doesn't know about such things," she said to herself.

She went into the back room, which was the kitchen. Robert had made a sink here, and had put up shelves over it. He was very "knacky" with carpenter's tools. He had bought the place at a bargain. It had been "marked down," like the carpet, for the former owner had been obliged to sell. It was not near a village, and house and land had gone for five hundred dollars. Robert had felt as if his father might easily enough buy it and give it to him. It was a grievance that he had not done so. But the young man had not mentioned this thought to any one. He knew that if he had been going to marry Isabel Keating something would have been done for him. His father never stormed nor scolded, but he had let fall a few words one day which told him that much.

Olive strolled through the house. It had three rooms below and two above.

At the window of the east chamber she knelt down and gazed out. It was a pleasant view. Her eyes roamed over it tenderly. Could it be possible that she and Robert were going to live here? What was she, that a man like Robert should choose her? Tears came into her eyes—happy tears that did not fall.

"I hope God will make me worthy of him!" she said, reverently, aloud.

When her vision had cleared she looked again over the country, which undulated down to the shining river, which was called the Creeper, because it rarely rustled or hurried, but crept softly along between the low hills, rippling sometimes against a stony bank, but usually sliding by a black peat that it had cut straight down. '

Right in front of this window, and more than half a mile away, Olive could see the red bridge that crossed the Creeper, and a few rods of narrow white road leading to the bridge. At the left, and still farther away, she saw the chimneys of the large two-story Nawn place. Though it was large, it was blackened from lack of paint, and some of the roof-shingles blew off in every high wind.

Old Mr. Nawn said that he slept just as well and ate just as well as if his house were newly shingled ; and he guessed he wasn't going to lay out seventy-five or a hundred dollars just to please his neighbors.

Olive's gaze dwelt longest on this building ; then it wandered away and saw, scattered here and there, eight or ten houses, each house standing in the midst of a farm. Nearly three-quarters of a mile away, and not in sight, was the shoe-factory where Robert worked.

This hamlet, almost the whole of it, was visible to the girl as she knelt by the window, and beneath this blue May sky it looked as peaceful as if no one in it had ever known sin or suffering.

"Oh, how beautiful the world is !" exclaimed Olive, delighting to speak the words aloud. "And here I am in my own home—our own home."

She blushed as she spoke, and her head sank down on her arms that rested on the window-ledge.

The sound of the cantering horse, which had died away somewhat, now became quite clear and near as the animal came out from behind the hill that rose at the west.

Olive remembered that she had heard it a moment before. She raised her head and saw a girl on horseback close to the opening in the fence where the bars had been removed.

The horse was now standing still; its rider was gazing intently at the house; then her glance took in the little shed, barn, and the enclosure Robert had made for his vegetable garden. She sat very straight on her horse, her head well up. There was the crimson of exercise on her dark face; her lips were deeply red.

This new-comer had not yet seen the girl at the window; but the girl at the window was staring down with a painful intensity that was yet somewhat guarded, lest it should be surprised, upon her face.

Olive was asking herself, sharply, "Why has *she* come here?"

Suddenly Miss Keating's eyes encountered those looking down at her. A great confusion seemed to envelop her whole person for an instant, but only for an instant. She made a quick, involuntary movement in her saddle, stooped as if to adjust her skirt, then called out, briskly:

"Now this is lucky, Olive Newcomb. I was just wishing somebody were here to show me over the house. Come down and let me in—that's a good girl."

The voice had a curious, commanding ring in it. This quality was nearly always present in Isabel Keating's speech, and it went quite well with her general carriage.

"You can walk right in," replied Olive; "the door's wide open."

"So it is. Stupid of me not to see it at first. It's such jolly good luck that you're here."

Olive rose from her knees. She stood a moment before turning to go down. She passed both hands over her face as if she were brushing some expression from it.

Then, hesitatingly, and as if she hated to do it, she began slowly to descend the stairs. Half-way down she heard a peal of laughter that filled the small building. She began to hurry.

She found Isabel standing in the middle of the room, her tall figure swaying as she laughed, her teeth gleaming, her eyes shining.

"Oh, isn't it funny?" she cried. "It's too funny for anything? I declare!"

Olive grew stiff.

"What is so funny?" she inquired, coldly.

"Oh, you needn't be mad about it!" was the response. "Don't you see? It's this carpet. Look at the size of the roses! Are they six inches across? Only eight of 'em to fill the room—or are there ten? Good gracious! I call it funny. Why, these roses would be large for the floor of a Saratoga hotel parlor. Did Rob select this carpet?"

Olive felt her hands growing cold.

"Yes," she answered. Why did that girl say "Rob"? Olive had hitherto liked Isabel Keating well enough; but now—well, she must try not to be unjust. They had both known Robert Nawn in childhood, and Isabel had been his playmate.

"Oh, you needn't be huffy because I make fun of such a thing as this," went on Isabel. "I'd say as much to Rob as I would to you. I think it's a great joke. Let's have a dance on the carpet and christen it."

Without waiting for any assent, Isabel seized her companion about the waist, and the two waltzed back and forth over the little space.

"It made me think of the only time I was ever at a ball in a hotel," remarked Isabel, when they stood still

again. "So this is where you and Rob are going to
live?"

"Yes."

Olive had a foolish feeling that it was sacrilege to
speak so lightly as Isabel had done.

"It's dreadful small, isn't it? I was riding over to
the great road, and just at the corner back here I happened to think I was near the place Rob bought of
Raymore, so I turned this way. Sha'n't you be just
terribly lonesome 'way out here? The neighbors ain't
so near as they are where you've been used to living."
Isabel's glance roved everywhere, but did not rest on
the face near her. Perhaps she was not so much at
ease as she seemed. "Sha'n't you be lonesome?" she
repeated.

"I don't think I shall be," was the reply.

"Oh, I s'pose you think you won't be 'cause you're
in love"—lightly, and still more sacrilegiously. Isabel
now turned squarely towards her companion, and
laughed as she looked at her. The daring black eyes
did not shrink as they probed the face before them.
"You'll be happy for a few weeks," she said, "then
you'll begin to wonder why in the world you married.
Worse than that, Rob will begin to wonder too. Ain't
you afraid?"

Olive's heart was growing yet colder, but she answered, bravely, "No, I ain't afraid."

"That's because you're ignorant, then. Everybody
speaks that way about marriage, and I guess everybody knows; and Robert's going to be a hard man."

"What do you mean?" indignantly. "You needn't
talk so about Rob!"

"Yes, I will, too. He's going to be a hard man. He
comes of stock that's just like a flint. You won't be any
happier than Rob's mother was—and you know she
wanted to die long before she did die."

Olive turned away; she was white.

"I won't hear any more about the Nawns!" she cried out. Then, impelled to turn back, she exclaimed, "You won't deny that you like Rob yourself. Folks say so, anyway."

The instant that she had spoken thus Olive wished that she could withdraw the words, but they had gone forth. Olive was ashamed.

Isabel drew away a little and did not immediately reply. Olive could not look at her. She stood staring down, and the pink roses made a blur in her sight. Those dear pink roses! Why had this girl come?

At last Isabel spoke. "Do folks say I like Robert Nawn?" she asked, very slowly.

"Oh, Isabel," cried the other girl, remorsefully, "I didn't mean to speak so; it was just horrid of me! I wish you'd overlook it."

"It doesn't make any difference whether I overlook it or not," was the answer. "Did you mean what you said? Do folks say that?"

Olive hung her head. "I've heard folks say it," she responded.

Isabel stood in the middle of the room. She had pulled off her gloves and was now twisting them about in her hands, and she was watching the work of her fingers. Her whole face was flushed, and there was a tender expression about her mouth. Her countenance had undergone an instantaneous transformation. But Olive's head was drooped, and she did not see this change.

Presently she heard Isabel's voice saying, just audibly, "What you heard was right."

"Oh!"

This exclamation burst as if in terror from Olive, who raised her eyes to meet those of her companion. There was a kind of defiance now on Isabel's face, and she met Olive's glance fully. There was a foolish imagining in Olive's heart that there was a literal stream of fire coming from those eyes which looked at her so intently. She moved uneasily. She was tempted to run out of the room, but she did not wish to leave this girl there. She was to lock up the house, and hang the key in the place agreed upon by her and Robert. In the intensity of her feeling at this moment she believed that she should never care for this home as she had cared an hour before.

"Yes," said Isabel, "it was true — it is true. I've cared for Robert ever since I can remember anything."

Olive put out her hand as if warding off something. "Oh, don't—don't !" she cried, in a sharp whisper.

The two girls tried to look at each other, but even Isabel's bold eyes drooped. Olive's swift glance had told her, however, that Isabel's face was at this moment more beautiful and winning than she could have imagined it could be.

The question plunged into her heart by the sight was, "What would Robert think if he should see her face like this?"

"Don't? Why shouldn't I?" returned Isabel. "You needn't think I'm going to tell anybody else. And I never dreamed I could tell you, but somehow I felt as if I must speak just now. You needn't care. You can come and live on these roses, and be as happy as a queen, for a little bit of time—only for a little bit of time."

Here Isabel began to laugh loudly, the sound filling the room and running over into the utter quietness of the yard. But the next moment the laugh had changed to a sob. The girl dropped her gloves and covered her face, swaying as she stood.

CHAPTER IV

THE MOTHER

OLIVE made a step forward as if she would put her
arm about her companion, though she did not do so.
She felt that she could not touch her. But she was sorry
for her; oh yes, she told herself, she was very sorry for
her. At the same time she was thinking that nothing,
no imaginable torture, could have made her thus confess her love for a man who was just going to marry
some one else. She was repelled, but she made a great
effort to conceal that repulsion; the fact that she felt
it made her think herself wicked.

"I can't tell you how sorry I am," she murmured.

Isabel still kept her hands over her face. But soon
she stopped sobbing.

"I don't want any of your pity," she said, indistinctly. Then her hands dropped and she flung up
her head, her eyes flashing through tears.

Olive involuntarily stepped away a few paces.

"But—but," she began, stammeringly, "I can't help
pitying you. It won't do you any harm. I was thinking what if—if 'twas you that Rob loved instead of
me—"

At this point Olive paused, becoming aware of how
stinging such words must be to the girl whom Robert
did not love. She felt helpless.

"Well, you can stop thinking that," remarked Isabel,
brusquely. "You needn't think of me at all. I shall
get on well enough, never you fear." She picked up
her gloves from the floor, and pulled out the fingers

carefully. "I ain't blind," she went on, "even if I do
love Rob Nawn. I know what he is going to be : he
is going to be a hard man. You're starting by just
adoring him. Now I tell you you make a mistake.
Stand up. Hold your own. Oh, I can fancy his grind-
ing a woman to powder. He wouldn't grind me, though.
Come, let's stop this kind of talk. Show me the rest of
the house. You'll have to live awfully close if you live
on Rob's wages. It's trying to love to have to live on
eight dollars a week, you'd better believe. Is that the
kitchen?" looking towards the next room, the door of
which stood open.

"Yes, that's the kitchen. But I don't think I want
to show you."

Olive had tried to refrain from saying these words,
but they seemed, as she thought afterwards, to come in
spite of her. She felt cold and dejected.

Isabel laughed again. She had laughed often during
this interview.

"All right ; you needn't," she replied. "You're a
stuffy little thing, aren't you? I s'pose you think I
shall desecrate the place somehow. Perhaps I shall.
I'm going now." She walked out of the house. Presently she turned. "I needn't ask you not to tell Rob
what I've said. He's the very last person you'd tell.
Just let him know some other woman besides you loves
him, and he'd begin to think of her. Good-bye."

Olive had advanced to the door, where she stood as
she now responded "Good-bye," and then she watched
Isabel mount from the fence and ride away without
looking back. She remained there motionless a few
moments, listening to the sound made by the cantering feet. Then she deliberately locked the door.

"I don't want any one else to get in here now," she
said, in a whisper. She tried the door to see if the bolt
had obeyed the key. She walked up-stairs to the east
chamber, and knelt down for the second time by the

open window. But when she looked out she did not
see the "gentle dimplement" of small hill and dale, the
bright sunlight over all. She saw nothing but a tall,
handsome girl saying that she loved Rob.

Olive put her head again on her folded arms upon
the window - shelf ; and now she began to cry. She
dimly wondered why tears could be so different—there
was no happiness in these salt drops.

After a little time she remembered that she ought to
go home to her mother. She rose from her knees and
slowly made her way down the steep stairs. She felt
puzzled and bewildered that she should be so deeply
affected by Isabel's coming. As long as Robert loved
her, and not Isabel, the sun should shine and the world
turn happily.

Olive looked sadly at the carpet as she walked over
it ; she could not smile at it now. She passed out of
the house and locked the door again. There was no
dear and intimate sense of possession when she put
the key in that secret place in the shed that she and
Robert had agreed upon. Instead of hurrying homeward, she plodded slowly.

Her mother was sitting at the kitchen window. She
was drinking tea from a saucer, blowing the liquid between her sips.

"I declare," began Mrs. Newcomb, "I didn't know
what had become of you ! I declare I had a good mind
to be frightened 'most out of my wits ! I felt sure something must have happened, Olive, else you wouldn't
have left me all alone all the morning ; and here 'tis
goin' on nine o'clock, 'n' the clothes ain't put in soak
yet, 'n' Clas'y Jane's jest be'n spreadin' her sheets out
on the grass. It's the early mornin' that whitens clo'es
most, I tell 'em. But when you can't do much yourself,
you have to wait for folks to do it for you ; 'n' if you
have a daughter that's courtin', you'll have to wait a
good while, most likely. I didn't do so when Israel was

courtin' me. I kep' right on takin' care o' my mother,
'n' she with her hands drawn up with rheumatism so
'twas hard work for her to do 'most anything. Now
you are here, Olive, will you pass me the teapot? 'N' I
wish you'd fill up the sugar-bowl with sugar."

Olive stepped to the stove and took the vessel her
mother had mentioned, carrying it to the little table
by the window.

"I don't think you ought to drink so much tea,
mother," she said, earnestly. "I believe you'd sleep
better if you didn't."

"No," returned Mrs. Newcomb, "I shouldn't, either.
I guess I know what keeps me awake ; it's my nerves.
The doctor told us, you remember, that I came within
an inch of nervous prostration. An inch was what he
said, Olive ; and an inch is pretty nigh, I call it."

The girl drew a long breath, but she did not speak.

Mrs. Newcomb took up the teapot and poured more
tea into her cup. It was very black stuff that came
from the nozzle. Her method of preparing her almost
hourly drink was to put in fresh tea leaves on the already soaked ones in the pot, turning in more water,
until at last the pot was crowded with the solid mass.
Then she emptied these leaves into a large stone crock
which stood on the floor under the shelves in the buttery, and began again. This stock of steeped leaves
was sacred to the faded three-ply carpet on the sitting-room. Whenever that carpet was swept, Mrs.
Newcomb liberally sprinkled it with the wet leaves,
which were brushed up as the sweeping went on. She
had read, as she said, "in print," of this method of clean-
ing a carpet. What she saw in print was of great weight
with her.

"I didn't know 's you were goin' to stay so long,"
she said, fretfully. "I s'pose you've given up washin'
for the day, 'ain't you? It always seemed real slack to
me not to wash Mondays. Monday to wash, Tuesday

to iron, Wednesday to visit, Thursday to mend, Friday to sweep, Saturday to bake—that's my way. When you git to house-keepin' for yourself, Olive, you'd better make it a rule to go on that plan. Then things 'll come out right, 'n' they won't any other way you c'n fix it Ain't the sugar 'bout out? Sugar's risin', too, I hear. If we c'n spare the money, I think we'd better git a dollar's worth, don't you, Olive?"

Olive had been placing a large tin boiler on the stove, pumping pails of water and pouring them into it. She had not listened to the words that trickled in a small stream by her ears.

"Don't you, Olive?" repeated her mother.

The girl stopped pumping; she held her hand on the pump-handle and did not turn her head as she now responded, "What say?"

"I guess you 'ain't be'n listenin'," said the elder woman. "You wa'n't thinkin' of what I was sayin'; you was thinkin' of your beau." Mrs. Newcomb smiled as she said this. She had a face that was still fair and pretty, and now, as she smiled, it was prettier still. "Say, Olive, wa'n't you thinkin' of your beau?" she asked.

The water from the pail swashed into the big boiler. "Yes, perhaps I was," answered Olive.

"I made sure you were"—with a small giggle. "At your age I was thinkin' of your par. But, land! you'll soon git over doin' that; you won't think of Robert from the time he goes off in the morning till he comes back at night. You'll have your mind on your housework. That's what women are for. Monday to wash, Tuesday to iron—"

Olive was pumping violently, and the rest of the days were lost in the louder sound. "I s'pose," said Mrs. Newcomb, reflectively, "that Robert 'll finally have his father's prop'ty. There ain't no one else."

As her mother frequently made this remark, the girl did not think it necessary to give any response.

"Has Robert got anything new over to the house?" were the next words Olive heard distinctly. She answered that he'd got a carpet.

"Ingrain, I s'pose?"

"No—Brussels."

"Why, how extravagant! I thought Robert was one not to be extravagant."

"It was marked down," said Olive.

"Oh! Was it? How I do wish I could have something marked down! I guess I'll soap them clothes for you, Olive."

Mrs. Newcomb rose and came to the tub, which her daughter had now placed upon the wash-bench. "You 'ain't had no breakfast, have ye?" she suddenly asked.

"No; but I don't want any," answered Olive.

There was silence for a few moments, during which time Mrs. Newcomb thoughtfully rubbed soap upon different places in the garments to be washed.

Presently she paused, with the cake of soap in her hand, and turned towards Olive, who was sitting for a brief space. "I've be'n thinkin'," she said, "that if anything should happen that your aunt Ruth shouldn't want to come and live with me after you're married, why, I guess I could make up my mind to live over on the Raymore place with you 'n' Robert, after all. There ain't much passin' there, 'n' I've be'n used to passin', bein' right here on the straight road from the Junction to the Falls. But I know I mustn't be too partick'lar."

Olive rose suddenly and began to crowd the stove with wood. There was a set look on her face and a glitter in her eyes. What would Robert say to such an arrangement? It had been her mother's own planning to have her sister Ruth live with her after Olive's marriage. Mrs. Newcomb had objected strongly to living in what she called that "out-of-the-way place that Robert had bought." She could barely manage to support herself on the income of the money her husband had left—she and Olive—and now sister Ruth would take Olive's place.

Have you any idea how little will provide for two women living in a hamlet like this? You would not believe me if I should name the sum; and these people are comfortable, too. It had never occurred to Olive to think that she and her mother were ill used because they had so little income. For three terms the girl had taught in the school-house just the other side of the bridge. She had been paid four dollars a week, and she had been rich. But a daughter of one of the trustees had wanted the school, so it was taken from Olive.

It had been immediately on her return from caring for her grandfather at Falls Village that she had taught. Since then she had only kept house with her mother. And Rob had begun to love her. She could not get over the astonishment caused by this fact. So the beggar-maid may have felt when the king noticed her.

Mrs. Newcomb went on placidly rubbing the soap into the clothes.

"Yes," she continued, "I s'pose I could make up my mind to live on the old Raymore place. You never c'n quite tell what sister Ruth will do, she changes her mind so often. But 'twill seem quite thick settled to her here, she's so used to livin' 'way back on that farm. I guess I won't spend no time thinkin' 'bout that, though. You still expect to be married the last of June, don't you?"

"Yes; that's what we're planning."

"June's a real lucky month. Your father 'n' I were married in June. I wonder what old Nawn's got against you, Olive."

"Got against me, mother!" Olive turned as she was passing through the doorway.

Robert had hinted that his father did not approve of his marriage, but now she had seen old Mr. Nawn and he had been so kind. She stood waiting for her mother to go on.

"Yes," said Mrs. Newcomb. " Esther Rice was in here while you were away this mornin'; she come to borrow a teaspoonful of saleratus; she said they forgot to send for some yesterd'y when Mr. Rice went down to the store, 'n' her mother wanted biscuit for breakfast; they'd got the creamy tartar on hand. Do you think this soap is as good as the other kind?"

"Well?" said Olive, with patient interrogation.

"Esther was tellin' of meetin' old Nawn the first of the week, 'n' somethin' had riled him, 'n' he talked right out. He said Bob was stan'in' in his own light marryin' you; that he'd told the boy if he'd give you up he'd make over ten thousand dollars to him right away, besides settin' him up in business over to the Falls Village."

"Did he say that?" asked Olive, in a low voice.

"Yes; he told Esther Rice with his own lips, 'n' she told me with her own lips; so you see it come straight 'nough, didn't it?"

"Yes," answered Olive. A sudden resolution had entered her mind.

CHAPTER V

OLIVE'S CALL

OLIVE hurried at her washing. Her mother rinsed the clothes, and before noon the girl had spread them on the slope of green grass back of the house. She hastily ate her dinner, scarcely hearing her mother's talk, which flowed on as slowly as the Creeper flowed between its banks. But often Mrs. Newcomb did not mind whether she was listened to or not.

Olive went to her own room as soon as she had " done" the dishes. She was tired, and there was a spot of red on each cheek. But she did not sit down. She stood before the bit of a glass and carefully dressed her hair. She put on her best gown, and she was very particular about pinning a ribbon at the throat. When she was dressed she stood hesitating in the middle of the little chamber. Her eyes were very anxious. She looked at herself again and again.

" I do want him to be pleased with me," she murmured. " But perhaps I'm doing wrong. I wonder if I am? There's no one for me to ask. He seemed to like me. Would Rob scold?"

She walked to the window and looked out. The ground fell away to the river. She could just see the water as the willow-trees swayed in the warm wind.

" It's borne in on me to do it," she said, more decisively.

She put on her hat and took her sunshade. She went softly down the stairs, hoping her mother would not hear her. As she walked swiftly along the path to

the road a window was flung up, and Mrs. Newcomb
called :

"Where you goin', Olive ?"

The girl paused.   She tried not to be irritated.

"I'm going to do an errand," she answered.

"But what ?"

"I'd rather not tell now."

"I declare, I hope you're secret enough !   D' you
know you'd got on your best dress ?"

"Yes, I did."

"Well, you *are* secret !"

The window slammed down.

Olive hurried until she was almost running.   But
when she came to the bridge she slackened her pace.
She stopped midway and leaned over, seeing nothing
as she gazed.

"What if I'm doing wrong?" she was saying to herself.   Then, more bravely, "But I don't see how it can
do any harm.   I'll go on."

She walked across the bridge and steadily along until she was entering the yard of the Nawn house.   The
gate swung slanting over on one hinge; the gravel
walk was half covered with tufts of "pudding-bag
shrub"; knotgrass and horseradish and dandelion were
everywhere.   Three or four turkeys stalked about,
and fled crying as the girl walked towards the door.

She would not pause again.   She lifted the blackened brass knocker and let it fall.

While she waited the wind came swooping under the
roof of the portico and snatched off her hat.   It was
a sweet wind, with the scent of white-clover and vio
lets in it, and the peculiar odor of the yellow-centred
daisy.

Olive ran into the grass for her hat, and as she did
so the door was opened by an elderly woman, who did
not try to conceal her surprise at sight of the girl, who
was now trying to fasten her hat on her head.

" Goodness me !" she cried, in a husky voice. " Ain't you the Newcomb girl ?"

" Yes, ma'am," answered Olive, coming back to the door.

The woman, who had kept house for the Nawns ever since Robert's mother had died, did not invite Olive in. She stood squarely in the doorway, and stared down at this unexpected visitor.

" Is Mr. Nawn—old Mr. Nawn—in ?" inquired Olive, as bravely as she could.

Before any answer could be given to this question a door was heard to open violently somewhere, and an angry voice demanded :

" What's all this noise ? Mrs. Barlow, you knew I was trying to get a nap. It's a damned agent, I s'pose. Send him away. I'll tie up that knocker."

" 'Tain't an agent," called back Mrs. Barlow.

Mr. Nawn's curiosity made him linger and ask, " Who is it, then ?"

" It's the Newcomb girl."

" What ?"

Olive had thoughts of running back among those pudding-bag plants to the hanging gate.

" The Newcomb girl," repeated Mrs. Barlow, in her raised tone.

" The devil ! Tell her Bob isn't here."

There was the muffled sound of stockinged feet coming over the floor ; and Olive, now tolerably certain that she ought not to have come, compelled herself to say, calmly :

" I didn't come to see Robert; I came to see his father."

Mrs. Barlow laughed, not in an agreeable manner.

The man above called out, " Let her in," and the house-keeper stood back while Olive walked into the large hall that she could not see had once been grand. It looked dingy and lonesome to her. Her face was burning, her hands cold.

"Come up here," said Mr. Nawn.

She went up the stairs. The man in his shirt-sleeves met her at the top. He took her hands. She hoped he wouldn't kiss her, but he did, and then said :

"Well, my dear, so you've come to see the old man. What do you want? For of course you want something. Everybody wants something. Did Bob send you?"

"Oh no, no. He doesn't know anything about it," hastily. "And I think I'm sorry I came, Mr. Nawn."

"Oh, are you? Well, now you're here, you might's well sit down."

Mr. Nawn pushed a chair towards her over the ragged carpet, and she placed herself in it.

He had led her into what seemed a kind of sitting-room, dirty and unkempt and desolate, like the rest of the house.

The man, whose big, unwieldy shape seemed bigger and more unwieldy as he stood there without a coat, thrust his hands into his pockets, and gazed at his guest. He smiled as he gazed. He glanced about the apartment.

"By George !" he exclaimed ; "a pretty face does light up a room, doesn't it?" He pulled one hand from his pocket, reached forward, and put the tip of a finger under Olive's chin. "By George !" he said, again ; "Bob's got eyes in his head."

The girl sat still and tried not to shrink. She was not thinking now that old Mr. Nawn was lovely, as she had thought when she had met him that morning. She felt sick, but she made a great effort to recall her courage and the motive which had brought her there.

Mr. Nawn now flung himself into a large chair which stood by the window. The sunlight came in and fell upon his fat face with its baggy cheeks and puffy eyes. These eyes were small and sharp, and they scanned his visitor, going from her head to her feet, and back again to her head, taking in every detail of her costume. But, manlike, he could not tell that this costume was inexpensive; he only knew that it was pretty and becoming. Therefore he argued that it must have cost a great deal of money — a great deal, that is, for a poor person to have, still worse to spend.

"So you don't want anything, and you come here because you don't want anything, eh?"

Mr. Nawn had drawn a key from his pocket, and he began to twirl the key round and round on his forefinger.

Olive fixed her gaze on this bit of metal, for she could not just now raise it to the man's face.

When she had resolved upon coming here she had thought that she could have a comfortable talk with Robert's father, and explain to him how she wished that he would be good friends with his son; and that she cared nothing for his money. She only wished that they all might care for each other, and so on in the strain of love and hope and good-will that filled her heart. So ignorant was she that she believed, if she could only talk a little while with her future father-in-law, they could come to an understanding, and things would be so much pleasanter. She couldn't bear to have Rob so bitter against his father, and since the morning she had thought Rob unjust. In her guileless heart she felt that Mr. Nawn, now he had seen her and been kind to her, must have changed his mind, so that he would not say again such a thing as Esther Rice had reported. At any rate, the impulse to see him had been too strong to resist; though she had dreaded to go, she could not stay away.

With her eyes still on the key, Olive said, in a very low voice, "I wanted to see you, sir."

"To see me, eh? Now I call that good of you. Young and pretty girls don't visit me, as a general thing." Mr. Nawn stopped twirling the key, put it into his pocket, leaned back in his chair, and looked persistently at the face opposite him. "No, by George! they don't," he repeated. "It's a great treat to me to see something like you in this room."

He did not audibly smack his lips, but his companion felt as if he had done so. She wondered if this was like all old men. She had only known her grandfather, to be sure, but he had, she thought, only been like an old animal which wanted its food, and, unlike other animals, its tobacco. She did not believe her grandfather's bleared eyes would have told him whether a woman were black or white, much less young or old.

The girl was greatly confused. She made an effort to bring things clearly to her mind. But she was not conscious of much save that she longed to get away, and she was resolved not to go yet.

She had now given up all hope that Mr. Nawn would help her any.

"I used to think your mother was one of the han'-somest girls anywhere near the Red Bridge," went on the old man, "and so she was. You ain't so han'some as she, but you've got something else that she didn't have. I guess they call it charm, or attraction, or some of those words. Oh, Bob's got an eye in his head. He's his father's son, he is, about that."

Mr. Nawn chuckled, and his eyes almost disappeared in the surrounding rolls of flesh as he did so.

Olive tried not to quiver in her repulsion. She was saying to herself, "Oh, how could I have been so mistaken?"

In the morning she had been grateful that he had been kind. Now she saw that this was not kindness. She shuddered as she endeavored to think what it was. She unclasped her hands, which had been lying in her lap. Involuntarily she extended them slightly towards her companion as she said, pleadingly, "Oh, I don't think I can understand you, Mr. Nawn. I came because I longed so for you and Rob to be friends. Can't you be friends with him, Mr. Nawn? Can't you?"

CHAPTER VI

MR. NAWN'S PROPOSITION

MR. NAWN looked surprised. Instead of replying directly, he said, with unction, "Oh yes, by George! she's a great deal more fetching—isn't fetching the word they use nowadays?—than her mother ever was."

Olive forced back the tears that came to her eyes. Hastily she rose from her chair. "I'll go home," she said, in a half-whisper, and as if speaking to herself.

Mr. Nawn rose also; he displayed a remarkable agility as he stepped forward and took the girl's hand.

"No, indeed, you won't go yet," he said. "What do you mean? Here I am admiring you. You're a queer kind of woman if you don't like to be admired. Sit down again. I don't have lovely visitors. Do you think I like to look at Mrs. Barlow from morning till night? Sit down, I tell you."

She obeyed him.

Mr. Nawn began to walk about the room, his feet in his stockings making no noise. He was smiling as if he were enjoying this call.

" I thought we might talk together," now began Olive again, desperately, "and perhaps I might get you to be real friendly with Robert—"

"Why, I'm friendly enough with him," interrupted Mr. Nawn; "we don't quarrel very much—not more 'n a father and son usually quarrel when the son thinks it's time the old man stepped out and left his money."

"You're all wrong, if you think that," said Olive, now speaking firmly, her head raised high and her eyes flashing. "We don't want your money unless you want us to have it. It's your good-will and friendship we long to have. You don't know how noble Robert is. He's the noblest, best man that ever lived; and I'm so proud that he loves me, and that I'm going to be his wife."

The light in the girl's eyes was very beautiful; her voice rang true.

The sceptical old eyes gazing at her took on for an instant a slightly different expression.

"By George!" exclaimed the man. "Damn me, if I don't believe she means it!"

"Means it?"

Olive sprang to her feet. She walked towards the door, and again the old man stopped her. This time he put his hands on her shoulders and not ungently pushed her back into her chair.

"This is mighty refreshing," he remarked, after a moment. "It's worth ten dollars to believe in anybody for five minutes. Yes, ten dollars."

Olive was silent. She had done a very poor thing when she came here.

Now Mr. Nawn began to grin.

"So you think that Bob is the noblest and best man that ever lived, eh? You're proud that he loves you, eh! Well, I don't say but that he's well enough. He's some like me, and I never thought that I was specially noble." Here the speaker paused an instant before he added, "I s'pose a man generally finds at least one woman who for a short time thinks he's noble. It all makes me laugh." But Mr. Nawn did not laugh any more just then. "You needn't worry about Bob and me," he went on. "We sh'll do very well. I wasn't going to give him any money, as he chose to marry a poor girl; but, since you've come here, I guess I'll make him a present of a hundred—no, I think fifty dollars 'll be enough. I'll give him fifty dollars as a wedding present. How 'll that do?"

"You needn't give him anything."

"Yes, I will. I like you. But he ought to have taken that girl with black eyes. She's got some prop'ty her- self—prop'ty and black eyes; that's a combination a young fellow don't often meet. You see, I s'pose he would have married Isabel if you hadn't come home just as you did. He hadn't seen you since you were grown up, and novelty is a great thing—a great thing to a man, though folks talk a lot of stuff about faithful- ness, and constancy, and so forth. Men ain't faithful. They like new faces and new ways. Don't you think a man's going to get mighty sick of any woman he sees under his feet every day of his life? Now I tell you he is. And who's going to blame him?"

Mr. Nawn had resumed his chair, and was lolling back in it as he talked, looking at his guest, watching the color rise and ebb in her face. Her eyelids were drooped. He could not tell whether she was following his words, and, in truth, he did not care. He liked to talk in that manner. He thought there was a "great deal of rot about love and marriage punched down people's throats—but he didn't swallow it."

If he had often expressed himself in this way to his wife she may have come most thoroughly to agree with him.

But Olive Newcomb hardly heard the last few sen- tences; nothing, in fact, after that phrase, "I s'pose he would have married Isabel—"

She hadn't known that; she hadn't known he thought of the girl in that way. He had told her that he used to go home with Isabel from evening meetings, but—

Olive gathered her courage together. She raised her eyes bravely; but she was not quite aware of the full significance of her words.

"I hadn't heard—" she began. She paused and began again. "I want Robert to be happy. If I know anything about myself, I want Robert to be happy, even if—even if he isn't with me."

She ended with her voice pitched rather high and quavering slightly. In spite of his appearance, all she thought at this moment of her companion was that he was the father of the man she loved.

As for the old man, as he heard her voice and met the glance of her limpid eyes, he said to himself, "I've a great mind to make that fifty a hundred, after all."

But he had no sooner thought this than he began to consider that the smaller sum would do just as well, and he would save fifty. Still the mere thought had given him a rather unusual sensation of kindliness and warmth. What a white-souled little thing it was! He was sorry for her; yes, he was truly sorry for her.

"I guess you needn't worry about Bob," he remarked, at last. "If I'm any judge of anything, his best chance of happiness lies with you—though you two won't start with any money. Money's a thing you can count on—love isn't anything; you can't touch it nor see it; you—"

At this point in his talk Mr. Nawn's eyes left Olive's face and casually glanced from the window. They saw the elderly figure of the house-keeper at Nawn house bent over a pile of chips. Mrs. Barlow was filling a basket. She moved rather stiffly; she was really getting old.

Mr. Nawn suddenly sat upright. A keen look sprang to his eyes. Why hadn't he thought of such a thing before? But then he had not seen Olive until to-day.

"I say," he exclaimed, with animation, "why can't we make an arrangement like this—you and Bob come here and live. It'll save the boy keeping up a separate home. I'll send Mrs. Barlow away. She's too old. I've thought for some time she's too old.

She potters. She's broken two plates lately. I can't have folks breaking things here. We'll let the Raymore farm. It's exactly the thing, eh?"

He turned to Olive, not as one expecting any dissent. She was white. She could not speak when Mr. Nawn said "Eh?" again. Her lips were stiff, but she did at least frame the words:

"I'll think about it—I'll ask Robert."

"Yes, do. But you'll find Bob 'll take to anything that 'll save money. You see, he could pay his own board, just as he's doing now, and you could work for yours. Capital idea! If there should ever be any brats, why, we could make some arrangement. I sha'n't undertake to support any of Bob's brats."

Olive rose. This time Mr. Nawn did not oppose her going. At the door she said "Good-bye, Mr. Nawn," and he nodded without leaving his chair.

When the latch had shut the man began to laugh silently. He sat up erect and put his thumbs into his waistcoat pockets.

"We'll see what they'll do. It's a good idea. If I'd only seen the girl before since she is grown up, I'd have stopped Bob from bargaining for that Raymore place. But if he'll let me manage, I c'n let it for more money than the interest on his mortgage. What so natural as for Bob to bring his wife home? There's room enough here. I'd rather see that girl round than to watch old Barlow stalking about. Guess I'll go up to the store and mention that I'm trying to have the young folks settle here."

Mr. Nawn went cumbrously down the stairs. He put on a shabby, out-at-elbows coat, and took his hat and stick. As he stood for a moment in the desolate yard he saw Olive's lissome young figure going swiftly along the road towards the bridge. He leaned on his cane and gazed at it.

"If she knew life as I do," he muttered, "she'd jump

into that river rather than try to live it. She thinks she loves Bob. Pooh!"

He turned and walked in the opposite direction, for in that way were the store and post-office and school-house. In the school-house a sermon was preached on alternate Sabbath afternoons by the minister from Falls Village. But Mr. Nawn did not attend these services. He said all they wanted of him was his contribution, and if he couldn't have the gospel free he wouldn't have it at all. Then he laughed deep down in his chest, as was his habit.

Olive hurried nervously until she came to the middle of the bridge. The narrow, railed space for foot-passengers ran only on the north side. It was not likely that any one would be coming over the bridge at this hour of day. There was little enough travelling there at any time, and the most was at night and morning.

Olive had always liked to stand and lean on the railing, looking down into the Creeper going so deliberately on its journey. It seemed now to be moving more slowly than usual. Indeed, it did not seem to move at all.

The girl's hot eyes grew cooler as she gazed, and her pulses became calmer. Her slender, work-hardened hands were clasped on the top rail. She was trying to think. But she could not think. And presently, between her and the water, there formed, with the vividness of life, the broad, heavy face at which she had just been looking, and, in spite of its heaviness and its aspect of age, this countenance bore a dreadful resemblance to Robert.

Olive moved uneasily and endeavored to banish the vision. It was as if a lifelike photograph of Mr. Nawn's face and head were suspended right below her vision and just above the water. She stepped back, then advanced again, always looking at the river. She began to be frightened. She could not, being ignorant

in many ways, explain this phenomenon by telling herself that it was caused by her overwrought brain—the
intensity of her feeling during the past hour when she
had been gazing at Mr. Nawn, and thinking of him as
if she could think of nothing else.

There was a great horror over her now. To live
at Nawn house! What would Robert say? To live at
Nawn house ! She must do as he decided.

Oh, if that old man's face would only move from
above the water there !

She must stay until it did move ; for if she did not,
it would be likely to be always awaiting her there, and
would stare at her every time she crossed the bridge.
That would be too terrible.

CHAPTER VII

ALL OVER

WHILE Olive leaned there over the railing she suddenly remembered the carpet with the big roses on it — remembered it as we recall comparatively trivial things in moments of mental stress. And, as we do in such moments, she gave undue weight to the thought — what would become of the carpet if they should go to Nawn house to live?

She shuddered violently. "Oh"—aloud—"I can't go there! It would be like trying to live in hell!"

The emphasis of the last word startled her. She had not known that she was going to speak it. Then she took comfort from the conviction that Robert would not wish to live in his old home; he would be as much opposed to such a plan as she herself was.

All the time she was gazing down into the water, and all the time there was that face, old and fat, with small, sensual eyes, gazing back at her. She would not have cared so much if only that face had not been in some strange way rather handsome, and like Robert.

An ox-team, dragging a creaking load of gravel, came slowly over the road and on to the bridge. The gentle oxen turned deliberately moving eyes towards her, and the sight of their faces comforted her.

Before she could resume her former position, quick steps came on to the planks; a youthful laugh mingled with the rumble of the cart-wheels, and a voice said:

"I thought that was you, Olive. I was laughing to think you might not want that carpet, after all. Perhaps Rob can sell it to some hotel—if there were only more of it !"   Another laugh, as Isabel finished speaking.

The girl came up and leaned on the railing beside Olive, who asked, quickly :

" What do you mean ?"

As she spoke she glanced furtively towards the water, and then drew a long sigh of relief — that broad face was gone.

" Oh, don't you know ?" was the reply. " I should think you'd know that you and Rob are going to live with old Mr. Nawn, after all, and the Raymore place is to be let. Oh, how horrid—horrid—that will be ! What shall you do ?"

Olive took a good hold of the railing before she answered.

" I can't imagine how you heard that so soon. Nothing is settled. It isn't more than an hour ago since Mr. Nawn proposed such an arrangement, and Robert doesn't know it yet. Of course, he won't consent."

" Won't he ?"   Isabel scanned her companion's face. " Well, I don't know that he will. I've just come from the store. Old Nawn was there. He was telling two or three men that he guessed the young folks might better come home to roost—said he was a fool not to have thought of it before ; but he'd take the Raymore place off of Bob's hands. So, now, what are you going to do with that carpet ?"—laughing—" and it's too bad Rob has worked so hard there for nothing ; and it's no matter, now you're not going to live there, if I did go into the house and desecrate it this morning," laughing again.

Before Olive could think of anything to say in response, Isabel remarked that she guessed she'd go right along home. She paused at the end of the bridge to call out, but in a subdued voice, that she didn't know that she should ever dare to call on Olive at the Nawn house; and should Olive have those pudding-bags in the front yard cut down?

To these words Olive made no reply. Very soon she left her place on the bridge and walked towards her home. But she shrank from meeting any one until she could see Robert. What would he say?

Old Mr. Nawn had been in earnest, then. She had had a faint hope that he had been joking—talking thus to see how she would appear. It was quite an unaccountable thing that she had not disliked him in the morning. She recalled now that he had once made her conscious of that sense of repulsion from him which was now so powerful in her. It seemed quite impossible that he could be Rob's father.

She came to the place where a path, made by many feet, ran across a field at the right. The men from this neighborhood who worked in the factory had worn this path going and coming.

Olive paused here, looking anxiously over the field. It was a long time before it would be the hour for the day's work to be over and for Robert to be returning. It was not certain that he would come this way, but it was probable. She must see him—she must see him at the earliest possible moment. But that would be more than two hours later, and she would give much to be alone during those two hours.

After a great deal of hesitation, Olive went into the field; she walked on until she came to a clump of birches; there she sat down and prepared to wait, and the time sped on much more rapidly than she had expected. She thought of many things, but she was not extremely depressed; the depression vanished, and that subtle elation which love can give to the heart where it dwells came to this girl. Why should she worry about anything since Robert loved her? And, was that his step? Could he by any chance have come so soon.

She sprang to her feet, peering out from among the birch leaves. Yes, there he was, striding along, his hat pushed back, his face intent. Ah, how handsome he was!—how fine !—how distinguished from all other men !

And he loved her ! That was the most wonderful thing that she could imagine—that he loved her.

She let him get by the birches, her gaze fixed on him. Then she stepped out and ran silently after him, cheeks and eyes glowing.

"Robert !" she called, softly. He stopped short, and almost staggered, like one who has been lassoed. Brilliance took the place of a rather stern intentness on his face.

"What, you ?" he cried, just as softly as she had spoken.

He snatched her hands and held them fast, gazing down at her. Then an anxiety came into his face.

"Has anything happened ?"

"No—that is, not much," she replied, quickly. "I wanted to talk with you. I knew you were not coming to my house to-night, and I must see you, Rob— must. So I waited. Can you sit down here a minute? You're out early. Are you in a hurry ?"

"Yes, I am out early. Something happened to the engine, so we all had to stop. I was going over to the house—our house— to work a while. Oh, Olive, you're a darling to wait for me ! I'm so glad to see you !"

He paused, as if he could look at her better if he did not speak. The next moment he asked :

"But what is it ?"

"I've been to see your father to-day," she answered, boldly; but her eyelids quivered slightly, notwithstanding her courageous appearance.

"My father? Olive, I'm sorry."

"So am I. But I went. It isn't any matter now

why I went. The thing I must have off my mind is that he wants us to go there and live with him."

Robert's jaw dropped.

"Yes," went on Olive, as fast as she could speak, "I'm to work for my board, and you're to pay as you do now, and he's to turn off Mrs. Barlow, and it will be cheaper for us than to keep house by ourselves, and he'll see that the Raymore place is let. Oh, Robert!"

Here Olive suddenly covered her face with her hands. But she did not sob, nor laugh hysterically. She stood quite still, and her companion gazed at her.

"He's a regular hyena," said the young man, at last.

Olive breathed heavily. Then he was not going to ask her to live at the Nawn house. She was weak with the relief this conviction brought. She wished to throw herself into her lover's arms and weep delicious tears of delight and gratitude. But she did not move.

The next moment Robert seized her, and drew her rather roughly into that clump of birches again.

"Some of the men will be coming along," he said, in a harsh voice, "and I can't have them see us now."

He made Olive sit down on the grass, but he would not sit. He stood in front of her, leaning his back against a tree. He flung his hat on the ground. His head suddenly felt hot and compressed, as if a strong, burning hand had grasped it.

"Now tell me every word," he exclaimed. And he could not help adding, "You were an idiot, to go there, Olive—a blind idiot. You ought to have known better. Father will tell me about it, and he will laugh. I'd rather he'd knock me down than laugh as he does. How could you have been such a fool?"

Olive's lip trembled before she was able to speak. Robert had never addressed her in that way before. She glanced up at him, and then her body cowered a little. She thought his face was cruel—that it was not like his face.

"How could you have been such a fool?" he repeated.

Then he tried to get some control of himself. He began to feel as if he were crushing a butterfly.

"It didn't seem foolish to me," she began, in a very low voice, not looking at him. "I thought, since he was so kind in the morning—"

"Kind!" interrupting, in a savage tone. "I don't know what you're made of, Olive, if you think my father is kind."

The girl waited. She sat with one hand pressed to her bosom. Was it possible that it was Robert who was speaking in that tone to her?

She must wait still more before she began again. She was not going to keep anything back.

"I thought, if I should see your father, Rob, and have a good talk with him, that perhaps you and he would be better friends—"

Robert burst into a loud laugh. He was beside himself with angry surprise that Olive should have done such a thing.

"I fancied you had some sense," he said, in the same rough voice he had used a moment ago. "I'll bet a thousand dollars he took it you came for money; didn't he?"

The girl hung her head.

"Yes, I think he did believe so," she answered.

"Oh, the devil!—the devil!" The young man flung out his hand with a gesture of impotent irritation.

Silence upon Olive's part for a brief space; then she said, softly:

"Oh, I'm so sorry!"

But Robert's anger was not yet nearly spent.

"I guess you didn't get any money out of the old fellow," he said.

4

Olive raised her head.

"I didn't go for money," she answered, firmly. "I tell you, I went because I felt as if there could be a better understanding, somehow. I'm sure he didn't think I wanted money—I'm sure he believed me when I told him I didn't."

"It 'll be the first time he ever believed any one, then, on that subject."

Olive winced visibly, but she went on and related, briefly and accurately, every particular of the interview with Mr. Nawn. Then she sat and waited again, her colorless face and wild, dilated eyes raised towards the man who stood in front of her, and whose own eyes did not meet hers.

Robert was staring off towards the Creeper, which he could see glinting between the birch leaves. At last he moved restlessly.

"I s'pose we shall have to live there," he said.

"What! Oh, Robert!"

Olive cried out sharply. She had not in the least expected this—had not expected it, notwithstanding Mr. Nawn's prophecy and Isabel Keating's words. Did they know Robert better than she knew him?

"What did you go there for, then?" demanded the young man, looking swiftly at the girl. "There's no likelihood that he'd ever have thought of such a thing as having us live there if you hadn't meddled. He expected us to live on the Raymore place. But I s'pose, when he saw you in the house, all at once it came to him that you'd be a good hand to do the work, and he could turn off old Barlow; and he'd be sure to think that we shouldn't dare to refuse—and I don't dare to. If we don't go, since he wants us, it would be a dead sure thing that he wouldn't leave me a cent. He'd chuckle in his grave to think some asylum, or something, would have his money instead of me. He doesn't care anything about me, nor about his son's taking his place, and all that stuff **that** other fathers care about. Oh, I've heard him talk, and **I know how he feels. It's just** damnable **to** think **you went** there. **I declare I can't** stand it. **You** may thank yourself that we **have to** live at the **old house. It 'll** be a regular **slavery. Yes, you** may **thank** yourself **for it."**

The young man shook **a clinched hand in** the **air. He felt that this state** of things was intolerable—intol**erable. It** was just like a girl **not to know** any better.

Olive **rose.** She stood an instant before she spoke. Young Nawn was still gazing off towards the river. The girl **had never** seen his face at all like that ; it was a new **face to her.** Was it really her lover who looked thus ?

"**Robert," she** whispered. **He did not turn towards her, but** he made a slight, involuntary movement that **showed** that he heard her. "**Dear** Robert," timidly, "**don't let** us **think** any **more about this. Let's** go **right** on getting ready to live in your own **little home."**

"**Not** think any more of **it?** That's as much as **a woman** knows, anyway."

Silence ; in the silence **a** bit of a song-sparrow came **and perched on** the top of **one of** the birches, **and trilled and sang, his little body** vibrating with his melody.

"Yes"—from Robert—"as much as a woman knows. We've got to go **and live** with father. I thought I should get **out from** under **his foot when** I married, but it 'll be worse than ever. **I swear it's** too bad !"

" We won't live there," said **Olive, her v**oice sounding **very still and strange.**

Robert turned to her.

"**Won't ?** Yes, **we must, too.** He'll be sure not to **leave any money to me if we don't."**

"**No,"** repeated the girl, **in** the same voice, "we needn't **live there.** I don't think it's **our** duty, if you feel **like that."**

"You don't know anything about it, I tell you. If we get married we must do as father says. I can't go against him in that as I did in—"

The young man paused abruptly. He had never thought it best to tell Olive that his father had wished him to marry Isabel.

"I know about you and Isabel," said Olive, mechanically. She was thinking that Robert had just used the phrase—"If we get married." Was there any doubt in his mind? If there were— She raised her head and looked at him. She saw that his eyes were bright and hard. How angry he was! How could he be so angry with her? She did not think that anything could make her feel in that way to him.

"We've got to live there," repeated Robert.

"No," said the girl.

"No? I tell you yes. Or we needn't marry," fiercely.

"Very well; as you say, we needn't marry," in that almost inaudible voice.

"Then it's all over between us, is it?"

Robert was in such a fury that he could hardly speak.

"Just as you say," was the response.

"All right. That's the way a woman loves, then. Oh, all right! I ain't going to whine. Good-bye!"

"Good-bye!" in a half-whisper, which the young man did not hear, for he was already going at a furious rate down the field. He tore along like some mad animal, having only sense enough to keep out of the highway lest he should meet some one who would speak to him.

He kept up this pace until he came to the house he had bought. He found the key where Olive had put it.

He was in a wild haste to get into the house. When he did enter he threw himself down on the carpet, caught hold of a place which had not yet been fastened and pulled at it, tearing up tacks, wishing the fabric itself would rend in his hands. In a moment the thing was lying in a heap in the middle of the room, and Robert was standing with his hands in his pockets, staring dully down at it.

CHAPTER VIII

A LITTLE BALM

So it was all over. The cold fit had come after the hot fit. Robert Nawn stood for a long time thus, his hands shut tight in his pockets, glaring at the heap of carpet. At last he lifted his foot and pushed the mass away from him. He raised his head and looked at the room ; he glanced beyond, into the bit of a kitchen where he had expected to see Olive at work ; and he had meant to see that she did not work too hard. He had intended to be very careful of her—the sweetest girl in the world.

He drew a hand from his pocket and pressed the palm to his forehead. The action made him think mechanically of his hat. Where was his hat? He must have lost it as he ran here. Some of the fellows would find it ; perhaps they would chaff him about losing it. His mind, in a puerile way, tried to decide what he should say if they made jokes because he lost his hat.

But what did he care ? He moved uneasily.

So it was all over ; and those vegetable seeds he had planted in the garden—there would be potatoes and beets and squashes — they would be growing, and he and Olive wouldn't be there. They would never be anywhere together. And that hen which was sitting —how Olive had counted upon taking care of those chickens ! In three weeks they were to have been married.

A quick, hot fury came again upon young Nawn.

"Oh, damn it! Damn it!" he cried, in a frenzy.

Then he rushed out-of-doors. He ran to the garden. He thrust his heavily shod foot violently into a hill of squashes; it relieved him to see the tender plants uprooted from the black earth. He trampled through the beet-bed. But he stopped as quickly as he had begun. "I'm acting like a fool," he said.

He recalled the paroxysms of anger or disappointment he had known as a child; he had never been taught to control his fury. He ought to have been taught—he proclaimed now aloud that somebody ought to have made him quell his violence. He could remember that his father had laughed and his mother had wept. But he had always been afraid of his father; he had feared and disliked him. He feared and disliked him now. At this moment he could almost have feared the strength of the hatred he felt towards that vigorous old man who sneered and chuckled, and never let the reins go from his hand. Aside from the fact that old Archibald Nawn held the money, his son knew very well that his father was the stronger man.

These thoughts, and a thousand vague and terrible ones, were making Robert's brain swim with the swiftness with which they galloped about.

"Hullo! Good land! What ye be'n doin' to your garden?"

A high, nasal voice asked this question, and the owner of the voice put his long legs over the fence that separated the bit of land from the field beyond it.

Robert wheeled about; he swallowed; his mouth was so dry that he could hardly speak.

There was Eben Lunt, his curious eyes going from the ruined vegetables to the face of the young man, and then back again.

"I swow," said Lunt, "you ain't goin' crazy, be ye? I thought you sot a sight by this garden."

"So I did," answered Robert; "but—but I got so

mad with the cut-worms and the squash-bugs. I was discouraged."

"They be discouragin'," was the response.

Lunt shuffled a little as he stood by the fence; then he shuffled off across the field in the direction of the post-office. He wanted to tell what he had just seen, and Robert knew he would tell, and he knew that he had not been believed when he had given his explanation of what he had just done.

When the factory-engine had given out that afternoon, Robert had felt like springing with one bound across space to this house that he might work here. Every stroke was a joy to him. Visions of a happiness that was both dazzling and sweet were with him as he labored. A home with Olive—that phrase expressed it all.

But now—

The young man staggered back to the house. He moved as if he were drunk. He entered the parlor and sat down on the pile of torn-up carpet. He covered his face with his hands as a woman might have done; and, like a woman, he began to weep. In the reaction he was weak and tremulous. But even then the tears came with difficulty—they were like drops of some searing, hot metal.

It was while he sat thus that Isabel Keating came riding along again on the highway near the house. The girl rode a great deal—the sense of power and exhilaration that comes from horseback riding made this exercise a favorite one with her. And she often came this way of late. Because, as she thought, with a sneer at her own weakness, "it hurt her so to see the house." Now she reached the place where the bars had been removed, and she stopped as she had stopped when she had found Olive there.

"After all," she was thinking, "they won't live here."

She leaned forward in the saddle. Was not that a

human figure in the front room? Yes, that was Robert's head, and it was bent. What was he doing? Anyway, it would do no harm to go up to the door. But Robert must be in the factory at this time in the afternoon.

Isabel slipped from her horse, as she had done once before. Holding her whip and her skirt in one hand, she walked softly over the grass to the open door. The occupant of the room had not heard her. He was sitting there with his face in his hands. He was sobbing. The aspect of the girl changed swiftly. Her face melted into a soft splendor. She gazed an instant.

Her eyes swept over all the visible space to learn if there were any one else there ; but Robert would not sit like this unless he were alone. She seemed to sway towards him, even before her feet moved. Then she stepped almost noiselessly forward—almost noiselessly, but not quite.

Robert became entirely motionless, listening. Surely no one had come. He did not wish to be seen like this.

A faint swish, swish across the now bare floor. Isabel put her hand very lightly upon the young man's shoulder.

"Oh, what is the matter?" she whispered.

Robert raised his head. His face was crimson.

"Isabel ! You !" he exclaimed. At first he wished to hide himself, but that impulse died the instant he met the girl's glance.

"Oh, Robert, what is the matter?" she whispered again, her hand still on his shoulder. "You—crying like a girl ! Oh !"—more softly yet—" how you must suffer !"

Robert gave a rapid brush of his hand across his face. He rose and stood beside his companion. In spite of the briefness of his years he thought he felt like an old man.

"Yes," he answered, "some things have happened— and I've made a regular baby of myself."

His eyes roved about the place, then came back to the eyes looking at him with tender sympathy. That mutual gaze soothed his spirit as a cool hand may soothe an aching head.

"A regular baby," he said, again, not knowing that he was repeating his words. "But"— he raised his head higher—"I think I sha'n't give way so again."

"I feel as if I had intruded," said Isabel, hesitatingly. She made a movement as if to go. Her voice was not steady as she added, "You'll let me be sorry that you are suffering, won't you, Robert?"

"Don't go—don't go," he responded, hastily. "It— it makes me better to see you, Isabel. I've had a hard time—a hard time."

He stood looking at her in silence.

"Do you think you can tell me what's happened?" Her usually authoritative voice was softly pleading.

Robert did not reply immediately; he was still looking at her. He roused himself.

"Of course I can tell," harshly. "You see, father wants us—Olive and me—to live with him—"

Here Robert stammered. Those words, "Olive and me," seemed to cut like daggers into his consciousness. He couldn't use those words any more—must not use them, though the thought of Olive as belonging to him was in his blood, in his breath. Whatever happened, though he never saw Olive again, though she married some one else, he believed that he should always think of her as belonging to him.

And yet—it was lovely that Isabel happened to be here now. He could have killed a man who pitied him; but to be pitied by this girl with the lustrously soft eyes—that was very different, very different indeed. He could bear that. He had an inclination to put out his hand and take Isabel's hand, but he stood straight and stiff beside her.

"Yes," she said, after a silence, "I know your father

means to have you and Olive live with him. I wondered if you would consent."

"You know it?" staring. "I don't see how you happened to know that."

"Easily enough. I heard him say so at the store to-day."

"At the store? Oh, well, it makes no difference, if he has begun to tell that. It makes no difference."

Robert now reached forward and took Isabel's hand. He held it fast; he looked down at it. It was a different hand from Olive's. This was long and soft, not hardened by work.

But even the touch of Olive's hand was helpful. Though she was so gentle, and deferred to him, and looked up to him, and admired him so, she was always as helpful as a strong, young comrade would be—and how he loved her! That was what he was saying to himself as he stood now holding Isabel's hand. But it was a comfort to have this dark girl near him.

"Why doesn't it make any difference?" she asked.

She moved closer to him. There was something of protection in her manner—as if she would stand between him and suffering. He felt this.

"Because—because—"

Here that dry, hot feeling came to his throat and mouth again. He tried to overcome it. Could it be really true that he was not going to marry Olive? He was angry that he had to suffer so. He made a fierce gesture with his free hand. He turned his head and met Isabel's eyes. What was there in them?

Suddenly he bent forward and kissed the girl's lips. Did she draw his head to her shoulder? She was tall, as tall as he. He gave a sob of relief as his forehead touched her shoulder.

But he sprang up quickly, though he was obliged to make an effort to do so. He was a strong man, and it occurred to him that he was acting like a woman.

" It's all over," he said, in a low voice.

Something flashed across Isabel's face, but she did not speak.

" Yes," continued Robert, conscious of a sense of ease in the prospect of telling Isabel what had happened. He did not wish to tell any one else, but this girl, whose presence helped him to bear his pain, he would tell her.

So he went on hurriedly. But he found that, when he attempted to grasp the particulars, everything concerning that interview was indefinite—everything but the one fact that he and Olive had quarrelled—though their difference did not seem like an ordinary quarrel —and that it was all over between them. That was certain. He dwelt upon that fact.

When he had finished, Isabel smiled as she assured him that it was only a "little tiff." Lovers were always disagreeing. She spoke in a friendly, commonplace way, but her whole face was curiously brilliant.

"And now I must go," drawing away a little. " Wasn't it odd that I should happen along here now ? You and Olive will make it all up in a day or two."

She looked at him in a way that drew him. He followed her to the door.

" Perhaps you'll let me come and talk with you ?" he said. " It does me good to talk to you."

Isabel's eyes fell. With the lashes still drooped, she answered :

" Oh yes ; come any time."

CHAPTER IX

AND Olive ! Was there any one ready to comfort her ? Alas, no !

When Robert had rushed away from her she stood gazing after him, seeing only indistinctly a figure flying over the field. She had a vague idea that that figure could not be Robert ; he would not go from her like that. She was suffering, and Robert would have stayed with her. She was half stunned ; she looked about her with glazed eyes that saw without carrying any definite impression to her mind. When lovers quarrel, it is to them as if the whole universe were convulsed ; the heavens are darkened, the sun has ceased to shine — nay, worse than that, it never will shine again.

Olive felt none of that frantic intolerance of suffering which Robert experienced. Perhaps a woman views suffering as something that must inevitably be endured ; while a man looks upon it as something from which he must escape—it does not matter so much how he escapes, so that he is released.

At first, as Olive saw Robert going away from her, she expected him to turn back. Of course he would not really leave her. But he did not turn. When he was out of sight she resumed her seat among the birches. She moved so calmly that it was as though she were deceiving herself by her own physical serenity. When she was seated she began to watch a large black ant as it toiled along, bearing the body of a fly. She watched this ant with such concentrated attention that her form stiffened. The creature had reached a long twig that was so embedded in the loose earth that it could not go under it. The ant became satisfied of this; then it tried to mount the twig with its burden in its mouth; it fell back.

Instantly Olive staked her hopes of reconciliation and happiness upon this possibility : if the insect succeeded in getting over the twig with its prey, she and Robert would yet be happy ; but if the ant failed—Olive shuddered. Her eyes grew hot and strained as they watched ; she became more rigid, bending forward, her hands resting on the ground.

How that little thing struggled ! Olive counted its attempts. She recalled that story of Bruce and the spider which had been in her reading - book at school. Was the ant going to give up the effort. She thought ants never gave up. It was standing still now. It had dropped the fly, but was evidently guarding it. Now, once more, it essayed to take its treasure over. It went up bravely, it was on the top—it fell rather than walked over — it scrambled after the dead fly, which had dropped ; taking it firmly, it marched off victorious.

Olive drooped forward, with her face to the cool grass. She was trembling, still thinking of the persistent creature she had been watching. She began to cry ; she said, brokenly, to herself, that it was a sign —it was a good sign. Then she cried harder than ever.

A brown thrasher alighted on the top of one of the birches, apparently with intent to sing. But he flew away, affrighted. What was that large thing lying on the ground, he asked himself as he flew. That was no place for him and his song.

For a long time Olive hoped and expected that Robert would come back. She was hoping this when he was holding Isabel's hand and looking into her eyes.

But finally she gave up this expectation. He would not come now; but perhaps he would call at the door that evening. She would sit where she could see the road along which he would walk. It would be dark, but she would know him; no darkness could prevent her from being aware of his coming.

So at last she went home. She listened dutifully to her mother's talk; she even joined in it as well as she could. Her mother told her that Esther Rice had been in again, this time to borrow some tea; and Esther Rice had heard that old Nawn had said at the store that he was going to have the young folks come home to live.

"I told her 'twa'n't no such a thing; 'n' she stuck to it, 'n' said her uncle Joe was in the store after m'lasses, 'n' he heard old Nawn with his own ears. 'Tain't so, though, is it, Olive?"

"I believe Mr. Nawn does want us to live with him," answered the girl.

"My goodness! ain't that odd? But you ain't goin' to, are you?"

"I don't know certainly what Robert has decided."

"Merciful sakes!" Mrs. Newcomb stared hopelessly. Then her gaze wandered to her daughter's gown, and she noticed again that the girl had made a change. "I s'pose you know, Olive, that you've got on your best dress."

"Yes, ma'am; I know it."

"Where've you been?"

Olive had placed herself in the nearest chair when she had entered the room. She now rose, finding that she must move about as her mother's words flowed on.

"'N' you look kinder strange, seems to me, now I come to notice you. Yes, you do look strange. Where've you been, I say?"

"I had an errand to Mr. Nawn's," was the answer.

"Mr. Nawn's? Gracious! No wonder you look

strange. I sh'd ruther go into the lion's den in the Bible than go there. What 'd he say? Do tell me what he said."

Olive looked pleadingly at her mother.

"Don't let's talk about it, now," she exclaimed. "I'm tired; my head aches a little. I guess I'll go 'n' take off this dress."

She hurried out of the room. Presently Mrs. Newcomb went to the door and called up the stairs:

"Olive! Olive, I say!" There was no answer. She called again, and added, "What sh'll we have for supper? Le's have griddle-cakes—them last I eat set first-rate; le's have some more?" Still no answer. "What in the world 's the matter with the child?" to herself. "She's as queer's she c'n be. I s'pose she'll come down when she gits ready, but she might jest speak."

Mrs. Newcomb walked to the wood-shed, brought some wood, and put it into the stove. Then she went again to the "chamber-way" and listened. There was no sound. The woman's face changed as she stood there. Had anything happened? It did not seem to her that anything could happen to Olive—she was always so "tough" and well.

Mrs. Newcomb was suddenly conscious of a quick, stabbing fear. She hurried up the stairs. The girl's door was shut. The woman pushed against it, having a faint feeling that she would find it locked. But it yielded immediately.

Olive was lying on the bed with her face towards the door. She was so white that Mrs. Newcomb grew still more frightened.

"Olive! Olive!" she cried, shrilly, as she ran across the floor. The girl stirred. "Why didn't you answer me? Why didn't you speak? You scared me 'most to death," querulously from the older woman.

"It didn't seem 's if I could speak," was the reply.

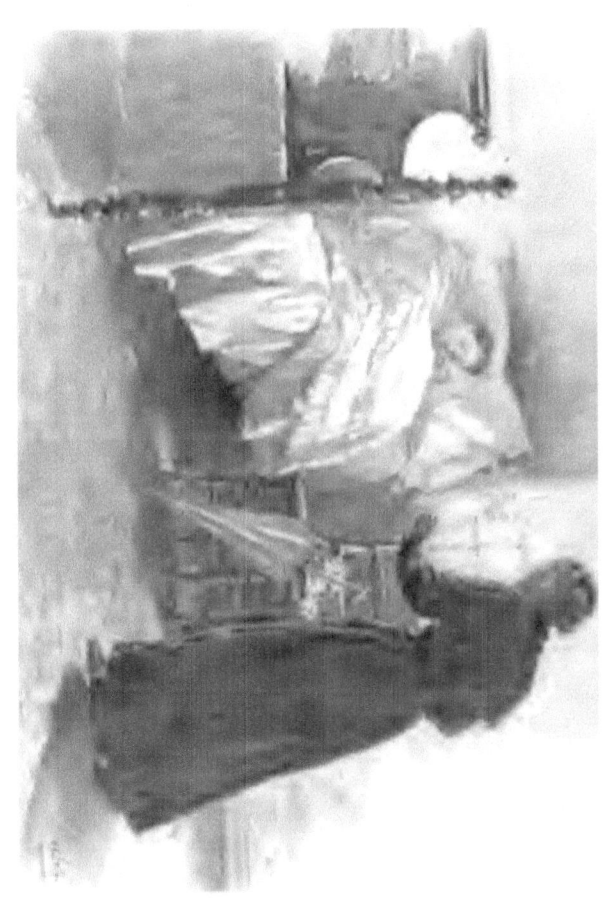

Then, with a great effort, Olive said, " I wish you'd go down-stairs, mother. I want to stay here a little while all by myself."

" But ain't you faint? You're 's white 's a sheet."

The mother put her hand on her child's forehead with solicitous movement.

" I guess I was faint at first. Things went black, and I dropped on to the bed. Then I didn't want to stir. I wish you'd go down-stairs, mother. I want to stay here and rest. I seem to be tired."

Mrs. Newcomb lingered.

" I'll bring you some of that currant-wine," she said, anxiously.

" No—no. Please, mother, go down. I sh'll be all right in half an hour."

Mrs. Newcomb went slowly to the door. Pausing there, she remarked that she would send Esther Rice for the doctor.

Olive raised herself on her elbow. " If you send for the doctor I shall never forgive you !" she exclaimed, in a piercing half-voice.

"Oh, I won't—I won't," hurriedly, and the woman went down the stairs.

But every few minutes she would go to the door that opened into the passage, and call out :

"Olive ! Olive ! Do you feel any better yet ?"

She would reiterate this call until the answer came :

" Yes ; but I'll stay up here a little longer."

Perhaps at the end of a couple of hours Olive became convinced that it would be easier for her to join her mother. She rose and carefully took off her gown, shaking it out of the window to remove the dust from it. She dressed in her every-day suit, studiously refraining from looking in the glass as she did so.

" Be you any better ?" was the question that met her as she entered the room.

Instead of shrieking and rushing out-of-doors, any-

5

where, so that she might be by herself, the girl made reply in a mild voice that she was well now ; she supposed that she must have been more tired than she knew. Should they have griddle-cakes for supper?

Oh no, Mrs. Newcomb "had got all over wanting" griddle-cakes, but would now take some toasted bread ; and would Olive open one of them tumblers of quince?

So the two sat down at dusk to a very late supper ; and it might have been husks that she was trying to swallow for all that Olive knew. Every moment she was listening for the sound of a step coming to the door. The kitchen window was open and the two could hear every sound in the neighborhood, and they knew what every slightest noise meant. There was a faint creaking, and then a snap ; that was Mr. Rice shutting his rolling barn door, and then snapping his spring-padlock into the staple. There was Esther Rice calling her cat to come and be put down cellar for a night's watching for rats. Farther away the storekeeper's dog was barking to be let into the house ; and Skip almost invariably barked at a quarter after eight. Beneath everything else was the soft, soothing sound of the Creeper as it moved slowly between its banks. Sometimes a carriage went over the bridge with a loud, bold kind of a sound.

Olive listened. She felt as if she were listening with her whole body, so intent was she. And she was obliged to reply to her mother's remarks. But at last it came to be the half after eight, when Mrs. Newcomb always went to bed, invariably making her daughter promise not to let anybody in, and not to make the slightest noise, for if there should be any disturbance she shouldn't sleep a wink all night. So Olive promised, as she had done hundreds of times before, and she went up-stairs to her own room. But why should she try to sleep?

She sat down on the side of the bed, and sat until she

was cold and stiff. Then she rose and groped for a shawl which, having found, she huddled about her and sat down again.

Could she pass the night in that way? Would she not be a raving maniac by the time daylight came? But she was quite sure that people did not become maniacs through great suffering—or did they?

The clock in the kitchen struck ten in its prolonged, hoarse tones; it struck slowly, and Olive remembered that she had not wound it before coming up-stairs. When the strokes had all been given, the girl suddenly became convinced that she could not — no, she could not — stay in her room just now a moment longer. She was quite sure that madness awaited her between these walls. She would go out, and when she came back perhaps she would be able to spend the rest of the night there. She stooped and took off her shoes. With the shawl over her shoulders and her shoes in her hand she went down the stairs, pausing at every step, fearful lest her mother should be roused and should speak. If she should speak Olive was positive that she could not bear it—no, she could not bear that.

But Mrs. Newcomb slept on soundly while her daughter was creeping out of the house. Once outside, Olive stood on the step-stone, dropped her shoes, and stretched her arms above her head. The cool, damp air blew benignly over her hot face. Her lips parted to receive it as though it were water which she might drink.

Soon she sat down on the step and drew on her shoes. She sat there for a time, wrapped in her shawl. She had left her room with no set purpose, save to leave it and get into the world outside. But finally she rose and walked towards the bridge. The bridge was hardly an inanimate object to her; it was something she had known, and with which she had been intimate ever since she could remember. When anything had troubled her as a child she had gone to the foot-path on the bridge and looked off up the winding stream or down into it. She went there now, having no definite consciousness of the direction her feet were taking.

Wasn't it time for the moon to rise? It was so damp that there must be a mist lying over the Creeper and along its shores. How many times had she watched the mist come up from the banks and spread itself all over the farms, softly, as if it were embracing the houses and trees.

CHAPTER X

WHEN Olive had reached the bridge, to her great surprise she felt too weak to stand. She was not used to weakness. She could not bear to think of going back to the house. She sat down on the wet planks and leaned her forehead against the uprights of the railing. Between these uprights she looked down towards the water, which she could not see, the fog lay so thick upon it. But she could hear it washing gently against the posts below. From the banks came the low, indefinite sounds made by the insects.

And now Olive began to think of Robert. It did not seem to her that she had been thinking of him since she had watched him flying from her. She had been trying to pull a knife from her heart and to keep herself from bleeding to death as she did so. But now Robert's face was before her, surrounded by flame, so vivid was it. It was his face of love and tenderness.

"Oh!—my darling!—oh!—oh!" she moaned.

Why, she could not live in this way! How did women live if they lost what she had lost? But he would come back—he loved her, and he could not help coming. She moaned again; it was a distinct relief to her to make this sound. She was glad that she had left the house. She might have wakened her mother.

As the moments passed she often uttered this little groan. She was telling herself that she had never been really unhappy, and she did not know how to bear unhappiness. She had heard old people say that a person "got over" anything. How very little old people, forty years old and more, knew! They must have forgotten that they had ever been young.

Suddenly she hushed the soft exclamations she had been making. Surely that was the quick crunching of gravel on the bank, made by a hasty foot. What if some one should come over the bridge? She had not thought of that; and if she had done so she would have known that there was slight probability that any person would be abroad at nearly eleven o'clock in this neighborhood.

Yes, that impetuously moving foot approached, and now it was on the planks. It was as if a man were almost running. Olive could only think that some one was going for the doctor. She did not try to rise. She pressed yet closer to the fence. This person, whoever he was, would dash by her, and then she would be alone again. All she asked was to be alone; surely that wasn't much to ask.

The fog was very thick; you could not see through it at all. Olive was thankful for that.

But when the man—for surely this new-comer was a man—had really begun to cross the bridge, he seemed to hesitate; and directly Olive knew that he had stopped. He had stopped not far from her, for she could hear him breathing. It gave her rather an eerie feeling to listen to the coming and going of that breath when she could see nothing.

All at once, for some reason which was too vague for her to grasp, she became convinced that this person near her was Robert. Indeed, she had no reason. She simply said to herself, "It is he," and straightway she began trembling again. She grasped the rods of the railing, half stifling her own breath lest he should hear it.

He had not been able to rest, then; he was wander-

ing in the night; he was suffering. At the thought
of his suffering, Olive's heart gave a great beat of
tenderness and sympathy. It was cruel that Robert
should suffer. She held fast to the uprights; she was
fearful that she had moved.

"Is anybody here?" cried a voice, harshly.

Yes, it was Robert. Olive did not reply—she could
not. She crouched still more closely against her support.

"I say, is anybody here?" again, and more loudly.
"Because, if there is, I tell you, I'll make you speak!"
Then lower: "The devil! Can't a fellow be alone
anywhere?"

It suddenly occurred to Olive that perhaps Robert
had been to her home. If he only had been there! She
wished to speak, but her voice would not come.

Robert swore furiously. Then, though she could not
see him, the girl became mysteriously aware that her
companion's mood had suddenly changed. He made a
quick, groping movement.

"Who is it?" in a sharp whisper. "Oh, who is it?"

This voice unloosed Olive's speech.

"Robert," she said, in a just audible tone.

"Oh! oh!" from the young man, who moved rapidly towards her, his hands gropingly outstretched.

"Where are you? Olive! Olive! Give me your
hands!"

Their fingers met and clasped each other. Then he
drew the girl to him, silently. He kissed her, fiercely,
again and again. Between his caresses he asked, im-
peratively:

"How could you—how could you treat me so?"

Even in the midst of this emotion, Olive thought
his question strange. But she clung to him as she
answered:

"I—I treat you? Oh, Rob, it was you—it was you!"

She felt him grow rigid.

"Be reasonable, Olive," he said, in a moment, and as if he were trying to be calm.

"Yes, yes," she replied. But a chill had come to her.

"You know it was very wrong of you to go to my father. You shouldn't have meddled." Silence on Olive's part. "No," more emphatically, "you shouldn't have meddled. Then he wouldn't have asked us to live with him. Seeing you made him think of it."

"But we needn't live there."

"Olive!"

Robert stamped his foot on the planks. How utterly unreasonable women were!

"He let us go on and get a house ready; then he took this whim—for it is a whim, isn't it?"

"But he won't leave his money to me, I tell you—"

"We can get along without it."

"Olive!" sharper than before. Then Robert tried again to be calm; he tried to explain, but he broke off to assert that women never could be reasonable.

All the time he held Olive fast in his arms. He was wild with the surprise, and doubt, and suffering he had been enduring. He had never dreamed that Olive would try to thwart him — for that is the way he thought of her behavior.

"Yes," she said, "we can get along without it. You told me that it wasn't certain at all that he would leave you his money. But "—a pause; Olive put her hand up to Robert's face and stroked it—"I am sorry I went to Nawn house—yes, I'm very sorry."

He kissed her again.

"And we've got to live there now, you see."

"Give me a little time to think about it," she pleaded. "I'm not convinced that it's necessary."

"Time!" fiercely again. "Not convinced! I wish you loved me enough! I wish you loved me as well as Is—"

Here the young man caught himself up. He was

ashamed that he had begun to say such an atrocious thing. But he was too late. He seemed now to be holding a statue in his arms.

Olive could not escape, but she leaned away from him.

"As well as Isabel loves you." She finished his sentence. "You were going to say that."

Robert's arms fell from her. "Yes," he answered, "I was going to say that."

"I'm sorry," responded Olive, now standing by herself. "I love you as well as I can love any one. That is all that I can do."

"How cool you are !" cried the young man. "You can stand there and talk like that !"

· No answer. The girl had been stung to her very soul by Robert's reference to Isabel. How could he have spoken in such a way ? And when would he go ? She could not long endure this. And why couldn't he understand that she could not immediately assent to living at Nawn house ? Why couldn't he understand that it was pulling at her very heart-strings to think of giving up that little home ? He gave her no time ; he was so impetuous, so arbitrary. And to mention Isabel ! Olive choked. Her blood was on fire. She was very well aware that she was going to consent to live at Nawn house ; dreadful as that would be, she would still be with Robert. But that mention of Isabel— something hard and stiff rose in the girl. She told herself, however, that she was above being jealous.

"You never loved me !" cried Robert, like a spoiled child. Still no answer. Olive's hands were hanging down, shut tightly. "Oh, very well !" he exclaimed, in a fury of excitement.

He turned and walked away. The girl heard him tramping on the planks, and then crunching on the gravel. Should she call him back ? No, she could not speak ; her throat was closed, her tongue frozen.

As soon as she could no longer hear Robert's footsteps, Olive seemed to be let loose. She ran towards home, stumbling and gasping, but keeping up her pace. She crept noiselessly up to her room, slipped off her damp gown, and got into bed. Once there, with the blankets pulled up about her, nature asserted itself ; she fell asleep directly.

As for Robert, he did not pause, either, on his way home. His furious sense of having been wronged grew with every moment. When he came near the house he saw that there was a light in the room where his father usually sat. It was sometimes late before Mr. Nawn went to bed. He said he couldn't sleep, and why should he put himself where he expected to sleep, just to be disappointed? Now, as he heard the outer door open and shut, he went to the landing. He was particularly wakeful, and perhaps he might be able to amuse himself with that boy of his.

When Robert was half-way up the stairs the old man called out :

"Come in and have a talk. I don't suppose you're any more sleepy than I am. Rheumatism and love keep a man awake."

Robert's impulse was to decline this invitation, but he dared not do so. When he came where the light from the lamp struck him, his father burst into a laugh.

"By George!" he cried, "I think I'll stick to my rheumatism."

He let himself down into his big chair. His son stood before him, haggard, his hair wet with the fog, his eyes gleaming, his lips pressed together.

"Did you want me?" asked the young man.

"Yes, of course, or I shouldn't have called you in here. What in the devil have you been up to?"

Robert dropped into a chair. He was beginning to feel weak.

"I s'pose you've seen that girl," remarked his father.

"What girl?" sullenly.

"Why, how·many are there? The Newcomb girl, of course."

Robert leaned his elbows forward on his knees.

"Yes," he answered; "I've just left her. It's all over between us."

"All over? What? Have you been such a damned fool as that?"

Mr. Nawn smote his leg with the palm of his hand as he spoke.

The younger man gazed at him in a sort of surprised stupor. Finally he said:

"I thought you didn't approve of Olive."

"That was before I saw her. Well, Bob, I must say you're a greater jackass than I thought you were—and that's expressing a good deal."

Here the speaker smiled and his hearer's face flushed a deep red. But he succeeded in keeping silent. Mr. Nawn lounged back in his chair. He put one large, corded hand on the table where the lamp stood, and drummed with his fingers, eying his son meanwhile.

"It's hard to know what you'll like," at last said Robert. "You didn't want me to marry Olive."

"Pooh! You were going to, all the same. You haven't been and quarrelled with her to please me. You needn't tell me that. And now, when I'd made a little plan for you both to live here, and have it cheap all 'round, you go to see her and come home looking as if you'd killed her, and a few others. I s'pose your nasty temper got the better of you. You have a vile, nasty temper, Bob—you know you have. I'm half in the mind to go over to-morrow and congratulate the girl on getting rid of you—only, I s'pose, I'd have to meet that ninny of a mother of hers. Well, who's going to be the next one?"

CHAPTER XI

MRS. NEWCOMB INTERFERES

ROBERT looked up savagely. "The next one?" he repeated.

"Yes. Don't say my words over after me. What are you going to do now? There's Isabel Keating. Very likely she loves your handsome face. You look a mighty sight as I did when I was your age."

Here the old man smiled once more. Robert dropped his head down on his hands, his fingers thrust into his hair. Still keeping this position, he said:

"You wanted me to marry Isabel. You swore at me because I loved somebody else. Now the very devil himself would be puzzled to know what you do want me to do."

"Oh, I've concluded to be a spectator merely," was the answer, the bony fingers still drumming on the table. "I'm not going to meddle any more. I'm going to sit still and see what kind of a mess you'll make of your life. You've got enough of your mother in you to—to—"

The old man's voice ceased. His mind had suddenly travelled back to that time when he had first seen the girl who became his wife. How beautiful she had looked to him then!—how quickly her beauty had faded, and how soon he became tired of her! But that was the way. Who expected a man to remain in love with his wife?

"I suppose," he said, aloud, "that young men will go on thinking they're in love and calling themselves idiots afterwards. There's nothing to stop them. Now you, Bob," with an incisiveness of manner that roused the young man like the thrust of a knife, "may do just as you please. I'm not going to advise—I tried it once. You'd better go to bed. I didn't know but you might make me forget my rheumatism." The young man rose. "Hand me that long pipe, will you? 'Baccy has risen—somebody's making a lot of money on 'baccy just now. Off with you, Bob. I'm going to make a bet with myself as to what girl you'll marry. I'll tell you some day how I bet. Why don't you go? If you will get in love you must expect to suffer."

Robert was standing near the door, his hand on the latch. "Father," he said, hurriedly, "tell me which one you'd rather I'd marry, and I'll go and ask her to-morrow."

"I sh'n't do it. Make your own choice. It's a great pity that you think you have only to lift your finger to either of them."

Robert flung out of the room. It was surprising how irritating his father could be; he "took all the conceit" out of his son every time he gave himself the trouble to talk with him.

The next day the young man did not go to the factory, though word was sent him that the engine was repaired. As soon as he had made a pretence of eating his breakfast he hurried to the little house he had bargained for. On his way he borrowed a wheelbarrow. Into this he put the carpet with the large pink roses on it, and he trundled his burden the three miles to Falls Village to the dealer of whom he had bought it. He took a wheelbarrow because he would not hire a horse and wagon; and he drove a rather good bargain with the furniture merchant; but of course he had to lose some money. He hurried back. The sitting-hen he sold to the nearest neighbor, who would not disturb her; and he endeavored to sell the prospective garden crop, but the man demurred at that; he said the ground had been "kicked up too much."

"That's because I was a fool," said Robert, to himself.

Another thing he did when he was in Falls Village : in the local paper he put an advertisement of a small house and farm for sale, on easy terms. He did not want his father to meddle with this business.

Then he went to the small house. He sat down in the doorway and gazed about him. He was thinking that he was the most wretched man in the world. He didn't know how he was going to endure existence. It would be a good thing to make an end of it all. His heart was full of love for Olive and anger towards her. How could she have hesitated? Isabel wouldn't have hesitated, he felt sure ; she wouldn't have weighed her answer. He tried to think of Isabel, and of how her face had looked when she had come there to him a few hours ago. But his thoughts would slip away and return to Olive.

After a time he bethought him of the good bargain he had driven with the man who had bought back his carpet. He pulled his pocket-book out and counted his money. He was conscious of a kind of pleasure, dull, to be sure, in the feel of the money in his fingers. He was sorry now that he had not stopped at the savings-bank and deposited this money. He should have no special need of funds now.

He thrust his purse into its place, and leaned his head against the casing of the door where he sat. His mind became more and more dull. Presently he was asleep. He woke half an hour later—woke with such an intense longing for Olive that he thought she must come to him. He said, aloud :

"I will forgive everything. Only let me have her again."

He gazed eagerly about him, as if expecting to see her. But he could not find her. At last he locked the door. This time he did not put the key in the place agreed upon by him and Olive; he dropped it into his pocket and strode away, frowning heavily.

He did not go home. Why should he go home and run the risk of having his father talk to him? And to-day he was not going to the shop. At a turning of the road he hesitated, then he walked on towards a large white house that stood behind pines and elms on a hill.

Isabel Keating lived there. It was her place. She had no father or mother, but an aunt lived with her, and there was a woman who was "hired help." At the gate, that stood open between two stone posts, Robert hesitated again. He was, at the last moment, turning away, when an authoritative voice exclaimed:

"Why, Rob, is that you? Come and see these new rose-bushes—they're just lovely."

The young man was glad to go up the carelessly kept gravel-walk; as he fell into step with the girl it was as if he had been transported a thousand miles. His spirits rose; he kept gazing at his companion. How alive she was! How red must be the blood that ran in her veins! And she was so gently gay; she referred to nothing unpleasant; it was as if there had nothing unpleasant happened.

Robert stayed on and on. When two hours had passed he was ashamed that he had not gone away long ago.

"You've done me good, Isabel," he said, looking wistfully at her as he held her hand in good-bye.

She smiled. "Have I? I wasn't thinking of doing good. That isn't much in my line."

"I wish you'd let me come here sometimes, Isabel."

"Of course; come any time."

And now she looked at him. He met the gaze an

instant. He sighed, dropped her hand and walked away.

Within the next few weeks Robert was often at the Keating place. If he had been a man to reason concerning his emotions, he would have said to himself that it was like an opiate to see Isabel. The girl did not mention anything disagreeable; she was peculiarly gentle and deferential. Strolling of an evening among the rose-bushes of the old Keating garden, with its present owner beside him, Robert was like one whose memory was partially benumbed. Half a dozen times he was on the point of begging the girl to marry him, but something restrained him. He feared that she would laugh at him for his fickleness.

When he left Isabel and walked back towards his home it was as if a tiger leaped at him and mangled him, so keenly did memory awaken. He would set his teeth and mutter oaths between them as he hastened on.

He wondered that he never saw Olive on the road anywhere. He longed to meet her, and he was afraid; for one part of him would spring forward with intensity of joy, while another part would scowl in hatred of anything that should make him suffer so. He was as one rent in twain. Many evenings, after he had said good-night to Isabel, he hurried over the fields to a hill back of Olive's home. From there he could look down on the little house. There was always a light there; he wondered at that. He would not speak Olive's name to any one, and naturally no one spoke her name to him.

Thus nearly two months went on. It was very hot weather now, and it was dry; the greenery was dusty and seemed shrunken. Robert had just left the factory. He was thinking of how Isabel had looked the evening before, as she sauntered in the garden, wearing a white dress, with a sweet-smelling flower at her throat. He had told her that he wanted her to be his wife. The hour, the fragrance, Isabel's eyes—but he did not analyze anything. He drifted on the tide that carried him pleasantly. He had been sure that she would say yes, and she had said it. He was aware that people in the neighborhood told each other that " Rob Nawn is going with Isabel Keating." His father had informed him, with a questioning grin and nod of the head.

The young man now stood a moment at the road edge. He was in his shirt-sleeves, his coat was on his arm, his hat pushed back from his forehead. He was asking himself whether he should go home across the field till he came to the Creeper. It was so dusty in the highway ; the Creeper had shrunk between its banks.

A small figure appeared from the group of pine-trees across the road, a figure with a sun-bonnet on its head, a white apron over a dark calico gown. Robert at last became aware that this woman was Mrs. Newcomb. She did not try to climb the rail-fence, but put one hand upon it, beckoning to him with the other.

He walked towards her. He thought she looked worn and almost ill.

" I wish you'd come into the field here," she said, speaking in a low voice, as if she were afraid of being overheard.

He sprang over the fence. She began directly to re-trace her steps, and he walked beside her. He waited, and she did not speak. Finally he remarked that " it was a dreadful dry time."

" Yes," she responded, " we do need rain." A pause, and then she added, " Sometimes I feel 's if, mebby, if we could have a shower, she'd be better." Robert opened his lips to speak, but no sound came to them. " I wish we could git some rain," said Mrs. Newcomb. " Esther Rice said she heard they had a tempest at the Falls day before yesterday. When I told Olive,

6

she smiled.   I d' know what made her smile, I'm sure.
She's dretful thin."

"What?"   Robert took hold of his companion's arm.
He held it so closely that she gave a little cry.   He
dropped it and moved away a step.   "Yes," he said,
hardly knowing that he spoke, "I don't remember
when there's been such a drouth.   Ever so many of
the wells round here have given out."

What did this woman mean by coming to him and
telling him that Olive was "dretful thin?"   And why
didn't she speak if she had anything to say?   And
wasn't Olive in the habit of smiling in these days?
He remembered her smile and the adoring look in her
eyes.

Mrs. Newcomb untied and then retied her sun-bonnet.   She was perplexed as to how to bear herself.   But
she would not retreat.

CHAPTER XII

FORGIVENESS

"I s'pose you hadn't heard Olive's be'n sick," said Mrs. Newcomb, at last.

"No," from the young man, his face growing yet paler.

The woman looked at him with a keen question in her faded eyes.

"Is that true?" she asked.

"True? Yes," impatiently; "do you think I'm lying?"

"That's strange."

"No, 'tisn't. Nobody speaks to me about Olive. Everybody else would know but me."

"Mebby that's so."

"I tell you 'tis so."

Mrs. Newcomb twisted her bonnet-strings.

"I wish I knew whether I'm doin' wrong or not," she exclaimed. "I can't do nothin' with Olive, anyway. She won't have a doctor. I told her she wanted tonin' up. She needs bitters, but she won't take a thing. She don't eat nor sleep. I've steeped thoroughwort 'n' yeller-dock, but she won't have nothin' to do with it. I arst her what kind of a quarrel you 'n' she had had, 'n' she jest looked at me 'n' wouldn't speak. She ain't a grain like herself. She's been failin' for 'bout two months, but she didn't take to her bed till a week ago yisterd'y. In the mornin' that day Esther Rice come in to borry a cup of granulated sugar. We both thought Olive was up-stairs. Esther was tellin' that folks said

you 'n' Isabel Keating were going to be married 'fore
fall. 'N' she said Jim Larkin saw you kiss Isabel one
night in her garden. You know everybody knows everything here. It turned out that Olive wasn't up-
stairs; she was in the next room, 'n' she had heard
every word. When Esther was gone, she come into
the kitchen. She was jest as pale as ashes, and her
eyes were blazin'. 'Mother,' she said, 'I heard what
Esther told you. I d' know why you need to be so
private about it. If Robert Nawn did kiss Isabel
Keating, and if he is going to marry her, he has a
right to.'

"I didn't ask her no questions. I thought if she
wanted to tell me anything, she would. She said that
night to supper that she felt better than she had sence
she hadn't been well, and she guessed she'd go to work
the next day. But the next day she didn't git up.
'N' she ain't be'n up sence. She says she ain't in no
pain.

"I thought "—here the woman raised her eyes to her
companion's face and gazed at him a moment before
she finished her sentence—"I thought that you ought
to know, Robert, and if you was to blame—"

Robert moved uneasily. His features worked. He
was thinking of Olive lying in her chamber. She had
been lying there when he had been walking among
sweet flowers with Isabel in her garden.

Mrs. Newcomb wished that Robert would speak.
She guessed that she didn't understand young folks.

"I hope I ain't done wrong," she said, feebly.

"Wrong?" Robert spoke the word mechanically.
He felt like one groping in blackness. He was thinking of what he had said to Isabel the evening before.
He had told her that she must be his wife. She had
given him her promise, and he had taken her in his
arms and kissed her. She had clung to him. He had
thrilled with the knowledge of her love for him. He

had thought then that, after all, perhaps he could be
happy. But now? He would have given everything
in the world if he had kept away from Isabel.

Poor Mrs. Newcomb's heart was sinking lower and
lower. She gazed at the handsome, scowling face before her. She wondered what had happened.

"I guess"—she began, in a half - whisper—"I guess
'twould kill Olive if she knew that I've been to you.
But I felt 's if I couldn't have things goin' on in this
way ; 'n' I didn't see how Olive could hold out many
days, if she didn't take a turn for the better, 'n' I
jest resked it. But don't you ever let her, nor nobody, know I've be'n to you. Will you promise you
won't ?"

" Yes, I promise."

Mrs. Newcomb stood looking intently at the young
man for a moment ; then she turned away. She
walked slowly, her head bent. There was no hope,
then. She didn't know what had happened to separate
these two. Of course it was trying that old Nawn
wanted the young couple to go there to live ; but that
wouldn't separate them. Her mind, never very broad
nor strong, feebly turned the matter over and over, and
could make nothing of it. She had done what she was
able to do.

She walked on, stumbling over mossy hillocks. She
would send for her sister Ruth. She must have somebody to help. It was a great pity that Olive had
become interested in young Nawn. She didn't like
the Nawns ; she didn't care if they did have money.
Tears gathered in the woman's eyes and blinded her.
She brushed them away ; but they would continue to
come. She stumbled still more ; she fell over the root
of a tree. Instantly she felt herself picked up by
strong, impatient arms.

"Can you walk now ?" asked Robert, hoarsely " Because I'm going on."

He kept his arm about her till she answered that she thought she could get along. She caught hold of his sleeve. He had no coat now. Holding him thus, she asked, eagerly :

" Are you going to her ?"

" Yes—yes."

" Don't you tell I told you—don't you tell !"

" No—no—I won't."

Robert ran on in uncontrollable haste. Mrs. New-comb hurried as fast as she could. She wished to be in the house, lest Olive should ask for her. Her spirits began to rise. Perhaps she had done right, after all. She thought she knew by Robert's face that he loved Olive. She didn't believe he was going to marry Isa-bel. Yes, she had done right ; and she couldn't have Olive die before her eyes and not do a thing to help her ; and the girl wouldn't take thoroughwort and yel-low-dock.

Robert vaulted over fences and stone walls and tore through thickets of briers. From the instant he had decided to go to Olive that instant his mind was filled with the fear that she might die before he could see her again. He did not give a thought as to what he should say to her. He must see her. Death might snatch at her before he reached her. He could keep even death away.

When he came within a few rods of the house he slackened his pace and compelled himself to walk de-corously up to the back door, which stood open, save that the screen door was latched. He stepped in softly, and paused in the kitchen, trying to breathe more easily, and listening as he stood. The door leading to the chamber-way was open. He stepped to this place, and paused again.

In a moment a weak voice above-stairs said, " Moth-er ! Mother, is that you ?" The voice that spoke was the sweetest voice in the world to Robert Nawn.

Without waiting for any answer, Olive said, "I wish you'd bring me a glass of cold water, mother."

Robert turned and looked about him. He saw the water-pail standing by the sink with its cocoanut dipper in it. He caught up the pail and hastened down the slope to the well. He would bring a fresh drink. His hand trembled as he hooked on the bucket and let it run rapidly down. But how long it was in going! At last he hurried back to the house, swinging the brimming pail. As he stepped to the stairs with the dipper in his hand, Olive cried out again, this time shrilly:

"Mother! Mother! Oh, who is it?" The young man made but two or three strides to the top of the stairs. He heard that penetrating voice call once more, "Oh, who is it?"

Then he had reached the door of the little chamber under the roof. This door stood open. He saw Olive sitting up in bed. She had a red shawl wrapped about her, for she was shivering. The white ruffle of her night-gown showed at her throat. Her face was so white and thin that Robert's heart gave a great beat of fear. Her eyes were distended, but a lovely light filled them as she saw who had come. Then she shrank away, putting out her hand as if to ward off this new-comer.

"I s'pose you and she are married," she said; "but you needn't have come to tell me. You needn't have done that."

Robert stepped gently and quickly across the floor. He bent over the bed, extending the dipper he held.

"Here's your water," he said. "Drink; you need it."

She obeyed, unsteadily, and drinking quickly. She handed the dipper back, saying:

"Take it, and go away."

Robert pushed it one side, not noting that it fell on the floor. He seized the frail hand; it fluttered and struggled, then was still in his grasp.

"It's cruel of you to come here," she whispered.

"No—no," he whispered in return. "I've come because I love you so, Olive."

He sat down on the bed and put his arm about her, and her head dropped to his breast. She breathed a long, unsteady breath.

"And you and she are not married?"

"No—no."

"But Esther Rice said that—"

"Esther Rice is always carrying tales."

"So she is—so she is. Then it wasn't true?"

"No—no."

"And you're not going to marry her?" trying to draw herself away, and being held more closely in consequence.

"I'm not going to marry Isabel Keating," with great emphasis.

Another long breath parted the girl's lips. "But," she began, then she shuddered. In a moment she continued, "Esther Rice said that Jim Larkin saw you kiss Isabel. Oh, Robert, did you?"

The young man hesitated an instant. He drew Olive to him with both arms. He bent down and kissed the dishevelled brown hair; he kissed it again and again. He gave a great sob. Two tears dropped from his eyes upon Olive's forehead.

Olive reached up a thin hand to his cheek. "What!" she exclaimed, "are you crying, Rob?"

"Yes," he burst out, violently, "I did kiss Isabel. P'r'aps men are different from women. I can't tell. I've been mad for the last two months. I wanted to forget you. I thought I should die if I couldn't forget you in some way. But I can't keep up that sort of thing, and I'm not going to try. I want you to marry me, Olive, right away—this afternoon. Will you? Then I'll go and get the minister. We're all ready to be married, you know—we were ready last June."

Olive lay very still in the enfolding arms. "Are you sure you love me more than you love Isabel?" she asked, finally.

"Sure. You needn't ask me that."

"And yet you kissed her?" in a solemn, wondering voice.

Robert moved uneasily. He was wondering why Olive couldn't understand some things.

"I hope you'll forgive me for that," he said. She was silent. "Olive," in a louder voice, "I hope you'll forgive me for that?"

"Ye—s. Yes, I shall forgive you."

"And you'll marry me this afternoon? I'll bring the minister here."

"But perhaps I shall be feeble and a burden. You know, Rob, men get so tired of a feeble wife."

"I want you, anyway."

"And I must be a help to you, you know." She put her arms about his neck. "Do you really want me, dear old Rob?" Her face was radiant, her eyes like stars.

"Yes—yes—ten thousand times, yes! I can't live without you!"

The girl looked at him intently, happiness, returning life in her gaze. She did not smile. Her face was too rapt for smiling. All at once a cloud came over her countenance. "Before I marry you, there's something I want to ask you," she said.

CHAPTER XIII

AGAIN Robert stirred apprehensively. But he held his burden still more closely. He had made up his mind that nothing should take her from him. He was telling himself that he had been a fool and a knave. But nothing should take Olive from him.

"Well, what is it?" he asked.

"It isn't much. Only this — has mother spoken to you about me? I've been afraid she'd go to you and tell you I was ill. Has she?"

"No," was the answer, quickly and emphatically.

Olive's face lighted still more. "Oh," she said, softly, "I'm so glad! I couldn't have borne that, anyway. I was so afraid she'd go to you and tell you I was pining away, and then you would, perhaps, be sorry, and come back to me for pity's sake. No, I couldn't have borne that anyway. I should always think you came back because you pitied me. I'd much rather die— much rather. I've been thinking in these days that it's real easy to die, and I was so thankful that it was easy."

Robert pressed the girl yet closer to him, a terrible fear overshadowing the consciousness of the lie he had just told.

"But you are not going to die now," he cried; "you're going to live and be happy with me?"

Olive kissed Robert's cheek. "Yes," she answered, "I'm going to live and be happy with you. If I'm only with you I shall be happy. Oh, I'm going to live now."

A foot-fall sounded below-stairs.

"There's mother!" joyfully. "Rob, you go down and tell mother I'm better. You tell her I don't need thoroughwort and yellow-dock," smiling.

And Robert thought his heart would break, even in his joy, as he saw how wan and thin she looked in spite of her happiness.

Olive withdrew from her companion. "Go. Mother will be so glad."

Robert rose. "And I shall go for the minister, too," he reiterated. "I shall bring him this afternoon. I'll tell her that, too."

"Yes, you may tell her that."

Robert bent over her, murmuring, "Oh, how I love you!" then he left the room, and presently Olive heard him speaking hurriedly to her mother, and then she heard her mother's exclamation of surprise; then Robert's footsteps quickly going down the road.

She raised herself higher on the bed so that she might look through the window. She could see the end of the Red Bridge, and the shining of the Creeper below it; very soon she saw Robert; he had reached the bridge, and went swiftly over it and out of sight.

She sank to her pillow. She clasped her hands together as one sees hands clasped in the recumbent statues on old tombs. A smile, full of a heavenly effulgence, was on her face. She was saying to herself, "Dear Rob! Dearest Rob!" She could allow herself to say that now; for, after all, he had come back to her. He had loved her all the time. And, after many happy years as his wife, she could, perhaps, forget that he had kissed Isabel. Still, it was very strange that he could do that. She couldn't understand. It would not be possible for her to imagine herself able to kiss any young man save Robert. But, perhaps, men were different; they must be.

After a few moments Mrs. Newcomb came into the

room. She exclaimed, "Why, how much better you
do look, Olive! I guess you'll be pickin' up right
along now."

"Yes, I'm going to get well. I'm going to be a help
to Robert, not a burden."

She spoke proudly. She caught her mother's hands
and pulled her down to her. "Oh, mother, are you
crying? Don't cry now!"

But Mrs. Newcomb's tears would gather and fall.
She said, brokenly, that "'twas a dretful thing to have
a daughter married; and then no human being knew
how she had worried about Olive."

So she talked on, and the girl listened, a vague smile
on her face.

When the elder woman ceased speaking, Olive asked
if her clothes might be brought to her; she thought
she would dress; and she would like a bit of toasted
bread and a cup of tea.

Mrs. Newcomb joyfully assisted her. She was saying in her own mind, meanwhile, that Olive would
have died if she hadn't seen Robert. And the mother
congratulated herself on what she had done. Nevertheless, there was a bitter drop in her gratitude—the
knowledge that she had been obliged to go to Robert.
She hoped that no one knew that she had done so.
She wondered if Esther Rice had any clew to that
interview. If she had—here the woman shuddered.
She didn't feel that she understood her daughter very
well, but she knew that Olive's pride would deeply resent that she had done—that Rice girl found out
everything eventually. Having come to this conclu-
sion, Mrs. Newcomb stopped crying, and began to help
Olive to dress. It took a long time, for the invalid had
become weak from lack of food and sleep, but at last
she had on a pale-pink print gown which she had made
for what her mother called a "dress-up for afternoons,"
when the work was done. Then slowly and carefully

she went down the steep stairs, and was established in
the rocker in the sitting-room, a shawl wrapped about
her. To Mrs. Newcomb it was as if some dearly loved
guest had come, and she forgot that she herself liked
to play the invalid.

For the first time in many weeks Olive found that
food was not as chaff in her mouth. Having eaten and
drunk, she lay back in her chair and watched her
mother tidy the room. Robert had said he would try
to bring the minister at three that afternoon.

At ten minutes after two Esther Rice came over to
borrow half a nutmeg, and, incidentally, to return two
table-spoonfuls of tea that she had borrowed the week
before.

Miss Rice paused in the doorway, to gaze at Olive
with uncontrolled astonishment. " I do declare!" she
exclaimed, " I never expected to see you down-stairs,
Olive, 'cept 'twas in your caskit. How be ye, anyway?"

" I'm ever so much better," was the reply.

" Well, I sh'd think you was! I s'pose' 'twas the
thoroughwort 'n' dock, wa'n't it? But you look 'bout
's pindlin' 's I ever see anybody look." Esther's sharp
little eyes roamed over the two women. It seemed
to her that there was something unusual in the air.
" Mother thought she seen Robert Nawn goin' towards the bridge to-day ; 'n' she thought he went jes 's
if he'd been here," she now remarked.

" Yes," said Olive, " he was here."

" Gracious me! was he? I wouldn't have him play-
in' fast and loose, nohow," severely. " I ain' much
opinion of them Nawns, anyway, though they have
got money. 'N' we all know that young Nawn's been
courtin' Isabel Keating. Jim Larkin seen Robert—"

" We've heard that story," interrupted Olive, with
some dignity. She felt a shiver of fear go over her
lest Esther should relate again how Robert had been
seen to kiss Isabel.

"Oh, you have, have you? Mebby I have told it in here to your mother. But one thing I 'ain't told, for I didn't know it till half an hour ago, 'n' that is that Isabel told Kate Ray this mornin' that she was engaged to Robert Nawn, but there wa'n't no time set for the weddin'. Kate Ray told Nancy Troute, 'n' Nancy told me. You see, it came real straight."

"You can't tell nothin' by what you hear," remarked Mrs. Newcomb, glancing fearfully at her daughter, who was trying to sit strong and straight in her chair.

"That must be a mistake, Esther," said Olive, in a clear, precise way. "There's been a misunderstanding. Isabel couldn't have said that, for Robert and I are to be married this afternoon. Robert thought he should bring the minister about three o'clock."

Esther stared silently for an instant. "You don't say so!"

She looked out of the window, following Olive's glance. She saw two men just appearing in sight on the foot-path of the bridge. One was Robert, dressed in his best, the other was Mr. Lang, who had been the minister in the nearest Congregational Church at Falls Village for ten years, and who preached every Sunday afternoon in the school - house of the hamlet here. They came on quickly, the young man looking very pale and excited, and evidently trying to listen to his companion's words.

Esther rose. She was thinking that she would be the first to tell this news. But she believed, all the same, that Robert had been courting Isabel Keating. She believed that he had kissed Isabel. It was all very interesting. She walked to the door; then she remembered that her borrowed half-nutmeg lay on the table. She returned for it. Before she reached the door again it was opened, and Mr. Lang came in with his jovial, wedding manner in use.

"Good - morning, Mrs. Newcomb; good - morning,

Miss Rice," shaking hands; "and how is Miss Olive to-day? I must call her Miss Olive while I may—ha! ha! You're looking finely, Olive—and that's the way a bride should look."

He held the girl's hand a moment in both his own in a fatherly way, looking down at her, and thinking he had never seen a lovelier face, nor one with more truth and sweetness in it. And, strangely, his heart ached at the sight of it.

He turned. "Don't go, Miss Rice; stay and be a witness; I ask it as a favor."

So Miss Rice stayed and saw the ceremony performed, and stepped up and congratulated the bride and groom, and then hurried away home to leave her nutmeg, tell the news there, and then start on a trip through the neighborhood.

She did not quite dare to go in at the gate of the Keating place to disseminate her information, but she walked more slowly along the road in that vicinity, and considered it the best of good luck when she saw Isabel come sauntering down the drive-way as if she had started for a walk. The girl nodded a careless greeting, and was about to go on when Miss Rice hastened to say, in a jocular manner:

"You're too late for the wedding, Isabel."

Isabel paused just in advance of her companion. She half turned and put her question over her shoulder, "What wedding?"

Esther rolled her morsel under her tongue. She dilated with her knowledge. "Guess!" she responded.

Isabel wheeled around. "What do you mean?" she asked. "You look as if you were stuffed and running over with something."

Esther resented the words and the manner, but she did not mean to show her resentment. "You jest give a guess," she responded.

Isabel raised her shoulder in her irritation; but she

was too curious to walk away without any more words. "Oh, well, then, I guess that Martin Lecky has married his third wife."

Esther laughed. She was feeling that she had never had so good a piece of news to tell. She hated to part with it, and yet she was in a hurry to do so. "You're miles away," she returned—"jest miles. It's a young man, and he ain't never been married before. Now do you know? You're real well acquainted with him."

Miss Rice chuckled in her satisfaction.

Isabel's figure straightened slightly, and she lifted her head as if to confront an enemy. What could make Esther Rice look like that? Could it be— But no, that was impossible.

"You'll have to tell me if you want me to know," she answered, coldly.

"I was one of the witnesses," remarked Esther. "Mr. Lang, he asked me to stay. I guess 'twas real sudden." Miss Rice gathered herself together. She saw that her companion would not wait an instant longer.

CHAPTER XIV

"BRING HER HERE"

"YES," went on Esther, "Robert Nawn and Olive Newcomb were married about twenty minutes ago. I was the first one that called her Mrs. Nawn. I d' know 's I envy anybody that's got into that Nawn family; though I d' know but Robert's a good fellow enough himself."

While she spoke, Esther's eyes never left Isabel's face. She saw the features become strained and a gray hue overspread them. She was watching for the girl to topple over in a faint, but she stood erect and strong.

It was but the briefest time before Isabel said, steadily, "Yes, it must have been very sudden, indeed, for I saw Robert last night, and he did not mention that the day was set."

Esther stared disappointedly She loved melodrama, and she had had very little of it in her life. "Yes," she responded, "I s'pose 'twas jest as sudden 's it could be; though you know they were goin' to be married last June. Robert's been dretfully in love with Olive ever since she come back from her gran'-father's to the Falls Village."

She delivered this last shot straight between the girl's eyes and watched to see the ball hit. She was disappointed, however. Isabel said that she was in a great hurry, and couldn't stop any longer. She opened her parasol and walked quickly down the road, so that Miss Rice was obliged to go on.

7

As soon as she was around the corner and out of sight, Isabel paused. She looked about her, as if seeking an escape from something. She climbed a fence into a field and went across it at the same pace. She was making for her home, but she did not dare to go back by the highway lest she might meet some one ; and if she met some one she might scream out like an animal whom the sight of a human being infuriates.

It seemed to take Isabel but a moment to reach the back door of her own home. The house-keeper was sitting in the doorway shelling beans. She rose quickly, beans and pods dropping to the ground.

"Oh," she cried, "what's happened? Are you hurt, Isabel?"

The girl turned like a wild-cat towards the woman. "Hurt!" she repeated. "No, I'm not hurt in the least ; why should I be?" She stepped on the bean-pods, which crunched beneath her feet. She went through the rear hall and up to her own room. But at the head of the stairs she paused to call back : "Have something good for supper, Mrs. Gill ; I'm as hungry as a hunter."

She laughed as she shut her door and turned the key in it. She flung her hat and parasol on the bed. She walked to the window and looked out ; then she walked back to the door and tried it to find that it was locked. Having done this, she stood in the middle of the room. She had an impulse to put out her hand and grasp a chair-back, but she would not do so. Her face was colorless and set. After a while she opened her lips and said :

"So Robert could do a thing like that !"

But she said nothing more. She sat down and cowered forward as if she were an old woman cowering over a fire. The room was full of sunshine, and Isabel's figure was prominent, as if cut out and projected into a glare of light.

"OLIVE'S HEAD WAS UPON ROBERT'S SHOULDER"

In the little Newcomb cottage Robert and his wife were sitting in silence. They were on the shabby old lounge, and Olive's head was upon Robert's shoulder ; he held her hand fast. In the kitchen they heard Mrs. Newcomb as she walked about, getting supper.

The two had hardly spoken since they had been left alone. Robert was thinking—thinking ; but Olive was blissfully resting. It had all come out right, after all, and perhaps she would sometime forget the agony of the last two months, when she had lain on the bed up-stairs, or had tried to sit with her mother in the kitchen. This loving had seemed a dreadful thing to her. She had longed to be able to stop loving. But now there was no need to keep up that battle any longer. She was leaning against Robert ; he had come back to her.

The young man rested his cheek on the girl's head ; he kissed her hair, then put his cheek down on her head again. " I must go and tell father," he said, at last.

He spoke reluctantly. She raised her head directly. She looked weary, but happy. Even the mention of old Mr. Nawn did not cloud her face.

" Yes," she answered, " you ought to go. Don't let him hear it from any one else."

" Esther Rice, for instance," with a laugh.

She laughed too. Then she urged him to go. She declared that she shouldn't take a long breath until he had told his father. At last Robert rose. He was thinking of some one else who had not been told. But he could not see her. No, that would be impossible. Yes, he had been a knave and a fool. He believed that there were few men who could be both. But he was both. However, he wasn't going to think of that fact. He was going to be happy. He had risen, and was now looking down at Olive, whose face was upturned towards him. He felt, with a thrill of unspeakable joy, that it was no matter what he had done, since now Olive belonged to him. She was his. He stooped and lifted her quickly in his arms, holding her fast, whispering words of love which could not express much, being simply words.

She clung to him, then pushed him away. Tears shone in her eyes; her lips trembled. "Go to your father," she said. "Go—but come back quickly. Oh, I hope he won't be very angry! Do you think he will, Rob? Do you think he will?"

So Robert went from the little house, and Olive leaned forward that she might watch him again as he began to cross the bridge. Then she sank back on the lounge and closed her eyes. She was praying that she might be a good wife and make her husband happy. Presently she fell asleep, being happily tired and ready for rest.

And Robert hastened until he came within sight of the brown old house. The poplars at the end of the back L looked melancholy and forbidding. The young man's steps began to lag. He paused to lean on the wall that ran between the orchard and the yard. The sun was westering and shone full in his face. He pulled his hat down over his eyes. He was looking keenly about the yard and at the open windows, hoping and dreading to see his father. He hated to be afraid of his father, and yet he was afraid. He wished he had asked the minister to come over and give the information.

But what was the use in delaying? The thing must be done. And perhaps the old man wouldn't care, after all. He wouldn't tell his son whom he wished him to marry.

Robert put a hand on the top of the wall and jumped over, going through the scraggy, uncut grass towards the rear door. Before he was half across the yard his father came out of that door and sat down in the flag-bottomed arm-chair that stood ready for him. He had his pipe in his hand, and he pulled out from a pocket a package of tobacco. He had just opened this package when he saw his son.

"Hullo, Bob, why ain't you at work? Factory's running, ain't it? Thought I heard the whistle." The bright old eyes took in the young man's attire. "What are you dressed up so for? I didn't know when you came home to put on your toggery. Picnic anywhere?"

Mr. Nawn began to fill his pipe slowly, watching his son as he did so.

"There's no picnic that I know of," was the answer.

Robert was longing to say boldly, "I've just been married to Olive Newcomb," but he delayed, inwardly cursing himself for a coward.

Mr. Nawn leaned back in his chair and contemplated the tall fellow standing before him. "You look queer," he remarked. "Have you jilted somebody, or has somebody jilted you? At your age, of course, it's something to do with a woman. Who was that fellow who, when anything happened to a man, instead of inquiring what's the matter, always asked, 'Who is she?' Well, I s'pose you'll tell me when you get ready. I'm sorry you lost so many hours' work."

Robert put his hands in his coat-pockets and shut them there. "Father," he said, "I've married Olive. We were married at three o'clock this afternoon. I've come to tell you."

Mr. Nawn had lighted a match. He now held it over his pipe; but he did not put the stem in his mouth. He was looking at Robert and smiling. He kept silence so long that the young man found it difficult not to writhe in his impatience. Finally the old man said, dryly:

"I s'pose you don't expect to marry Isabel, too?— that is, not at present?"

Then he lighted another match, his first one having by this time burned out; and now he kindled the tobacco in his pipe and took a few puffs at it.

Robert, hearing those words, struck one hand violently against the house. He must make some swift movement, and he dared not say what came to him to say. He gazed at the man before him, his eyes burning and strained. He wondered how his father could think of such exasperating things to say. And why wasn't he like other men?

But the next instant the young man lowered his eyes, and said, sullenly, that it was insulting to talk to him like that.

"Perhaps 'tis," returned the other, "but I do hate to see a young fellow shilly-shallying round as you've been. What does Isabel say to it all?"

"She doesn't know it yet."

Mr. Nawn shut his teeth hard down on his pipe-stem. He stretched out his legs and contemplated them carefully before he spoke.

"I never thought I was very strict in my notions of things," he said. "I've always done about what I wanted to do, without any trashy questions as to whether a thing was right or not; but, I swear, you surprise me, Bob, in your dealings with those girls! They both adore you, eh?" Robert did not reply. He stood there and ground his teeth in silence. "Both adore you, eh?" repeated the old man.

"I don't know," morosely.

"Very likely they do. Girls are just the fools to be taken with your straight nose, and your cupid upper-lip, and your handsome eyes. Ha! ha! Women are fools, and so are men. You start out in married life under good sail, don't you? I'll bet a dollar against a cent that you'll hear from Isabel. She's no milk-and-water specimen. But then the devil only knows what she can do about it. Where are you and Olive going to live?"

This question was put with a sudden directness that was like a blow in the face to Robert. But the young man managed to reply, with tolerable calmness, "You asked us to live here."

"So I did; that was some time ago; Olive was well then. I don't want any feeble women here. If you bring a wife home, I must turn off old Barlow. I'm not going to have a lot of useless creatures hanging about. I can't afford it."

"I think Olive will get well."

"Oh, you do? If she does, she may come. I heard you'd let that place you bargained for."

"Yes," answered Robert, "I've found a tenant."

"So you can't go there, anyway. You let it when you thought you might take Isabel, after all. By George, Bob, I'm proud of you!"

Robert writhed again. He wished to walk away, but he must wait until he had learned whether he could bring his wife there. He wished also to break out into fierce words, but his behavior of late had not been such that he dared to indulge himself in that way. Besides, underlying everything in his interviews with his father was the fear that he might be cut off from his inheritance. Therefore he stood there and writhed.

"Yes, I knew you'd found a tenant," continued the old man. "That's the only sensible thing you've done lately. I knew all about it, and I knew about your philandering after Isabel. I know what you're doing. How many days' work have you lost in the shop?"

"Only one, except when the engine gave out." Then he asked, quickly, "Shall we come here to live? Say yes or no."

Mr. Nawn took his pipe from his mouth. "If Olive gets well enough to work, yes; if not, no."

"All right; now I understand you. I'll tell her."

The young man turned away, but his father said, "Stop a minute. What's your hurry?"

Robert paused; he did not look at his companion;

he gazed off towards the line of pines on the hills beyond the Creeper.

"You know if you'd taken Isabel you'd have got a
little bunch of money."

Mr. Nawn had resumed his smoking. What did he
mean by talking like this? Hadn't he approved of
Olive after he had seen her?

These questions were in Robert's mind as he stood
there gazing at the pines. And another question was
there, too—should he outlive his father? This query
came now with so much distinctness that it startled
him. If he should outlive him, he, Robert, would be a
free man.

Mr. Nawn was looking at his son, and as he looked
his hard face changed somewhat. With a quicker
movement than was usual with him, he removed his
pipe from his mouth, tapped the bowl on the edge of
his chair, and then thrust it into his waistcoat-pocket.

"That Newcomb girl is a good girl," he said, the
jeering tone all dropped from his voice; "yes, she's a
good girl. I hope you'll treat her well, Bob."

The young man flung around towards his father, his
face reddening. "Treat her well!" he cried out, angrily; "why, I love her!"

"I s'pose so; but you must confess that you haven't
begun remarkably fine. Now go back to her; bring
her here when she's able to do the work."

CHAPTER XV

OLIVE came back to health and strength with the rapidity with which youth is often able to walk that road. In less than a month she was as well, nay, better, than she had ever been ; or she thought that she was, which amounts to much the same thing.

During this time Robert had lived at her home, and gone back and forth to the factory regularly from there. He had brought nothing from Nawn house but his working-suit ; he had seen his father but once, and then to tell him that Olive was well, and that on the next week they would come there to live.

"All right," the old man had said ; " I'll send Mrs. Barlow off next Saturday night. I can get my own meals until the new house-keeper comes. I'm not going to hire anybody for a few days. 'Twon't pay. I say, Bob, Olive can wash and iron and scrub, eh ?"

" Yes," shortly ; " you know she's always done house-work."

"That's the checker, then. You understand, I'm not going to hire a woman to do extra work. If that's to be done, you pay for it out of your own pocket, Bob."

Robert stood irresolutely an instant ; then he asked, " Did you say some time ago that Olive might work for her board, and that I was to pay mine the same as usual ?"

" Yes, I said that."

" Then you're driving a hard bargain, father, and you know it. Mrs. Barlow gets more than her board."

Mr. Nawn laughed, his thick shoulders shaking as he did so. "It makes setting up a wife come rather easy to you, though, Bob." '

Robert frowned. "But she ought to be paid something," he persisted.

Mr. Nawn still laughed. But he was examining his son's face carefully. "It's just my good-nature that makes me let you both in here," he remarked.

"No, it isn't," returned Robert, courageously; "you're making a good bargain."

"And you're a chip of the old block, Bob. Well, I'll give Olive just half what I've been paying Barlow. Now take it or leave it."

"Oh, I shall take it. I haven't any choice."

It was under such conditions that Robert and his wife came to Nawn house to live. They walked over one night after supper. Robert wheeled on a barrow the one trunk which held Olive's possessions, and on top of the trunk was a grip-sack containing the suit of clothes he had carried to the cottage.

It was a warm night in late September, and the fireflies were among the clethra-bushes by the way-side as the two came in sight of the old house. Mrs. Newcomb's "sister Ruth" had arrived the day before. Olive had not objected now to going to Robert's home. Her dream of life in the little house was dreamed out. She had thought that she had lost Robert; now that she had not lost him, she cared comparatively little about any less important circumstance.

The young man walked on ahead along the narrow track that led by the carriage-path. It was very still and very sultry. There was Nawn house, looming black and ominous before them. A sudden terror came to Olive's heart—a terror which she did not understand. She stepped up and put her hand on Robert's arm. He paused and set down his barrow rather quickly.

"What's the matter ?" he asked.

Olive hesitated. "I suppose I'm kind of fanciful," she said, "but don't you think the big house looks forbidding, somehow, and as if—as if— Oh, Rob, I was going to say, as if we shouldn't be happy there—only I shall be happy anywhere in the world where you are, you know."

"I'm glad of that," with just a touch of brusqueness, for the young man was weary with wheeling their belongings ; but he had decided to do it rather than to hire them carried. "But you are fanciful. There won't anything happen there. It's a lonesome old place, all the same, and I've always hated it. It's cheapest for us to go, tight as father is."

Robert wiped his damp face with his handkerchief. Olive had by this time become accustomed to hearing her husband speak of this or that as being available because it was "cheap." They could not have a thing or do a thing unless it was cheap. She had been a poor girl all her life, but she had not been brought up to think much of cheapness. There was a great deal that she could not have, and had never thought of having. Robert took up the handles of his wheelbarrow again, and the two resumed their walk, Olive behind.

Just then they heard a sound of horse's hoofs close to them, and immediately, from a cart-path in front, there galloped a horse with a woman on its back. It was still light enough for the two to know directly that the woman was Isabel Keating, and for her to know them. She looked very handsome and prosperous ; her habit was becoming, her eyes shone in the half-light.

Robert dropped his barrow again. From the red caused by fatigue and heat, his face went purple. He took off his hat. How poor, how menial he and Olive seemed to him in comparison with this girl !

He had been able to avoid meeting Isabel since his marriage. This was the first time he had seen her since he had asked her to be his wife. At this moment he remembered how she had looked at him that evening. She loved him. He could not doubt that she loved him. A flash, as of lightning, went through his soul, leaving wretched confusion behind.

All this in the space of an instant.

Meanwhile Isabel had stopped her horse and was looking down at the two. She said, "Good evening," in the most affable way. Her very position, sitting in her saddle, while they were afoot, gave her an advantage, and the dusk helped her. Robert wondered if she were smiling.

"I thought at first of being afraid," said Isabel, easily, "because of you two tramps. Are you moving?"

Robert had put on his hat. He pulled it far down over his brows. He left it to his wife to reply.

"Yes," answered Olive, "we are going to Rob's home to live. And Rob thought he might better wheel our things over himself. You know," with a soft little laugh that was full of happiness, "we are not like you ; we have to save pennies."

The young man breathed a sigh of relief. It was much better to speak in this way than to pretend to ignore the fact that they were trying to save pennies ; but he couldn't have spoken so. Now, however, he said, lightly :

"You forget, Isabel, that Olive and I belong to the poor laboring class."

"Oh, well, as long as you can make a joke of it, you won't suffer," was the retort.

Olive left Robert's side ; she approached the girl sitting above her there. Her voice trembled a little in her earnestness as she spoke. "Isabel, I wish you'd come to see us ; won't you?"

There was a just barely perceptible hesitation before the reply came. "Why, of course, I shall. Why shouldn't I?"

Olive reached up her hand and put it on the pommel of the saddle. Her heart was full of love and peace towards all the world; particularly was it tender just now towards this girl who had missed so much.

"You have so many other places, you know," responded the sweet voice, "that I was afraid you'd forget us; and then people have dropped the habit of calling at Nawn house, I suppose."

Isabel's horse, irritated by something, pawed uneasily and backed away a few steps. Olive stood in the place she had taken, gazing at the girl, what light there was from the sky all seeming to fall on her face and figure. Isabel gazed back.

There was something hard and ringing in her tone, though it was very low, as she replied, "Thank you, Olive. I will come." Then her horse cantered away.

Olive went quickly to her husband's side. She slipped her hand into his as she asked, anxiously, "You're not sorry I asked Isabel, are you, Rob?"

"No."

"Because," grasping the hand more closely, "I couldn't help feeling sorry for her; perhaps she isn't as happy as I am."

Robert took the hand in both of his. His thought then was one of passionate emphasis—that Olive was his good angel, and that he wished he was worthy of her. He stammered some ardent words to that effect, and Olive bade him hush. She added, in an awed half-voice, that it was wonderful how good God had been to her, and that she prayed that she might be grateful. Then, in the solitude of the highway, the young man kissed her; and a few moments later the two entered the yard of Nawn house; the dew-wet clusters of pudding-bag shrubs brushed against their ankles; and the cat came out from somewhere and walked around them, slowly curling and waving her snaky tail as she walked.

CHAPTER XVI

ROBERT and Olive had come to the door which opened on to the back porch. It was here that old Mr. Nawn sat and smoked, and the flag - chair was standing in its place now. Robert tried the door and found it locked. He shook it.

"Here's a jolly home-coming," he exclaimed, bitterly. "Wouldn't you have thought father might have left the door unlocked? Evidently Mrs. Barlow has been sent away. She, at least, would have let us in."

The cat rubbed against the grip - sack which the young man had set on the floor of the porch. She was purring loudly. Robert restrained his wish to kick the animal.

"Perhaps he had to go away," suggested Olive.

An owl, not far off, made his melancholy call. Olive moved and stood a little nearer her companion. She felt her hands growing cold.

Robert shook the door again. A moment later a heavy step was heard somewhere up-stairs; then a voice at an open window asked, "What's the row down there?" It was Mr. Nawn; and now the odor of to-bacco-smoke came on the air.

"I wish you'd let us in," exclaimed Robert, crossly. "I thought you were expecting us."

"Oh, it's you, is it?" in a leisurely manner. "I was expecting you by daylight. I'm having my smoke up-stairs, where I can have screens in the windows to keep away the mosquitoes. I'll let you in."

Then the two waiting below heard slow steps. At last the key was turned and the bolt shot back, and Robert and Olive entered the house.

"I hope you've had your suppers," remarked Mr Nawn, "because you'll find mighty little food in this house, I can tell you. I've eaten up everything old Barlow left, and to-day I had to bake some johnny-cakes for my dinner. I couldn't eat much. Don't throw 'em away ; give 'em to the hens, Olive. Mind you don't throw anything away, either of you. What we can't eat, the hens 'll eat, and what the hens won't eat, the pigs will."

As he finished speaking, Mr. Nawn, having taken a match from his waistcoat-pocket, drew it across his trouser-leg and held it up, examining the new-comers by the light of the tiny flame.

"Hand me that lamp—the little one will do—from the shelf, Robert, 'fore this match goes out."

Robert sprang forward to obey, and the lamp was lighted.

"I don't keep a lamp going when there's no need of it," said the old man, "and this small one is generally enough, anyway. You don't expect to paint or draw by lamplight, do you, Olive, eh?"

"No, sir," said Olive, in a low voice.

She had placed herself in the first chair she found. Robert was standing by the stove — for they were in the kitchen ; Mr. Nawn's bulky form, in his shirt-sleeves, and with only stockings on his feet, was at the other side of the stove. The kerosene-lamp was indeed small ; it cast a faint light over the figures in the dingy room.

Mr. Nawn pulled his pipe from his pocket, where he had thrust it for a moment. He sucked hard at it, found to his satisfaction that it was still alight, then he remarked that he had "saved a match that time." He puffed out several whiffs in silence, standing with his stockinged feet planted far apart, his hands in the pockets of his great, baggy trousers.

To Olive's mind the dim light magnified the size of the man standing there. She did not wish to look at him, but her glance persisted in returning to him.

Robert did not seat himself; he stood leaning against the wall; he was staring morosely at his father.

"You see," said Mr Nawn, at length, "old Barlow was as mad as a sitting hen when I told her to go; and she's left things all at sixes and sevens, I guess. 'Twasn't worth while to hire as long as you two were coming so soon. I hope you've got back your strength, Olive, so you can put your shoulder right to the wheel."

"Oh yes," was the hurried reply, "I'm well and strong now."

"That's the talk. I thought you were. You see, we've only had one cow for a year or two, because Barlow couldn't manage much butter‐making. I bought another yesterday of Isaac Sands; he had to sell to raise money to pay the doctor for doctor‐ing his daughter through the measles last winter. I offered Sands about half what the cow was worth, and he was obliged to take it. That's the way to buy, Bob—when folks have got to sell. I always wait till then; I manage to go without till then."

Mr. Nawn took his pipe from his mouth and laughed deep down in his chest.

"The pigs have been needing a little more skim-milk," he went on. "I've been feeding 'em since Bar-low left. I'll teach you to-morrow, Olive. You ain't squeamish about taking care of pigs and hens, are you, Olive?"

"No, sir; not a bit. I've taken care of hens ever since I can remember."

The fresh young voice answered bravely, and the fresh young face was upturned towards the old man.

Robert stirred perceptibly, and his eyes melted as

they looked towards his wife. He was thinking that he had brought her to a horrible place ; and he was wishing that he had the resolution to face round to his father and announce that he had changed his mind ; that he was going to take his wife away and make a home for her somewhere—anywhere away from that house. But he did not make any such announcement. He stood silent and glowering, and then he remembered that it would cost more to go away, and that his father would be offended, and no one could reckon upon how such a man as Archibald Nawn would leave his property.

" Now, I call that lucky," responded the old man, with some heartiness. " I shall take care of the horse myself, and that's about all I intend to do. I thought we might as well have this talk the very first thing, you know, so that we'd start out with a fair understanding. You ain't calculating on having company much here to meals, are you, Olive ?"

" No, I had not thought of it."

" Well, you needn't think of it, then. Company 'll make you a lot of work, and it's expensive. I set my foot down there. Why, Barlow's own sister, that lives at the Falls, has only taken one meal here in the ten years that Barlow kept house for me. I didn't know but your mother, or your aunt Ruth, might get into the habit of coming here to supper or something."

" No," from Olive, " I don't think they will."

Robert saw the look of wonder that was creeping over her face. This was a home-coming, indeed !

" Just in raw material, company costs a lot in the course of a year," continued Mr. Nawn, " and it's just a devilish waste. I don't visit, and I'm not going to have visitors. I think I've made this quite plain."

" Yes, father, perfectly plain," hastily, from Robert.

Mr. Nawn looked at his son with a grin on his face. Then he turned a little towards Olive, and said, more

8

gently than he had been speaking, "Perhaps you don't think you're welcome, Olive, but you are. You'll get the hang of things here soon, and if you don't turn out to be wasteful, we shall get on all right."

Having spoken thus, Mr. Nawn took his pipe from his mouth and put it once more in his waistcoat-pocket. Then he walked out of the room without saying good-night. Perhaps he thought it was an expensive habit to say good-night; anyway, he very rarely said it.

When the door had closed behind him, the two were silent and motionless for a moment; they were listening to the heavy foot-falls that were going up the stairs in the dark. When these foot-falls had ceased, Robert knew that his father was in his own room, and that he probably would not be seen again that night.

The young man crossed the floor to where Olive sat. He knelt down by her and put his arms about her, drawing her close. He had never before had so keen a sense of the sordid atmosphere in which he had been nurtured. At this instant he was sensitively alive to the fact that Olive's nature was a higher and purer one. He felt as if he were stretching his hands upward to her. He asked himself humbly how it had happened that she had cared for him. He was sure that he had never loved her so much as now, when she was sitting like some lovely thing that was foreign to this dingy room with its miserly light, which made the place dim rather than brilliant.

She knew that he was grieved and ashamed. She bent towards him as a woman bends towards the man to whom she has given all her heart. "Don't you worry, Rob," she whispered; "we shall get into the ruts after a little." She rested her cheek on his forehead as she added, with a slight laugh, "You'll be surprised to see how economical I can be. I shall remember that what we can't eat the hens can; and what the hens can't eat the pigs can. That's going to

be my motto as I begin house-keeping. And what do
I care so long as I have you, Rob, and you are happy?"

So the two began their lives at Nawn house, and
Robert kept on steadily at work in the factory, and it
was not long before old Mr. Nawn perceived that his
meals were better served, the house was brighter, and,
somehow, he was happier than he had been for many
years. To tell the truth, he had forgotten all about
happiness, or, if he thought of it, it was to doubt that
such a state of mind could be. Strictly speaking, he
was not happy now, only more comfortable; and to be
comfortable is sometimes all that the elderly person
asks. He forgets that there is such a thing as happiness in the world, and he looks incredulously or mockingly at the youth who has happiness in his eyes. He
is sorry for that youth. He is thinking of the crash
that will come sooner or later.

Mr. Nawn, before the first month was out, had formed
the habit of sitting a while in the kitchen on forenoons
and watching Olive as she made butter, or cooked, or
washed dishes. Sometimes he would walk up to her as
he entered and put his broad forefinger under her chin.

"Ha! ha! Bob's a lucky dog!" he would say.

And Olive, for Robert's sake, would try not to shrink.
But Mr. Nawn did not care whether she shrank or not.
He had two reasons for sitting in the kitchen. One
was that he liked to be with a nice girl like Olive, and
the other was that he wanted to watch to see if she
were wasteful in any way. "He'd stop that; he'd nip
it in the bud," was what he said to himself, his great
cheeks wrinkling as he shut his mouth tightly.

"Now, don't throw that away!" he exclaimed one
morning as Olive was about to pour the dish-water she
had used into the sink. "Here, I'll get the pig-pail.
You ought to have it stand in the wood-room and put
everything into it. Have you been brought up to pour
out your dish-water, I should like to know?"

Olive paused. She set her dish-pan into the sink and rested her wet hands on the sink's edge. The sleeves of her calico gown were rolled up above the elbow. Her arms were very beautiful. Mr. Nawn, who read books of almost any kind when he could borrow them, recalled something he had read once about a woman's arm, and as the remembrance came to him he exclaimed :

" By George ! it's a pity to get such arms all tanned up. You'd better pull down your sleeves when you hang out clothes, and so on."

Olive did not speak ; her head was drooped slightly, and her eyes saw nothing but the hand on which her wedding-ring was shining, shining as if it were a sentient thing that was appealing to her to be brave, to be cheerful. And she was not cheerful just then. That morning Robert had reproved her for using too much wood ; he said that there was no need of taking three sticks when two would do the work. She had dropped the third stick back into the box, her throat contracting and her eyes stinging. But she had not looked at Robert until she had her face under control. When he had hurried off to his shop, she had still kept command of herself, as she had gone on with her duties without yielding a moment in which to think over things. But she was conscious of a dull sense of terror, because she was afraid to think over things.

The day before, when she had been buttering the toast for supper, Robert, who was sitting in the kitchen, had said, suddenly, " There, there, Olive, one would think butter could be picked up on the road to see you spread it on. Take more salt and less butter, can't you ?"

She had waited then, expecting that her husband would refer to his father as the instigator of his reproof ; but he did not. An arrangement had been made between the two Nawns, after much chaffering,

to the effect that the money for the butter that was
sold should be divided equally between them.

Since that arrangement, Olive was obliged to own to
herself that Robert had been as careful in the use of
that food as his father ; and she herself was conscious
of a certain sense of guilt when she put butter on her
bread.   She was moving just now in a cloud of painful
bewilderment.

Mr. Nawn, having given his advice and brought the
pail, walked out of the room.

Olive went on hurriedly with her work.   She poured
the dish-water into the pail ; then, it being time to
feed the pigs, she went out into the yard with the pail
in her hand.

When she was midway across the yard a clear, ringing voice from the road called out, " Is that you,
Olive ?   Whither away, my pretty maid ?"

CHAPTER XVII

THE BUTTER-MOULD

OLIVE paused and set down her burden. She was surprised to find herself trembling. That gay, dominating voice seemed to fill the air about her.

Isabel Keating walked into the yard briskly, her fall jacket unfastened and revealing the bright-red rose at her throat. She came up close to Olive and looked into the pail.

"Mercy!" she exclaimed. "That looks like pig-swill."

"It is pig-swill," was the answer.

"Good heavens! What are you going to do with it?"

"I'm going to take it to the barn, stir in a little meal and more bran, then give it to the pigs."

"I'll go with you."

Olive resumed the pail, and the two walked on and entered the barn.

"Do you mean that you take care of the pigs?" asked Isabel.

"Yes."

Isabel laughed. She examined her companion yet more closely, and then she laughed again.

"I'm glad you are amused," said Olive.

"Oh, you needn't get up on any high horse, Olive. I'm going to say that I should think Robert would be ashamed. I'm ashamed of him."

Olive grew red to the edges of her hair. "You sha'n't talk like that to me!" she exclaimed. "I feed the pigs because I—because I prefer to do it."

She spoke loudly and emphatically

"SHE DIPPED UP A SMALL MEASURE OF INDIAN MEAL"

It was an instant before there was any response. Then Isabel said, in a low voice, "I wouldn't say that, Olive, because I don't believe you. I don't believe there's a girl in the world who prefers to feed pigs. If I see Robert, ever, I'll tell him what I think."

"Then, if you do that, I never'll forgive you—never!"

"Gracious!" Isabel drew back as if in alarm.

Olive hurried to the meal-chest and opened it. She dipped up a small measure of Indian meal and carefully smoothed it down with her hand. She knew, even then, that she must not use a heaping measure. She was feeling that she could not endure this girl's presence—this girl who seemed to make her humiliation take shape and stand out as a visible object.

But she remembered that she had invited Isabel to come and see her, and this was the first time she had called. She was, indeed, the first caller, with the exception of the minister and Mrs. Newcomb, that had been to see Olive. Mr. Nawn's reputation was too well established for people to venture to begin to visit at his house now, even though his son had taken a young wife there.

While Olive was stirring the stick about in the pail, she remembered the pan of sour milk in the buttery. She ran back after it, aware of a sense of fright that she had come so near to preparing this food without it.

When she returned, she found Isabel sitting on a bunch of hay that was lying in a corner of the barn. The sight of the girl was, somehow, like a pain to her. She tried to be cordial, and to make up for the quick words she had spoken. She invited her guest into the house, but Isabel shrugged her shoulders as she answered that she was afraid that, if she went in, she should help to wear out Mr. Nawn's carpets. But she lingered at the barn, and Olive was thus compelled to stay with her, though she knew that the fire was burning in the kitchen stove, and that she ought to be making use of it.

Olive poured the pail of food into the spout that led to the trough in the barn cellar where the three pigs lived ; then she sat down on the hay by Isabel's side. Isabel had selected some long stalks of herds-grass and was braiding them together.

"You look tired," she remarked.

Olive inwardly winced. These words seemed a sort of reflection upon Robert. "I've had extra work to-day," she answered.

"And thin," went on Isabel. "I suppose you know, Olive, that if you turn yourself into a drudge for those Nawn men you'll soon lose all your good looks."

Olive winced again ; and this time she said nothing.

"Don't you know it?" insisted Isabel.

"I've always been used to working," she now responded.

"But not as you do now. Esther Rice told at our house the other day that your mother said you'd break down before the year was out. She said that you were being worked to death."

Olive flushed and paled. She pulled up a handful of hay and seemed to be looking for something among the dried stalks. "I'm sorry mother said that."

"Olive," suddenly and quickly, "did you expect to be happy?"

No answer for a moment, and the question was repeated.

"Yes," replied Olive, slowly, "I think I did ; but I'm sure that, before everything else, I wanted to make Robert happy."

Isabel turned and looked fully and intently at the face near her ; but Olive was looking down at the spears of hay that she was twisting in her hands. She was not thinking of Isabel just then ; she was repeating to herself the question which had been put to her,

and saying, inwardly, "Yes ; certainly I expected to
be happy. But am I?" And immediately Isabel pronounced that question aloud. What right had Isabel
to probe in this way?

Olive was so weary that it was only by an effort that
she now flung up her head and laughed as she re-
torted : "Are you happy yourself, Isabel Keating?
I'll turn the tables on you if you go on catechising
in this way."

"Oh, you needn't laugh," responded Isabel. "I'm
going to tell you what I've thought every Sunday
when I've seen you sitting there with Robert in the
Nawn pew."

Isabel was very serious now ; she was still braiding
the grass. But she gave a quick turn of her fingers
and pulled her braid apart.

"Well?" said Olive, interested, in spite of her resolve not to be interested.

"Well, I've thought of a little Sunday-school book
I read when I was a child. The name of it was *The
Curse of a Granted Prayer.*" Having said this, the
girl rose and shook the grass from her skirts. "Now
I'm going. I don't suppose it 'll do any good to ask
you and Robert to call on me. Esther Rice says
you haven't either of you been to a neighbor's house
since you were married. Good-bye. Oh, dear, there's
Mr. Nawn coming out, and I shall have to speak to
him ! Good-bye, again. I wish you and Robert would
come and see me."

Isabel walked into the barn-yard and met Mr. Nawn,
who was approaching slowly, his hat on the back of
his head.

He smiled when he saw Isabel. "What's your hurry?" he called out. "Come with me and see how my
pigs are growing. I shall make more money this fall
on pigs than I made last year. But Mrs. Barlow didn't
take an interest. Olive does first-rate ; she puts her

mind on it, you see; and my bill for shorts and meal isn't as large as 'twas this time last fall."

"Perhaps Olive has found her vocation then," was the mocking reply. But Isabel did not go to look at the pigs; she hurried on down the road, and Olive, standing in the barn, watched her. But directly she remembered that the wood was burning in the stove, and that she was not using the fire.

It was the next day that something occurred which was to Olive, always in her memory a prominent thing, as if it were a door through which she passed into a state of things which was never again precisely like the former state. The man from the Falls Village had come for the butter. He came every week, and Olive had her six lumps ready as usual. They lay on the broad white platter, and were stamped with the shape of a thistle, each piece weighing a pound.

Mr. Nawn entered the room as the cart drove into the yard. He walked to the table and looked down at the yellow lumps on which tiny drops of water glistened. "First chop," he remarked. "Better than Barlow did." And then he smiled, thinking that he paid this house-keeper just half what he had been paying Mrs. Barlow. But his smile ceased as he continued to look at Olive's handiwork. "What!" he exclaimed— "this is a thistle stamp! What does that mean?"

Olive came from the pantry with a pan of milk in her hands. She heard his question, but she could not reply, for just then the man from the Falls came in.

"Butter's gone up two cents since last week," announced Mr. Nawn, standing in his favorite attitude, hands in pockets and feet wide apart. Standing thus he was accustomed to sway gently backward and forward, and the boards would creak under him.

When the man had gone, Mr. Nawn walked to where Olive was stooping over the wood-box. Without looking at him she yet knew that he was frowning heavily.

"What made you use that thistle mould?" he asked, sharply.

Olive stood up. She was quite pale. She answered, gently: "I used it because the other one split last week, and I found the thistle mould on the top-shelf. I thought it would save buying to use that."

"H'm—h'm! You might have told me. I should think that thistle mould makes a full pound lump."

"A full pound lump?" she repeated. "Isn't that what we've been selling all this time? Wasn't the cluster of acorns a full pound?"

Mr. Nawn coughed, and then he laughed. "No, it wasn't. I had the acorn stamp made. That mould makes a lump of butter that weighs just half an ounce less than a pound. Nobody suspects it, and in the long run half an ounce makes a difference, I can tell you."

"But it's cheating?"

Olive's eyes were dilated as she gazed at the man opposite her.

"Oh," easily—from Mr. Nawn—"you look at it in that way, do you?"

"Yes."

"I guess you'll get over that. I'll mend up the acorn mould, or get another, and you can go right on using it."

There was a just perceptible pause before Olive answered. "No," she said, "I sha'n't go on using it—as a pound mould."

"Eh?"

Olive looked about for a chair. She crossed the room to reach one and sat down quickly in it. She felt weary and wretched.

"Eh?" repeated Mr. Nawn. "What did you say?"

So Olive said her words over again, not looking now at that man standing there, but down at her reddened, hard hands which lay on her calico apron. She was not thinking of anything. It was as if a dull ache were pervading her whole consciousness.

"Oh, I reckon you'll change your mind about that."

No response. Olive had lifted her eyes, and they roamed over the kitchen floor, following out the stiff pattern of the shabby oil-cloth carpet.

"I shall get the mould mended. I can fix it myself, probably, and then I hope you'll use it."

Olive now raised her eyes to Mr. Nawn's eyes, and the two looked at each other for an instant. The man had a curious feeling that he was gazing into the eyes of a bird which he had wounded ; or that an outraged dove was solemnly staring at him—a dove with a subtle strength not belonging to a dove.

"Mr. Nawn," whispered Olive, at length, "please don't ask me !"

Mr. Nawn shuffled his feet on the floor. "You talk like a fool," he said, roughly. "What's a half-ounce of butter, I should like to know !"

"Don't ask me—"

"Pooh !" moving his feet again.

"For I sha'n't do it."

"Is that so ?"

"Yes, surely."

Mr. Nawn withdrew one hand from his pocket and passed it over his face. He said, "Bob 'll tell you to do it."

A frightened look came into Olive's eyes. "Oh no, he won't !"

"Yes, he will. You'll see. You're a regular little idiot, Olive ; but, then, what can one expect? And for half an ounce of butter !"

Mr. Nawn burst into his laugh as he left the room. He returned directly and asked for the broken mould. "I can mend that without its costing a cent—wire it right together." And now he went away with the mould in his hand.

It was not until after eight o'clock that evening, when the old man had gone up-stairs to bed, that Olive had a moment alone with her husband. Then she told him what had happened. She was standing by Robert's chair with her hand on his shoulder. She felt him start beneath her touch.

The young man restrained the impatience he felt. He kept silent until he could say with tolerable calmness, " I'm sorry."

"So am I. But you wouldn't have had me try to cheat in that way, would you ?"

"Oh, well," irritably, " a half-ounce of butter isn't much."

"Oh, Robert !"

And now Olive's nerves gave way and she began to cry ; which, of course, was very ill-advised in her.

Robert jerked one shoulder. " Father never 'll forgive you ; and every time you offend him makes it more likely that he won't leave me his money."

CHAPTER XVIII

INSUBORDINATION

OLIVE did not reply immediately. She was making an effort to stop crying. She had seen that jerk of Robert's shoulder. He was tired, poor fellow, and she must not annoy him. But she could not let him think that she would go on measuring butter in that mould. All the old Puritan sense of uprightness in every smallest detail was roused in her. People had often said of her father that he was too honest — that he flung away money many a time because he wouldn't "take advantage." But people had respected him, and liked to deal with him.

After a few moments Olive had dried her tears. She went to where Robert sat leaning one elbow on the table. She put her hand on his head, stroking his thick hair. The young man moved, turned quickly towards her, and took her in his arms. He was still in love with his wife. Olive's face brightened indescribably.

"Oh, I'm happy, after all," she whispered.

"Even here, in this den?" he asked.

"Yes—yes; anywhere with you."

"And you're not going to be a foolish girl?" looking down at the face on his shoulder.

That sensitive face changed. A cloud came over it. "Oh, Robert!" in a voice of inexpressible tenderness.

He hesitated; then he said, "Olive, you mustn't displease my father. I want him to leave his money to me."

Olive raised her head. There was a rigidity coming to her frame. "I can't make butter that way," she said.

"But it isn't your responsibility; you put the butter into that mould and father sells it. Olive, are you going to be stubborn? I didn't know that you were ever stubborn."

And now the young man was frowning, and that square look was coming to his face, the look that caused him to resemble his father

"I can't make it," she repeated.

She was sitting up straight on Robert's lap now; his arms had been removed from her.

"He said you would tell me to do it," she began, "and I was sure you wouldn't. He laughed: 'Oh! oh!'"—in an intense voice. "I wish he wouldn't laugh like that! Sometimes, when he laughs like that, I feel as if I should run out of the house." She shivered. Then she turned again towards her husband. An expression of ineffable tenderness was in her eyes. "I've always looked up to you so, Rob," she murmured, "and I can't bear it if you agree with your father about this—"

"Nonsense! Don't let's make a mountain out of a mole-hill."

But the speaker flushed and was uneasy. It is not a pleasant sensation to know that you are falling below some one's ideal of you. Still a man can't be expected to live as high as the pedestal on which he is placed by the woman who loves him; and it sometimes gets to be very tiresome trying to do so.

"It isn't a mole-hill." A spark had come to Olive's eye. "It's a principle. And I want you to tell me that you'd rather I wouldn't use that mould."

"No, I sha'n't tell you so," with a masculine air of knowing what is the thing to do.

Olive rose to her feet. "Robert!" she cried, looking down at him.

" Olive !" not glancing up at her.

Young Nawn had been absolutely positive that he had but to give the word about anything and his wife would run to obey him. And wasn't such obedience a part of a wife's duty ?

He moved in his chair ; he stretched out his feet in an attempt at an appearance of ease. But his soul was not at ease. The thing he wished to do was to take his wife back in his arms while she told him that he knew best, and she would do precisely as he wished. Robert had never given the matter any special thought, but he would have said promptly that the mere fact that a human being was male gave that human being the superior wisdom that enabled it to dictate to the female.

Now here was Olive acting in a perfectly ridiculous way. She was making a half-ounce of butter stand between them and the chance of having his father's money. Why, it was worse than ridiculous ; and it must be stopped ! He must assert himself.

But always in the man's heart was the wish to take his wife back in his arms and caress her, and instruct her, knowing that she would follow his instructions. He was fond of her. He didn't object to having her take up this notion about the butter ; that was nice, and sweet, and all that. A woman, of course, would naturally have ideas concerning honesty and uprightness that were a little higher than a man's ideas on the same subject, and impracticable ; but, when he asked her to do so, of course Olive would give up the intention of acting on such ideas. It was ridiculous, indeed. In resisting the wish to take his wife in his arms again, Robert became severe in his manner.

" I insist that you go on using that stamp," he said.

Olive was standing a few feet from him. He thought he had never seen her so tall.

" I can't do it," she responded. The spark in her eye had deepened to a fire.

The young man gazed at her. Wasn't he going to be able to control this soft, gentle, loving thing?

"You'll have to do it," in a still harder tone.

"No ; I can't."

"Don't tell me that !"

"I can't."

It was maddening to hear that voice repeat the refusal.

Robert sprang up, his temper rising like a flood. "Do you dare to refuse?" he cried out. His pulses were hammering in his temples. No answer. "If you do refuse, you'll lose us all father's money, I tell you." Still no answer, though Olive's lips moved. "Can't you say anything?" furiously.

"I've just told you twice."

"Do you understand that we mustn't displease father ?"

"I mean to try to please him in every way that's right."

"Right ! Don't I know what's right ? I can tell you what to do, and then you're to do it."

Robert's voice was thick. It seemed to him that he had never been so angry in his life. Was Olive going to stand out against him ? Olive ? Why, he could break her in his two hands ! And then, if his father should die, and should leave his property somewhere else—

Hardly knowing what he was doing, Robert made a stride forward and took hold of his wife's arm. She shrank, and then stood quiet. But she grew yet whiter.

"Will you do as father says ?" he asked.

Olive's lips quivered, but she shook her head.

Robert dropped his hands. "Damn you !" he cried.

He walked out of the room. The door from the porch slammed heavily.

Olive remained standing there for a moment. With a mechanical motion she put one hand to the place on her left arm where her husband's fingers had clutched.

9

CHAPTER XIX

GOLD

No tears came to Olive's eyes. Presently she sat down in a chair by the kitchen-table. She folded her arms upon it and put her head upon them, still wondering curiously why she did not shed tears. She would have said that at such a time a woman would weep her eyes away—yes, her very life.

She knew that Robert had what was generally called a "quick temper." Everybody knew that. But she had never imagined that he could be so angry with her—with her.

And he was very "close"; she could not deny that. Perhaps others would call him penurious. She had not known this part of him; and even now she called the trait thriftiness. Yes, he was very thrifty.

The bewilderment that was ruling her at this moment was accompanied by a scorching light upon her husband's character. This was the man she had married; she had nearly died because she thought he was lost to her. This was the man she had married—more than that, this was the man she loved. She must love him. But, of course, she must give up all thought of happiness. I think youth is always very ready to give up all hope of happiness.

Olive raised her head and looked about the dingy room. Here she was to drudge all her life; here she was to save pennies for the Nawns. And, perhaps, if Robert had married Isabel— She started up—that thought was intolerable.

She was stiff with having sat so long, and the room was not very warm. She never dared to have the room quite warm enough, and sometimes she wondered how she should be able to be comfortable in the winter. But if Robert were only good to her she could bear any-thing. She supposed that other women ceased to love —she had heard of such things. She wished that she was one of the kind that could cease to love. She was thinking now that love was not an armor to shield her from the ills of life, as she had once believed it to be; instead, it was something that made her suffer still more—as if she were clad in a garment of cruel sensi-tiveness.

Was that the sound of the outer door? How long was it since Robert had left her in anger? She mustn't stay up longer. And she had kept a lamp alight all this time, when she had not needed it for any work. She had wasted oil.

She stood listening for the sound she thought she had heard. She could hear nothing now. The moon-light would enable her to reach her room. She extin-guished the light, and on the instant she was standing in a broad bar of white brilliance. The moon was up in a clear sky, and the curtain was drawn. She saw the figure of a man standing in the yard. It was Robert, and he was looking at the window by which she stood. Involuntarily she extended her arms; she thought that she cried out, but she made no sound.

The figure moved rapidly towards the house. Olive remained motionless, listening. Oh, if he loved her, he would come to her now! Yes, there were steps lead-ing from the long back entry to the kitchen—but would they turn and go up the stairs? No, the door opened, flung back impetuously, and Robert came in. He did not hesitate. In a breath he had his wife in his arms, and she was clinging to him as if she had just found him after years of separation.

He was speaking, but at first she did not distinguish a word. She was crying now, with her head pressed on his shoulder ; and she was thinking that it was a terrible thing to love as she loved Robert. You see that she was somewhat of a primitive kind of woman ; she took love seriously, and not as a pastime, as some philosophers argue that it ought to be taken. Are those philosophers right ? If they are right, there are a great many women gone wrong in this world.

At last she heard what Robert was saying. He was repeating again and again that " he was a brute—an infernal brute. He didn't deserve that she should ever forgive him."

And Olive kept on crying until her sore heart was eased somewhat. As soon as she could speak she assured him of her pardon, and cried again because she must have seemed stubborn ; but, indeed, it was not stubbornness—and then she paused abruptly, because she had not meant to refer to the subject of their disagreement.

Young Nawn was now so gentle and tender that Olive began to wonder at herself for suffering as she had suffered a few moments ago. They sat side by side on the rickety lounge, the moon filling the room with light, and glorifying even that kitchen.

" And you've changed your mind about the butter, haven't you, Olive ?" the young man asked, after a time. The sudden quiet that came to his companion's form gave answer to the question, and Robert himself felt his muscles becoming tense and a heat rising to his brain again. " Haven't you ?" he repeated, in a studiously quiet voice.

She replied in just the same voice, " I don't see how I can change my mind about that." A silence, during which the two sat close, but with a difference. " You see," she added, " it would be wrong."

No answer, until Robert could speak as calmly as he

wished to speak. "I think you're mistaken. You're not selling the butter. And perhaps father 'll leave his money to somebody else."

The moonlight turned dark to Olive. She went back to her old words, "I can't do it."

And this was the girl whom Robert had thought was as wax in his hands — almost too yielding—if he compared her to the spirited Isabel. It must be owned that he did sometimes compare her to Isabel. Isabel would have yielded; she wouldn't have cared. And here they were in precisely the same place. And this time he was convinced that he could not move her. But the cold fit came on him now. He rose.

"I don't think we'll talk any more about it," he said, in an extremely calm manner.

The next day, when Robert came home from his work, he met his father just starting out in the old buggy, behind the old horse. He raised his hand to sign to his father to stop; then he walked up and leaned on the wheel. It was not light enough for the two men to see each other distinctly, and the younger one was glad of that.

"Do you want anything?" asked the old man, for his son seemed to hesitate. "Folks are most generally wanting something, I notice."

"I was going to speak about that butter-mould business," began Robert. "You see, I'm afraid Olive's going to be contrary; in fact, I'm afraid she has a contrary streak in her."

"Oh, has she?"

There was something in Mr. Nawn's voice that grated upon his son's ears.

"Yes," he went on, more crisply, "I've been talking to her, and I can't persuade her to use that mould for a pound mould. I wanted you to understand that it's my wish that she should do as you say."

"Oh, you do?" And somehow Robert felt meaner

than before. " So you couldn't bring her round, eh? And you were afraid, if you didn't, that I shouldn't leave you my money? Why didn't you marry Isabel? Then you wouldn't be so dependent on my money. I tell you what 'tis : I'm going to leave my property exactly as I please—to you, if I want to; to somebody out in Hindostan, if that pleases me. And I've got a lot more than you think I have." Mr. Nawn leaned back on the buggy-seat, and his form shook with his laughter.

Robert did not reply. His face was white ; his eyes full of anger.

"Yes ; why didn't you marry Isabel, I say?" repeated Mr. Nawn. "If you find your wife contrary, why, I can't help it. Her father was always contrary when anybody else would have cheated."

"You told me," said Robert, in a scarcely audible voice, "that I might marry either one. You must remember that I asked you."

"Yes, I remember. The devil! Do you think, at your age, I'd have asked any one a question like that? You went against me, to begin with, but you couldn't stick to it like a man. I wonder what Olive would say if she knew?"

The contempt in the old man's face and voice was unmistakable, and the son felt withered by it. He made an attempt to hold up his head as he began :

"We had a quarrel—Olive and I—I thought 'twas all over between us—I—"

"We needn't talk any more, Bob."

Mr. Nawn gathered up the lines, and Robert took his hand from the wheel. As the horse walked away its driver muttered to himself :

"That boy 's got a lot of his mother in him."

As the fall days shortened in that year of Robert's marriage, life at the old Nawn house seemed to contract. Olive grew to imagine that the days were something like the walls of a room which gradually shut in closer and closer about the doomed occupant. She had read a story of somebody who was suffocated in that way once. And she worked harder than ever. She was hurrying all day long through the chilly rooms, or she was bending over the wash-tub, or the ironing-board, or she was cooking, and always endeavoring to cook with less and less material. Sometimes Mr. Nawn or Robert, as they sat at the table, would remark :

"Seems to me, Olive, you've put in too much butter into this squash—butter's expensive ; we can't afford to eat much of it." Or, "This is a cut of meat that we can't afford, Olive. You should make the butcher give you a cheaper cut ; and you needn't buy meat every time the cart comes round."

Olive would say, "I'll try to remember."

And she did remember, until the daily food on their table, well and carefully prepared as it was, was of a quality which seemed too poor even to Olive, who had always lived so frugally. She thought that each month showed a perceptible difference in her father - in - law ; each month he hated, worse than he had previously done, to spend any money.

Once, in December, Olive entered his room, prepared to sweep the floor. She knew that he had gone away a short time ago, and she did not know that he had returned. The door had opened softly, and the old man had not heard her. He was sitting at a little table, the top of which, to Olive's suddenly dazzled eyes, seemed covered with gold.

Mr. Nawn was sitting on the edge of a chair, bending forward over the table. She saw the side of his face, and the sight of it was like a blow to her ; it made her forget the gold and everything else for a moment. She had heard of the word "gloating." She had been told that misers gloated over their gold. That look of eager adoration and possession ; that strange, concentrated expression that hardened the features at the same time that it brightened the eyes ; that, in some inexplicable way, made a human being have the appearance of an ogre without human emotions.

Olive paused and shrank there in the doorway. She dared not move lest she might disturb this man. And she herself immediately was conscious of the power of fascination there is in a heap of gold. When her eyes left the old man's face they fixed themselves greedily on that yellow pile. How wonderful it must be to own so much money as that ! How much good might be done with it ! What a power it had !

She breathed heavily. Mr. Nawn heard the breath. He moved quickly. His first impulse was to cover his hands over that shining heap ; but he restrained that impulse and leaned back in his chair, staring at the figure with the broom and dust-brush in the doorway. He was frowning blackly.

"What are you creeping about the house in that way for ?" he asked, savagely.

Olive drew herself up. "I wasn't creeping," she answered. "I thought you were away, and I came to clean your room."

She spoke with dignity. She had schooled herself not to seem so afraid. She felt that she was leading a slave's life, but it was a kind of satisfaction to her to pretend not to be a slave. The timid girl had changed somewhat. Having made this reply, she turned and was going ; but Mr. Nawn said, hastily : "Come back a minute." Olive obeyed. The man beckoned her to approach still nearer. He lifted a handful of gold and held it towards her. "Take it ; try the feel of it in your hand."

His heavy face was both absorbed and alert, and it was more alight than she had ever seen it.

Olive extended her hand, and the pieces of gold were slowly clinked into her palm.

CHAPTER XX

A GIRL IN A SLEIGH

OLIVE did not know that gold pieces were so beautiful. She had seen a five-dollar piece twice in her life—but handfuls of broader pieces ! She sighed. Her eyes were filled with the yellow lustre. She sighed again. She tried to ask herself why she should be so excited at sight of this money. A pile of bank-notes would have been interesting, and would perhaps have represented more wealth ; but this metal was more agitating.

"Hold out your other hand."

She extended the other. She stood there with open hands held together and heaped with the stuff.

"What would you do with it ?" asked Mr. Nawn.

"Give it to Robert."

The answer came without the slightest hesitation.

"Then you are silly. But I'm not going to give it to you, for I'm not silly. So you've found out that Bob loves money, eh ?"

"Yes," in a very low voice, "I've found that out."

She leaned forward and dropped the money on the heap lying on the table.

Mr. Nawn had now thrust his hands into his pockets and was sitting back in his chair. "I s'pose you think I'm a miser, don't you ?" he inquired. No reply. "Don't you ?"

"Yes, I do."

"That's right ; I am. I reckon I'm the first miser that ever owned up to it. I'd rather accumulate money than do anything else in the world. I always keep several hundred dollars in gold by me just to look at and handle. I look at it a good many times a day, but I mean to lock the door when I do it. I neglected to lock the door to-day. But it isn't much matter if I did. You're a good sort, Olive. If I didn't love this gold so well I'd give you a few bits. But I can't do it. You needn't tell Bob I've got it in the house here—you needn't tell anybody. I always say I don't keep a cent by me. I don't want burglars to think I do. There isn't much else in this old house that burglars want, and it's pretty well known."

Mr. Nawn reached forth a hand and took up a gold piece; he contemplated it lovingly; he replaced it and pushed the pieces up in a mass; then he scattered them over the top of the table. Olive watched him.

"Mind you don't tell anybody," repeated Mr. Nawn. "You're the only person, besides myself, who knows I've got this here. I didn't mean that any one should know. But you're a safe sort. Promise you won't tell any one."

Olive promised. She disliked to make promises, because, once made, they were sacred to her. She had hesitated now, but she gave her word.

Mr. Nawn looked at her steadily. "Mind, I don't want Robert to know. Bob 'll be a worse miser than I am when he's as old. You know they say avarice is a vice of old age. So 'tis; but I guess it belongs to some young folks, too. Bob's a fellow that wants to have his cake and eat it. He'll have to find out he can't do that. We all find that out sooner or later. Pity somebody can't discover a way in which we can spend money and hoard it, too. Now I like to hoard it. It's better than victuals and drink, better than love itself, to have a good strong-box and a safe place to hide it in—to come and open the box and add a piece to it, and count the whole, and roll your hands

around in it, and chink it, and gaze at it until everything looks yellow—yellow."

The old man's voice had a tone that Olive had never
heard before, and his eyes gleamed. But the light in
his face was such a strange light that it made him look
older instead of younger.

Olive moved to the chair where she had laid her
duster and hand-brush. She shivered. It was one of
the cold, short days of early winter. Although there
was a stove in the room, there was little fire in it. Mr.
Nawn wore his overcoat. His thick gray hair made a
covering for his head.

" What are you hurrying for?" he asked, with some
impatience. " Did you leave a lot of wood in the kitchen
stove to be burning out for nothing ?"

" No ; I only left one stick, so that the fire would
keep."

" That's all right ; I'm glad you've learned that.
There's no earthly need to burn out so much wood as
most folks do — economical folks, too. I'm thankful
you're learning. Don't you think you made the coffee a bit too strong this morning ? Coffee 's risen a
cent and a half a pound since last week. And we don't
really need cream in it ; boiled skim-milk will do first-
rate. The cream ought to be saved for the butter, for
we can sell butter. Let's have the boiled milk."

" Very well," responded Olive.

She stood waiting a moment to learn if her companion had anything more to say. She was thinking that
when she and her mother had lived together in poverty in the little house near the Creeper they had been
rich—rich—and that this wealth was poverty.

Mr. Nawn had turned towards the table of gold
again ; he put his hand upon the metal. He was smiling. " I've got a place where I keep the strong-box
that holds this," he said. " I've got a place that nobody knows, not Bob himself. I mean to tell you,

Olive, before I die, where I keep it. You see, I like to
have about a thousand dollars to look at. It doesn't
draw any interest, and it's a weakness of mine. It
ought to be drawing interest. Other folks take a
pleasure-trip, go to the theatre, have a dram, and so
on ; I come in here, lock the door—only I didn't lock
it to-day—get out my box of gold, and enjoy myself.
Run along now, Olive, and don't burn too much wood
in the kitchen stove. Wood has sold for twenty cents
more a cord than it did last year."

Olive did not linger after that permission. She
hastened down the stairs; she passed through the
great square front room that was on the south side
of the front door. In summer this was the sitting-
room, but in winter no fire was allowed save in the
kitchen, unless Mr. Nawn chose to have one in his
own room. But he sat much by the kitchen stove, his
chair drawn close up to it, while he smoked endlessly,
watching Olive as she worked. It seemed to her that
she had no solitude, now that winter had come and
she could not stay out-of-doors or in any of the cold
rooms ; and when Robert came home from the factory there was his father present.

Life settled itself down into the tramping round of
house-work—into moments when she could sit at the
kitchen window with quiet hands and look into the
back yard where the snow lay, and at the five Lombardy poplars, which stood in a row at the head of the
lane which led into the pasture. Beyond those poplars the sky looked a hard blue. Was it really a hard
blue, or did it only seem so ?

By the middle of January, Olive felt as if she had
been living at the Nawn house for a score of years.
Usually she worked so hard that when night came she
lay down like a log on her bed and fell asleep. She
loved Robert. She watched for his coming, and she
would leave the kitchen, where the old man sat ready

with his cynical laugh or word, and hurry to the outer door to meet her husband. They would kiss each other and clasp hands, and look in each other's eyes, and Olive would smile ; and when she was alone she would sometimes tell herself how happy she was, and then would sigh.

But since that time when she had refused to use that scant butter-mould there had been something between her and Robert—a thin veil—a something which she could not remove, try as she would. She could not yield her point ; that was impossible.

On the night of that day Mr. Nawn had come in from the barn and sat down, pulling out his pipe as he did so. He had gazed at Olive while he pressed the tobacco down in the bowl with his finger. Then he had said :

"About that butter business, Olive; you may go right on using the large mould. We'll give 'em a full pound after this." Then he had chuckled to himself.

When Olive had told her husband, he had exclaimed, "That's odd! But he won't forget — he'll lay it up against you." And Robert evidently was not going to forget.

One day in the last of January, when Robert came home to his dinner, he announced that he was going to the Falls Village after work that night, and he might not return until late. He glanced at his wife and requested her not to sit up. He expected to see a man who was talking of buying the little house, the Raymore place, and he might have to wait for him.

"Don't sell unless you make something," remarked Mr. Nawn. "Who is it ?"

"Name is Garrett—lives in Boston—wants a small place to come to in the summer."

"Make him shell out, then. He won't know values in the country here," was the old man's advice.

Robert nodded. He had immediately adopted the

habit of not telling his wife anything about his affairs. He was naturally reticent, and he hated to be questioned. She knew his daily wages, and if he had any other business he kept it to himself. If you did not tell anything you didn't have to explain anything.

Now, as Olive followed him to the door, the keen air swept over them. He put his arm about her and said, kindly, "You're such a good girl, Olive !"

She smiled at him as he stood on the step below, and she touched his cheek with her fingers, her face flushing at his words. He was in his best suit, and was very handsome and striking-looking.

The next moment he had hurried away. She shut the door, for the air was full of frost. She went to the window to watch him until he was out of sight. He walked on until he came to a place where a road branched from the main road. He hesitated an instant, then he took the branch road. This way led also to the factory, but it was farther. He had not gone many rods before he heard the sound of sleigh-bells coming rapidly ; then a horse and sleigh wheeled into the road in front of him. The driver was Isabel Keating, and she was alone. She wore a fur cap and jacket, and her face was brilliant. She pulled in her horse, and he took off his hat.

"You were not coming to call on me ?" she asked.

"No."

"I thought not. You and Olive aren't a bit neighborly."

He stood gazing at her. Then he said, "No ; we don't have any time to call. We are working-people, you know."

Robert felt his cheeks glow. He was asking himself if Isabel had not grown beautiful.

"Yes, I know," she responded ; "but you look rather fine to be on your way to the shop."

"I was going to the Falls after working-hours."

"Oh, were you? I'm going there now. Would you—"

Here the girl paused and did not finish her sentence, save by a vivid blush.

The young man stepped hastily forward. "Would you be so kind as to let me go with you?" he asked. "It 'll be such an accommodation, if you will."

Isabel laughed, gayly. "I didn't know whether I ought to ask you or not," she responded; "but it would be silly enough, wouldn't it, for you to walk over when you could have a seat in my cutter just as well as not? I suppose you were going to walk?"

The girl threw back the fur robe, and Robert stepped into the sleigh and sat down by her, tucking the fur about his legs.

"Yes," he said, "I intended to walk. Father don't often offer his horse to me; and, anyway, the old sleigh has lost a runner; it broke last week in that big thank-you-ma'am on the Farley Hill. Of course, it never 'll be mended."

The young man's face was animated; his eyes shone. He supposed that his heart beat all the time, but now he was conscious that it beat.

CHAPTER XXI

MONEY LOST

"WHAT if we should meet Esther Rice?" Isabel made this inquiry after they had fully started down the road. She was sitting up straight; she had the lines in one hand and the whip in the other. She did not glance at her companion as she asked the question, nor as she continued, a laugh in her voice and face, " She would hurry through the neighborhood and tell that she had seen Isabel Keating carrying off Robert Nawn—just as a hawk carries off a chicken, you know."

The girl's laugh sounded clearly on the cold air. She touched her horse lightly with her whip. She knew that her companion was gazing intently at her, and that his face was serious.

He did not reply, and the next moment, beneath his gaze, the girl's face suffused with a yet deeper red.

Robert withdrew his eyes. " I don't think Esther Rice would say you were carrying off a great prize," he said, with some bitterness. After an instant's silence, he added, " It is I who would have the prize."

Then he turned and looked at her again ; but their eyes did not meet. The young man was conscious of a certain excitement. He said to himself that he was excited because he was remembering so clearly that evening, not yet six months ago, when this girl had told him that she loved him, and had put her arms about his neck and had kissed him. The next day he had married Olive Newcomb, because, after all, he had loved Olive—oh yes, he had loved Olive. But he wondered what would have happened if Olive's mother had not come to him. He thought he was sure that his father had preferred that he should marry Isabel— he thought so now, though a person couldn't always tell what old Mr. Nawn did think. And now Olive was going against the old man. That was very annoying. She ought to know better than to do that. It was unaccountable that she didn't know better. Well, he had been crazy with love for Olive ; but still he didn't know how things would have turned out if Mrs. Newcomb hadn't come to him that day. And Olive was really dying for him. Yes, he did know how things would have turned out—he would have been Isabel's husband by this time, and he would have had her money ; and he was almost sure now that Isabel was the one the old man wanted him to marry; and, besides, Isabel had always possessed for him a sort of bewitchment. She was sumptuous and tropical. She had a way with her eyes. Robert's thoughts ran on hither and thither. He felt just now as if he had acted idiotically in every way. He did not wonder that his father often called him an idiot. He was an idiot.

Isabel's clear voice, with the imperative ring in it, now asked, "What are you thinking of, Rob? You look as black as if you were planning a murder."

They had crossed the Red Bridge and had left the hamlet behind them. The horse was walking up a hill through a pine wood. A squirrel had just run across the narrow track in front of them ; sometimes a solitary flake of snow fluttered through the gray spaces of the air ; a chickadee sang somewhere in the wood.

Robert turned fully towards his questioner. His fine face was set in gravity, but his eyes were lustrous. "It's enough to make a man look gloomy to know some things about himself," he replied. Isabel uttered

10

a little exclamation, as if she were feigning alarm. Robert was thinking how meanly, in what an unpardonable manner, he had treated the girl beside him; and yet he thought that she must have forgiven him—because of her love for him.

"So you know something about yourself?" Isabel asked. "You speak as if it were unusual for a man to have that sort of knowledge."

"It's maddening to have it too late," was the response.

Isabel sat silent. She whipped the horse, which started into a surprised trot, then fell back into a walk, for it was still climbing a steep hill.

"I don't know whether it's unusual or not," was the answer; "but I hope it is—to have it—too late."

As he spoke the last words Robert felt the color rise to his face, and at the same time a dull consciousness came to him, a consciousness of disloyalty and falsehood and meanness. He made an impatient movement, as if to shake off that consciousness, for it brought him discomfort. After all, what had he said? Why, nothing—just nothing at all.

He wished to meet Isabel's glance, but she was gazing straight ahead. She was lovely to look at this afternoon. Robert had a fleeting wish that Olive did not have to drudge so constantly, and so never have time to wear a fine frock. And Olive had lost something of that soft bloom of youth which is so attractive in a man's eyes; and as for the fine frocks, he wondered that he had thought of them, since she had never had any such aids to beauty. But she had worn light, fluffy gowns in the summer; they were cheap things, but beautiful, nevertheless. She must dress according to her work, and she worked all the time now. Again Robert's thoughts ran after each other confusedly, like things he could see and could not control. And that subtle and delightful excitement grew stronger.

"Isabel," he said, suddenly. Yes, it was a sort of intoxication to be alone with this girl. If he had not turned into that road, which was not the direct way to the factory, he should not have met her. It was a very strange thing that he had met her thus. "Isabel," he began again, "I've wanted to see you and ask you if you could—but no, it is impossible that any woman could ever forgive a man for doing what I've done. I don't mean not marrying you—" now hurrying in his speech—"you are well off in escaping that," bitterly; "but I treated you horribly. I hate myself when I think of it—and I think of it a good deal. You can't forgive me! I know you can't!"

Robert had placed his arm along the back of the seat, and he was leaning eagerly towards his companion. He saw her face slowly lose its bright color. He saw her lips tremble. She drew slightly away from him.

"Oh, Isabel!" he exclaimed, in a whisper. Now she turned to him. At the end of a long mutual gaze, Robert said, again, "Oh, Isabel!" But this time in a different tone. Then he sat up suddenly and stiffly away from her.

The horse had reached the top of the hill, and now began to trot down the long slope in front. Isabel gathered up the loosely hanging lines. She seemed intent upon holding them in a certain way. She reached forward and placed the whip in its socket. Then she sat gazing forward at the horse's ears.

The animal went faster and faster down the hill, and its driver presently had all she could do to attend to him. But she was fully able to control him. She hung back steadily on the leathers, her eyes sparkling more and more as the pace increased.

"You're not afraid, are you, Rob?" she inquired, not removing her eyes from those forward-pointing ears.

For answer, young Nawn laughed. He was grateful

for the swift race down over the snow. He knew that a false step made by that flying horse would send them toppling and rolling over the hard crust ; but what of that ? He sat close to his companion ; he put out his hand with an involuntary motion, and the next instant he was holding her closely to him, but only so that she should not fall from the seat. His blood was rushing through his veins. Oh, what a dull, stupid life he had been living !

As soon as the horse had reached a more level place, Isabel soothed him into a slow trot ; she talked gently to him, her voice soft and sweet. It seemed to Robert as if that voice was addressed to him, though the girl had immediately moved away from his protecting arm, and was sitting as far from him as possible.

The quick ride, the exhilarating cleaving of the air, had had upon Nawn the curious effect of making him feel more reckless—as if he had taken a heady wine. But when he turned to Isabel, hardly knowing what he was going to say, there was something in her appearance that made it impossible for him to speak. He questioned her with his glance, but she did not reply.

Presently she made some common - place, unimportant inquiry, and he replied in the same manner. But he resented the change in her, and was sulky all the rest of the way. Was she going to have that look in her eyes and then pretend not to have had it ?

Very soon now they entered the one long, populous street of the Falls Village. Here the Creeper grew stronger and faster in its flow, and turned mill - machinery, and was in every way different from the still stream that glided under the Red Bridge.

Robert got out of the sleigh ; he turned to thank Isabel. Just then a young man came up quickly, doffing his hat to the girl—a well-dressed young fellow, with a city "style" in his appearance. Isabel seemed to know

"SHE NODDED CARELESSLY TO ROBERT'S 'I'M MUCH OBLIGED TO
YOU, ISABEL,' AND BEGAN TO TALK WITH THIS STRANGER"

him. She nodded carelessly in response to Robert's formal " I'm much obliged to you, Isabel," and directly began to talk with this stranger, who leaned against the sleigh, very much at his ease.

Robert stalked away, his head in the air, a bitterness in his heart which he could hardly understand, and which made him furiously indignant with the girl he had just left. And he had lost a half-day's work by means of her ; that meant money. He did not like to lose money. He had intended to work until night, and then walk over to the Falls. Although it was cloudy, there was a moon, and he was used to walking.

He hurried into a more quiet street. He wished to get out of sight of those two whom he had just left. He thought that it would be a pleasure to him to go back and knock that young man down. He did not know that Isabel had such acquaintances. But, then, why should he know ? He looked at his watch. If he lost no time he could be on his homeward way in an hour. It might set in to snow at sunset. The flakes continued to drift down irresolutely and apparently with no object. Perhaps it would clear, after all. It was almost the full of the moon, and there was not often a storm then, or if there were one it was terrible.

Robert now hastened to the house on the main street where he was to meet the prospective purchaser of the Raymore place. He perceived instantly that this man really wanted the place, and so he named a high price and rigidly adhered to it, putting on an appearance of not wishing much to sell ; being indifferent, and whistling softly to himself as he gazed through the window. The man, after declaring that the price was outrageous, ended by buying and paying fifty dollars to hold the bargain. Robert's eyes sparkled, but he kept his lids lowered as he slowly counted the money and placed it in his pocket-book.

Did you ever fancy that there was much self-re-

vealment in a man's purse? This little leather re-
ceptacle tells if it belongs to a spendthrift; money
easily leaves it; but the shabby, rubbed purse, where
bank-notes seem to cling and multiply—who doesn't
know that kind? This was the kind that Robert drew
from his pocket; and when he had placed the money
in it he looked at it with a loving glance before he
thrust it back into its place.

There was one more errand. He examined the sky
as he stepped into the street. It was still a filmy gray,
and still those hesitating flakes came drifting towards
the earth. Going down the sidewalk Robert's eyes
were caught by the displays in the shop-windows. He
was moved to buy stuff for a new gown for his wife.
There was something brown, with a tint of a bright
color shot through it. He put his foot on the thresh-
old; then he hesitated.

"She won't miss it if I don't get it," he thought,
"and I might better save my money. Money 'll be
better than anything else."

He walked on; but he felt a faint glow at his heart
just from the impulse he had smothered. He went in
at a door that had a modest plate upon it which bore
the words :

T. H. DRAKE

Stocks Bought and Sold

A thin man with a long white beard was sitting within,
reading a newspaper. He looked up and then took off
his spectacles.

"That's you, is it, Mr. Nawn? I was hoping you'd
come in soon. Great break in S. & W. Gone down
like a stone in a mill-pond. Do you want to sell
out?"

"What?—and lose?" asked Robert, his face growing
white.

He had put in one hundred dollars two years ago.

Twice he had sold out, and each time he had made money — the first time twenty dollars and the next time twelve. He had told no one ; but he had hugged the knowledge to himself. He wondered if his father ever made money in this way ; he had never dared to ask. Robert was still very young and inexperienced, but he was bound always to do a safe thing, he told himself. Mr. Drake had said that there was nothing safer than S. & W., and there was nobody more shrewd than Mr. Drake ; besides, he knew the market.

"Yes, lose half now, rather than the whole later," said Mr. Drake, easily. "S. & W. is dead. I'll bet it 'll be in a receiver's hands in three months. Better sell."

"How much is it ?"

"Forty-two this morning." Robert gasped. He had thought perhaps he could sell again and gain enough to make another hundred with what he had in his pocket. "Going down," tersely, from Mr. Drake. "Save what you can."

So Robert gave orders to sell the next day, and Mr. Drake said "he'd wire in early in the morning." Then he began to talk on the hard times, but Robert could not listen. He could hardly understand what the man said. He was continually counting up the money he had probably lost. He had never lost a cent before. It was horrible.

He was thankful that he had not bought that stuff for a new gown for Olive. He wondered if Olive really made as much butter as could be made from that amount of milk. Winter butter always sold at a higher price. It seemed to him that Olive was somewhat inclined to be lavish in her house-keeping. He must talk with her about it. He was sure that she could save more than she did. He had often heard that Olive's father had been a wasteful man, that he gave more to poor people than he ought ; and everybody knew how Israel Newcomb had once lent fifty dollars to a man who had been unfortunate, and Mr. Newcomb had refused to take any interest.

Robert began his walk home in great gloom of mind. He strode on with his head bent, thinking of the money he had lost. The wind was at his back ; the air was thickening with snow. As soon as the sun had set the storm began to come on in earnest. But the young man did not think much about the storm. His mind was dwelling on his loss, and magnifying it. He wanted to stretch out his hands and clutch at those vanishing dollars. It was so depressing to lose money. How should he make up that amount ? He must make it up in some way. But even then there would always be the consciousness that he might have had that much more if he hadn't lost it. His father ought to give him an allowance ; his father—but Robert could hardly be coherent on that subject.

CHAPTER XXII

AT home Olive was working. When was she not working? She sat close to the stove, bending over a coat she was patching. Old Mr. Nawn had brought it to her a half-hour ago, suggesting that she "go over it."

She had turned it about despairingly ; it was not fit for a tramp. But she said nothing ; she began on her task. Her father-in-law sat at the other side of the stove, smoking. He smoked nearly all his waking hours. He often said that every man had his extravagance, and tobacco was his. There were two things he liked to do, he would add, get money and smoke.

" Have you fed the hens ?" the old man asked, after a long silence.

Olive started. Her thoughts had been far afield. "Yes," she answered.

"What are you giving them now ?"

" Cracked corn and oats, and sometimes meal and shorts, scalded."

A silence, during which Mr. Nawn gazed at the figure bending over his old coat. He was saying to himself, " How that girl has faded ! I wonder if Bob has noticed."

Then Olive glanced up, and Mr. Nawn saw the beautiful eyes. Yes, Olive's eyes were still beautiful and clear and sweet as truth itself.

Mr. Nawn took his pipe from his mouth and held it as he asked, "Ain't you ever sorry you married Bob ?"

She looked at him and smiled. As she did so the old man's face softened.

"Oh no," she answered, promptly.

"That's odd—that's devilish odd." He put his pipe back and whiffed at it. " I s'pose you think you love Bob, eh?"

" I know I love him," warmly.

"And you'd rather live in this den with Bob than anywhere else without him?"

"Yes."

" I say, Olive, look up at me a minute."

Olive raised her eyes again. This time she spoke, timidly, but with courage, "Oh, Mr. Nawn, I wish you'd take some of your money and be more comfortable. We might be happier. Don't you think we might be happier?"

"I don't know about you young folks," was the immediate reply, "but I can't be any happier; why," with a laugh, "I'm just as happy as I can be. What more can any one ask?" He smoked harder than ever. Presently he said, " You're a brave girl, Olive."

" Am I?"

"Yes; to ask me to spend more money. You wouldn't catch Bob to ask me that. He'd be afraid I'd be mad and wouldn't leave him my property."

Olive said nothing. She threaded her needle and began to sew with it. She heard her companion laughing down in his chest. She always felt like shivering when she heard that laugh. And she knew he had just spoken truth about his son. She wished that it wasn't the truth. In the silence that followed, Olive seemed to think of everything, and she felt as if she had lived here for years, and had mended that old man's coats since she could remember.

Mr. Nawn rose to empty his pipe into the stove. As he raised the cover he remarked that there was a great deal of wood in the stove, more than was necessary.

There was no need to make a room as hot as an oven. Then he filled his pipe again He smoked and watched the woman's hand flash back and forth until he became somewhat dozy and forgot to draw on his pipe. But he roused himself immediately and inquired if she knew what business Robert had at the Falls. No, she didn't know.

"Bob doesn't tell much, that's a fact."

He was fully awake now, and began to speak about what he had done when he was a young man, and how he had resolved to be rich. He talked on with interest, his face gained animation. He had fallen into the habit of relating many incidents of his early life to Olive. Finally the two ate their supper silently, Olive waiting upon her father-in-law with a deft kindness which he did not appear to notice.

The night had fallen in thick with snow. The old man went to the door and held his hand out. "The storm has come," he remarked, "and I guess it'll be a rough one. It's growing cold, too."

Very soon he left the room and Olive heard him on the stairs. She knew that he would not return again that evening. She sat by a small lamp now, with one of Robert's stockings drawn over her hand, filling in a hole with coarse yarn. She was expecting her husband with every moment that passed, but not until the clock had struck nine did she begin to feel anxious; and then she remembered that he had said that he might be late, and that she must not worry. Nevertheless, when ten o'clock struck, she did begin to worry.

She extinguished the light, mindful of the waste of oil. She sat cowering over the stove with a shawl drawn about her shoulders. She did not replenish the fire for the same reason that she did not keep the lamp burning. But she grew colder and colder. The mercury must be falling fast, and her heart beat solemnly, not slowly, but with a hurrying solemnity.

It was about three miles to the Falls. Robert was strong and a good walker; and the wind was behind him. She was sure that he had not meant to stay so late. She wondered what was his business, and she wished that he was a little more frank. It was curious how he kept things to himself.

She put her shawl over her head and went to the porch door, opening it softly, lest she might disturb Mr. Nawn. The sound of his snoring came down the stairway, and a draught of icy air swept in as she drew the door back. The soft, cold flakes rushed in also, and came on her forehead and cheeks. It looked light outside, for there was a full moon behind the clouds, but it was an impenetrable light, that kept things almost as safely within it as darkness keeps objects.

As she stood at the door, she recalled Robert's advice to her; he had said that she must not sit up for him. But she must — she could not go to bed. The floor about her became white in a moment, and she closed the door, pressing up against it that she might latch it.

It was very strange that Robert did not come. As she stood there in the entry she was sure that she heard the sound of sleigh-bells down the road. Then, for nearly ten minutes, she was certain that Robert had caught a ride with some one, and that he would soon appear. But, no; the time passed, and then she was obliged to own that he had not been in that sleigh.

The kitchen seemed warm after she had stood in the open door-way, and she huddled down in Mr. Nawn's large chair and told herself that she would not be silly; she would sit there calmly for half an hour. She did not know how long a time had passed, and she thought that she must have been asleep, for when she started up suddenly, as if she had been awakened, the clock struck one.

"Oh," in a cry that sprang from her heart to her

lips, "where is Robert? Something must have happened to him."

She moved as quickly as she could in the dark to
the door again. But she changed her intention and
did not open it. She would go to an outer door that
was towards the south—there the snow would not
drift in. She rubbed the glass in a window near and
looked out before she touched the latch. As she
looked, her heart gave a great beat of thankfulness.
So near the window that even in the thick smur she
saw it, walked a man's tall figure. He had come!

She hurriedly drew the bolt and tried to pull back
the door that she might tell him to enter here. But
the door stuck at first, and when she had succeeded,
she could see nothing but the wall of snow, the moving wall rushing past her.

"Robert!" she called softly—"Robert!"

CHAPTER XXIII

AFTER GOLD

She waited an instant for a reply, and as none came she called for the third time, raising her voice. But there was no answer. She dared not call as loudly as she wished, lest she might awaken Mr. Nawn, whom she could still hear breathing.

But it was of no consequence. Robert had gone around to the north door, which was the one ordinarily used. In a moment more she would be brushing the snow from his clothes, and he would be laughing at her for her anxiety.

She hastened through the rooms to the north of the house again, expecting to hear him stamping his feet there on the thick rug. But no ; it was still, save for the beating of the wind and the melancholy sough of the snow on the window and house-wall. With a pang of ungovernable terror she now believed that the man she had seen could not have been Robert. Then she made herself think that it was Robert, and that he had gone to the barn to look after the cow and horse before he came in. She must be patient.

She sat down on the edge of a chair, rigid and expectant ; expectant, though in the bottom of her heart she knew that it was not in the least likely that Robert would go to the barn now. The moments passed as moments do pass at such a time. Then, at last, the clock struck two. Olive grew calm with the calmness that sometimes comes from a conviction of misfortune. Something had happened to her husband ; but

perhaps it was nothing evil that had kept him. She
wondered coolly why we always immediately suspect
that it is misfortune that is coming.

With the word " coming " forming itself in her mind,
she started from her chair and ran to the door. She
had heard a sound in Mr. Nawn's room. She stumbled
against something in the darkness, recovered herself,
and went on, running up the stairs with arms out-
spread, and calling, as she went, " Mr. Nawn ! Mr.
Nawn !"

But no one answered. It was not a voice that she
had heard in the old man's room, but a noise as of feet
scuffling on the floor. She wished now that she had
lighted a lamp and brought it with her ; but it was
too late to wish that. She knew that Mr. Nawn's cus-
tom was to keep his door locked. She fumbled for
the latch ; it was very black in this hall. Her hand,
instead of finding the latch, passed through into space.
Then she knew that the door was not only unlocked,
it was open a little. She pushed it wide and entered.
There was some light in the chamber, for the blinds
of a window were flung back, so that a pale illumina-
tion from outside entered.

There were two men struggling with each other. One
was in a long, white robe—that was old Mr. Nawn ; the
other's form was more vague and yet more dominant.
It was the other who was getting the advantage ; not
too easily, however, for Mr. Nawn, though old, was still
powerful, and he was now defending his gold, or he
thought that he was. Neither uttered a sound.

Confused and frightened as she was, Olive did not
hesitate. She flung herself forward and clutched at
the neck of the stranger, attacking him in the rear.
She knew that a little help would avail much. And it
did. From the instant she touched him it was the
effort to escape that absorbed the intruder. He had
a black veil so tightly fastened on his face—Olive felt

it—that even in the scrimmage it did not fall off.
He flung himself about; he threw Olive heavily from
him with one hand, and she fell with a thud on the
floor; he succeeded in freeing himself from the old
man's clutch.   He dashed at the door; he could be
heard running down the stairs; the outer door resisted
him for an instant, then that slammed open, then com-
plete silence.

The cat, which had been shut into the wood-shed,
walked noiselessly into the room, purring comfortably.

Mr. Nawn, from the push that had been given him,
had fallen forward on the bed. He now raised himself,
put his hand to his head, and sat quiet for a moment.
Then he carefully reached forward to a stand that had
stood at the head of his bed with matches upon it. But
the stand had been knocked down and the matches
scattered.

Then the old man opened his lips for the first time.
He swore roughly. He crouched to the floor and
groped about with flat palm and extended fingers until
he touched a match. The sound of the contact of the
match on the wall was curiously distinct in the silence.

Mr. Nawn scrambled to his feet with the match held
upright. He found the lamp on the shelf and lighted
it. Then he turned with it in his hand and looked at
the figure lying on the floor. Olive was as motionless
as if she had been dead. He knelt stiffly down by her.
He was becoming stiff now, and it was cold in that
room, so cold that the man began to shiver.

"She's stunned," he said, aloud.

He rose to his feet laboriously and carried the lamp
to the shelf. He went back, stooped, and lifted Olive
in his arms. He laid her on his own bed and spread a
heavy cover over her. Having done that, he dressed
with remarkable swiftness, now muttering to himself.
His heavy steps shook the floor. When he had drawn
on a garment he would stoop over the figure on the

bed, with the light held close to the face. Once he laid his thick, heavy hand over the heart.

"She'll be coming to soon—she'll come to. She can't help it. She's young." So he kept muttering. He brought a bottle of brandy from a closet, and he poured some of the liquid into a spoon and forced the spoon between Olive's teeth. "They say it's water of life," he whispered. "I should hate to have her die like this. I want her to live to see that scoundrel punished. After my gold ! Great heavens ! my gold !"

He put the bottle and spoon on the stand, which he had placed upright in its old position. He grasped a post of the bedstead and held it fast as he stooped over Olive. Yes, she was reviving. She moved her head uneasily ; she spoke, but indistinctly at first ; then, more distinctly, she asked :

"Has he gone?"

"Yes, to the devil !" was the prompt answer.

Olive sighed. Presently she said, "If Rob had only been here !"

"He couldn't have done much better than you did," was the response.

Olive lay still a moment ; then she raised herself on her elbow and gazed about her, her eyes wild. "Oh !" she cried, "where is Rob ?"

"Hasn't he come back ?" asked Mr. Nawn.

"No. Something has happened to him. I must go." She tried to rise, but Mr. Nawn pushed her down.

"You can't go. It 'll be morning before long now. You lie still. I'll make a fire here. I'll sit by the stove and smoke. By-and-by I'll get a sleigh of somebody and go over to the Falls."

The man set about making a fire, and Olive watched him. Her head was so strange when she lifted it that she dared not try to rise. When the fire was roaring in the air-tight, Mr. Nawn came to the bed again.

"Another sup of brandy ?" he asked.

11

She made a negative sign. He put the bottle in the closet and locked the door. It appeared to be his habit to lock all doors. He wrapped a blanket about him and sat down by the stove. He crowded in the wood in apparent forgetfulness of the fact that he was lavish of the fuel. He lighted his pipe and smoked fast, the blue clouds filling the room. As for Olive, she lay looking at him, aware of a strange haziness enveloping her brain. This haziness was so great that she gave up trying to think clearly; and she could not prevent herself from falling asleep.

Mr. Nawn, sitting by the fire, after a while felt his head drooping, wide awake as he had thought himself to be. He put his pipe on the stove-hearth, leaned back in his chair, and he also was soon asleep, the room becoming breathlessly hot. The cat sat in a little heap, sometimes blinking inquisitively. So the time went on until the late daylight began to creep into the room. Outside the snow was swirling about, apparently as thick as ever.

Olive opened her eyes, then sat up, throwing the comforter quickly back. She rose to her feet, standing irresolutely a moment. Then she asked, in a whisper, "What is it? What is it that has happened?"

But even as she put the question she remembered every detail of what had occurred. And Robert had not come back. Mr. Nawn was still sleeping. The room was in disorder from the struggle of a few hours before. The lamp was burning palely in the light. She stepped forward and extinguished it. How much oil had already been wasted!

Then she went down-stairs as quickly as she could. Her head was unsteady, and hurt her when she turned it. There was the north door unlatched, and the entry was heaped with snow. She waded through it to the wood-house and brought back a shovel with which she began to pile the snow, so that she might open the door. As she did so, she heard sleigh-bells coming. She dropped her shovel and ran to the front of the house, but the snow and frost had so curtained the window that she could see nothing, and her hand stuck to the glass. But she knew that the bells had stopped.

A sound at the north side of the house! She hurried back.

"Olive! Olive, I say!" impatiently, in Robert's voice. "Why, how came all this snow here? Why didn't you shut this door? It must have been open all night."

The young man had crowded through the aperture, and he now took the shovel and began to fling blocks of the white stuff outside. He did not glance at Olive until he had cleared the mass somewhat. Then he dropped the tool and his wife caught his arm.

"Oh, what has happened?" she cried.

The two entered the kitchen.

"I'm awfully sorry you've been worrying," he answered. "I knew you would, but I couldn't send word to you. You know I told you I might be late. Well, it was almost midnight before I started from the Falls. Had to wait to see a man on business, and the storm was pretty thick by that time. I was struggling on, the wind at my back, luckily. But I didn't have much luck all the same. I fell, and somehow I twisted my ankle—not much, I'm only lame a little. A man on a wood-sled came along just then, on his way to the Falls. He said he'd take me right back; that I was a fool to try to go on; that I should freeze to death, now I couldn't go fast. It was terribly cold, you know. How you shiver, Olive! I knew you'd worry your life out, almost; but I rode back on the sled, and I stopped the rest of the night at Mr. Hayden's, and got him to bring me home this morning."

Young Nawn's words were spoken quickly, and as soon as the explanation was over he exclaimed:

"But what has happened here? I would as soon

think of the world's coming to an end as of father's leaving a door unlocked.   And haven't you been in bed at all, Olive?   You ought to have thought that the storm delayed me and have gone to bed and slept."

Here Robert stooped and kissed the white face on his shoulder.   Then he lifted Olive in his arms and said, with a laugh, that he should put her to bed now, and she must stay there while he kindled a fire.

She made no reply; she let him do as he said.   Their bedroom led from the kitchen, and she lay there quietly until she heard the fire crackling in the stove.   It was very cold—the first "cold snap" of the winter. Although the water had been let down from the pump the handle was frozen stiff, and had to be thawed from water in the teakettle.

"Don't get up yet," Robert called once ; "it isn't warm enough."

She listened to his movements.   She knew by the sounds just what he was doing.   If one had looked at her face it would have been found singularly inexpressive.   Her eyes were fixed on a certain figure in the paper on the wall.

After a time Robert came into the room.   He sat down on the bed and leaned tenderly over that quiet face.   "You look as if something was the matter," he said—"something more than my being so long away. And how came the door open?"

"The man left it open," answered Olive.

She was now looking intently at her husband, and he was meeting the gaze with questioning eyes.   But his eyes seemed somehow to recede as he looked.

CHAPTER XXIV

"THE man?" he repeated. Then he asked, hastily, "Olive, are you well?"

She smiled slightly. "Oh yes, I'm well, and perfectly sane. The man, when he ran away, left the door open, and neither Mr. Nawn nor I thought of shutting it." She spoke with apparent effort, and she now seemed also to meet her husband's eyes only by an effort. She took his hand and held it pressed to her bosom. "Oh," she murmured, "I'm so glad you've come! I have suffered so! But you've come back."

He kissed her again. "I'm so sorry—so sorry!" he said, gently. Then he resumed, "But you must tell me about the man. Was he a burglar? Did he get anything? How is father? Does he know? It's dreadful to think that you were alone, or as bad as alone— my poor Olive—my poor darling!"

He bent over and caressed her. She clung to his hand, gazing up at him. He had not been so gently kind of late, not for a long time. But she supposed that it was not a man's way to be demonstrative. A man was so different after marriage: he left his wife to take many things for granted; he was busy; he couldn't be continually turning to her and saying, "I love you—you are dearer than ever to me." If he did not become cruelly indifferent, it was all the woman could expect.

"You must think that I want to know what has happened," urged Robert, after a short silence.

So Olive hesitatingly told him every particular of what had occurred, and the young man listened with an intentness that appeared to take the word from her lips almost before she spoke it. He suddenly put his arm about her when she came to the telling of how the burglar had flung her to the floor and then run away. And when everything was told, he still held her and questioned again and again as to whether she was really much injured. He was once more the tender and impassioned lover of a few months ago. She lay back on the pillow, her worn face happy, her eyes softly brilliant through their anxiety.

At last Robert limped into the kitchen to attend to the fire. He would not allow Olive to stir. He said he would get the breakfast. Everything would be late anyway, now, and he should not try to go to the factory until noon. Oh yes, in answer to her remonstrance, he could walk if he took time—and a cane. He laughed; he hung over his wife and petted her. He said he was so thankful that no worse had happened to her.

When he went out he should stop at Mr. Ames's house and tell him of the burglary. Mr. Ames was chairman of the Selectmen, and it was his business to do something. That fellow must be caught; he, Robert, couldn't rest until he was caught. He wished his father would offer a reward. If he were able, he would offer a reward himself.

Young Nawn made some tea and carried it to his wife. She drank it, but she said that she could not eat; she could not even try to eat. At last Mr. Nawn's step was heard on the stairs; then the kitchen door opened and he entered. Robert was standing by the sink. He turned quickly and gave the old man a sharp gaze, which was returned by one fully as keen.

" I hope you're all right, father," said Robert. "Olive's been telling me what's happened. I wish you felt like offering a reward."

Mr. Nawn had reached his chair by the stove, and he now dropped into it slowly, supporting himself by putting a hand on each arm.

"Reward for what?" he asked.

"For finding that man who tried to rob you last night."

"Pooh! what's the use? The Selectmen are fools; and if they got some police out here, the chances are that they'd be fools, too. I sha'n't offer any reward. You may do that if you want to."

"I would if I had money enough," was the response.

"Then you'd be a bigger jackass than I take you for. Where's Olive?" looking about the room.

"She's lying down. I wouldn't let her get up yet."

Mr. Nawn leaned back in his chair and grunted. He said he was too old to be broken of his rest. Then he gave his chuckling laugh and rubbed his hands.

"The fellow didn't get anything," he said, presently. "I guess he'll try another place next time. What in the deuce did he come here for? Did he think I kept gold lying about where he could grab it? Not much. Put a little more coffee in the pot this morning, Bob. I feel as if I'd like a stiff cup."

His son obeyed him, and presently the two sat down. The old man ate a hearty breakfast of the ham and potatoes, but Robert could not eat, though he made a pretence of doing so.

"What's the matter?" asked Mr. Nawn, eying him across the table.

"I've been startled—and to think that Olive was flung down!"

"But she wasn't hurt badly, was she?" reaching for another potato.

"No," shortly.

"Then there's no harm, is there? I wonder what Isabel Keating would have done?" Mr. Nawn laughed again, and Robert frowned. "She's a great, strapping girl, Isabel is. Perhaps she'd have flung the burglar, instead of letting him fling her. If you'd married Isabel, Bob, you'd have had money enough yourself to offer a reward."

"Hush!" Robert glanced towards the bedroom door, which was not quite closed. "Olive will hear you." The young man's face became red, then faded to an unnatural pallor. He pushed his chair back from the table. "I wish you wouldn't talk like that, father!" he exclaimed, in a half-whisper.

"Like what? Ain't you very delicate? You know you didn't really know which to take—now, did you?" Robert's eyes dropped as his father sat looking at him intently; he noticed a purple mark like a bruise near the young man's left temple. "Have you had a fall?" asked Mr. Nawn, suddenly.

"Yes; that's what kept me. I started for home last night, and I fell and got a little sprain. The going was bad."

"I shouldn't think soft snow would have been so bad to fall on."

"'Twas ice," answered Robert, shortly.

Then, with an effort, the son related to his father the circumstances that had detained him. When he had finished, Mr. Nawn remarked that it was a pity Bob hadn't been at home; that he probably would never be so greatly wanted again as long as he lived. Then the subject was dropped.

All the neighborhood discussed the affair. The Selectmen came and examined the room; they sent for a detective from the nearest city, and he examined everything. Of course the snow obliterated all tracks. The town officials, perhaps, were stung into unusual efforts by Mr. Nawn's open scorn of their powers. He sat by the air-tight in his room and scoffed at their suppositions. Presently they gave up the affair. The neighborhood held on to it a while longer, and every-

body made a guess as to how much money old **Nawn**
kept in the house. The store-keeper did not scruple
to assert **that "they"**—meaning by this collective pro-
noun the burglar—wouldn't stop there; "they" would
make another attempt. **He** shook his head wisely over
the molasses which was trickling slowly through a tun-
nel into Esther Rice's **stone** jug. It took a quart of
treacle a great while in **the** winter **to go** through a
tunnel.

"**I pity** Olive," **said** Esther   "I declare **I** do pity
Olive. I s'pose she was **in** love with Robert Nawn,
but she don't look none too happy now; **'n'** she don't
hardly ever come to her mother's; 'n' **Mrs.** Newcomb
she's about given up goin' over to old Nawn's, anyway.
She says she'd rather see the old Harry than to see
him; she says she always feels **'s** if he was lookin' her
through 'n' through, and **'s** if she was all to once goin'
to be found **out** in something dreadful. How much
money do you s'pose old Nawn keeps in the house?"

Esther tried to peer over the counter at the molasses,
but found that she could not quite succeed.

"Not **a cent**," promptly, from the store-keeper.
"**He's too bright** to keep money by him."

"**I know** he's jest **as** bright as the Evil One," spoke
up a voice near the stove, " but he's got **a** weak point.
I'll bet a dollar ag'inst a cent any time, that old Nawn
keeps a pile of gold somewhere, so 't he **c'n** go 'n' roll
in it jest 's a dog rolls in carri'n. You'll find I'm right."
The speaker slapped his hand down **on the** top of a
sugar-barrel as emphasis.

It was some **time** after the attempted robbery that
the minister called at Mr. Nawn's. He was the same
minister who had **married Robert** and Olive. He drove
over and hitched his horse **to** the fence, taking a long
time to tie the rope. **It** had begun to grow warm
now; a thaw had set in, and everything was dripping.

At last he walked up the path to the front door.   The
weeds and the pudding-bag shrubs were all gone.   The
minister's rubber boots sank into the "sposh" and spat-
tered large drops about.

Olive came to the door in response to his knock.   She
was pale, and there were dark marks under her eyes.
The man's heart went out to her in a great throb of
sympathy.   He stepped quickly into the hall.

"You'll have to come to the kitchen," she said; "we
don't keep a fire in the sitting-room."

He followed her through the desolate house, expecting to find Mr. Nawn established in a warm corner, but
his chair was empty.   The visitor sat down ; he looked
again at Olive ; then he said, earnestly :

"I wish I'd brought my wife with me.   You look lonesome, Mrs. Nawn ; you must excuse me for saying so."
Olive drew herself up more erectly.   She folded her
hands with a prim movement in her lap.   She opened
her lips to speak, then closed them again.   "Yes,"
went on Mr. Lang, "I do wish I'd brought Mrs. Lang.
You're too much alone — you need to see a woman
sometimes.   I wish I could say something to cheer
you.   Olive, are you well?"   .

The minister was an impulsive man.   He spoke
rapidly, and he leaned forward as he spoke.

Now Olive succeeded in speaking.   "I thank you,"
she said, formally ; "I'm quite well ; and you're mistaken about my being much alone.   Mr. Nawn is here
most of the time.   He's gone over to the Falls to-day.
He heard that a grocer there was selling sugar at a
quarter of a cent a pound cheaper than you can get it
here."

"Oh !" Mr. Lang uttered this exclamation and then
was silent.   He sat looking at this woman whose eyes
were lowered, and whose lips were so reticently closed.
He glanced at her hands ; they were folded so closely
that the nails showed white.   What should he say?

He felt a strange inclination to weep. Was this Olive
Newcomb? And was she beginning to think of nothing but that sugar was a quarter of a cent a pound
cheaper at the Falls? If his wife were only here she
might go to this girl and put her arms about her.
"I'm sorry you are troubled, Olive," he said, gently.

She raised her eyes. "Troubled?" she repeated.
"What should I be troubled about?"

The man made no reply. He sat there gazing about
the room, hoping he could think of something to say.
At last he remarked that he should suppose that Olive
would like to have her mother come and stay with her.
As old Mr. Nawn had requested his daughter-in-law
not to have visitors stop to take meals with them, this
remark was not particularly happy.

"Mother has Aunt Ruth with her," replied Olive.

The minister grew more and more embarrassed. He
rose and walked to the window, making some irrele-
vant remark to the effect that the Creeper was more
swollen than he had ever known it to be so early in the
spring.

"Yes," said Olive, dully ; "Robert was saying the
same thing yesterday."

Mr. Lang returned to his chair and sat down. He
resolutely began to talk, not caring much what he said.
He sat for half an hour, and then he rose. Olive rose
too, the same fixed expression on her face that had
been there since her guest had come. The minister
shook hands with her, and she invited him to call
again, speaking monotonously. She followed him to
the door, and closed it when he was walking down
through the melting snow to his horse. While he was
unfastening his hitch-rope the door opened again, and
a voice called, hurriedly :

"Mr. Lang, please come back—come back !"

There was a penetrating entreaty in that call.

CHAPTER XXV

Mr. Lang dropped the rope and hastened to retrace his steps. Olive was standing there holding to the latch of the door. With her other hand she touched the minister's sleeve. She looked up at him with a heart-breakingly wistful glance.

"I couldn't bear to have you go, after all, without praying for me," she said.

"Yes, yes," he answered. He took her hand and led her to the kitchen. Her aspect had wholly changed. The man's eyes blurred as he walked through the hall with that small, cold hand in his warm palm. He had been in many households where there was sorrow, but it was not often that his heart was so moved as now, where there was no visible grief.

When the two had reached the room they had just left, Olive withdrew her hand and sank into a chair. She looked up again, intently, absorbedly, as some women and some children can look.

"I thought," she said, in a whisper, "that perhaps God would be more used to hearing your prayers. As for me, I pray night and morning, but I suppose God is tired of having me do it. Do you suppose He is tired?"

"No—no. Impossible. A father doesn't get tired of his children," was the hurried response.

"Doesn't he? But I think God is weary of me, anyway." Mr. Lang drew his hand across his eyes. He was silent a moment. Before he was ready to speak,

Olive broke the silence. "I don't want you to think that my husband isn't kind," she said. "Robert is a very kind man, and I love him with all my heart. But I suppose I get morbid staying here without going out-of-doors. The walking has been so bad, and I don't think I've been very well. And the going has kept mother at home, you see. But no, I won't pretend that I could talk freely to mother—she isn't the kind, somehow. But there's a look in your face, Mr. Lang—there's something about you that made it seem as if I couldn't let you go without calling to you. Do you think it was weak, Mr. Lang—do you think it was weak?"

And again the man answered with his monosyllable, "No, no."

In truth, there seemed nothing else to say ; and he was also wise enough to know presently that it was best for Olive to talk all she felt to talk. He sat with his elbow on the arm of his chair, his hand shading his eyes, as he listened. He had a feeling that it would not be right to look at her persistently.

Olive went on : "When I saw you coming just now I was so glad. I thought I'd ask you to pray. I've wanted to get out to meeting at the school-house this winter, but the road has been slippery, and I was afraid I should fall. I didn't want to fall. You remember, Mr. Lang, that I always used to be regular at the service ?" The minister nodded. "Perhaps you'll think I'm very wicked, but I thought 'twould be lovely if you were a priest—a Roman Catholic priest, you know —and I could kneel and say everything there was in my heart. Do you think that was wicked ?"

"No." Mr. Lang's kind eyes met Olive's for an instant, as he replied.

"I didn't know but it might be wicked," in a relieved tone. "You see, when you're shut in the house so, you take up fancies. I've only been out to the barn to feed the pigs and the hens. I put ashes down on the path, and was real careful not to fall." Olive was sitting far forward in her chair, her hands on the arms, as one who would rise in a moment. Mr. Lang was silent. "I want you to pray for—" Olive paused for so long a time that the minister looked at her inquiringly. He had been under the impression that she had asked for prayers for herself. "I hope—" A painful blush slowly colored Olive's face to the hair that hung loose on her forehead. "I hope," she began again, "that you won't think strange if I tell you that it's for the child that I want you to pray; it wasn't for me—though maybe I said it was."

"The child?" repeated the minister.

Olive's blush had subsided. "Yes," with more dignity than had yet been noticeable in her manner. "I haven't even told mother; I thought she'd worry so about me. We expect a child in June. I've been afraid it would be a miser. Oh"—Olive rose; she extended her hands with a gesture that was indescribably touching—"you must pray that it won't be a miser!—pray so that God will have to hear you and answer! I've prayed so much that I'm confused, and I sometimes think—did I tell you?—that He is weary of me. But you are a minister of the gospel; He won't get tired of you. If my child should be a miser I should die—I mean I should want to die—for I've heard that people don't often die when they want to the most. But, then, I should long to live for him, unless I could be his angel before the throne—to be my child's angel before the throne!—that would be something to long for—wouldn't it, Mr. Lang? You remember how 'their angels behold'—but I can't remember quite the words of it. Now will you pray?"

Olive rose from her chair and stood with her hands clasped in an attitude of entreaty.

The minister rose also. He felt that he hadn't a

"'PRAY SO THAT GOD WILL HAVE TO HEAR YOU AND ANSWER!'"

word, and yet he must not disappoint this woman. He looked at her with dazed eyes. He was longing to be inspired as he never yet had been inspired.

"Now will you pray?" repeated Olive. She had the air of one expecting great comfort.

Mr. Lang began. He said: "Dear Lord!—dear Father!" And then he knew nothing more coherently; he was only aware that he wept as he besought God to make this woman's child noble and generous; not to let it love money. What else did he say? When he tried to tell his wife afterwards about this interview, he stammered and ceased speaking, and his wife suddenly rose from her chair and came to his side and kissed him.

"John," she said, "you needn't try to tell me. I want you to take me over there the next time you go."

Now, when he had said "Amen," he turned blindly about to look for his hat.

There were no tears in Olive's eyes. She brought the minister's hat to him. He thanked her in a vague manner and walked towards the door with it in his hand. He left her without saying even good-bye. She stood watching for many minutes after he had gone. She was listening now, however, to the sound made by the Creeper—a sound very different from the slight rustle that marked its course in the summer—if, indeed, it made any noise at all then. A muffled rushing was in the air—an undertone to the continual dripping from trees and eaves, and the running of melting snow all about. The sun was not shining; one could see the warm fog rising in the meadows and drifting before the southerly wind.

Olive's spirits were rising. She suddenly wished that she might go to her mother's. She had not seen her mother for more than two months. Mrs. Newcomb had not been able to walk on the snow on account of a touch of rheumatism; but the store-keeper had brought her in the early winter to the Nawn house one day when the ground was bare, and she was able to walk back.

Olive felt as if she could not combat this longing. It suddenly seemed to her to be cruel that she had not told her secret to her mother. It was so mild, perhaps she might try to go. She found some old rubber boots that had belonged to her husband ; to be sure, one of them leaked on the top, but she might be able to step so carefully that she would not get her feet wet. She did not expect Mr. Nawn until night. She was surprised at the strength of her wish for her mother. Soon she was on the way. She took one of Mr. Nawn's canes ; it would help her not to slip, and she could sound the depth of the slush as she went.

The water was running fast down the road as she started out. Things were not so bad as she had thought. She found the bridge entirely cleared. It was a distinct joy to her to set foot on the planks. She paused in the middle of the footway and leaned over. She could see the water directly below her, but all behind and before was enveloped in the mist. She hung over the rail, happier than she had been for many a day. Yes, she had been growing morbid staying there alone, and she had not been well. But she would be cheerful now ; and she had a conviction that God would aid her. Ought she not to be the happiest woman in the world?

She smiled as she looked down into the river. As she smiled, the thin, transparent image of a face formed itself at the surface of the water and smiled back at her. It was old Mr. Nawn's face that was gazing at her—its large cheeks hanging flabbily, just as she saw them every day. Just this thing had happened to her once before. But then presently Robert had come to her. Robert had loved her ; they had married ; and in her absorbingly busy life she had not often thought

of this appearance. She had shrunk away from the
railing; but now she approached it again and looked
down with a resolute gaze. There was no hint of a
face there; the dark, turbid water went hurrying un-
derneath. In her relief she laughed aloud.

"Good land!" cried a voice, a few yards away.
"Who is that laughing? Mercy! Is that you, Olive?
I couldn't be more surprised if I'd met the Pope of
Rome out here on the Red Bridge!"

And Esther Rice advanced from the fog and paused
beside Olive. Esther had a tin quart measure in her
hand, and explained that she was going over to Mr.
Day's to "borry a half-pint of vinegar, for their'n had
froze in the last cold snap, and though 'twas a good
deal thawed, they didn't want to draw from it now,
for if they did, what was left wouldn't be fit to use."

While she was making this explanation her inquisi-
tive gaze was fixed upon her companion in that gim-
letlike way that is so trying to bear.

Olive said, in reply, that she knew it wasn't best to
draw off vinegar when any part of it was frozen. Then
she turned and leaned on the railing again and looked
down. Esther ranged up beside her, the tin quart
clanging against an iron upright.

"It's jest as funny 's it can be, that I should meet
Robert, 'n' then I should meet you!" remarked Esther,
presently. "I arst him how you was, 'n' he said you
was well, but you hadn't be'n out none this winter; 'n'
then that I sh'd come along to the Bridge 'n' find you
laughin' here 's if 'twas summer, 'n' you was viewin'
the landscape."

Olive gathered herself together. "'Twas so mild,"
she responded, as if it were necessary for her to make
an explanation, "that I thought I'd go to mother's for
an hour."

"I know it's mild, but it's dretful weather to take
cold," said Esther. "It wouldn't do for you to have

pneumonia there at old Nawn's, for there wouldn't nobody dare to go 'n' take care of you. Odd, wasn't it, that I should have met Robert, too? He was comin' out of the drive up to the Keating place; he was in a great hurry, and only nodded. He couldn't stop to speak."

Olive put her hand on the rail as she looked at her companion — looked calmly and unflinchingly. " It doesn't seem very odd to me," she answered. " Work isn't very driving at the factory now. I suppose I ought to be going to mother's, if I'm to be back in time to get supper."

So the two women separated. Olive went on, with her head held high. But when Esther was out of sight she paused in her walk, hesitated, then turned.

" I don't know as I can see mother, after all, now," she said, aloud.

She hastened up the slight ascent from the river, and was breathing heavily when she reached the house. Her great rubber boots all at once seemed to weigh her down.

CHAPTER XXVI

OLIVE was surprised, however, to find that, as she moved here and there to get the supper, she was not depressed. A fine sense of exhilaration buoyed her up. She recalled Esther's words and smiled at them. What if Robert were coming away from Isabel Keating's? When he came home perhaps he would refer to his having been to the Keating place—though she owned to herself that he rarely mentioned anything he had done. She had learned that, though she had not before her marriage been aware of this trait. She had thought that he told her everything then. She sighed, but she smiled also.

When Robert returned he did not speak of where he had been until Olive mentioned that she had gone out and had stood on the bridge; but even then she did not allude to the face she had seen floating above the water. She said that Esther Rice had been going over the bridge to borrow vinegar; and Olive smiled.

Robert raised his eyes from his plate. "I saw Esther," he said. "I'd been to the Keating place on an errand."

And that was all. Robert scowled slightly. He did not relish being obliged to say even that; not that he had been obliged to do it, but he knew very well that Esther Rice always told everything.

"I reckon your errand was to see a pretty girl," remarked Mr. Nawn; and he added, with unction, that "that would be errand enough for him, any time."

When Robert sat down by the stove after supper, he
watched Olive as she cleared the table. Once he rose
and followed her into the shed.

"Let me take that pail," he said; "it's too heavy for
you." There was in his voice that soft cadence that
his wife knew so well. She glanced up at him. He
had never been more gentle than since that night of
the attempted burglary. "I wish," he said, now, "that
father wasn't always in the room. A man likes to
have a moment when he can speak to his wife."

Olive's glance grew yet brighter, and her good spirits continued, week after week. The spring came on
apace after the great thaw. Mr. Nawn, one mild day
in April, told Olive that she needn't feed the hens any
more; they might pick up their food now. It was all
nonsense to keep on feeding hens after the snow was
off the ground. If they couldn't find their own living,
they weren't worth owning.

"And you'd better not take any meat of the butcher
oftener than once a fortnight. Butcher's meat runs
up like the devil."

Olive bowed her head. She was not greatly troubled
by these things. She thought it strange that she was
not more troubled. A subtle sense of exultation was
with her all the time. What did she care for butcher's
meat? But she was sorry for the hens. When she
went to the barn they flocked about her and pecked at
her feet, and seemed unable to understand; but at last
they would scatter over the yard, searching for something to eat.

Olive went about the house with a lovely light upon
her face. Old Mr. Nawn, as he sat smoking, would
stare at her, sometimes taking his pipe out of his
mouth as he did so. There never was such a beautiful June since the world began. The Creeper ran
through a country that smiled up at heaven. The hills
were green; the new growth on them seemed promis-

ing something more wonderful than anything the sun had ever shone upon. The water of the little river curled and dimpled by its banks ; children played on the Red Bridge. Many times a day Olive stood at the open door and gazed down the valley. This month her child would be born. All the world knew it ; all the world was glad, and showed that it was glad.

"Of course, I know better than that," she said, aloud; "but I like to think so ; and the world is such a happy place. It is plain that God heard the minister's prayer ; and my child won't be a miser."

She went on with her work as usual, or almost as usual. The heavier things old Mr. Nawn put his hand to. He said there was no need of having a woman come—hired help always wasted and ate as much as their wages ; and he wasn't going to spend his money in that way. Robert said "that was so ;" it was foolish to have a woman—yet.

Olive listened and made no remark ; the fine light was in her eyes ; she seemed to walk in her own radiance. On the morning of the 15th of the month the child was born—a boy.

Olive's mother was with her, very teary and nervous. Old Mr. Nawn was walking up and down in front of the house, among the weeds and grass. Robert was leaning on the gate. It was not yet five o'clock ; but the sun was shining through a beautiful mist, and the birds were singing as if their little hearts would burst with triumphant joy. Some one knocked sharply on the window-pane within the sitting - room. The two men turned quickly. Robert strode up to the house.

"All right !" cried Mrs. Newcomb, joyfully. "It's a great boy. Don't you want to see it ? I must run back this minute."

Robert entered the house and ran up the stairs. His eyes were gleaming, his lips parted. He stepped softly into his wife's room and up to the bed. He stood looking down at her, and he choked as he looked. She turned her head slowly, and her gaze was instantly absorbed in his.

"I wish I were half worthy of you," he muttered.

She feebly put out her hand. "That's silly," she said. He had grasped her hand. "I'm doing so well," she said, in a whisper, "that there needn't be the expense of a doctor, I'm sure. Mother 'll stay with me, and she won't cost anything, only her food."

The young man reddened until his face was almost purple. "I deserve that," he said. Then he restrained himself and answered, "You must have good care."

A moment later he went away. In the next room he met Mrs. Newcomb with the baby in her arms. Young Nawn stooped over it ; and he wondered if the infant human being were always so uninteresting as that—a pink, wrinkled, squalling thing.

"It's splendid!" exclaimed Mrs. Newcomb, putting a flap of blanket over its face.

"I suppose so," responded Robert, and he hurried down the stairs.

When he started he was thinking that he would go for the doctor immediately; but by the time he had stepped from the outer door he paused, and was asking himself why he should be at that expense, after all. Perhaps Olive was right, and it wasn't necessary. He would wait ; there would be time enough. He walked to the fence and leaned over it, pulling his hat down that the brilliant sunlight might not strike his eyes. How bright the world was to-day ! And that was his son up there—that muling thing with red, aimless claws. He wondered if some men loved their children when the little animals were like that. And then he wondered, in a dull, half-resentful way, if Olive would get back her good looks now. He didn't know that women could fade as she had done. Very likely she had worked too hard ; but it wasn't as if she were not used to work.

He stood up and looked, as if involuntarily, off across the Creeper to the opposite slope where, among newly leaved maples and horse - chestnuts, he could see the chimneys of Isabel Keating's home. Isabel had not faded. She was more beautiful and bewitching than ever. The young man shut his eyes, and before him rose a vision of that dark face ; a seductive vision that led him on and on. He hoped that his father would never ask him again why he had not married Isabel. He believed that he had found out positively now that his father had really wished him to marry her. And his father's money ? The old man puzzled the younger one. The son had never been able to understand the sneers and the cynical remarks — they confused him. And the young husband still had what might be called spasms of tenderness for his wife— these confused him also. Who was that fellow who had come up to the sleigh that time when Isabel had driven him, Robert, to the Falls ? The neighbors were already saying that he was Isabel's "beau." Well, and what if it were true ? It was nothing to him. Robert extended his hand and grasped the rickety old rail of the fence ; beneath that powerful touch the rail dropped from its place in the post.

"What are you doing?" asked Mr. Nawn, who had kept his place, not stirring after he had heard Mrs. Newcomb say, "All right ; it's a great boy."

"Nothing," was the short reply. "This fence isn't worth paying taxes for."

Robert walked off with his hands in his pockets. He had thought he should feel more emotion if he should be the father of a son ; he had always hoped it wouldn't be a girl. He had read a lot of stuff about the emotions of a father when he first saw his infant son. That didn't mean anything — that was all made up by somebody who did writing as a business. Perhaps, by - and - by, he should care for the boy. But the child would be an expense. Perhaps the old man would want to be paid more board - money. At this thought Robert fumed. Then he asked himself if Olive loved that brat even now. And she had looked lovely with her head on the pillow, and her beautiful soft hair about her face. And what eyes she had — not seductive, like Isabel's, but beautiful, true, and deep, and full of a sweet light.

Robert felt his heart warm again as he thought thus. Then a petulant feeling came to him, and he wished that Olive hadn't quite such a high ideal of him—if she had. It made him uncomfortable ; he couldn't live up to it ; and he felt somehow to blame because she had taken such a notion. Yes, he had been tremendously in love with her ; he was in love with her now, of course : only it was different when a woman was a man's wife. Then the question went like a flash through Robert's mind, "Would it have been different if he had married Isabel ?" He tried to shake off these questions ; they were worse than useless, and they worried him. Then over him again swept the tenderness that had come to him just now when he had stood by Olive's bed.

"Bob," called his father. The young man turned. "I'm glad it's a boy," said Mr. Nawn. "A boy can generally get hold of more money than a girl."

"Yes," said Robert.

"I say," presently, from Mr. Nawn again ; "I suppose the old lady won't make any charges for taking care of her own daughter, will she?"

"I should think not. I sha'n't pay her if she does."

"Well, that's your lookout, not mine." And the old man walked away, a trail of tobacco-smoke floating behind him.

Up-stairs the next fortnight passed in one absorbing monotony. Olive grew in strength steadily, and so did the boy. He developed a terrific pair of lungs—so his grandfather said. Olive was fed with nourishing food ; her mother brought it to her, and she did not reveal that it was purchased with her own money and privately prepared. She thought that she would tell Olive some day, for Mrs. Newcomb was not one to bury any fact in her own mind. She was going to inform the neighbors, when she was where she could see them, what those two Nawn men let her do ; and how neither of them thought of getting " anything decent for a sick woman to eat."

" She didn't see how Olive had borne it, living there alone with them two Nawns," she confided to her sister Ruth when she went home one day while her daughter and the child were sleeping. " Robert's as bad as his father ; I d' know but he's tighter, if anything. I always feel 's if he was watching me when I sweeten my tea, 'n' wishin' I wouldn't use so much sugar. I guess he'll find it's cheaper to let me have my tea sweet than to hire a nurse. I jest wish he did have to hire a nurse. And only to think ! He ain't had no doctor come near ! I don't call it respectable. If Robert lives as long 's his father, I guess he'll starve himself to death ; 'cause victuals cost money anyway you c'n fix it. No, I declare, I don't understand how Olive lives with them two Nawn men."

Sister Ruth, who had a fat, placid face, with good eyes, now remarked that burdens were made for the backs that bore them, " and you must remember that Olive 'bout died when she thought she'd lost Robert Nawn. Them love-matches don't turn out first-rate half the time. But Olive 'll have her boy now." And Ruth went on piecing a sleeve-lining.

" Mebby her boy 'll be a Nawn," responded the mother, " 'n' if he is, he won't be no comfort to anybody. Well, I must be hurryin' back."

She found Olive lying happily awake. Her face was

turned towards the crib where the boy lay, though she could see nothing but the posts of it. It was the crib in which Robert himself had slept, and, from its appearance, generations before him. He had brought it down from the attic, and it was put in use immediately. Mrs. Newcomb bent over it, while Olive said :

"Did you meet Rob ?"

"No, I didn't."

"He says work's shut down at the factory, and he won't be earning anything for a few weeks. We've got to be as saving as possible. I shall be able to do the work soon, I hope."

Mrs. Newcomb's face grew red. "That means that you don't want me any more, I s'pose."

"Oh, mother !"

"Yes, it does. Well, I must say I ain't cost anybody much, save for the victuals I've eat. I declare, I don't see how you stan' it ! I don't wonder old Mis' Nawn died, and was glad she could die. I've been sorry a good many times since that I went to Robert that day. You'd a good deal better have lived without him all your days, I do think !"

So they didn't want her there any more—and she had saved them doctors' bills and nurses' bills ! She sat down in the nearest chair and began to snuffle slightly.

Olive, who was dressed, rose from the bed. She was quite pale. "You went to Robert ?" she asked. "What do you mean by that ? When did you go to Robert ?"

CHAPTER XXVII

A BUNCH OF ROSES

Mrs. Newcomb ceased snuffling, suddenly and completely. She was frightened. She had never meant to speak of what she had done when her daughter seemed to be fading away into the grave before her eyes. She had not meant to tell, but being a woman who sooner or later revealed everything, of course she had spoken thus. She was silent now. The baby in its bed stirred and made a gurgling sound, but its mother did not notice it.

Mrs. Newcomb was wondering what she should say. She knew that her daughter was stronger than she; but she would hesitate as long as possible.

"What do you mean by that?" repeated Olive, and her voice was clear in the room.

"You needn't get excited, Olive, as I know of," began Mrs. Newcomb; and she added, artfully, "You'd better remember that it 'll be bad for the baby if you 'low yourself to git excited." The young mother turned her eyes for an instant on the child; but only for an instant. Then she looked at the elder woman. Mrs. Newcomb spoke quickly. "You know you 'ain't named him yet, Olive. I s'pose you'll call him Robert, sha'n't you?"

"I've sometimes thought I should call him Robert," answered Olive, slowly, "but I don't know; I've not made up my mind."

She walked to the open window and stood there a moment. Beneath her a thick honeysuckle-vine clambered up the sides of the house and spread its branches over the lower part of the window. The vine was full of blossoms, and the humming-birds were darting into the sweet recesses of the blooms. The air was poignantly fragrant. Olive bent over and put her finger on one of the blooms, as if she were caressing it.

"Robert's mother planted this vine," she said, aloud, not knowing that she spoke.

"Did she? I want to know!" exclaimed Mrs. Newcomb. "I guess 'twas when she first come. I don't believe she'd feel much like puttin' in honeysuckles after she'd been here a little while with old Nawn; though, to be sure, he wasn't old then. I guess I'll go down and see 'bout startin' a fire for supper."

She rose and was walking to the door. After all, Olive wasn't going really to notice what she had just dropped. How lucky that was! She hurried; but her daughter was beside her the next instant, with her hand on her arm.

"No matter about the supper," she said; "wait, I want to ask you something."

Mrs. Newcomb stood with the door in her hand. She told her sister Ruth afterwards that she "never felt so nervous in all her life as she did then; and there was the curiousest look in Olive's eyes—so she knew there wa'n't any use in trying to keep anything from her."

But Olive was silent for so long a time that her mother again asserted that she must see 'bout startin' the fire for supper.

"No," was the peremptory response. "Mother"—sternly—"did you go to Robert before we were married?" Hesitation on Mrs. Newcomb's part. "Answer me, mother. Did you go to Robert before we were married?"

Mrs. Newcomb hastened to sit down. She gathered her apron in a bunch between her hands.

" I d' know 's you need to look like that," she answered. " If I did, I guess he's glad 'nough of it ; for
'tain't in the least likely that Isabel Keating would
have done near 's well 's you've done here. Olive, I'm
sure you 'ain't nothin' to reproach yourself with, 'n'
that's more'n' most folks can say."

"Mother !" Mrs. Newcomb started ; she grew pale
at the sound of that voice. "Did you go to Robert
and tell him that I was pining for him ?"

"You know, Olive, you was wastin' away 'fore my
face 'n' eyes—'n'—."

" Stop ! Did you go ?"

" Wall—yes—I did go. I thought if he only knew—
'n' Isabel Keating—"

" Will you stop ?" Olive moved a step until she
could lean against the partition. Mrs. Newcomb was
thinking that she would speak again about starting a
fire for supper, and that this time she would escape,
when her daughter broke the silence. Her words were
so clearly spoken that the other woman had what she
called a crazy notion that those words were things
which were presented to her. " When Robert came to
me that day—when he came up to my chamber, where
I lay longing to die—you had been to him ?"

" I thought—you know—"

" Answer me !"

" Yes, I'd been to him."

" He came to me because you had been to him. He
didn't come because he loved me so that he had to
come. You sent him. Oh, my God ! my God !"

Olive's arms were hanging straight down by her
sides. She was looking fixedly across the room. She
made no gesture as she uttered that exclamation.

Mrs. Newcomb jumped up, and hastened to her
child. She attempted to put her arms about her, but
she was repulsed. " Now, don't you take it that way !"
she cried out, " Robert loved you all the time, I tell

ye—he was thankful to come back—'n' he didn't know
you was sick till I told him.   I had to tell him."

Olive faced around.   "I would have died a hundred
times before I would have had you go!" she cried.
"And you let him think I sent you—that I knew—"

"No—no! I told him I wouldn't have you know
for all the world—and I made him promise that he
never 'd tell you."

But Olive did not seem to hear her mother's words.
She made a vague movement, as if to prevent her
companion from touching her, while she said, again, "I
would have died a hundred times first!"

But she did not raise her voice, though there was a
penetrating intensity in it that made her listener
shrink.

"You don't seem to understand," began Mrs. Newcomb, helplessly—"you don't take in what I'm telling
you. He was thankful to come back—he loved you all
the time—can't you understand that, Olive Newcomb?
Oh, dear!   You look jest as set 's your father used to
sometimes.   Olive Newcomb, I say! stop lookin' like
that!"

And now the alarmed mother would press nearer,
and she caught hold of her daughter's arms and pushed
her down into a chair, standing over her as if fearing
she would spring up and escape in some way.

But Olive made no attempt to escape; she seemed to
settle down in the chair as if she could not rise.   She
gazed beyond her mother.   "It was not because he
loved me that he came back," she said.

Mrs. Newcomb ran to the closet; she brought back
a bottle of something; she had an indefinite hope that
it was camphor.   It proved to be brandy.   She dashed
some of it at Olive's face.

Olive sat up and put the bottle aside.   "I don't need
anything like that," she said.   "I need nothing at all.
When I remember how my husband was asked to

marry me to save my life, I think he has been very kind—very kind, indeed. He never would have come back. He would have married Isabel Keating. But he had to marry me. And I've been so foolish and blind as to have had many happy days — yes, many happy days. But they're all over now."

"Olive!"

"I wish you wouldn't talk to me," averting her face.

"But I did it for the best—I did it for the best!"

"I tell you, I wish you wouldn't talk to me. Can't you leave me alone now? I'd like to be alone. Do you understand me? I want you to go away."

Mrs. Newcomb took up the brandy-bottle again. "I'm afraid to leave you," she said, piteously. "I'm afraid you'll do something to yourself. Can't you think of the baby?"

Olive sprang up from her chair; she did not know what she thought of doing, only that just then everything was intolerable. She must run off somewhere if her mother would not leave her.

"Oh, I'll go — I'll go!" exclaimed Mrs. Newcomb; and she hastened away with the bottle in her hand.

Olive returned to the window and looked out again upon the honeysuckle. She wished that the place were not so full of fragrance—it stifled her. She threw back her shoulders that she might inhale more air. She wondered why it was so difficult to breathe. The sense of suffocation was dreadful. Then for a moment her mind became so confused that she asked herself repeatedly what had happened. She gazed about her. Her mother had told her something—what was it? Then the cloud lifted, and she laughed. She was not very strong yet, and she did not think she could endure as well as she could when she had regained her strength. She would soon be strong now. A slight movement on the little bed made her go to the crib and bend over it. The baby lay on a pillow, its small face turned, its eyes fast shut. With a sudden, quick movement, Olive lifted the pillow with its burden still upon it ; but she lifted it gently and did not disturb the child. She carried it to the window and studied its face with intent, burning eyes.

"Are you going to look like your father ?" she asked, with an accent of ill-subdued fury in her voice.

She sat thus for many minutes, gazing down at the sleeping baby. At last she carried her boy back to the bed, and this time she knelt down by it and covered her face. But she was not praying ; she was only suffering. She was in that position when, a half-hour later, some one noiselessly appeared at the door and looked in.

It was Robert. His Apollo-like face was particularly gentle and tender as he gazed. He seemed to hesitate an instant, then he softly stepped within the room and walked towards his wife, who raised her head, then rose, and stood quiet, one hand resting on the frame of the crib. The young man was immediately aware of some indefinite change in his companion ; but the next moment he thought that this impression was only a fancy.

"Is he asleep ?" he asked, coming to Olive's side and looking down at the crib.

"Yes," was the answer.

Robert raised his hand, which had been hanging down, held somewhat behind him. He carried a large bunch of magnificent roses. He extended them towards Olive, who gazed at them and then retreated a step.

"Don't you like them ?" he asked.

She returned to her former position, and distantly inhaled the odor, saying, as she did so, "They are beautiful. I know where they grow." She did not offer to touch them.

"Yes, you'd know that. Isabel was just driving by ; she was bringing these to the boy, she said." Robert laughed with a hint of embarrassment. "She made me promise to take them right to him. She said it was her first offering to the prince. He is our prince; isn't he, Olive?"

"Yes, I suppose so."

The woman stood in the same position, not looking at her husband. The sweet, winning tone had been in his voice as he spoke the last sentence. She was thinking that no man, surely, could be more winning and lovable than Robert when he was in the right mood.

He now held the roses down towards the little face on the pillow, saying, as he did so, "This small fellow doesn't yet know that roses are lovely — and have thorns."

The man's arm was caught sharply back. Olive's eyes were flaming.

"Would you give those—*those* to my boy?" she cried.

Robert wheeled about and away a few paces. Impatience, anger, flared up into his face. He stared an instant, then he exclaimed, "I always did think I couldn't endure a jealous woman!" The ghastly look that came into his wife's face made him add, hastily, "I hope you don't imagine these things were given to me, Olive. Isabel brought them for the baby—just to be polite, I suppose. I didn't know you were so childish."

As if to illustrate his own freedom from childishness, he flung the flowers violently on the floor and put his foot on them; the roses sent up a pungent perfume. Robert's face was not pleasant to see.

CHAPTER XXVIII

Olive made a movement as if she would take the
baby in her arms, but she did not. She walked to the
bed and sat down upon it. She was saying to herself
that she was asked to bear too much. And she was
crying out to God to be good enough to take away her
love for this man. That was the only thing she could
think of just then for which she could ask God. For
she loved him. She sat gazing at Robert and saying
to herself that she loved him. She could not yet help
loving him ; in the exaggeration of her thoughts just
now she believed that, as her heart phrased it, she was
made to love him.

Robert stood looking down at the crushed flowers on
the floor. " I didn't mean to lose my temper," he said,
in sullen apology. " I've got a devil of a temper, you
know."

There was no reply to this. In the uncomfortable
silence which followed, the young man was wondering
how he could get out of the room ; and he was thinking also that this was the first time that Olive had
shown any feeling about Isabel ; he ought to give her
that credit ; and—he raised his eyes—she was lovely to
look upon—her face had been more beautiful than ever
since the baby was born. He had thought her faded
before. He was a great brute, he was telling himself.
A keen, exciting sense of his wife's loveliness and attraction suddenly seemed to overwhelm him. He had
been so used to having her adore him—how would it

be with him if she should change in that respect? And
what had she been thinking of when he had come into
the room just now?

"You've always been very forbearing about my temper, Olive," he said, now, with a touch of humility and
gratitude.

Olive held out her hand. "Come and sit beside me,"
she said, entreatingly.

He obeyed. He seized both her hands and kissed
them repeatedly. The revulsion had come to him,
aided by the attraction of Olive's face, and that something in her personality that had drawn him from the
first. He abandoned himself to this attraction, at the
same time having a certain half-acknowledged conviction that, after all, he must be a good sort of man, and
not a bad husband, since a woman like this woman loved
him.

Olive smiled sorrowfully. "One would almost think
that you were fond of me," she said.

"Fond of you!" he cried out, passionately. He held
her to him and kissed her on the lips, murmuring that
she did not know how he loved her; and again and
again, that he was not worthy of her.

"Why do you always say that?" she asked, drawing
away somewhat.

"Because it is true—true," he answered. "You're a
thousand times too good for me."

"That is foolish," she responded; and then, with
another smile, "you remind me of Deacon Webster—
you know he seems to think that the more often he
can tell God how wicked he is, and how unworthy—
what a vile worm of the earth—"

"Please don't!" interrupted Robert; "you make me
ashamed." He pressed his face down on his wife's
shoulder.

It was a few moments before either spoke. Olive
was so pale that she looked as if she would fall back

onto the bed ; but she sat upright and held her hand
on the close-cropped head that was against her shoulder. It seemed to her that she was learning many
things, and that she was too young to be obliged to
learn them. And God was not yet ready to take away
her love for Robert ; and she could not hurt nor grieve
what she loved. She must learn not to hurt nor grieve
any living thing, because she must, in a way, love all ;
perhaps that was one of the lessons of life—to love.
Oh, the tender and sweet spirit that looked out from
her eyes at this moment ! If Robert had seen this look
would he— But how worse than useless such questions are—and yet we are continually asking them !
If, at such a moment of my life, a particular woman
had smiled upon me, I should be the happiest mortal
in the world to-day. Nay, if that woman had smiled,
you might to-day be the most wretched man on this
globe. Who dare make such assertions?

After a little Robert raised his head. He still kept
his arm about his wife. "We don't care for the roses—
they are crushed," he said. "Tell me you don't care,
my darling."

"I'll tell you that I'm sorry I spoke so about them,"
replied Olive, "and I'm sorry they're ruined—the boy's
first gift."

She did not say that she wished the first gift had
not come from Isabel Keating.

Robert began to be more light-hearted—and he
could at times be very light-hearted if he were not
crossed. Like a great many of us, he seemed to have
two natures—when one was in play he was apparently
an entirely different man from what he was when the
other was to the front. He was dimly aware of this,
and used sometimes to ask, "Who's to blame?" But
that was only when he was particularly reckless, or
particularly tempted. It's a fine refuge, that same
question—"Who's to blame?"

Robert rose and walked to the bed where the baby lay; he drew his wife with him. "What shall you name him?" he asked; "the naming belongs to the mother, you know."

He did not in the least doubt what the answer would be, and he could not wholly conceal a displeased surprise when Olive answered.

"I've always expected to name it Robert, or Roberta, if it should be a poor feminine creature," smiling; "but I've changed my mind."

The father was silent and wondering. Was it that bunch of roses that had changed her decision? But Olive was never petty like that—that would be more like him.

"For a little while, just an hour or so, Rob, I've felt as if I should like to call our boy Victor. Are you willing?"

Olive thrust her hand through her husband's arm and leaned upon it. She was gazing down at the baby.

"Certainly. But I supposed you might give my name; and I was going to propose Archibald, for one name, to please father, you know."

Usually this would have been enough to cause Olive to relinquish her own wish and assent to that of her companion; but now she said, with firmness, "I'll call him just Victor — no other given name. There, he is waking. Rob, do you know, he has my father's eyes?"

When, ten minutes later, Olive was left alone with the child, she sat holding it closely to her, while the tears fell fast down her face. The pressure of the little warm body against her was like a healing touch; but the tears did not stop falling. Still, she sometimes smiled as she sat through the hour. Once the child looked at her in that intent and yet semi-blind way with which infants first gaze into the world.

"Yes," she said, almost joyfully, "they are really my father's eyes, and no man with that kind of eyes can be a miser." Then she fell to thinking how strange it must be to be made so that you loved money above all else in the world. She sat leaning far back in the large rocker, her eyelids drooping, drooping. She held the child up against her with a gentle fervor that went like some sweet wine through her consciousness.

But her thoughts were with her husband. She had not said what she had meant to say to him. She recalled something she had once read : "The inner core of things is silence, and in every conversation the important words are those which are not said." Would she ever be able to speak to him just the right, the important, word ? Surely if she could do so the word would fly like a well-shot arrow and penetrate to his heart. Then her eyelids grew more heavy ; she let her head fall against the back of the chair. She was asleep ; but in her sleep she remembered to hold the baby softly close to her, and in her light dream she was saying to herself, "He is my Victory—God will give me the victory—my own little Victor—mine !" She was conscious of a vivid sense of annoyance that those words that she was repeating should suddenly change to a song that was sung in a loud, untrained voice. She woke from her slumber and heard plainly through the open window a woman singing these lines :

> " Here's to him that grows it,
> Drink, lads, drink !
> That lays it in and mows it,
> Clink, jugs, clink !

> " To him that mows and makes it,
> That scatters it and shakes it,
> That turns and teds and rakes it,
> Clink, jugs, clink !"

Olive stirred uneasily. She did not recognize the
voice, and she leaned nearer the window as she listened. People did not come about Nawn house singing as they came; the sombre aspect of the place was
usually enough to make a singer dumb. The voice
went on, and it was still more audible. It was a tune
with a grand swing to it :

> "And here's to thane and yeoman,
>   Drink, lads, drink !
> To horseman and to bowman,
>   Clink, jugs, clink !
>
> " To lofty and to low man,
>   Who bears a grudge to no man,
> But flinches from no foeman,
>   Drink, lads, drink !"

The singer was coming nearer still. She must be
just on the other side of those fir-trees. And why was
there a ring of triumph in her voice?—or did Olive
imagine that? Olive thought it was a cruel thing
that, just at that moment, the story her mother had
told of going to Robert should come back to her and
strike her—for it seemed to strike her. While she
slept, holding her Victor to her heart, she had forgotten ; but now the keen pain returned. And that
girl outside could sing with exultation ! That was
Robert's voice now speaking near the firs.

CHAPTER XXIX

"I DIDN'T know you could sing," said Robert, animatedly.

"Oh," answered the girl, "I have a thousand accomplishments that you haven't heard of. How is the little Robert now? Did you give him the roses? Did he smile—or did he claw at them? Babies can't do anything but claw for the first six months."

"Can't they? His name isn't Robert."

"Not Robert!" exclamatorily.

Olive, listening to Isabel—for of course it was Isabel—felt that not for all the world would she let this child be called that name. And she could detect the pique in her husband's tone.

"No," he said, "Olive wanted to call him Victor. I sha'n't oppose her."

Isabel laughed. She had laughed in that way, Olive remembered, when she had come to the small house, and they two had danced on the new carpet. Oh, that had been long ago! And since then Olive's mother had made Robert come back to her daughter.

"Perhaps," she heard Isabel say, now, "Olive once had a lover whose name was Victor."

It was Robert who laughed this time, not quite pleasantly. Then he said, shortly, "That's not likely."

"The most likely thing in the world—somebody whom she knew when she lived at the Falls. You didn't know anything about her when she lived there, did you?"

"No."

The laugh that now sounded through the firs jarred so upon Olive that she walked hastily across the room. Then she returned and shut down the window with a crash. As she turned away her foot pressed upon the roses that Robert had flung upon the floor. How like him that had been! She stooped and picked up the poor, bruised things. They were pathetically sweet. They would never revive. Roses could not revive after they had been stepped upon.

Olive had a certain sense of something dramatic about those flowers; but she reproved herself as being imaginative. The next moment she wondered why her mother had not called her to supper; and just then the door opened and Mrs. Newcomb came in with an air of mystery.

"I've been keepin' back supper," she said, "'cause I think Isabel Keating's coming to call on you, 'n' I can't ask her to tea, 'cause, you know, Mr. Nawn don't want folks eatin' up the victuals. She's out there talkin' with Robert, 'n' I heard her say she wanted to see the new Nawn and his mother. There, she is comin' now. Lem me take the baby. I wish you had on your other wrapper."

"I'll keep the baby," responded Olive, decisively; "it's no matter about the wrapper."

She advanced towards the open door and met Isabel as she entered. Perhaps it was because of her burden that she did not extend her hand; but she smiled at her guest, who exclaimed that she had just told Rob that she, for one, wanted to see if a new baby were really such an uninteresting animal as Rob thought it. Olive drew the child yet nearer to her as Isabel approached; then she feared lest the girl had noticed the movement. Isabel bent her head, reaching out a finger and touching the soft cheek.

"Why, it's awake!" she cried out. "It's eyes are open."

"Yes, it can open its eyes," responded the mother.

"You're making fun of me now." Isabel gazed a moment, then she looked up and asked, "Is it really, truly true that you love it?"

"Yes."

"That's odd. I never believed that a woman loves a child until it gets old enough to amount to something—be a plaything, at least. I know there's a lot of nonsense talked on the subject, but if you tell me you love it, and have that kind of a look on your face when you say so, I suppose it must be true." The speaker looked at the door; it was open, but Mrs. Newcomb had gone down-stairs. "I wanted to see you and ask you a question. Why, Olive, I didn't know you could be so pretty—no, not pretty—attractive! If I were a man I'd fall in love with you this minute."

Isabel's large, black eyes were full of a bold light that the other woman felt that she hated. Had this girl come merely to talk in this way? Olive made no reply whatever to these words.

Isabel glanced about the room, taking in its bareness and lonesomeness. "I suppose now you'll be just like other women," she remarked; "you won't be a wife or a woman any more—you'll simply be a mother."

"Is that to be like other women?"

"Yes, you know it is." Isabel came nearer; Olive thought that she was going to touch her, and she involuntarily moved back a step. "Oh," bitterly, "I'm not going to lay my hand on you—you shrink from me! Of course you despise me because I told you that time that I loved Robert. It's no strange thing to love him, is it? You ought not to think so, surely. I wanted to ask you this question again—I asked you once before: are you happy? You have the one thing in all the world that you wanted most, and now are you happy? You must answer me!" This time Isabel did touch her companion; she seized her arm and held it closely. She seemed eager, feverishly eager, and her eyes interrogated even more strongly than her words. "You can't evade," she said, "for I'm watching your face. You won and I lost; you ought to be happy. Are you?"

There seemed something coarse in these last sentences, as if, Olive thought, she and Isabel had been contending for Robert. And then over her, in a bitter wave, came the consciousness that, but for what her mother had done, she might not have been Robert's wife; more than that, this girl who was now inquiring so sharply might have stood in her place.

A sudden sweeping fury of indignation and futile resentment swept along in Olive's soul. For that moment she felt that she couldn't bear it—no, she could not bear it. She walked away from Isabel's side and laid the baby carefully on its bed. The boy cried out a little, then subsided into slight murmuring sounds as its mother stood a moment with her hand on its breast. When the sounds ceased, Olive came back to where Isabel remained standing and watching her. In those few moments Olive had been fighting with herself one of the fiercest battles she had ever fought. As she stood with her hand on the child there came to her, as if it were a whisper from Heaven itself: "Why did you name him Victor? You thought you could conquer?" But that was fanciful. Olive had had plenty of time to become fanciful as she labored alone about the house. When she returned to Isabel her pallid face was luminous.

"Have I been happy?" she repeated in a low voice. "Yes—and unhappy too. That's all I can tell you, Isabel."

"But that is no answer at all. You know what you dreamed of and hoped for—have you got it? Have you got it?"

As Olive looked at her companion now she saw that

there were dark marks under Isabel's eyes, and a tense line at either side of the mouth.

"No," answered Olive, gently. "Do we ever get that?"

Isabel shut her hands, then she opened them and flung them out with a swift movement. "How strange that is! How diabolical that is!" she cried, with rebellion in her voice and attitude. "You passionately long for something—you know you will be miserable without it, and if you get it you're miserable! I tell you, God must hate his creatures. Why did he make us?"

As she ceased speaking, Isabel walked away from Olive; she went hurriedly up and down the room two or three times. At last she paused by the bed where the baby slept. She gazed down at him. As she gazed, tears gathered in her eyes and fell; she did not seem to know that they were falling.

"You think Victor will comfort you," she said, "but don't be too sure of that. Perhaps he'll be your greatest sorrow—perhaps he'll be the one to break your heart." She raised her head and looked at Olive as she continued, "When I heard that you would not name the baby Robert, I said to myself, 'I will ask her if she is happy.' That word Victor is a symbol to you. Oh," with a tremor of the voice, "you won't get the victory, though. Nobody gets it. Now I'm going." She took a few steps towards the door, then she paused. "You know I do pretty much as I please," she said, in a different voice. "I don't have any one to consult. There's that man who wants to marry me—you've heard of him—Mark Plummer. I wish I could decide. One day I say yes—to myself, you know—and the next day I say no. I can't imagine how it 'll turn. I'm watching myself as if I were somebody else, and in the morning I say, 'I wonder how it 'll turn out.' And all the time I'm just sweet enough to him to keep him from dying of despair. We are queer creatures, we women. But, then, you know exactly what you'll do; you'll be a mother—you won't be an individual—you'll simply be Victor's mother. Good-bye; I'm going now."

At the top of the stairs Isabel paused again to say that she had a great mind to stop to supper, because she knew that it would be such a trial to old Mr. Nawn if she did so. "And how much do you suppose he saves in a year by never having company to a meal?"

With a laugh that was immediately followed by a chuckle at the foot of the stairs, Mr. Nawn's voice said, "Is that you, Isabel? Save? Why, I mean to save enough this year to get a silver cup for my grandson when he can say 'gold.' I'm going to teach him to say 'gold.' Come down, Isabel, and let me see your handsome face."

Olive heard the bantering, cynical tones, and she closed the door to shut out the sound, as she had closed the window a short time before. "Teach him to say 'gold!'" she whispered. "No: no!" She flew to the crib and made a little swoop down to the face lying there, holding her own face against it for an instant, half breathless, lest she might waken the child.

Mrs Newcomb stopped two weeks longer, and then went home; and Olive took up the work again. But, to her astonishment, it was drudgery no longer. All the time, as she hurried from one task to another, there was a secret, blissful excitement in her soul. When the butter was made, she would run up to see if " he " slept. If he waked, she would sit with him in her arms. But if he still slept, could she not do more work, all the time knowing that he was there—that, sleeping or waking, he was there, and he was hers?

Sometimes a smiting terror came to her, a terror that paled her face and contracted her heart. What if Victor should not live? But God surely would not be so cruel as to take her boy. God might do other things, but He would not do anything so cruel as that. Then she would feel as Mrs. Browning felt, that " it was a terrible thing to have all her fortune in one coin." But, as the days went on, she began to be more and more sure of her treasure, and the sense of possession was dearer and stronger.

Robert noticed the child sometimes, but mostly he seemed absorbed, absent. He went oftener to the Falls Village, but he never made any remark concerning those visits. Sometimes Olive saw Mr. Nawn contemplating his son with a concentrated gaze, and once he inquired, quickly, " Bob, what are you up to in these days?"

" Nothing; I work every day in the factory, that's all."

The next week Robert asked his father to lend him five hundred dollars.

" No; I sha'n't do any such thing. What are you up to, I say?"

" Nothing," morosely.

The young man was sullenly silent, or when he spoke he was irritable. He complained when he had to spend a penny. He said his wife was extravagant—she might save more. When he said such things, Olive answered him bravely; she looked at him with courage.

" I shall not try to be any more economical," she would say; " there is no need."

At first Robert stared in astonishment. She had been so silent, so meek, so acquiescent. She was different; she was no longer cowardly. She was on the defensive. The most timid animal may be courageous when it has young.

Mr. Nawn watched Olive also, and every now and then he would say to his son, " Bob, you were a thundering fool. Why didn't you marry Isabel?"

As time went on, when Mr. Nawn said this, Robert

"'BOB, WHAT ARE YOU UP TO IN THESE DAYS?'"

would start impatiently, gaze at his father, and look as
if he were about to speak—but he kept silent.

"Olive is getting more extravagant every day," Mr.
Nawn remarked to his son; "she'll be wasteful the
next thing. There's nothing too good for that brat of
hers."

This was when the boy was four years old.

"Can't you speak to her about it?" asked Robert.

Mr. Nawn was sitting in his old place in the porch.
It was June, as it had been when Victor was born. The
old man took his pipe from his mouth. He grinned
maliciously at his son before he replied.

"Speak to her? I've done so. But it doesn't do any
good. She's changed. She looks full at me, is perfectly respectful and perfectly resolved, and she tells
me that she thinks that we must have good, nourishing
food; that we can afford it, that skimmed milk isn't
good enough for Victor. Victor! There isn't much
Nawn in that boy, now, I tell you. He has a monstrous
look like Newcomb—and why shouldn't he resemble his
grandfather, I should like to know? I caught him the
other day giving his banana to that Easton child that
was here. He gave him the whole of it, and went without himself. Where did he get his banana? Oh, from
his mother; she says fruit is good for him. Not much
Nawn blood in him—eh?"

"She'll spoil the boy," harshly, from Robert.

His father whiffed leisurely at his pipe. "No, I
guess she won't spoil him. He has to obey. He seems
a fine chap enough; but there's no Nawn blood in
him, you see. You must have been crazy when you
didn't marry Isabel. It seems she and Plummer didn't
make a match of it, did they?"

"No."

Mr. Nawn sat smoking and gazing at Robert.

"Bob," suddenly and sharply.

"Well?"

The young man seemed to find it difficult to withdraw his thoughts from the road they were travelling.

" Do you visit Isabel Keating?"

Robert frowned; he moved his hands restlessly.
" What cursed gossip has been talking?" he asked,
furiously.

" Esther Rice—and a dozen others. But I reckon
Esther Rice set 'em agoing." The old man smoked
on serenely. " You're an improvement on your old
dad, ain't you?" Robert swore in a whisper. Then
he turned to go away, but his father said, " Stop !"

CHAPTER XXX

THE young man stood with his face averted, his hands pocketed, while he waited for what his father was going to say.

"I found out something yesterday," Mr. Nawn began; "I've been a ninny not to have found it out before. You've been gambling in stocks—in your small way—old Drake, at the Falls, has been doing it for you. Well, you *are* a fool, Bob. Just enough of your mother in you to spoil you. And you've lost—of course, you've lost. By George! you make me wonder at you. Letting old Drake invest your money!"

"Is that all you have to say now, father?"

"About all. You deserve to squirm. I s'pose you've lost a lot."

"Sometimes I gain."

"Sometimes! Just enough to make you bite again, I reckon. With your handsome face and taking ways"—here a pause—"you've made out finely, haven't you? I s'pose you're waiting for me to die. But I'm tough; I'm going to live a long time yet. Naturally, you'll inherit finally. I don't think it's likely I shall ever make a will, and you're the sole heir, you know. It's a great bother to make a will. You're tighter than I am, Bob; but I'll bet you never can pile up as much money. If I were you, I wouldn't make a scandal by visiting Isabel, even if you do find her entertaining. They're a set of dunces in this village, anyway. That Rice woman 'll be coming and telling Olive a pack of stuff. Do you want Olive to know you go there?"

14

Mr. Nawn rose, thrust his pipe in his waistcoat-pocket, stretched his arms above his head, and yawned. But he kept his eyes on his son, and there was a contemptuous expression in them.

"There's no harm in my calling on a neighbor, is there?" Robert's voice rasped on the sweet June air.

"Calling on a neighbor!" repeated Mr. Nawn. Then he burst into a laugh.

As he laughed, a small figure came in sight around the corner of the house—a sturdy figure, wearing a clean and patched gingham frock; its light hair was flying in the wind as it ran, its eyes sparkled. It hurried so that it seemed as if it would pitch forward head-first; but it kept its feet.

This was Victor. When he spoke he spoke plainly, without any of the lisp or impediment usual in childish speech.

"What's so funny? What's so funny, gran'pa?" he cried, eagerly. "I want to laugh, too."

And he flung back his head, opened his red mouth, and laughed lustily, showing some small white teeth in front on the upper jaw as he did so. Then, in his laugh, he lost his balance and rolled over in the grass. He did not try to rise, but lay there, clutching at the broad blades and gurgling in the delight of being alive.

The two men gazed at the child in silence. While they looked the mother came to the open door.

Had Olive grown tall? Or was it that she carried her head higher? There was a light on her face, a loveliness there that made Mr. Nawn sometimes give her a scrutinizing glance and then turn to his son as if he would exclaim, "Dolt! blockhead! are you blind?" But he would not say those words, he would only smile derisively.

At this time in her life Olive Nawn was a magnificent woman, with the shining of an invincible happiness in her eyes.

" Victor," she said.

" Oh, he's all right," responded Mr. Nawn ; " we were just laughing."

Olive glanced at her husband, but he did not return the glance ; he walked away, having drawn a hand from his pocket and snapped a thumb and finger at the boy.

Olive could never quite understand why she always remembered this morning so plainly. There was the picture of Robert in the background, standing tall and handsome ; the old man nearer, with his usual cynical face ; and in the middle-distance the boy lying on the grass, kicking up his heels and laughing to himself. She remembered this picture with the brilliant June sunlight on it, and to - morrow would be the baby's birthday. But nothing happened that day, nor the next, nor the next.

She stepped forward and picked up Victor from the ground. He clutched her tightly about the neck and rubbed his face against hers, making a little noise in his throat, which he presently explained by saying that he was "purring." Olive disappeared within the house. Glancing through the window, she saw Robert going across the field. In the stillness she heard the Creeper flowing by that place in its banks where the stones lay.

A few days later she walked down to the bridge, leading Victor. The two stopped midway in the foot-path. The boy, hanging on his mother's hand, peeped between the uprights, talking to himself, as was his habit. Vaguely Olive heard his chatter about "wild eels and the duck that swam down to the bottom." Then some one else came on to the bridge. It was Olive's mother, and she came straight on to her daughter's side, and said, quickly :

"I've be'n hopin' I should see you, Olive ; I've be'n watchin' for ye. I knew you come to the bridge sometimes, 'n' I never did like to go up to the house."

Olive turned to her mother, and her grip on the boy's

hand tightened as she asked, " Has anything happened ? What makes you look like that ?"

And now Mrs. Newcomb hesitated. " I don't know how I look, I'm sure," she said.

She examined her daughter's face. She was thinking that Olive looked happy ; but she " didn't see how she could."

" What's happened ?" repeated Olive. Then, more quickly, " Has there been an accident at the factory ?" She had the appearance of being ready to fly, with the child in her hand.

" Accident ? No, there 'ain't been one. Wall, I'm goin' to tell you, anyway. I thought that was you goin' on to the bridge, 'n' I told Ruth I'd jest run down. I s'pose you'd be the last one to know it, any- way ; but I was bound to run down, as I told Ruth."

" Know what ?" Olive was growing white about her mouth.

" What the whole neighborhood's been talkin' of for ever so many months. 'Ain't you heard nothin' ? Or are you pretending ?"

" I'm not pretending," coldly. Olive was wishing that her mother was a little different ; and her heart was beat- ing so that she hardly dared to trust herself to speak.

" Wall, it's Robert 'n' that Keating girl ; that's what 'tis."

" Robert's my popper," said Victor, still peeping in- tently down at the water, hoping to see a wild eel.

Neither of the women appeared to notice that he spoke. Indeed, it was only a slight outer sense in the boy that recognized his father's name ; he was really thinking of the river and the strange things he might see in it. He hung on to his mother's hand and strained forward. He could thrust his arm and shoulder between the uprights of the railing.

" When I'm bigger, mammy, I sh'll come here alone," he said ; but no one made any response.

"I thought 'twas high time you knew; everybody else has known this long while. It's a burning shame, that's what it is. He's jest bewitched. He goes there a lot. They walk 'round in that garden of hers; 'n' she takes him to drive in her buggy. She's a shameless critter, 'n' I 'ain't no words for her!"

"Shameless critter!" repeated the childish voice; and then Victor gave another lurch, crying out, "A horn-pout! a horn-pout!"

Olive's fingers were clutched tightly about the small brown hand. She wished to speak, but found her lips curiously stiff. She tried again, and said, in a quiet voice, "You've been listening to Esther Rice, mother."

"Esther Rice! It's all over the neighborhood. Ask anybody. I've seen them myself walkin' 'n' talkin' 'mong the rose-bushes in that garden at dusk—'n' he a-bendin' his head down to her, 'n' she a-lookin' up to him. It's jest sickenin'; and he a married man with a boy four years old."

"I'm the boy; I guess I'm the boy," from Victor. "Oh, mammy, I do think that was a trout!"

"You needn't pretend not to believe it," excitedly went on the elder woman. "You'll find you'll have to believe it; 'n' you might 's well come to it now 's any time."

"You seem to wish it to be true," said Olive, bitterly; and then immediately she was sorry she had spoken thus.

"No, I don't, either; but 's long 's 'tis true, you might 's well believe it. 'Tain't no use shuttin' your eyes 'n' makin' believe something ain't so when 'tis." Mrs. Newcomb was standing with a hand on the rail, her small, excited face reddened, and her eyes flashing at her daughter. "Robert ain't what he should be. He's in love with Isabel Keating, 'n' everybody but you knows it."

Olive insensibly drew herself away from her mother.

"I do not believe it," she said, in a concise, distant voice.

Even as she spoke her heart seemed to turn to lead in her bosom. A flashing, blinding vision of Isabel, sumptuous among the roses of her garden, with Robert by her side, came across the wife's eyes. And Isabel had made no secret of her love for Robert. She had lured him on; she had— But here Olive's thoughts stopped abruptly; they stopped against that wall of fact—the fact that her mother had brought Robert to her; he had not come because he must come, as she had thought. That memory was always lying in her mind ready to insert a venomous tooth. But of late there had been days, nay, weeks, when she could rest in the belief that her child had made that poison in-nocuous. Her child! She had him. She turned now with an ardent movement and drew the boy to her; a hard, dry sob came to her throat; she was gazing down at Victor as she pressed him close.

He caught at her skirts, his eyes held by that strange look in hers. "Oh, mammy! mammy!" he cried; "are you hurt? Has anything hurt you, mammy?"

"Yes, Victor," she answered. She was singularly truthful with the child, only evading his questions when she must, and then frankly telling him that she could not answer him. She stood silent a moment with the boy clinging to her. He began to sob. "Hush! hush! Victor! be mammy's brave boy. When we are hurt we must bear the pain. Come, we'll go home."

Olive was moving away when her mother touched her arm. Mrs. Newcomb knew that she did not under-stand her daughter—that she never had understood her.

"Olive," she said, unsteadily, "I felt 's if you ought to know it. Somebody 'd tell you some time. It's a dretful thing to be tied to them Nawns."

CHAPTER XXXI

A FIT OF ANGER

OLIVE walked along the bridge towards her home, or she thought that she was walking towards her home. She held Victor by the hand, and his small feet trotted to keep pace with hers. She did not know whether her mother remained there ; she forgot her mother. It was true what she had just heard ; she knew that it was true. "His head bending down to Isabel, and she looking up at him." Olive blenched as she recalled those words ; each word was a distinct wound to her ; she had an insane notion that she could see her heart bleeding.

"Mammy, you hurry so, I can't keep up."

The child's voice penetrated to her understanding. She had reached the end of the bridge. She knelt down by the road-side and put her arms about Victor. She held him so close that he panted, but he did not struggle. She kissed him with a solemn passion ; her lips clung to the sweet young mouth with a significance that had never been in her kiss before. When he could do so, the boy drew away a little and looked wistfully at her.

"Victor—Victor !" she exclaimed, but not as if the boy could understand ; "you must be a good man—be a true man—oh, be a true man !"

"Like popper, you mean," he said.

He saw wonderingly the expression that came to her face. She answered, gently :

"I'm sure your father would want you to be a good man."

The boy shook his head slowly. He was conscious of something strange; he did not know in the least what it was, but it must be a strange thing that would make his mother's face like that. "Yes," he said, " I s'pose popper does want me to be good — I guess he does; but I know what he wants more'n that."

Olive did not seem to hear what Victor said. She still knelt there under some willow-trees. The place for the moment seemed as solitary as if it were not near the road; but there was the white, winding highway climbing up the low hills from the Creeper.

"I say, mammy," began the boy, pulling on the hand he held, "don't look like that—you look 's if you'd got frozen, somehow; you can't get frozen in summer, can you?" She made no response. He continued to gaze at her, his eyes growing more and more strained. "Say, mammy, you can't freeze in June, can you? It's June, ain't it?" No answer. "Ain't it? Ain't it June?"

"Yes, Victor."

"I was sure 'twas. I heard gran'pa say there were some of his dividends due in June. What are dividends, mammy? Are they any like huckleberries?"

"No."

Victor hung back as far as he could on the hand to which he was clinging. His open, frank face grew more and more overcast. "I know what papa wants more'n he wants me to be good," he exclaimed, reverting to his thought.

"What?" was the mechanical answer.

"He wants me to keep putting pennies in my bank, and never shaking 'em out. He says he never shook his out. I say, mammy, what's the good of never shaking 'em out? He looked real cross when I shook one out yesterday to give to Lizzie Fuller. He said I was a regular Israel Newcomb. Am I, mammy?—am I a regular Israel Newcomb?"

Olive suddenly bent forward and caught the child

in her arms again. Her face reddened and grew pale. It was on her tongue to cry out, "Oh, I hope you're not a Nawn !" but she checked the words. She had an impulse to shout at the top of her voice—to shout that the Nawns were mean and false—mean and false. But she checked those words also. Victor's father was a Nawn.

The boy's arms were about her neck, but he drew his head back to gaze at her with the wide, all-questioning eyes of childhood. He was persistent, and he repeated his inquiry, "Am I a regular Israel Newcomb, mammy ?"

"I hope you'll be as good as he was," she answered. She rose from her knees.

"What makes you hug me so just now, mammy ? What makes your face like that ? Oh, I'm frightened ! I'm frightened !"

The boy's own face snarled into a knot ; he was about to thrust his fingers into his eyes, but his mother took his hands. By a great effort she succeeded in looking and speaking with an appearance of calmness.

"You're a foolish boy, Victor. You needn't be frightened. You needn't ever be frightened unless you have done wrong."

The child leaned against his mother The puzzled look on his face deepened into a shadow. "I am frightened ; I'm scared lots of times when I've been good," he said. "I guess, mammy, you're mistaken 'bout that."

Victor looked up at her with contracted brows. Olive received her boy's fresh bright glance and held it in hers a moment. Then she drew a deep breath of utter delight in him. Yes, strange as it may seem, at that instant all trouble was swept away as she gazed into Victor's eyes. He loved her ; he had never deceived her ; he was her own—her very own. Every drop of blood in him was hers ; every pulse of that true infant heart was hers. Oh, God had been good to her—God had given her this boy! Thank God! Thank God! She restrained a desire to take him in her arms again. She must not be hysterical. She stood quietly under the willows, hand in hand with Victor. Yes, she could face the world yet.

"Mammy," said the boy, suddenly, "what did gran'-ma mean? What's Isabel Keating done to you?"

"We won't talk about that; you can't understand."

"Well"—Victor stood up as high as he could; his tanned cheeks reddened—"you just wait till I'm a man, that's all. You just wait. I'll get a gun—that's what I'll do—and I'll shoot everybody that you don't like, mammy. Won't that be splendid? And we'll live together; and I'll shingle the roof so 't the shingles won't fly round so when the wind blows, and then the attic won't leak."

"You may shingle the roof," responded Olive, smiling and stroking the red cheeks, "but you won't shoot any one. Come, now, we'll go home."

Then she found that, in her confusion, she had crossed to the farther side of the river. So the two walked back over the bridge, and Olive could not help pausing in the middle of it to look down into the placid water; and as she gazed she remembered the large fat face that had come like a spectre and gazed up at her from below. She half expected to see it now; but no, perhaps the presence of her son had driven the shape away; perhaps, indeed, she had never seen it, but only thought that she had. She heard Victor's prattle about horn-pouts and turtles, heard it as some indefinite, pleasant sound. She wondered again why this bridge and this slow-moving stream had always been so dear to her—they were part of herself; she could never have been Olive Newcomb unless she had lived by the Creeper and played half her childish days on the Red Bridge.

Presently mother and son went on home. Nawn

place was precisely as it had been, only more shingles had blown off, the crop of knot-grass and pudding-bags was more rank than ever in the front yard ; and there on the north stoop sat Mr. Nawn, smoking, just as if he had not changed his place nor stopped whiffing once during the years since Victor was born. And he appeared not to be a week older. He took no notice as the woman and the boy drew near. He often proclaimed the fact that he had no particular interest in brats. Why should he like a human being just because it was young? There was a great deal of tommy-rot talked about children. He supposed women liked children ; they made an awful fuss over a baby, anyway. As for Victor, well, the boy's mother worked enough for his board and hers, so far.

That night, as the family sat at the supper-table, they were as silent as usual. If old Mr. Nawn had not changed in the five years, the same could not be said of Robert. He looked to be thirty as he sat there silently eating his supper. The perpendicular line between his brows had deepened, his lips seemed to have grown thinner ; and what was the expression that sat permanently on his face? His wife often furtively studied her husband's countenance—studied it with a deathly sinking of the heart. She was a foolish woman, for she still loved this man, who now never gave her a loving glance ; who, after he had broken out into furious anger, never had moments of passionate repentance when he was tender and loving as few men could be—that time was over. Silent, absorbed, Robert came and went. The lover who had made love so winningly, Olive never saw now ; but she could not forget that lover. Surely no man had ever known so well how to woo a woman. It had never come to Olive's mind that her husband could be fickle. But she had Victor. Her eyes turned to the child, who was eating bread and milk with hungry diligence.

As he met his mother's eyes, something seemed to recur to Victor's mind. He dropped his spoon back in his bowl as he exclaimed, " Oh, popper, what did gran'-ma mean 'bout you 'n' Isabel Keating? Mammy said I couldn't understand, but I guess you c'n make me understand—can't you, popper?" The childish treble rang through the room as the boy spoke.

Old Mr. Nawn leaned back in his chair, his shoulders shook with his laugh. " Ha, ha, Bob," he cried, " score one for the boy—score one for Victor !"

But Robert did not laugh. He made no immediate reply. He reached forward and took a piece of bread from the plate. Olive tried not to look at him ; notwithstanding her effort, her eyes would go to her husband's face. They found it flushed, the line on the forehead deeper than ever. She would not reprove Victor ; to do so would be to be making too much of his words. She could only hope that the child would drop the subject ; but she expected him to persist, and he did so.

" What did gran'ma mean ?" repeated Victor, gazing at his father. " It plagued mammy ; mammy grew white. Gran'ma said the whole neighborhood knew it ; mammy said it wasn't true—she said it couldn't be true. Say, popper, what is it that can't be true ?"

" Hush !" whispered Olive. She reached forward to put her hand on the boy's shoulder ; she felt that she could bear it no longer.

At the same instant Robert turned with a ferocious exclamation. " Hold your tongue, Victor !" he shouted. " Who cares what your grandmother means ? She's a silly old woman."

The boy shrank in his little chair, but he kept his eyes on his father's face ; and his eyes had a childish courage in them. " Mammy cared," he persisted.

" She needn't, then ! If you speak again till supper's over I'll flog you within an inch of your life."

" Robert !" from Olive.

The young man turned with a movement that showed how uncontrollable his anger was getting to be. "Don't you meddle !" in the same loud voice. "You teach that boy to be disrespectful to his father ! You—"

Olive rose quickly. "Stop !" she cried out ; "that is not true, and you must not say it !"

This was the first time she had ever replied when her husband lost his temper in this ungoverned way. The boy sat white and still in his chair. The scene was disgraceful, and Olive felt this keenly She trembled always when Robert made an exhibition of temper before his son.

Robert's hot eyes glared up at his wife. He slapped his hand down on the table in front of him. "I don't care whether it's true or not," he shouted ; "I'm not going to stand this kind of thing ! No, I won't stand it !"

Olive made no reply. Her face was of an ashen gray, her eyes on fire. She pushed her chair still farther from her ; she drew Victor from the table. "Run out-of-doors," she said, gently. The boy hesitated ; he glanced at his father, then up at the woman close to him. "Run out-of-doors," she repeated.

Victor threw himself on her skirts. He clutched the folds with one hand ; he looked at his father again. Then his high voice sounded shrilly, "When I'm bigger you sha'n't treat mammy so—you sha'n't !" Then he thrust his face into the skirt-folds and began to cry violently.

Olive did not speak. She led the boy from the room. Once outside the door, she paused and gazed down at him ; she saw the top of his fair head ; he was still crying. There were love and sorrow on her face. She seemed about to embrace the child, but she restrained that impulse. "I must go back," she said, quickly.

"Don't cry—don't cry." She didn't even put a hand
on his head, as she longed to do.

She returned to the room where the two men sat.
Mr. Nawn had the appearance of a person interested
in an entertainment. Robert was still plying his knife
and fork, though he tasted nothing, and seemed not to
know what he was doing. There was a sense of something out of the common in the air. It was not an unusual thing for the young man's temper to burst forth,
but the two men were aware that this was not an ordinary occasion—and the something different was Olive.
She advanced and took hold of the back of a chair.
She was still ashen in color.

CHAPTER XXXII

A FINE FELLOW

OLIVE did not speak directly. She was looking at her husband, who did not raise his head. "Robert," she said, at last, "I shall have to ask you not to behave in this way before Victor."

This was so very different from what had been expected of this woman that the old man stirred a little; then he smiled.

Robert laid down his knife and fork and looked up. His face showed haggard as well as furious. "What is that you're saying to me?" he asked, as if he were speaking to a slave.

The sense of degradation that Olive always felt when Robert did not control his temper was now greater than ever. It was low—it was horrible—that a man should speak and look like that. And always at such times there was present with the wife a keen, heartbreaking memory of that man whom she loved—the man who was passionately tender; whose love seemed limitless, and who was so penitent if he grieved her. Where was that man? Always she was hoping, hoping and longing—thinking that he must come back to her —he must. Would not her love bring him? But her boy must not be hurt. She stood up bravely and met Robert's fiery scorn. Why should he scorn her.

"Yes," she said, "I must speak to you like this." Her voice trembled, but she went on. "It's bad for Victor to see you in such a temper. You must control

yourself before him. I can bear it, but he mustn't see
you in that way."

"Mustn't?" Robert seemed to choke as he asked
this.

"He must not," firmly. "You know that it's wrong."

Olive now put both hands on the chair-back. Her
very lips had grown white. Robert all at once became cold and still. She was used to these transitions;
she did not know which phase of her husband's temper
she dreaded more.

"I suppose," he remarked, sneeringly, "that you're
paying me off now for that infernal talk about Isabel
and me. I don't see as I'm responsible for what a pack
of gossips say."

"We will not talk about Isabel Keating," was the
quiet rejoinder. "I ask you to avoid letting Victor
see you in such a—such a fury. It's a bad example.
Oh, Robert"—her voice trembling again—"we want
our boy to be better than we are, don't we? I'm continually trying to live so that it will be good for him
to be with me. Don't you feel as I do about him?"

It seemed as if she would break down; but she did
not. Old Mr. Nawn sat back and looked at her steadily, save that two or three times he glanced at his son.

Robert rose from the table. He moved deliberately,
and he was careful to push his chair under the table
before he spoke. "I've had about enough of this," he
said, coldly; "I guess I've had quite enough. We don't
seem to get on very well together, Olive; do you think
we do?"

Olive's lips formed the word "no." She could not
imagine what was coming. She longed to beg Robert
to be kind to her; to entreat him to give them both
a chance to be happy, or at least comfortable, together
But she could only say, faintly, "no," and wait.

"Perhaps it's all my fault," continued the young man.
"I don't much care whose fault it is. I thought you

were going to be more saving; I thought you were
going to help me lay up money. But since that boy
has come you've been wasteful of food—"

"Wasteful!" she broke in. "Robert, you are wrong.
Nothing is wasted. I look out for everything. But I
mean that Victor shall be properly nourished; he is
growing. But I patch and patch his clothes; it doesn't
matter about his clothes."

She paused abruptly. She felt powerless. And the
meanness, the sordid lack of real life in this way of
passing her days—oh, the despicable smallness of it
all! Was this really Robert? Was this the real Robert. And that man whom she had loved with all her
heart and soul, her ideal, where was he?

The young man standing there curled his fine lips in
a sneer. "I guess we'd better not try it much longer,"
he said; "we don't hitch, anyway."

"Not try it?" she asked. "I don't know what you
mean," helplessly, an undefined terror coming to her.

"Oh yes, you know well enough what I mean. It's
been a dreadful mistake, anyway. I think we'd better
separate."

"Separate?"

Olive's eyes seemed to be glazing over, but they kept
upon her husband's face. Wretched as their life was,
the wife had never thought of separation. She knew
that there were married people in the world who
procured divorces; just as she knew that there were
earthquakes and dreadful pestilences. But for her and
Robert— And he was standing there and proposing
such a thing! Why, she hadn't been able to stop loving him. In a fleeting six years, how could she stop
loving him? That was not time enough in which to
make herself over and take Robert out of her heart.
She had not yet ceased to hope that his love would
come back to her. It was too monstrous that it should
no. Since God ruled the world Robert would surely

turn to her again some time—some time.   Was she not
praying with almost every breath?   In the simplicity
of her soul Olive was hoping, hoping always.   And she
had Victor.   She wished that she did not feel so weak.
She looked from her husband to the old man at the
end of the table ; he met her glance with an inscruta-
ble one.   She could not know that he was saying to
himself, " Now we'll see what stuff she's made of."

Robert had hesitated after he had pronounced that
word.   He kept his eyes averted ; he gazed down at
his plate on the table ; his mind, like a thing apart,
took in the scroll of oak leaves and acorns which surrounded the plate ; he could remember those leaves
and acorns ever since he could remember anything ;
for this was the crockery which had helped furnish
forth the Archibald Nawn household.   At length he
raised his eyes ; his wife saw how they had softened.
Perhaps she would have a glimpse of the man she had
loved.   A sudden beat of her heart rose to her throat,
making her face suffuse with blood.

" We might as well come to an understanding now,
Olive, and be done with it."

" Yes," in a whisper ; " what is it?"

" I've been to a lawyer at the Falls, and he says that
where the parties are agreed, it's an easy matter to get
a divorce."

Olive did not speak.   Presently she walked around
the table towards her husband.   She tottered as she
walked, still she kept on.   Robert did not see her, for
he had dropped his eyes again, but he heard her coming ; then he felt her hand on his arm ; the tremor in
her fingers was evident to him.   He tried to stand like
a man of wood.

" Did you mean for us to be divorced, Robert?—for
us?"   Her voice was just audible, but it pierced.

" That's what I meant ; we don't seem to hit it off,
someway."   A pause, and silence.   Robert spoke again ;

his mouth was very dry, but he managed to enunciate. Olive's hand was still on his arm; it was as if a bird had alighted there. "I suppose you won't oppose a divorce, Olive," he said; "if you do, it 'll be no use to try for one."

Another pause; then the wife answered, "No, I sha'n't oppose it." She came a little nearer to him. He felt that she was looking up in his face. He hoped that he would not feel any revival of tenderness; he distrusted his tenderness for her. And he wished that she would go away now. Was she going to plead with him? That would be very hard to bear. Then before him came the vision of a dark face looking love at him. Isabel knew how to love; Isabel adored him.

"Well?" he said, huskily.

"No; I sha'n't oppose you," repeated Olive. She was seeing before her that young man who had come wooing her — who had hurriedly persuaded her to marry him that afternoon six years ago. But her mother had told him that the girl with whom he had quarrelled was dying for him—Olive shuddered uncontrollably. She must be careful or she would entirely lose her self-control. "Robert—I won't oppose you—but—Robert, I love you." The voice was faint, but yet distinct.

Olive came nearer. It appeared impossible for her to do otherwise than as she did do. She extended her arms and put them about her husband's neck.

Robert suddenly sat down in a chair that stood close to them. Yes, certainly, he was a brute, a devil; but how could he help being himself? He felt his head drawn to his wife's bosom and pressed there, her heart beat against his cheek. They had entirely forgotten that they were not alone, and they hardly noticed when Mr. Nawn noisily and hurriedly moved his chair, and then heavily walked from the room, closing the door hard behind him.

"Oh no," whispered Olive, piteously, "I will never try to make you keep me when you don't want me. I don't think I can have any spirit, or I shouldn't come near you now. Perhaps if I'd had more spirit you wouldn't have grown tired of me so soon; would you?"

Robert made an inarticulate sound. He had put his arm about his wife and was holding her as she stood there. He was moved; a kind of pitying tenderness was in his soul; but at the same time he was never more conscious of his riotous passion for that other woman. He made an attempt to speak, but Olive hushed him.

"You needn't answer me if I do question you," she said. "Of course you want to get rid of me. You were made to marry me—"

"Olive!" remonstrantly. A spark of manliness began to glow within him.

"Yes," she went on, still keeping Robert's head pressed to her; "I may as well tell you now that I know you lied to me that day we were married. I asked if mother had been to you, and you said, no. How happy I was! You don't care to know that you are the only man in the world who could make me happy. I don't think many people are happy for more than a few months in the whole of a long life—do you, Rob? And I've had my few months. Let me talk, dear. It's just a mercy that I can talk; but it's odd that I can. Mother told me, that summer Victor was born; she told me that she went to you. It was that day when you brought in the roses that Isabel had sent to the baby. You remember?"

" Yes."

As he sat there with his wife's arms about him, and her soft voice speaking to him, a vision of a love and life transcending any mere passion passed before the man. But, nevertheless, passion held him.

"Mother did wrong," said Olive, "and we suffer for it. If she hadn't meddled, I might have died; but then"—with a start—"then I couldn't have had my child. Isn't it strange that I can talk? Robert, you loved me for a little while, didn't you?"

"Oh yes," brokenly. "God knows it! I'm a wretch! I'm torn by emotions I can't control."

Tears came into the young man's eyes. All the best there was in him responded to the touch of his wife's hand. It is a mistake to suppose that such a man as Robert Nawn is not capable of tender and fine emotions; but tender and fine emotions sometimes go for little.

"Poor Rob!" murmured Olive. "I know it. I've known it for a long time. I'm sorry for you."

The pity in her aspect and in her voice made the tears gather faster in Robert's eyes and drop over his face. In the depths of his consciousness was a hazy conviction that he couldn't be such a bad fellow; real villains did not feel like this.

"If you'll only let me tell you, perhaps you'll understand," was the response, when Robert could speak clearly.

"You don't tell me things," she answered.

She passed her hand over his hair; it was a familiar caress of hers, long since disused.

"No, I know I don't. I can't seem to. I have to be just as I'm made, don't I, Olive? A man has to be just as he's made."

There was no reply to this. A red spot burned on each of Olive's cheeks; her eyes were sweet. Was there a sweetness of renunciation in them?

In the silence that followed Robert was searching for words for what he wished to say, but Olive could hardly be said to be thinking.

CHAPTER XXXIII

THE TWO

AT last the young man raised his head. He drew back so that he could look at his wife. She had never been more lovely, she had never had more charm, and Robert knew this; he knew it at the same time that he asked himself, wonderingly, why she did not move him now in that wild way that he remembered and craved. To him, as perhaps to most men, love meant the delightful delirium of passion, the excitement of novelty, pursuit, and uncertainty. Love did not mean any depth of devotion and constancy and tenderness and sacrifice. And yet his mind perceived in a dim way that a great and noble love, while it never lacks passion, is not founded on passion.

Just now Robert was elevated and ennobled emotionally. He even had visions of the possibility of sacrifice; again he felt as if he were really not a bad fellow, after all. How could he be, when a woman like Olive loved him? And he was conscious of an expansion of the heart that was unusual with him. For the moment the image of Isabel grew dim. He was sure it would fade more and more. He had been blind, indeed—why, his wife was a glorious woman—and what an exquisite way she had of revealing her tenderness. The man's eyes shone as they dwelt upon the face near him. He would be thankful if he had shaken off the shackles of that unlawful passion. His mood rose higher and higher.

"You can never forgive me—never!" he exclaimed.

Olive was pale, but she smiled. She knew her husband better than he knew himself.

He gazed wistfully at her. "I don't know what it is in me that can lead me away from you." He gently kissed her hand; then he put his head down on her bosom again as he resumed, "A man with such a wife as you must be mad to think of any one else. Yes, that's just it; I am mad." Now lifting his head and hurrying in his speech, "You don't know—a woman can't know, maybe—how I long to see Isabel—how the longing springs at me and tears me, rends me, conquers me! I have to go to her house just to look in her eyes for a moment. I tell you"—more quickly still—"I have to go. You don't know anything about it—you're calmer. But I don't see her much. The neighbors are liars," raising his voice and flinging out his hand; "they want to make me out worse than I am. They always make a great story. I hate them all. And then to come to you with the tales—"

Robert made another gesture, and smothered the oath that came to be uttered. He endeavored to control himself somewhat, but neither as man nor boy had he ever known how to do that.

Olive sat very still in her chair. As her husband turned towards her again, as if for help, she smiled. She had hardly heard his last words. She was thinking of what he had said of his longing to see Isabel. It was true, then—it was true. And Isabel loved him. Isabel could not make up her mind to marry because she loved him. And Robert had been brought back to her by her mother. The horror of it all! But Robert had loved her then; there could be no mistake about that, Olive thought. And then in bitterness her spirit cried out that question which many a woman has asked, "Why was I allowed to love this man?" To love a man as weak as this, as lacking in moral fibre— but Olive checked herself. There was a terror to her in this perception of what her husband was. She could almost have prayed to be kept blind to his character. Her memory hastened back to the time when she had been blind ; when she had believed the man she loved to be noble and high-minded. But he was not—no, he was not. What greater curse could befall a woman than to love where she could not respect? And at this moment the fact that she did not respect Robert flashed luridly and unmistakably over her mind. And he had never been worthy of respect. From this time she could never be deceived again. But a strong pity and tenderness remained ; and the sting of a helpless jealousy thrust itself deep into her soul.

"Why don't you say something to me, Olive?" asked Robert, after a silence.

She roused herself. She felt sick and weak. "What shall I say?" she responded.

"How can I tell? You see I'm not one to be frank— I can't be—but I've told you how I feel about Isabel— how I long—"

"Please don't !"

Olive had not meant to speak, but the cry came from her in spite of herself.

Robert frowned, but his brows smoothed again immediately. In his absorption in himself he could not notice acutely how another felt, but he could not help knowing that such words could hardly be pleasant to a wife. "You can never forgive me," he repeated. "But it seems now as though, if you could try to forgive, perhaps I might be a better man ; I might be able to forget Isabel. I—"

Olive shook her head. She extended her hands and took Robert's face between them, holding it gently but firmly. Her mournful eyes studied that face intently. A prescience that it was for the last time, the very last time, was upon her. Only God in heaven knew how dear this man had been to her. But she knew him

—at last she knew him. She let her hands drop heavily.

"Don't you believe I can succeed?" he asked, quickly.

"I'm sure you can't."

"You mustn't say that; I won't have you say that," impetuously. He gazed at Olive admiringly. As she seemed to be withdrawn from him, his admiration re-awakened. "Only be a little kind to me. I've confessed everything; now, if you'll help me—"

"Oh, Robert, when wasn't I kind? When didn't I want to help you?"

Olive pressed one hand over her eyes. She was becoming worn out with this scene and with the realization of what her husband actually was. It had come suddenly, for we rarely are cognizant of the steps that lead to such a realization. Olive had gone on in the habit of thinking of Robert much as she had first thought of him. She removed her hand from her eyes. The man watching her thought he had never seen this look upon her face.

"Robert," she said, speaking slowly, as if she were weighing her words painfully, "I think you'd best begin about the matter of divorce."

Having spoken thus, Olive turned away and laid her head down upon the table. She struggled to keep her eyes open — a weight and blackness were upon them.

"Olive!"—loudly—"you are cruel now!" Olive tried to lift her head, but she could not; it also was weighed down as if with that weight, and she could not speak. He was calling her cruel. "I asked you to help me, and you answer me like that," burst out Robert. He began to walk about the room, stumbling against a chair and uttering an oath. "I might get over that infatuation if you'd only help me. If—"

"Robert," without raising her head, "you know I'd give my life for you, but I'm powerless now."

Before any reply could be made, the door opened a little way, and a voice called out, "Mammy! Mammy!"

Olive raised her head now. An ineffable light broke across the wretchedness on her face. "Yes, Victor," she said, hoping to make her voice as usual. "Run away now."

"Are you all right, mammy? Somehow I got kind of frightened."

"You needn't be frightened. Run away now."

"All right."

The door was slammed shut, and little feet could be heard running across the bare floor. Olive rose. The ineffable light was still on her face. That poor thing which served Robert Nawn as a soul was moved within him as he gazed at his wife. And something, he could not guess what, told him that he had lost her.

"I've been thinking," she said, with decision in her voice and manner, "that you'd best begin about the divorce directly. I shall not oppose it. So, as you say, there'll be no difficulty. Begin immediately."

Robert stood looking at his wife. For days he had been dreading to broach this subject. He had expected tears and entreaties, and he shrank from the thought of them. But now, with the contrariness of the human heart, he was disappointed. And perhaps, after all, Olive had never loved him so deeply as he had believed. This supposition galled him. She was a cold creature, anyway. He himself was full of fire—impetuous passion. But Olive—why, he could not understand it! He could not take his eyes from her. A few years ago she had been dying for him. Now, here she stood, tall, and with head up, telling him to begin about the divorce immediately. He had asked her to help him. Hitherto, if he had ever thought of the matter, he had been as sure of her aid as a religious devotee is sure of God's help. And curiously, at this moment, his wish for a divorce retreated into the background of his thoughts.

"I didn't expect you'd be so willing," he said, suddenly.

She turned upon him a flashing glance. "Willing!" she cried out. "Did you expect me to beg you to let me stay with you?" Then in a milder tone, "Do you think that we need to talk any longer now? I am tired."

She turned as if to go from the room. Outside, under the open window, could be heard a child's voice singing:

> "Let 'em alone,
> And they'll come home,
> Wagging their tails behind 'em."

This was repeated again and again, as a bird sings its little song.

The sound irritated Robert. He walked to the window and called out, "Can't you stop singing, Victor?"

Silence after that, save for the muffled noise of feet running in tall grass. Olive had winced when her husband had spoken thus to the boy, but she had kept silent.

"Do you think we need to talk any more now?" she repeated. She wished to say that she couldn't bear it, but she held back those words also.

Robert did not reply. He was moving restlessly about the room. At last the thought in his mind found utterance. "How odd that I should have been so mistaken! I thought you loved me."

Olive gazed at him without attempting any reply. If her disillusionment had been long delayed it was likely to be thorough and to seem sudden.

"Yes," Robert said, "I thought you loved me. But women don't know much about love, anyway," bitterly.

Olive walked to the door. She rested her hand on the latch. She opened her lips to speak, but, before

she had spoken, from down towards the Creeper came
the sound of singing :

> " Let 'em alone,
>   And they'll come home,
>   Wagging their tails behind 'em."

She listened; then she said, coldly, "You were not
mistaken, Robert. I loved you with all my heart.
Now," hurriedly, "I can't bear this any longer."

She opened the door, passed through, and closed it
softly behind her. Once without the room, she leaned
against the wall with her hands pressed hard upon her
bosom. She heard her husband stirring within the
room she had just left. She was afraid that he would
come to the door and open it ; she could not bear to
see him again now. She wished to run away from the
place, but her limbs were heavy, and she thought that
she could not move them. She felt as if she were losing control of her body.

Again, from farther off towards the Creeper, on a
waft of sweet, warm wind, she heard a child's voice,
piping high :

> " And they'll come home,
>   Wagging their tails behind 'em."

She moved. She fled from the house down the
slope. She saw the river shining between the drooping branches of the willow-trees—saw it, as one might
say, blindly, not with her outward eyes. She was so
thankful that she could stir. As she went on her mind
was absorbed in that one emotion of gratitude that she
could walk.

The willow-trees were swaying gently, catching the
sunlight on their narrow, polished leaves. Where was
her boy? She paused in her flight, for she seemed to
herself to be fleeing. She caught hold of a birch-tree
by which to steady herself.

"Victor!" she called; "Victor!" She listened. It was a long time that she listened. She was within a few yards of the river, and its sparkle just now offended her eyes. She was listening for a voice, and she did not notice another sound—that made by something rushing through the alder bushes at her left. A small body precipitated itself upon her, and a laugh rang on the still air.

Victor caught her hand and swung back upon it, as was his way. There was black mud on his shoes, his knees, and his chin; his hands streaked Olive's gown. "I heard you," he was explaining, "but I couldn't answer. It plagued me horrid to have you call then. I was building a dam. Oh, mammy, come and see my dam! A frog had just jumped on it when you called. What d'you call for, anyway?—and how cross popper was! Come and see my dam!"

He pulled her along, and she let him. But when he had led her to the bank of the river, where he had been digging in the mud, she suddenly broke down and began to sob fiercely, her frame rent by her heaving breath.

The child's whole aspect changed in a flash. He stood an instant gazing at her, his dirty face drawn in his intentness. Then he clutched at her skirts and tried to pull her down. "Mammy! mammy!" his voice loud and shrill. "Stoop down! stoop down, I tell you! I can't reach! Oh, I can't reach!"

Olive knelt down beneath the compelling voice and hands. She felt his vigorous young arms clasped about her neck, and his hurried, frightened kisses on her face. But for a moment all was black confusion in her mind. It was like being in a dream. But Victor was kissing her. This was surely Victor who was rubbing his muddy face against hers, and who was beginning to cry in his alarm. She had been selfish to let him know that she was suffering. He could not understand, and he had a tender heart. She wished to stop crying, but the strain had been great, and the reaction must be great also. Robert had told her that he desired to be rid of her. Her marriage had been one of those deadly mistakes that some women are allowed to make. She held the boy tightly.

"You ain't dying, are you, mammy?" he cried, wrenching himself away, and poised to run for help.

She pulled him back to her. She tried piteously to smile, that she might comfort him. "No," she answered, finally. "You needn't be frightened any more; I was bad to act so." She kissed him. She was getting herself in hand, but she was still panting.

"No, you wa'n't bad; I guess you ain't ever bad." Victor contemplated his mother with serious intentness. After a moment his blackened fists doubled themselves up. He scowled. "Was it popper?" he asked. "Did popper do something?"

"Hush! Oh, hush!"

The boy stood silent a moment. He was pushing his shoe into the soft earth and watching it. Then he looked up. His face was solemn. "I guess," he said, slowly—"I guess that I don't care much for my popper, anyway."

"Victor, you mustn't talk so!"

"Why not?"

"Because—"

The boy's gaze upon Olive confused her. She felt herself grow red; something red seemed even to come over her eyes. Victor's glance grew bolder.

"I don't think I care for my popper, anyway," he repeated; "and you can't make me, mammy. And Tommy Jones don't care for his popper, either. He told me so day before yesterday. We talked about it. He said his father struck his mother, and she hollered; and he struck her again because she did holler. Tommy said when he got grown up he was going to wallop his father for that, and I said I'd help him. I guess we'll wallop my popper at the same time. Sha'n't we, mammy?" Olive's features yielded, and she broke into an hysterical laugh. Victor danced, shouting, "That's right, mammy; I'm glad you're laughing. You feel better, don't you? Now come and see my dam."

He took her hand again, and she let him lead her down the Creeper's banks, and she listened to his chatter. But she was thinking, thinking, and she seemed to herself to be walking in a kind of red glow that she could not escape, and that penetrated to her brain.

CHAPTER XXXIV

WITH ISABEL

WITHIN the house Robert Nawn stood at the open window and watched his wife as she hastened towards the Creeper. His eyes glowed; his mouth made but a line of white across his face. He was indefinitely conscious of a sense of being wronged. And how splendidly his wife had looked when she stood up there!—and how curious it was to think that he had but to reach out his hand and take his freedom!

His chains had galled and fretted him; now he had but to say the word and they would drop from him. Olive would help him. Olive! Why, he could not take that in! He had been prepared to storm and command. Yes, Olive had been really magnificent. When she was drudging at her work he had not noticed her. And why didn't he long for his freedom as he had longed last night—nay, an hour ago? In an instant Olive seemed to change from a woman who loved him tenderly to a sort of queen whom he had no right to approach. It was all very strange, and he was filled with resentment.

A movement overhead made the young man start and scowl yet more deeply. His father came down the stairs and lumbered into the room. Mr. Nawn had not changed in his face perceptibly, but he walked more stiffly, and he used more frequently to curse the necessity of growing old. "What's the use?" he would say. "As soon as a man really learns the easiest way to hoard up money he has to die and leave it all.

And who knows what kind of legal tender they have over the other side?"—with that cynical intonation which even now made Olive recoil.

Mr. Nawn sat down in his own especial chair. As he did so his son walked towards the door. "Here, Bob, where are you going? Come back. You needn't run away now. You and Olive have been talking. I saw 'twas coming when I went up-stairs. Sit down. I hate to see you jumping about like that."

Robert sat down at one end of the table and rested his arms on it. He looked gloomily direct in his father's face, but he did not speak.

"I s'pose you've had it out, eh—you and Olive?"

"Yes, we've had it out."

"And she knows you want a divorce?"

"Yes."

Robert tapped the table nervously. He was angry that he did not feel triumphant, and he couldn't account for this lack of exultation.

"Don't be glum," said Mr. Nawn; "speak out. "I can't pump you for every word." But the young man did not speak out. He sat staring down at his hands that kept up their drumming. Old Mr. Nawn grinned as he gazed at Robert, showing his smoke-stained, strong old teeth as he did so. "Where's Olive?" he asked, suddenly, making a movement as if he would rise, then falling back in his chair with a grunt.

"I don't know—she went out. I tell you, father, it's a cursed, twisted-up affair. I wish I'd never got into it."

Mr. Nawn sneered, but he made no articulate sound for a moment. Then he said, "I reckon she didn't go down on her knees and beg you to keep her?"

"No. I used to think she cared for me."

Mr. Nawn smacked his hand down on the arm of his chair. "Oh, the devil!" he cried out. "What a son I've got! He's as weak as his mother and as wicked as his father."

16

Then the man laughed, and laughed still louder as his son looked frowningly at him. When his hilarity had subsided, Mr. Nawn asked soberly for a few particulars. He sat far back in his chair and refrained from looking at his companion. But he listened carefully.

Robert made his recital in these words: "There's nothing to tell. I said to Olive that we didn't seem to hit it off, and I had thought of getting a divorce."

"And she?"

"She seemed a little startled at first, but she gave her consent."

"Is that all?"

Robert was again staring at his drumming fingers. "It's all that's worth telling," he answered. "I've made a horrible muddle of my life so far, and if I am like my mother"—now morosely raising his eyes—"I don't see as I can help it."

He rose and violently pushed his chair back. He went to the door, and his father did not call him. When he was out-of-doors the young man hesitated. He looked down towards the Creeper. The day was so quiet that the sound of the river was more than usually audible. He could hear the voices of his wife and child; Victor's tones were pitched excitedly high. "I wonder what they're talking about," he muttered. Then with more emphasis, "That child doesn't care a rap for me—not a rap." He did not add that he did not care much for the child. He stood with his hands in his pockets gazing about him. "I wish I could get rid of the whole thing," he exclaimed, aloud. He kicked at a shingle that lay on the ground. He looked up at the roof where the shingles were growing looser and looser with every year. "I wonder if the old man will ever die," he whispered. Then a flush rose and subsided on his face, leaving it ghastly. He glanced up at the windows of his father's room. They were

open. "I'm positive he has gold there," he was thinking, "but the evil one himself couldn't find it. Everything has gone wrong with me. I'd like a few handfuls of that gold." He extended a hand, opened it
wide, and then shut it close. The sound of voices
down by the Creeper had changed to a gentle murmur. "How intimate those two are !" he thought.

A sense of disappointment and desolation came over
the young man. Life was such an unsatisfactory thing,
anyway. He wanted to enjoy life to its fullest. For
an instant he felt like a spendthrift willing to lavish
everything for the enjoyment he craved. Then the
crafty, hoarding spirit of his father came uppermost.
He was ready to drive a hard bargain with existence ;
he meant to get the best of it. The sound of his son's
voice come up the slope.

"Oh, mammy !" cried Victor.

A kind of fury took possession of Robert. He said
to himself that he was shut out from everything. He
turned and looked in an opposite direction. He saw
the maples and the lindens that did not quite hide the
Keating place. He hesitated; he gazed once more
down towards the Creeper, and he heard his boy laugh
with the shrieking laugh of childhood. "I'm shut
out," he said, grimly.

He started to walk rapidly in the direction of the
Keating place. He wished to run, but he restrained
himself. If his wife and child did not care for him
there was one who did. Half-way over the distance
Robert remembered how, less than an hour ago, his
head had been pressed to his wife's bosom. The memory was like a hand thrust forth from space arresting
him. He stopped still. He sat down on a rock of the
pasture, for he had left the highway. He understood
very little of himself or of the world or of life. He
was strongly conscious that he was ill-used, and that
he had lost something. If you have lost a precious

thing by your own fault, you resent its loss just as
keenly as if you were reasonable. Look back on your
own life and tell me if this is not a true saying. Who
is going to be reasonable in regard to his own pro-
clivities?

Robert leaned forward with his arms on his knees
and his chin on his hands. In the space of a moment
he thought of a great many things—of his unlucky
speculations, of how long his father might live, of that
moment when his wife's tenderness had pierced his
heart, and then of how Isabel's eyes had looked into
his but two evenings ago. Then he rose quickly, and
he did not pause until he had passed between the
stone posts into the drive that led to Isabel's home.

There she was, in a graceful morning-wrapper, walking among the rose-bushes. She had a bunch of red
roses in her hand as she came forward slowly when
see heard Robert's footsteps. She smiled and held
out her hand.

Robert took the hand closely ; but he was inclined
to be angry that this girl's presence did not immediately make him intensely happy. He perhaps wished,
like some others, to be able to summon a sensation at
will; but there is truth in the assertion that it is a "sad
fact that you cannot repeat a sensation." Here was
Robert standing in the midst of roses and holding Isabel's hand while she looked at him ; then why should
he remain insensate, and continue to think of that
woman he had just left, who had pressed his head to
her heart—ah, that true heart, that tender heart ! The
young man now smothered a groan. He dropped Isabel's hand and turned away. The sense of desolation
and loss was intolerable for the moment. He had
come here for his opiate ; was he not to get it ?

Isabel stood watching her companion. She was
much the same in appearance as she had been six
years ago, save that there was more opulence of figure,

"'OH, ISABEL, WHAT IS IT? HAVE I HURT YOU?'"

a deeper glow in the eyes, and a certain expression of unscrupulousness, or, more accurately, of recklessness, in the face, chiefly about the lips.

" Well ?" she said, at last.

Robert was gazing down the valley through an opening in the maples. He made no immediate response, and she repeated the word she had spoken. She advanced a step nearer him, and a whiff from the roses she carried swept to Robert's sense. His faultless profile was towards Isabel, whose glance dwelt upon it while her lips tightened slightly.

Having waited an instant longer, the girl turned shortly and walked in the direction of the house. She walked hurriedly, while her face grew red and her eyes flashed angrily. She had reached a thicket of syringa-bushes when she heard Robert's step hastening after her. She paused, for she had a mind that he should overtake her in the seclusion of this thicket. She saw him coming around the bend in the path. She dropped her roses and covered her face with her hands.

At sight of her thus the young man sprang forward eagerly. He was distinctly grateful to know that the thought of his wife dropped swiftly into the background. He paused close beside the girl. He restrained himself from touching her, but he bent over in an attitude of fondness as he whispered, "Oh, Isabel, what is it? Have I hurt you? I can't bear to have you suffer."

A subtle exultation because he had power over this beautiful woman was diffusing itself through his consciousness. After all, he was to have his sensation and his opiate. His pulses took on a new beat. He stooped and picked up the roses Isabel had dropped. He came yet nearer, and now he put his hand gently on the fingers that covered her face. No one had a more tender or more winning manner than Robert had.

"Dear, dear," he murmured in a half-voice.

He was aware that Isabel trembled slightly.   His spirits rose in a growing excitement.

"Why did you come here now?" asked Isabel, dropping her hands but averting her face.

"Why?   Don't you know?   You must know.   Are you going to desert me now, Isabel?   Are you going to be cruel to me?   I'm the most unlucky wretch in the world," passionately.

He had her hands now, and the two were gazing at each other.

The next moment Isabel laughed excitedly.   "Who has been cruel to you—who has forsaken you now?" she asked.

Robert grew red.   He dropped the hands he had been holding.   The roses fell again to the ground. "You like to taunt me," he exclaimed, "and no wonder. I've acted like a poor creature all my life.   But you— you, Isabel Keating—have bewitched me.   Don't you dare to deny it."

Isabel's laugh ceased.   A sweet expression came to her eyes, which she lifted fully to those of her companion.   "If I did bewitch you, I've suffered for it," she said, in a scarcely audible voice.   "I've suffered all these years, and I see nothing for me but to go right on suffering.   You have your consolations—you have your boy—"

"My boy!" roughly ; "what does he care for me?"

"And you have Olive," went on the girl, as if she had not been interrupted.   "She is devoted to you, whether you know it or not."

"Is she?" rudely.   "Isabel," catching her hand again and this time kissing it fervently, "do you guess why I came here just now?   I hoped you'd be glad," hurriedly—"I hoped you'd tell me we should be happier than any words can describe.   Isabel, don't turn away —look at me.   Oh, I'm free—free!"

CHAPTER XXXV

WITH VICTOR

NOTWITHSTANDING Robert's entreaty that she should not turn away, Isabel withdrew herself and walked to the distance of a few yards. She walked with bent head and drooped eyes. She had grown pale. As she went she stooped and picked up the bunch of roses Robert had let fall.

She felt blinded. She had not known Olive well enough to know that she would immediately consent to a divorce if Robert asked such a thing of her. She had misjudged Olive as one woman will sometimes misjudge another. As for herself, she was sure that she could never have given her consent ; she would have made it as difficult as possible for Robert to regain his freedom. That opposition would have been her revenge upon him for daring to make such a request, for wishing for such a thing. But Olive was different then. Olive—

Here the vision of Olive's face and eyes, the knowledge of what her old acquaintance must really be suffering now, came overwhelmingly to this girl. Isabel thought she knew how Olive loved her husband—and she had given him up !

With that sudden revulsion which some natures are capable of feeling, Isabel now flashed around upon Robert. "Oh, how wicked we are!" she cried. "How wicked! I hate myself! I hate you! Yes, I hate you, Robert Nawn !"

The young man made a furious gesture. Then he

stood perfectly still and gazed at the girl near him.
At last he began, with the endeavor to speak calmly,
but he found his tongue awkward and almost unman-
ageable.

"So that's all you care for me? So that's what a
woman means when she says she loves? It's enough to
make a man shoot himself! It's enough— Oh, good
Heavens! what's the use of talking? I can't talk."
He leaned forward quickly and seized Isabel's arm—
seized it rudely, so that she cried out with the pain.
But he did not release her. "Do you mean that you
hate me, Isabel Keating? Do you mean that?"

In the midst of his emotion there came the remembrance, like a shrewd thrust between the ribs, of the
fact that his father wished him to marry Isabel, and
that the marriage would be of pecuniary advantage to
him. So complex is the mind of man that it can contain several very curious and contradictory things at
the same instant of time.

Isabel hesitated as he insisted upon his question.
The gust of remorse had swept over her; but Robert
could not know that it was only a gust, and would
count for nothing in the girl's life and actions. It is
much easier to give room to praiseworthy emotions
than it is to perform praiseworthy actions; and the
emotions have a refreshing sense, as if one had done
well.

While Isabel hesitated, Robert, blind as a bat, was
growing more infuriated. He suddenly stooped and
kissed the girl on the lips; but the kiss had as much
of fury in it as of a caress. Then he swung about
and tramped off down the path, believing that the
world was ended for him, and not much caring if it
were.

Isabel looked after him, her distended eyes aching as
she looked. Once she seemed about to call him, but
she restrained the impulse. She stood silent among

the odorous syringa blossoms. She had a vague feeling that the heavy perfume made her sick. She
wished that she could cut down the bush—she wished
that she could annihilate every syringa shrub in the
world ; for any time in the years to come she might
happen to inhale that fragrance, and then she would
have to live over this scene with Robert again. Did
she hate him?

At last she walked slowly towards the house. She
succeeded in entering without being seen by her aunt
or the house-keeper. She went to her room and locked
herself in. As she did so it was as if she had gone
back the six years to that other time when she had
come and turned the key in the door after having seen
Olive at the little cottage where Olive had expected to
live after her marriage. She walked about the room ;
she paused to look in the glass.

"I'm six years older than I was then," she said, aloud,
"and I'm still the silliest woman in the world. What's
the reason I can't forget that man? Yes, what's the
reason? I know him. I know he isn't worthy of even
my love. Is it because he looks like Apollo, and has
such a way with his voice and eyes? Oh, haven't I any
will?" She stood before the glass, still gazing at herself as women will when they wish to torture themselves. She searched relentlessly for wrinkles and
signs of age. "In six years more of this I shall be
an old woman—a bitter, ugly old woman. But Olive
won't be old in that time. What is it that keeps that
lovely look on her face? Is it that boy? Pooh ! It
can't be. She was never so attractive as she is now.
Robert can't see. Are men like that? If I were in
Olive's place and Olive in mine, it would be Olive
for whom he would be half mad. I know that well
enough. Nobody need to tell me that. And here I
am talking to myself like the weak-minded creature I
am." She moved abruptly from the glass. She rest-

lessly traversed the floor for a time, then she went
to the barn, saddled her horse with her own hands,
and galloped away.

Robert had no horse to saddle and ride away, so he
walked as fast as he could go to the Falls Village and
had an interview with Mr. Drake, who still bought and
sold stocks for the young man. When he came out of
the office, Robert hesitated before the door of a liquor
saloon. He had never felt any temptation to drink
strong drink, and he had despised those who did feel
that temptation, as we do despise those whose weakness is not our weakness. But his last venture had
gone wrong, and Isabel—curse the women, anyway.
He pushed the swing - door and walked in, leaning
against the bar, where two other men were leaning as
they sucked something through a tube. The whole
place reeked with the smell of spirituous liquors.

"What 'll you take?" asked the man behind the
bar.

"Nothing," said Robert, shortly. He wheeled about
and the door swung behind him, vibrating back and
forth with the violence of his exit.

"It costs a lot to drink," he was thinking; "besides,
I'd rather gamble in stocks. A fellow may gain something there, and he can't by making a sot of himself."
So Robert walked homeward, his face setting itself
morosely as he went.

At the Nawn house "old man Nawn" was sitting
on the porch smoking as he waited for Olive to come
back. He had something he wished to say to her.
Every few moments he took his pipe from his mouth
and looked into the bowl of it—looked absently, as if
he saw nothing. After a time he forgot to puff, and
the fire in the pipe died out. But he did not seem to
know this, and sat with the stem between his teeth, his
body far back in the chair, his feet extended and resting on another chair.

The beautiful afternoon **waned** slowly. It **was a long June day**, and there were many hours to pass before the sun set. The frogs **were** calling in the lowlands near the Creeper. The chimney-swallows were swooping about the crouching **form of a** cat in the **yard. It was still** very bright, **but there was an indescribable aspect that** told that night was **on** its **way.**

For a long **time Mr.** Nawn heard occasionally the **high** notes of Victor's voice **as he** talked with his **mother** on the river-bank, and his fresh laugh came piercingly on the still air. Impossible to tell what **the old** man was thinking, or whether he was thinking at **all.** He was not asleep, for his eyes gleamed below **his** bushy, gray brows. After an hour had passed Mr. **Nawn** pulled a thick silver watch by a leather string **from** his pocket and looked at it.

"**It's after five** o'clock; time she was getting supper," **he thought.**

Then he remembered **that it** had been an hour, perhaps, since **he** had heard Victor's voice. That was **odd.** You could always hear **a** brat if he were within half a **mile.** The shadows were getting heavy **in** the **yard. The** grotesque outline of the house lay there plainly defined. The cat had walked away, the swallows flying **down** at her as she walked. Mr. Nawn rose and **went to** the south of the house and to the top of a **knoll,** from whence could **be** seen **a** stretch of the Creeper where there were no trees, a portion of the **bridge, and** a few rods of the narrow road that climbed **upward from** the bridge.

On this narrow road, walking **in a** broad bar of sunlight, Mr. Nawn saw two figures, which his far-sighted eyes told him **were** the figures of Olive and her son. They were hand in hand, and they were walking away from the house, moving steadily, as if with **a** set purpose.

Mr. Nawn gazed for a moment ; then he struck his stick on the ground as he exclaimed, "What the devil does that mean? Why, it's supper-time!"

The woman and the boy turned around a bend in the road and disappeared. They entered a thick wood, where the shadows were dark and green, the smell of growing leaves being strong on the air.

As Victor gazed about, the sense of coming night pressed upon him, and he moved nearer to his mother ; but the next instant he drew away and said, with an assumption of boldness, "If it gets real dark, mammy, I c'n take care of you, 'cause, you know, I'm a boy, and you're only a woman."

Olive looked at her companion and smiled as she clasped his hand yet closer ; then she drew a long breath as she answered, "Yes, I'm only a woman."

"That's so ; but you're my mammy. There ain't anybody else got such a mammy, has there?"

There was an intonation in the voice that said these words that made Olive start and look eagerly down at the sturdy fellow walking by her side. It was the intonation in a child's speech like the sweetest tones in Robert's voice when Robert's mood was tender and loving.

"Oh," cried Olive, before she could prevent herself, "don't speak like that, Victor—don't!"

The boy stared up at her, his lip dropping. "I didn't know 's I'd said anything bad," he exclaimed ; "I didn't feel wicked, anyway."

"No, no," hastily from Olive ; "but—" She prevented herself from saying that he spoke like his father. She hurried him on. He ran beside her.

"Will he be like Robert?" This question buzzed over and over in her brain, making her faint and sick. At one instant it gave her a delight to think of the possibility of this resemblance ; the next moment the very sky itself turned black at the thought that this boy might grow up to be a Nawn—a Nawn! She hurried yet more.

"I say, mammy," running fast to keep pace with her, "I guess gran'pa 'll be mad if supper ain't ready. Did you tell him you shouldn't get supper?"

Olive paused. She stood in the shadow, looking forward into the blaze of reddening light, which still she did not see at all. She wished to think clearly. She had been trying to do this every moment since Robert had told her that she must go one way and he should go another. They "didn't seem to hit it off." That was what he had said—that they didn't hit it off. And it was true.

Well, perhaps some time she should find her mind clear again, and be able to think and form plans; but thus far she could only long to get away somewhere with Victor; to be alone with Victor was all that Olive could plan now; but that thought was perfectly clear and well defined. The details might come later. She must wait until these details did shape themselves. Meanwhile—she paused in her walk and held back the boy from going on—meanwhile, what? If she had been alone, if there had been no Victor, everything would have been simplified. But, thank God! there was a Victor!

Olive had walked from home with a confused sense of wishing in every way to help Robert to get rid of her. She had an intense desire to make it easy for him to cast her off. Now, hurrying hand in hand with her son, she began to realize that she must have thought of going to her mother. There was absolutely no other place of shelter just now, but as soon as possible she would get work in one of the factories in the Falls Village. She was quite sure that she could support herself and Victor.

Walking thus, and not hearing the child's prattle, Olive and her companion turned a corner, that they

might partially retrace their steps and thus reach her
mother's house.   Ahead, and coming rapidly towards
them, galloped Isabel's horse with his mistress on his
back.   Always, Olive thought, that girl was galloping
through her life.

WHEN Isabel saw the woman and the boy, her horse swerved abruptly aside by reason of the violence with which his mouth was pulled. She was tempted to turn squarely about and ride away, but she hated to retreat like that. She rode forward.

Olive involuntarily stood still and waited, her brows drawn together. Of course Isabel would ride on; in another moment she would be gone. Isabel did ride on, bowing as she went by. Olive gathered herself together and walked a few steps. Then she was aware that the horse had turned and was coming back. She glanced about; to what refuge could she flee? But no, she would not retreat; she continued to go on, leading Victor.

"Ain't it a splendid horse, mammy?" Victor was saying. "Jacky Loud told me that gran'pa could get me a pony 's well 's not, only he was such a miser. What is a miser, mammy?" No reply. "I say, what is a miser, mammy?"

"Oh, hush! Hush, Victor!"

The boy looked up at his mother, was dimly conscious of the anguish in her face, and kept silence, wondering greatly. The horse rushed up and stopped, arching its neck and pawing. Olive stopped also; she would not continue her walk now. What was one pang more or less? She looked up fully into the face above her, and as the eyes of the two women met, Olive became aware that Isabel was suffering — perhaps as deeply as she herself, and the sight of suffering always disarmed her.

"I couldn't help coming back," said Isabel, speaking thickly. Olive said nothing. What had she to say to that remark? "I wish you'd send that child away," cried Isabel.

Olive's hand gripped still harder on the hand in hers. "No," she answered.

"But I have to speak some things, and he will hear."

"Don't speak things that he should not hear, then."

A brief silence after this. Isabel sat bending somewhat in her saddle, her eyes fixed upon the woman before her. But Olive was not looking up; she stood with lowered lashes, waiting, holding her boy's hand.

"You don't know how I've tried to give him up!"

These words came in a low exclamation from Isabel. She unconsciously put out one hand as if in entreaty. This was hard for Olive to hear. So Isabel was trying to give up Olive's husband? Olive's heart had a fire in it—a fire which she could not yet conquer; but even at such an instant she felt a pity for this girl.

"Do you think I've been happy these six years," went on Isabel, "struggling as I've been? You had a right, I had none. I was outside—always outside. I'm tired of it; I've been tired of it all a thousand times, and I'm growing horribly old. You're not growing old, Olive Newcomb. There's something in your face that 'll make it charming when you're ninety. He is a blind man, and he isn't worthy that any woman should love him—"

"Stop!" cried Olive.

"No, I sha'n't stop, either. I'm speaking the truth— and why shouldn't I speak it, I should like to know? He doesn't deserve to have a woman like me love him, much less that you should love him. Do you, Olive— do you care for him now?"

Olive trembled so that she leaned against the strong

shoulder of the horse that stood so near her. "You've no right to ask that," she answered in a whisper.

"No; only the right of suffering, and that gives rights sometimes—anyway, we think it does."

A silence. Victor was stroking the glossy chest of the horse and wishing his grandfather wasn't a miser, so that he might have a pony. And he was wondering, in a childish, vague way, what the talk was about. Who was that "he" that Isabel Keating was mentioning? He would listen with all his might and find out, if he could.

"I was sorry when I saw you on the road here, just now," began Isabel, at last. "You were the one person I didn't want to meet; but now I'm glad. You give me strength, somehow."

"That is strange, when I'm so weak—so very weak," still in the same whisper.

Isabel's eyes rested for a moment steadily on the bent head below her.

"If I tell you that I've driven him off," she said, hurriedly, "perhaps the telling you will help me to keep to my resolution; perhaps it will make you forgive him—when he asks you."

Olive stood up, away from the horse which had supported her. "He has been to you then—already?" she asked.

"Yes."

"I was sure of it. You need not drive him off, Isabel. Do you think, if my own heart were breaking, that I could find comfort in his presence—after you had driven him away? No; keep him—smile upon him. What is it to me? I say"—more loudly—"what is it to me?" Olive's whole face flashed fire. She stepped back. "Come, Victor," she said, "we must hurry; it 'll be dark soon."

The two walked away, and as they walked they heard the quick galloping of horse's feet.

17

"Who was she talking about, mammy?" the boy asked.
"Never mind."

"Yes—yes ; tell me.   Was it somebody 't I know?"
"Victor, I shall not tell you."

The boy was silent.   He gazed up at his mother ; he
seemed about to cry, then he controlled the inclination,
and went soberly on by her side.   Presently the two entered the yard of the little house that had been Olive's
home.   Aunt Ruth was sitting at the window, sewing.
Mrs. Newcomb was at the sink, washing the supper
dishes.   Since her daughter had left her, Mrs. Newcomb had ceased to be an invalid.

"Sakes!   There's Olive and the boy!" exclaimed
Aunt Ruth; and she rose, dropping her scissors with
a clatter to the floor.

Mrs. Newcomb, with the dishcloth in her wet hands,
came forward and looked.   "So 'tis.   It's kind of odd,
her comin' jes' now, ain't it?   She don't come here
much, anyway."

"She's so busy workin' for them Nawns that she
can't come," responded Aunt Ruth.   "Seems to me
there's something kind of queer 'bout her, ain't there?"

"No, I guess not," said Mrs. Newcomb.   "I don't see
nothin' queer."   The door opened.   "That you, Olive?"
continued her mother.   "You're quite a stranger, ain't
you?   How be you 'n' Victor?"

Mrs. Newcomb kissed the boy and told him that the
Williams-red would soon be ripe now.

"Williams-red apples are dretful sour for a boy," remarked Aunt Ruth.   She was looking over her spectacles at her niece, and again saying, this time to herself, that "there was something odd about Olive."

Meantime Olive had placed herself in one of the
chairs and Victor was leaning against her.   Mrs. Newcomb was standing in the middle of the room rolling
the wet cloth into a ball, and holding one hand under
it lest it should drip upon the floor.

"How's old man Nawn?" she asked.

"He's well. Mother," speaking quickly, "will you give me a cup of tea? I think a cup of tea would do me good."

"But what—" began Mrs. Newcomb.

She was interrupted by Ruth, who exclaimed, "Never mind, sister, don't stop to ask questions; you jest go 'n' git the tea, 'n' have it hot, too. Lukewarm tea ain't of no account."

And when Mrs. Newcomb went into the buttery for the teapot, Aunt Ruth refrained from even looking at her niece, who sat with her hand on her son's shoulder, her eyes drooped, her face held rigidly quiet. Olive was wondering how she should tell her mother, or, rather, what she should tell her. She could not be questioned—that was something she could not bear.

At last Mrs. Newcomb brought the tea. As Olive took the cup in her hand, her mother, looking across her and through the window, saw a figure slowly approaching.

"The old Harry!" she cried out, "if there ain't Mr. Nawn! And he's comin' in here, too. I don't remember 's he ever come here before, since that time he wanted to buy that lot of land of Israel, 'n' offered him half what 'twas wu'th." Mrs. Newcomb spoke rapidly. She bustled towards the door, and reached it just as Mr. Nawn's hand was on the latch. "Walk in 'n' take a chair," she said, excitedly.

Mr. Nawn came in deliberately and sat down. He told Mrs. Newcomb that everybody grew old but her, and her faded face flushed as she heard him; but she said:

"'Tain't so, Mr. Nawn, 'n' you know it, too."

Aunt Ruth glowered silently at the visitor, and waited for what might transpire.

The old man turned towards Olive, and said, "I thought I saw you coming this way, and as I was walking out, I made bold to call, so that we could go back together."

Olive did not reply. She met the man's eyes fully,
the shrewd, bright eyes that had a way of communi-
cation that was of keener power than the speech of
their owner. These eyes seemed to say, " Hold your
tongue and follow my lead."

And Olive held her tongue ; she drank her tea while
Mr. Nawn chatted in a leisurely manner with Mrs.
Newcomb, recalling old times and scenes. But, though
he appeared so leisurely, he remained but a few moments. He rose heavily on his stick, saying, " Come,
Olive, we shall be late to supper as 'tis," and he glanced
at her again.

She rose also, holding Victor's hand and following
the man outside. Once in the road, she said to the
boy, " Run on, Victor ; gran'pa and I want to talk."
The child hesitated, and she commanded, pushing him
from her. As he ran ahead she turned quickly towards her companion. " Why did you come ?" she asked, harshly. She drew herself up and walked apart.

" I came after you," was the brief reply.

" You need not."

" Oh yes ; I thought you'd be running away to your
old home. I wasn't going to have it."

Olive faced round upon the man. " You don't know,
then," she exclaimed ; " you can't know !"

" Pooh ! Didn't I hear enough before I left the room
to be able to guess the whole thing ? And don't I know
Bob ?" The speaker thrust out his lips and raised his
brows.

" He wants to be divorced." Olive spoke in a barely
audible voice, and she turned away as if she could not
bear that any one should look at her.

" Lucky thing for you if he does," said Mr. Nawn.
" I've advised him to do just that."

Olive stopped short. The old man thought she
swayed as she stood. He reached forward and took
hold of her arm.

CHAPTER XXXVII

AUNT RUTH

"ARE you going to care for a man like that?" Olive, trying to keep her senses under her control, thought she heard this question in a voice that was far away but that still was the voice of Mr. Nawn. She felt his hand authoritatively on her arm; but plainer than anything else to her was the little figure a few rods distant along the road, the boy, who often hesitated and looked back. And like a flash across a black cloud was the thought, "I must do what is best for Victor; I can live for Victor." "I say," repeated Mr. Nawn, "are you going to care for a man like that? It's astonishing how much he is like his mother—got her winning ways, too."

The last sentence appeared to be spoken to himself, and not to Olive, who, indeed, did not note it. But she heard the repetition of that inquiry. She stood still now, and her companion paused beside her, keeping his hold on her arm. He glanced over her shoulder and saw that they were within sight of the house they had just left, and he thought, "Those cursed women are staring from the window, of course. Well, let them stare."

"I've cared for him for years," now answered Olive. Her voice was piteous, and yet it was the voice of a strong woman. "Do you think I can stop caring? If God is good, He will help me to stop." She was visibly fighting for a semblance of composure—she felt it to be a cruel thing that this man had come for her now.

"I don't know about what God will do," was the bluff response; "but I guess 'tain't in you to go on loving a man who's mad after some one else." Olive winced, and her face stiffened in its pallor, but she stood firm. "I know what I sh'll do, anyway. I sh'll have you go right home with me, and go on keeping my house as if nothing had happened."

Olive's form seemed to dilate. "No," she said—"no. Do you think I will live in the house with Robert after what he said to me?"

The whole woman was indignant and rebellious.

Ahead of them Victor was singing:

> "Wagging their tails behind 'em."

And at the sound that old thrill of joy and hope which her boy's voice could awaken in the mother's heart came to it again, like a drop of brandy to the fainting. Oh yes, there was Victor.

Mr. Nawn saw the face before him flush suddenly, and a fine light come to the despairing eyes. "You needn't live in the house with him," he said. Olive looked at Mr. Nawn silently. "No; he'll go away; he won't stay there. But you will. You've got a backbone; you've got what I call integrity; you won't creep and crawl. You'll keep my house. Besides," with a laugh, "you've learnt to be real saving; you don't waste more'n Israel Newcomb's daughter 'd have to waste. Let's walk right along. We c'n talk as we go. I won't let Bob come back. He can board somewhere else while he's getting his divorce. There won't be any fuss. I hate a fuss, anyway. Olive, look here," with a sudden change of voice; "you needn't get that stubborn look on your face. Are you listening? Well, then, take this in : Do you want your boy to have a good start?"

Olive clasped her hands quickly. "Oh!" she exclaimed, softly, the fine light still in her eyes. But suddenly the light was gone. She did not believe much in this old man who was talking to her; and yet there was an air of verity about him now. Perhaps he would deceive her, as his son had done; she could not help thinking of that. She felt that she had need of all her armor, and she longed for wisdom.

Mr. Nawn stood looking at her searchingly. "You'd do anything for the lad, wouldn't you?" he asked.

"I'd do many things."

"I understand; but not anything mean?"

"I hope not."

Mr. Nawn smiled indulgently. "Do you think I'm going to get a new house-keeper broken in?" he asked. "I guess not! I'm going to keep you. You know what food to set on the table, and what to give to the pigs; and that's a lot to know, I tell you. You're coming back now with me, and you're going to get supper just as usual; and when Bob comes home, he'll leave; that's all there is about that. I've encouraged Bob in his talk of getting a divorce—you needn't stare at me. I put it into his head; he grabbed at it fast enough. He thinks you're wasteful, too," with a shoulder-shrug; "and he thinks I've never overlooked it in you for refusing to put the butter into that mould that was short-weight. You were rather set that time, Olive; you must confess that you were."

But Olive hardly listened to these last words. She was thinking, thinking, and her thoughts were gradually clarifying. "If Robert does not stay at his home I will go back with you now," she said, decisively.

"All right, now you're talking sense. Come, supper 'll be late. I like my meals on time."

The two started on. They had gone a few yards when Olive put her hand on Mr. Nawn's sleeve. "I don't want you to bribe me with promises about Victor," she said, earnestly. "It has come to me clearly that it is right for me to stay with you—at present."

Mr. Nawn nodded. They went on in silence until they reached the porch ; then the old man turned to his daughter-in-law ; he extended his hand to prevent her from entering the house until he had spoken. His eyes had a curious look in them as he said, " I thought I'd tell you that I ain't one of the kind that likes to make a will and cut off a son. I've been of the mind to let things go to Bob as they would naturally, and he knows it. So I don't know how you and the kid will fare. I don't relish giving money away while I'm alive. As long as I have the breath of life in me I want to handle my money. I just mentioned giving Victor a start ; if I can make up my mind, I'll give him a few hundred dollars before I die. You see—"

But Olive drew away with a proud gesture. " I will take care of Victor," she said, shortly.

At that instant the boy ran up. He heard those words, and he looked in a puzzled way from one to the other. " I'm going to take care of my mammy my own self," he announced.

Olive veiled the gladness in her eyes by lowering her lashes quickly.

" Run along into the house," ordered the grandfather ; and when the child had obeyed, the old man turned again towards his companion and said, " Don't you make a fool of him. There's another thing I wanted to tell you : I've respected you ever since that butter-mould business ; but I was mad with you all the same. I can trust you. That's all ; I guess I'll have another smoke. 'Baccy's gone down two cents a pound wholesale ; so I'll smoke again before supper."

The woman and the child passed on into the house, and Olive prepared the supper just as if nothing new had come into her life. But was this thing new? Was it not an old fear now put into words and made a fact? The meal was late, and it was dusk when Olive was washing the dishes. Victor lay asleep on the lounge in the kitchen, his hair tumbled over his moist forehead.

As Olive stood at the sink some one softly opened the south door. With the light shining in her eyes Olive could not at first see who it was, but she saw a hand beckoning to her and she hastened towards it. "Aunt Ruth!" she exclaimed, in a whisper.

"Hush! Is anybody 'round?"

"Only Victor, and he's asleep. Will you come in?"

"No, indeed; but I couldn't rest till I'd seen you again. Olive, I know something's happened, but you needn't tell me what. I jest wanted to see you 'fore I went to bed; I knew I shouldn't sleep a wink if I didn't, 'n' I d'know 's I shall as 'tis."

The small, gray-haired woman stepped nearer; she looked yearningly at her niece, but she did not touch her. She held that it was "flat" to caress a person merely because you love that person.

"I jest wanted to let you know, Olive," she went on, in the same hissing whisper, "that if you feel like coming home, you c'n come jest as well as not. I've got a bit of money—enough for us all to squeak along on—and you needn't have to explain too much to your mother. Sister always means well, but she don't have wisdom given her every time. I see you was troubled. Now, if you 'n' Victor care to come home, I c'n manage it. 'Twon't be no trouble, neither. What do you say?"

Olive could not speak; a tremor went over her. Something within her seemed to break up. Her eyes stung and then filled with tears that must be shed. There had been no chance for tears, and she had been so tense that they could not come. All at once she flung out her arms, and, literally, in the Old Scripture phrase, fell on Aunt Ruth's neck and wept. Ruth was so astonished at this outburst that she stood perfectly still, holding the shaking form in silence. She could only make that soft noise that mothers sometimes make to their children—"Sh! Sh! Sh!" long drawn out.

Even in the midst of this emotion Olive did not forget to subdue the sounds she made to a murmur, lest Mr. Nawn might hear from where he sat smoking. And the old man "hated a fuss." Besides, she shrank from making revelation of herself. "Don't worry about me," Olive said, as soon as she could speak. "Things have been rather hard to bear—"

"You needn't tell me," interrupted Ruth, and she added, sternly, "I can guess, and that's enough for me."

Olive lifted her head from its resting-place. She stood quietly for an instant; then she said, "I can't go home now. I don't know whether I ever can or not; but I can't now. My duty seems to be here."

"I wouldn't be trod upon!" cried Ruth; with a rush of fierceness. "I wouldn't let um grind me to powder. There's some things a woman ain't called upon to bear."

"I know it," was the response, with dignity, "and those things I sha'n't bear, Aunt Ruth; I'll go to you first."

"So 'tain't no use persuading of you?" hesitatingly.

"No."

"Then I guess I'll be goin'." But she stood still, gazing wistfully at her niece, whose hands were now in the dish-water, and upon whose face the lamplight shone. "I don't jest like the looks of you, somehow," she remarked.

Olive smiled. She shook her hands over the pan and went back to where her visitor stood uncertainly. "I'm just as much obliged to you, Aunt Ruth," she said, her voice not steady. "I don't think you'd better say anything to mother."

"No, I won't. Good-night."

"Good-night, Aunt Ruth."

"I hope you'll remember that I've got a bit of money, and I should like first-rate to share it with you," said the woman.

Olive raised her eyes to the slim figure in the half darkness, but she knew that she could not trust herself to speak. So Aunt Ruth walked away towards her home. She paused on the bridge to "stiddy herself," as she expressed it, before she entered the room where her sister was sitting without a light, watching the June night come over the earth.

When she was gone, Olive hurried still more with her dishes. Her hands twitched sometimes, but for the most part she controlled them.

CHAPTER XXXVIII

ROBERT GOES

WHEN the last dish was wiped and put away, Olive sat down a moment. She placed herself so that she could see Victor's face as he lay sleeping on the lounge. She unconsciously leaned forward as she looked. Her tired heart was full. To-day she knew for certain that she had lost her husband's love. Later she might learn that such a love was not precious, but she had not learned it yet. That is, if she knew it with her mind, there was something within her that would not accept the knowledge and that cried out against it.

But Victor was hers. She rose from her chair, and went with noiseless quickness to the lounge and knelt beside it. She softly put her head down close to the tousled hair, inhaling the fresh, out-of-door smell which clung to the boy. He stirred slightly and murmured something inarticulately, then fell back into deep slumber. She took one of the tanned, grimy hands and put her palm down closely upon its palm. Instantly the small hand clasped itself about the larger; but the boy did not waken in the least, and, directly, the clasp relaxed. Olive's pulses slackened somewhat in their strained beating. "That was good of Aunt Ruth," she thought. Her head sank still more heavily down beside the boy.

After a little time a man came quickly through the yard, his feet swishing among the grass and weeds. This was Robert, and when he saw dimly the form of his father in the porch, he swerved aside and went to

"SHE WENT WITH NOISELESS QUICKNESS TO THE LOUNGE AND KNELT BESIDE IT"

the south door, entering there and making his way to the kitchen. He had seen the light in this room when he had approached the house, but he did not see Olive as she knelt on the floor by the lounge. He came in quickly, but without much noise ; he was dreading to have his father speak to him, and he was glad to think that this room was empty. Immediately he saw the boy and his mother ; he stopped short.

Olive, roused from the half sleep into which she had fallen, rose to her feet. She stood for an instant looking at her husband. Then she turned silently and left the room, glancing back when she reached the door, as if to assure herself of Victor's safety. Robert made a swift gesture with his hand as if he would have detained her, but, though she saw the gesture, she did not heed it. She did not pause in her walk until she reached the porch where Mr. Nawn was half asleep. She touched his shoulder and, as he started, she asked, in a whisper, "Are you awake?"

The old man moved ; he dropped his pipe as he did so, and the stem broke. "There's more money gone!" he said, testily. "What did you come stealing along like this for?"

Olive made no reply to these words. She said, "Robert has come."

"Well, well," was the irritated response. "Let the matter drop until to-morrow, can't you?"

"No. You must keep your word." Olive's voice was cold and distant. "Either Robert leaves to-night, or I do—Victor and I. I've made up my mind."

"Oh, you have, have you? I'll see about it, then. You don't shilly-shally like Bob. I hate shilly-shallying. I was asleep, you see. Where's my cane?"

Olive picked the stick from the floor and put it into the man's hand.

"Your fingers are like ice," he said. He rose slowly. "Come along," he commanded.

She hesitated. "I'll go and get Victor," she said; "he's asleep on the kitchen lounge, and Robert is there."

"Come along," he repeated. "I want you to hear what I say to Bob; then you'll know I mean it; then it 'll be plain sailing between us."

Mr. Nawn grasped a fold of Olive's sleeve and pulled her towards him; then he guided her towards the kitchen door. They could hear steps in that direction, as of a man walking restlessly. Olive's resistance ceased. She went straight on into the kitchen, the old man's shuffling feet and sharp-tapping cane coming on behind her.

Robert stopped in his walk. He had his hat still on, and his hands were in his pockets. The low room looked very dingy by the light of the small lamp, but it was full of the sweet June air which came in through the open windows. Robert frowned as the two entered. His father sat down before he spoke. He opened the subject at once.

"I've been thinking," he began, "that you'd better get another boarding-place, Bob."

Robert pulled his hands from his pockets with an abrupt movement. His face reddened. At first his surprise prevented him from speaking. "What do you mean by that?" he asked, loudly.

"You needn't holler so," remarked his father. "Perhaps you can see yourself that you might as well move out, since you're going to start the divorce proceedings. Some men would have thought of this without being reminded."

"Yes," said Robert, "I'll go—I'll go. But I hadn't thought; I haven't been able to think. I'm—oh, I can't think clearly, though I've tried."

His eyes sought Olive's, but she kept her own drooped. She stood behind the old man's chair, holding fast to it. The scene seemed to her so paltry, so

low, so unworthy of any manly feeling, that she could
hardly remain. Suddenly, as Robert walked restlessly
to the other side of the room, she raised her eyes and
looked at him. He was ghastly pale now, and his face
was pinched. Olive was thinking that that face had
always seemed noble to her. She could not even yet
divest herself of the belief that it was noble, and
that it was an index to her husband's nature. She
had been dreaming something horrible. She shook
herself. Surely she would soon awaken. There was
Robert, her Robert, suffering. It hurt her to see him
suffer. Not yet could she adjust herself to the truth.
She told herself that she knew the truth. Why, then,
did her heart leap so involuntarily towards this man?

After that examination of her husband's face, Olive
held herself as quiet and cold as if she felt thus. She
was wishing that she might be able to cease to feel
even pity for him. It tore her heart to be obliged to
pity him.

"Olive was going," remarked Mr. Nawn; "but I've
put a stop to that. Of course, she can't go. She's got
to stay here. So you may move your things out. Take
'em out to-morrow, but you may go to-night. You
may let me know how the divorce comes on. You two
ought never to have married. I knew you ought not.
Isabel's the wife for you, Bob. But I reckon this isn't
very seemly talk. It's all been a mistake. But perhaps
you can patch up something all round. It's a damned
muddle; but that's what life is, anyway. Now, go
along, Bob. There's Mrs. Symonds takes boarders, you
know, and she's handy to the factory." Mr. Nawn
rested his hands on his cane, and looked at his son.
Robert did not move. He stood with his head bowed.
"Ain't it settled?" inquired the old man, irritably.

Robert walked a few steps towards Olive. His mouth
was dry, and he could not at first speak. "Olive," he
said, at last, "do you think it's all settled?"

"Certainly," answered Olive, promptly.

But she thought it was some one else answering with such decision, some one else whose word she would abide by. And Robert was suffering.

"Very well. I've got myself to thank for it all." As the young man spoke he walked towards the door. When he had gone thus far he stopped. "I don't suppose anything can be helped," he said. There was a note of pleading in his voice.

"Nothing can be helped," answered that person who seemed to be speaking for Olive, and whom she was to obey.

"Very well," again.

Robert passed out through the door-way. His wife heard his feet as they went slowly among the grass. She walked to the door as if she were going after him, but that person who was controlling her made her pause. She stood there listening to the sound of the feet brushing among the grass ; she listened as if the sound were something that she longed to hear, and that she should never hear again. When it had grown almost inaudible, she ran down the step from the door and into the overgrown path.

"Olive !" cried the old man.

She stopped instantly, as if the word had been a hand which had caught her at the throat, and she reeled slightly, as if the hand had come nigh to choking her. Then she turned and went into the house, where she found Mr. Nawn leaning forward in his chair as though he were about to rise and follow her.

"He has gone—Robert has gone," she announced, hardly.

"Yes, I know it," gazing at her keenly in the dim light. "What !" raspingly—"are *you* going to have half a dozen minds, too? It's enough for Robert to be that way."

But Olive apparently did not hear, though she stood

looking at the speaker. "I was sure I loved him," she said, mechanically. "I loved him with all my heart— oh, with all my heart !" She covered her face with her hands, standing quiet before the old 'man, who stared at her as one who was trying to remember how people used to act when he was young. And he was annoyed by the fear lest she should begin to be what he called, cynically, "womanish." But she made no sound. She stood in that attitude for a moment, then she dropped her hands and said, "I will put Victor to bed now."

She went to the lounge and lifted the boy in her arms, heavy though he was. As she raised him she was aware that the mere sense of his weight was a com- fort to her. She walked into the bedroom and closed the door fast.

Victor's head had fallen heavily on her shoulder, but his eyes did not open. She wished that they would open, but it would be a kind of cruelty to waken him. She placed him carefully on the bed, then she fumbled about for the match-box. She prolonged this search, for it occupied her ; she felt like making much of the smallest duty. She stumbled and struck her head against the corner of the shelf ; she stood dazed and aching for a moment, glad of the pain, for it was a counter-irritant. She heard Victor's soft breathing as he lay on the bed. At last the match-box was found and the lamp kindled. She began slowly to take off the boy's jacket.

" I wish you'd wake, just for one minute," she whis- pered. Nevertheless, she was careful not to waken him. As the firm, white chest and arms were uncov- ered, Olive stooped and kissed the boy's throat.

Victor half opened his eyes and whispered, " Oh, I'm so sleepy !"

" Yes—yes," she murmured. " That's right ; sleep and rest."

His head was continually nodding as she put on his
18

nĩght-gown. When the neck-band was fastened and
the sandy shoes and stockings drawn off, the mother
stood back from the bed that she might the better con-
template the figure lying there.

All at once the old, the intolerable fear that Victor
might be like his father came upon her again. She had
besought God to keep Victor from becoming a miser.
She remembered that in those days, long ago—hundreds of years ago, they now seemed—when Robert
had loved her, she had also pleaded with God that this
child might be like his father. She shuddered now
at that remembrance. How many women have shuddered at just such a remembrance?

Possessed by this memory, Olive, with a gesture as
of one who can resist no longer, took the lamp from
the shelf and bent over the bed with it in her hand,
letting its light fall full upon the boy's face. It was
as if she were examining that face for the first time,
though she knew every line of it more thoroughly than she knew anything else in the world—save the
face of the child's father.

Victor's regular breathing ceased; she did not notice that. He flung out one arm restlessly; then he
opened his eyes and blinked sleepily at the light. The
next instant he was staring up into his mother's intent
countenance.

"Victor," she said, sternly, hardly knowing that she
spoke—"Victor, are you going to be like your father?
Are you going to break my heart?"

CHAPTER XXXIX

"YOU'RE A GOOD GIRL"

THE boy's eyes dilated, his lips parted as he continued to look. His mother's face was so unlike what he
was used to seeing that he began to be frightened. His
mouth quivered. He thrust a fist up to his right eye.

"Oh, mammy," he blubbered, "what makes you look
so? I'm afraid!" But even then the masculine in-
stinct came to the front, and he snuffled out, "But I
ain't goin' to be afraid but a minute. I don't want
to be a coward. No"—taking his fist down and swal-
lowing hard—"I ain't goin' to cry. I 'ain't cried for
three days—I guess it's three days."

Then he shut his teeth, and his red lips became two
lines of white as he continued to look at his mother.
As for her, she was intent upon her examination, and,
in the way with which he was familiar, noticed him
not a whit. Therefore he was obliged to take another
grip upon his self-control; but this last was too much
for him, and he now burst out a-crying in good earnest.

Olive hurriedly set her lamp upon the stand. Then
she sank down on the bed beside her boy and drew him
into her arms, exclaiming, again and again, "There's
not one look—not one look!—and they are my father's
eyes. Thank God for that! Oh, thank God for that!"
Then a pang came to her, because she could thank
God for such a thing. It was the turning of her love
in its grave.

Victor went on sobbing; but now he felt that they

were indeed his mother's arms that held him so sweet and strong. But what was that? Was mammy crying, too? Victor stopped his sobs, save for an occasional, irrepressible heave of his whole body. He put one hand on his mother's face and brushed away a tear, but another came instantly and he used his other hand. His face twitched and snarled in his effort not to join afresh in this weeping. "'Tain't me, is it, mammy?" he said, at last; "'tain't 'cause I've been wicked?"

"Oh no, no." Then, fighting for a smile, "It's because I have you, Victor. I'm so glad I have you, my darling—my one love—my comfort—my blessing—my precious gift from God! Oh! Oh!"

Olive kissed the boy's eyes, his forehead, his hair, his cheeks, his lips, over and over, with a heart-breaking passion of tenderness. And Victor clung and clung to her, terrified and speechless.

In a moment more Olive became more calm. She began to reproach herself bitterly. She had meant to hold this accumulated excitement well in hand. She had no patience with hysteria, and she felt that she had been hysterical. And she had frightened Victor. She set herself to work to soothe him, and she soon succeeded. Presently he ceased to sob.

"I d'know why you should be glad you've got me," he said, as he lay with a hand on each of his mother's cheeks; it was a favorite caress of his to hold his mother's face in that way. "Course you've got me. You see, you've got me, 'cause you're my mother, 'n' I'm your little boy. Bime-by—"

But Victor could keep awake no longer. The small gust of excitement had passed away from his small ken, and he was asleep once more. His mother watched his long, refreshing breaths until she was outwardly quiet again. Yes, it was true, in a greater degree than ever, that all her fortune was in a single coin. Presently she took the lamp and left the room for her nightly round of locking up the doors. She found that old Mr. Nawn was still in his chair, and that he had fallen asleep. She put a steady hand on his shoulder and spoke his name. He raised his head and looked confusedly at her.

"Did you see where I keep my gold?" he asked, thickly.

"No—no. Wake up! You've been dreaming."

"Oh," shaking himself, "you think I've been asleep, do you? Well," defiantly, "I haven't slept a wink. Have you locked up?" Olive shook her head. She watched the old man get to his feet. She thought he seemed more unwieldy than usual. He went to the door, striking his cane down smartly with each step he took. Having reached the door, he paused and turned his face towards Olive. "I tell you what 'tis," he said, impatiently, "I d' know but I keep too much gold in the house. Mebby some night I sh'll be murdered for my gold."

Olive made a gesture of horror. "No—no!" she exclaimed. "Send it away if you feel so."

"Pooh! it's only a notion. I can't take it away. I want it where I c'n touch it 'n' see it. I s'pose you want Victor where you c'n touch him 'n' see him, don't you? Well, then, you ought to understand me. Now I'll go to bed." He went into the narrow passage that led to the stairs, and immediately Olive heard him pause again; then her name was called. "Olive, come here." She joined Mr. Nawn as he stood at the foot of the stairs. "You remember the time that fellow got into the house after my money?" he asked.

"Yes."

"You helped me a lot then, didn't you?"

"I suppose I did just as any one would," responded Olive.

"My dream made me think of that night," said Mr. Nawn; "and then I thought that now we're only an

old man and a woman in the house with that box of
gold. Victor don't count. He's only a baby."

"Do take it away!" exclaimed Olive.

Mr. Nawn struck his stick against the lower stair.
His face reddened. "I won't take it away either!" he
shouted. "Do you think I want to live if I can't have
my gold to count? Do you want to live yourself, if
you can't have Victor?" The old man did not see how
Olive shrank at hearing him again compare his gold
to her boy. "Besides," he resumed, more in his usual
manner, "nobody knows I've got gold here. They all
think"—here he chuckled—"that I'm too bright to
keep the stuff by me. And I wish I was—I declare, I
wish I was. But what's the use having it if I can't put
my hands in it? You 'ain't told, have you, Olive? You
'ain't told?"

"Never."

"Not even Bob?"

"No."

The two stood looking at each other; then Mr.
Nawn gave himself a slight shake as he said, "I believe
you. I knew I could trust you. Now I want you should
promise me something." He hesitated a moment, gazing at her. "'Tain't much," he resumed. "Only that
you'll stay here and keep my house 's long's I live. I'll
pay you decent wages; you can't ask for more than
decent wages; and you've got Victor; he's got to have
his board; you can't expect so much as if you hadn't
got him."

"I can't promise that," was the prompt reply.

"Can't? Why not, I should like to know?"

"Because—I couldn't. I might think I ought to go,
and if I had promised—"

"You're a little fool, that's what you are," broke in
the old man. "There ain't another woman within
twenty miles of the Red Bridge that wouldn't promise
for the sake of what I might do for the boy. But you

needn't count on my doing anything for you or the child, I can tell you that."

Olive drew herself up. Into her tired face there came a flash of fire. "I don't count on it," she said. "We shall have to take care of ourselves — Victor and I."

Her voice changed as it pronounced the words "Victor and I," but it was none the less firm.

"I guess you'll have to," was the rejoinder, "for I ain't one of those men who want to will away their prop'ty from their son. My son's a poor stick, and I wouldn't go and make a will in his favor, but I'd let the law take its course, and the law gives a man's prop'ty to his children." Olive made no response to this. She was turning away, thinking Mr. Nawn was ready to go up-stairs now. "You needn't be in such a hurry," he exclaimed, peevishly. "Go on ahead with that light," for Olive had the lamp in her hand; "I'm so thunderin' stiff I can't carry the cane and the lamp to-night."

Without a word Olive began slowly to mount the stairs in advance of her companion. She heard behind her the shuffle of his feet and the strike of his stick, and the sounds for the first time were to her somehow uncanny. She glanced behind, then she hurried on and waited at the head of the stairs, holding her lamp so that it should shine on the man's way. He came on slowly, and she watched him, noting his big, clumsy frame, and how pallid and pasty his thick cheeks were, how swollen his eyelids. All at once, as a scene flashes from a magic-lantern, there came to Olive's memory the time when she had walked to Nawn house to beg this man to be friends with his son. She saw her own figure coming hesitatingly up the rough path, and she felt again the same terror that was in her heart when she had lifted the knocker and heard the sound of Mrs. Barlow's approaching feet.

That was almost six years ago ; six years ago she had thought that she could not live without Robert Nawn. And he had seemed to care for her. Had that feeling of his been but the passion of a moment—absorbing, dominant for the time? How was one going to tell what was a permanent feeling? It was real, but not lasting. Well, perhaps there was nothing lasting in the human heart. Olive roused herself. Mr. Nawn had reached the last stair. He did not seem in any hurry to go to bed.

"Seems to me," he said, glancing at the lamp Olive carried, "that you've got that blaze turned up real high. There's no need of wasting kerosene." Olive turned down the blaze. Mr. Nawn stood before her on the landing. "You know that room next to mine here?" he said. She nodded. "Well, I wish you'd move into it. You'll find it more airy than that down-stairs bedroom."

"I'll fix the beds to-morrow," she answered.

"No, to-night ; do it to-night. I guess I'm getting old and notional. I want you up-stairs on this floor."

"But Victor may disturb you."

"I shall have to risk that. Do it to-night."

"Very well."

Now Mr. Nawn went forward into his own room. Olive set her light on the shelf and proceeded to grope her way down the stairs for another lamp. She had a strong repugnance towards taking this room, but she did not hesitate. As she fumbled down the steps, Mr. Nawn's voice called out from the open door of his chamber :

"Olive, you're a good girl."

"Oh, no, no," she answered, quickly.

A surprise, mingled with elation, came to her as he spoke thus. In all the time she had lived in the house with him he had never given her a word of commendation before. Perhaps he was going to die. She

worked quickly and with little noise. She made the
bed in the large chamber adjoining Mr. Nawn's room,
and then half led and half dragged Victor to it. He
whined, but soon he was as fast asleep as if he had not
been moved. Olive went from door to door and from
window to window, fastening them all. Before she had
finished the clock struck eleven. This was a late hour
for this neighborhood.

CHAPTER XL

LOCKING UP

THOUGH it was late, and Olive was very weary, she was sure that she could not sleep. She walked to one of the windows of the kitchen and leaned against it, looking out. There was no moon, but it was a clear night, the June stars were shining brightly. She removed the stick from above the sash and flung open the window, putting her head out, that the clear west wind might blow over it. A great many things had happened to her, she thought, within the last dozen hours. But everything was settled now. She was to live on here, but Robert was not to be with her; Robert was tired of her. The west wind made the leaves of the Lombardy poplars rustle, and the pine branches soughed softly back and forth. Olive felt as if she had come up against a high stone wall. So far as she was concerned, life was ended. She had had her day. A brief day it was, but sweet while it lasted.

Do you smile that a woman not yet thirty should say her own individual life was over? But Olive believed, nevertheless, that it was so. Only through her boy could she live now. Her boy! A glow spread from her heart through her frame; it lighted her eyes until they shone in the dusk. A man was crossing the Red Bridge. The gentle wind brought definitely the sound of his firm, decisive foot-fall. Olive listened a moment, then she drew down the window and carefully replaced the stick for a fastening Then, impelled by a nervous feeling of uncertainty about the locking up, she took her lamp and went all about the lower floor of the house again, pushing at sashes, trying locks ; she even went into the three disused rooms and saw that the dust and cobwebs were untouched on windows and doors. The musty smell rose and made her cough. Coming from the last of these rooms she heard Mr. Nawn calling loudly :

"Olive ! Olive, I say—where are you ?" She hurried forward, and, reaching the foot of the staircase, she looked up to see the old man, in his long night-gown, standing at the top gazing down at her. "Where've you been ?" he asked. Olive told him. "Is everything locked up tight ?" he inquired.

"Yes, everything."

"Then I wish you'd come up here. I wish you'd come into my room. I can't sleep. It's odd that I can't sleep, I call it. I want to show you something."

Olive went slowly up the stairs ; she did not wish to go into her father-in-law's room, but she went straight through the open door and saw him standing, leaning one hand on the table that stood by his bed. His lamp, the flame extravagantly large, was on the shelf ; but the room was spacious and the shadows in it were deep.

"You ought not to be up," said Olive, reprovingly. She glanced about to find what he had meant by his words, but she saw nothing out of the ordinary.

"Pooh !" he said, scornfully, "you can't expect a man of my age to sleep all night, can you ? Shut that door, will you, and turn the key. Now come here."

Olive obeyed. She felt dull, as one feels whose power of sensation has been used to the utmost. She was not much interested. Mr. Nawn was still standing with his hand resting on the table. Now that Olive advanced and saw him more plainly, she was aware that his whole appearance was keenly alert. His eyes sparkled under their thick brows ; his great crop of hair stood out more rampant than usual.

When she was within a few feet of Mr. Nawn she
stopped and waited. She wished that he would hurry
about what he had to say or do. And there was the
clock down - stairs striking one. The June morning
would soon be coming now.

"I thought I'd show you where I kept it," said the
old man.

Olive quickly put out one hand with a dissenting
gesture. "No, no," she cried ; "I don't want to know."

"That don't make any difference, as long's I want
to tell you," he responded. "It came over me, all at
once, after I got up here to-night, that I'd show you
where I kept it. Then, if anything should happen to
me, why—well, you see, it came over me that I'd do it,
and I'm going to. I might have known I could trust
Israel Newcomb's daughter. But I hated Israel Newcomb. Do you want to know why ? You needn't keep
standing there staring at me. Can't you sit down somewhere ?"

Olive walked to a chair and placed herself in it. Her
dull feeling was leaving her ; her pulse had taken on a
new beat. She had a distinct feeling of thankfulness
because she was well and strong ; she was very strong,
she told herself. But she wished again that she might
have been left to herself for the rest of the night. And
was Mr. Nawn going to be ill? How his eyes shone !
Though he held himself quietly and spoke quietly, he
seemed to be laboring under a subtle excitement.

"I'm glad you've sat down," he now said. "I feel
like talking. I s'pose a man does feel like talking sometimes. You see I sit and smoke, and there ain't anybody I want to talk to. Didn't I speak of Israel Newcomb ?"

As he waited for a response, Olive said, " Yes," and
again she advised her companion to go to bed and rest.

"Rest ? Ain't I resting all the time, I should like
to know ? There's Israel Newcomb—he was one of

the open-handed, generous kind; he'd always help a
friend." Mr. Nawn paused and glanced about the
room, his glance dwelling on a particular part of it.
Olive wondered why he should speak of her father.
"So, of course," resumed Mr. Nawn, "he died a poor
man. I wonder how much he got out of life? I've often
wondered about that. I had a notion for your mother
when she was a girl"—here Olive started; "oh yes, I
did; for she was a mighty handsome girl, and a young
man don't so much care whether a girl has any mind
or not. You know your mother isn't overstocked. You
don't take after her any. Newcomb must have found
her rather wearing as time went on—"

"Don't, please!" interrupted Olive.

"Oh, well, you needn't be sensitive about that; you
must know your mother's a shallow creature; not half
the woman your aunt Ruth is; but the men didn't care
about Ruth. I guess Newcomb must have got awfully
tired of his bargain. But he never showed it. He
stepped right in and courted Charlotte while I was
thinking about it; so she never knew that I had a fancy
for her. I hung her a May basket one May. I got it
cheap at the Falls, but 'twas a pretty one, all the same.
The next month she married Newcomb." The speaker
paused a moment, then he added, "Everything seems
as clear's a bell to me to-night, somehow."

"Aren't you tired? Won't you lie down?" inquired
Olive.

"Tired? What makes you keep harping on that?"
impatiently. "I never felt better in my life. And
things never were so clear." Mr. Nawn thrust his
hand into his night-gown pocket and pulled out a key.
He stood holding it in his hand and gazing at it for
some time before he spoke. Then he gave a little
laugh, as he said, "I reckon you've read lots of stor-
ies about where misers hide their money, ain't you?
You know they always have a secret panel, or some-

thing or other. You have to have some such thing as that. I've got mine in—but you give a guess where mine is—" looking at Olive with a sudden, knifelike directness. "You're bright enough; you guess."

Olive saw that she must obey without demur. She had not the least idea what to say, but she cast her eyes about the room and then pointed to an old desk. "Somewhere in that desk," she said.

"You must think I don't know much, then," he replied. "That's just the place that everybody would guess, that's where a burglar 'd go the first thing. No, 'tain't there. Try again."

"Oh, I can't!" cried Olive, impetuously. She felt an impulse to wring her hands, but she controlled it.

Mr. Nawn took little notice of this exclamation. He twirled his key over and over on his forefinger. "Speaking of burglars—I ain't ever been much afraid of 'em. You remember that time when one of 'em broke in here, 'n' you come to my help?" As Mr. Nawn asked this question he suddenly walked across the space that lay between him and his companion. Olive thought that he was going to grasp her arm, but he did not touch her. His heavy eyelids had flashed open widely, making his face different entirely in its aspect. "You remember?" he repeated, harshly.

"Yes," she answered. Though she did not move she yet appeared to shrink away, not so much from Mr. Nawn as from some thought in her mind. "I haven't guessed again about the hiding-place," she said, eagerly, casting her eyes about the room.

"Never mind; I'm thinking about that burglar," continued the old man. "He didn't know where my treasure was; if he had known he'd have got it and made off before I waked. He was a bungler, that's what he was. Odd there couldn't any trace of him be found, wasn't it, and he such a bungler?" Silence on Olive's part. Mr. Nawn repeated, "Odd, wasn't it?"

"I—I don't know."

Mr. Nawn raised his head as if the better to look at Olive. She did not meet his gaze; she had risen, and stood white and fearful before him as if she were dreading what he would say.

"Great Jupiter!" he cried out. "Do you—"

But Olive sprang towards him and flung herself upon him. "Oh, Mr. Nawn," she whispered, "what's the good of talking in this way? Let me guess where the gold is. You told me I must guess—don't you remember you told me I must guess?"

But the man only stared in silence for a moment. He cleared his throat as he began, "So you've known—"

"One can be sure of nothing—one is almost certain to be mistaken—I haven't anything to say—I—" Olive ceased speaking. She had spoken in gasps; but now she drew back in cold composure. "I am so tired that I'm horribly nervous, and you mustn't mind what I say."

"By George!" exclaimed the man. He glanced about him as if he were addressing some one. "If women ain't the most curious animals in creation, then I'll give it up!" He turned around and walked lamely towards his bed. He sat down upon it, and then he noticed the key which was still upon his forefinger. His face lighted at sight of this suggestion of his treasure. Then the light faded and he remarked, dully, "You haven't guessed—again. You see we got to talking of that burglar, and now I'm getting sleepy. Go to bed, Olive. You're going to sleep in the next room there, ain't you? Well, run along, then. If I want you, I'll call. No; bring me that bell from down-stairs —the old dinner-bell, you know. That makes a thundering racket. I'll ring that if I want you. Now go along." When Olive reached the door, Mr. Nawn said, "You're a good girl, Olive; but the best part of it is, you c'n be trusted." He raised his voice as he con-

tinued, " Now don't you ever let Bob blind you again ;
don't you ever do it. Do you hear what I say?"

" Yes, I hear."

" Then you mind. He could deceive the very elect ;
that's because he's in earnest at the time ; but it doesn't
last—nothing lasts with him, only his love for money,
and he doesn't know how to get that. And he's got his
mother's winsome ways; but his mother wasn't anything—she was just nothing, I tell you !" in a louder
voice. " I s'pose she had a hard time with me, but
then I had a hard time with her, so we were even.
She'd steal my money every chance she got. I had to
have a place to hide it in. I tell you "—still louder—
" if you let Bob blind you again I sha'n't pity you.
Let him have his Isabel. That's the one he ought to
have married. Why don't you go? What are you
waiting for?"

Olive hurried down the stairs. She brought back
the bell and placed it on the stand close to the bed-
head. Mr. Nawn was now lying down. Olive looked
at him, and a quick, strong pity came over her. She
bent and kissed his forehead. She was surprised at
herself as she did so, but the giving of this caress
brought a feeling almost like tenderness to her heart.

" Olive," said the old man, quickly, " you're a good
girl. Don't you let Bob blind you any more. Do you
hear me ?"

And again she answered, " Yes, I hear." She went
softly into the next room and shut her door. She
prepared herself for bed, wondering that she should
be so calm. She did not know that the reaction had
come, and she must be calm. She looked at her boy's
face as it lay on the pillow, and she smiled as she
looked. Then she laid herself down by Victor, and
began to listen for the sound of the bell ; but in five
minutes she was asleep, holding the boy's moist hand
close to her breast.

CHAPTER XLI

THE BELL RINGS

OLIVE thought it a curious thing that she should have slept so soundly. It seemed to her that she had but just closed her eyes when she became aware that some one was violently pulling her hand, and a voice very far off was calling out insistently, "Mammy! Mammy, I say!" Then presently the same voice said, "What makes that bell ring so? I say, mammy!"

When she did waken, Victor had begun to whimper because he couldn't make his mother hear, and a bell was ringing loudly in the next room.

"Be quiet, Victor; it's gran'pa."

She rose and hurried into the hall and to the old man's door. She turned the handle sharply and pushed, for the door had swollen and always stuck to the frame. The next moment she knew that it was now locked. The bell continued to make such a din that she was sure Mr. Nawn could not hear her if she shouted; nevertheless, she did shout. But she could not wait. She pounded and kicked at the door. If Mr. Nawn would only stop ringing the bell he might hear her, and let her in.

All at once the bell made a final clash and jangle as if it had fallen, and then all was still. And now the man would come and unfasten the door. But perhaps he was helpless and could not come. It was ridiculous that he should have fastened the door. The entire stillness was worse than the noise had been. In that stillness, bare feet came softly over the floor and a

19

hand grasped Olive's hand. Then Olive thought of a way.

"Come, Victor," she said, quietly. She led him down the stairs, and the two went out-of-doors into the beauty of the June morning. It was not quite three o'clock, but the light was making the east glow. The birds were singing everywhere; they were drunk with the mere joy of being alive with their mates. But Olive did not think of June or of the birds. She took Victor to the great honeysuckle which clambered up over half the house on the west. It was the same honeysuckle into which she had looked from the room where Victor was born five years ago; and then she had heard Isabel Keating singing:

> " Here's to him that grows it,
> Drink, lads, drink !"

She thought it strange that she should remember this so vividly when her mind was full of other thoughts. As she stood there looking eagerly at the stout old vine she was repeating mechanically:

> " Now here's to him that stacks it,
> Drink, lads, drink !
> That thrashes it and tacks it,
> Clink, jugs, clink !"

But it appeared to be something outside her mind, while it was yet of it, that said this at the very instant that she started back at the discovery that some one had clambered up by that vine and by the tough oaken trellis that had at first been its support. She glanced at the soft earth, already overgrown with the springing grass and weeds of June. There were the marks of a heel ground into the soil; the next glance told her that these marks had been made by feet flying from the house, not approaching it.

"Victor," she said, quickly, " I want you to climb up

by this vine and get into gran'pa's room. Then you
must unlock the door and let me in. I'll run up the
stairs. Can you do it?"

"Just as easy as nothing," was the instant rejoinder.

The boy began to swarm up the side of the house,
the gray flannel legs of his night-gown following each
other as if he were some kind of an animal whose mis-
sion in life was to climb.

"I'm afraid gran'pa's sick," called out Olive, as she
stood a moment watching Victor. And then a shud-
dering horror came to her. What would the boy see
when he reached the open window? In the flash of
an instant a dozen dreadful pictures went before her
eyes. She ought to run into the house and up the
stairs that she might be ready at the door. But her
feet held their place as she stared upward.

Victor reached the window-shelf. The top sprays
of the vine had been wrenched down and hung dan-
gling. The boy put his hand on the shelf and pulled
himself upward. His eyes were just on a line with
the first open space. Olive could see his profile. She
saw the grayness come to his cheek. He looked
through the opening.

"Mammy!" he shrieked.

"Hold on! Don't drop!" she called. "Go in! Go
in! Open the door for me!"

She saw how his little brown hand clinched on the
ledge. A chimney-swallow swooped down angrily at
the tousled head.

"I'm afraid! I can't!" he cried.

"My boy!" she called, "be brave! help your mother! I'm going up the stairs. I sh'll be waiting for
you at the door."

And Olive ran, not knowing that her feet touched
anything until she was shaking the locked door and
shouting encouraging words to Victor. Then she
heard something skurry across the floor, the key was

turned and the bolt drawn, a little form flung itself
into the skirt of her wrapper and hid its head in the
folds.   When she entered this form clung to her and
dragged on her, but she hardly thought of it.   She
stumbled over the bell which had rolled partly across
the room.   The bell jangled.   Why didn't she look?
For a breath she withheld her eyes from that thing
not far from the window.   But though she withheld
her eyes she knew it was there, on its back, with chin
upturned.   And on the floor two gold pieces lay, one
lying partly on top of the other.   They shone dully.

Olive violently pulled Victor from her skirts and
thrust him outside the door.   "Perhaps I can help
gran'pa," she said.   "You wait; I may want you.
Victor, be my brave boy!"

She shut the door swiftly.   There was no more hesitation now.   Without any perceptible repugnance she
went forward and knelt down by that ponderous form;
as she did so a gold piece rolled away from her foot
and went merrily over the floor.   There was a bloody
spot on the man's head.   Now that Olive was bending closely over him he did not look so stark as when
she had opened the door.   He was in his shirt and
trousers now.   He must have risen and partially
dressed.   She thought he had been sleepless, and had
been counting his money again.   She had her hand
on his heart, holding it steadily there as she thought
this.   Yes, his heart beat.   After all, she might help
him.   She rose to her feet and stood a moment, thinking.   One terrible fear ran through her mind.   She
went back to the door and opened it.   Victor was sitting on the top stair, and he turned towards her.   Oh,
the unspeakable comfort the sight of that tanned,
childish face gave her!   She restrained the impulse
which bade her catch him up in her arms and console
him for his fright.

"Victor," she said, her voice ringing somewhat, "I

want you to run to Mr. Jewett's, and ask him to saddle his horse and go for the doctor—quick! Tell him gran'pa's dreadful sick."

The boy rose. "I ain't dressed, you know," he said.

"Never mind; 'tis not cold. And, Victor, don't say anything but that gran'pa's sick."

"No, I won't."

The boy slid down the banisters and darted out-of-doors. Olive went back to the prostrate man. She used all the simple means within her reach to revive him, but nothing availed. All the illness she had known had been that of her grandfather, and he had faded away slowly. When she had done what she could she looked about the room. She picked up the bell. There was a little blood on one edge and a few gray hairs stuck to it.

Mr. Nawn had a thick mat of hair, enough to be some protection. He had plainly been struck on the head with this bell. Some one had wrenched the bell from his hand and struck him. Olive stood gazing down at the edge of metal to which the blood and hair clung. That same terror was in her mind.

"Why should any one know of that blow?"

She asked the question aloud, and then turned about quickly. She hesitated; then she hastened down the stairs to the sink where she pumped furious strokes, sending the water dashing over the bell. She gathered the three or four gray hairs and burned them in the stove. She took the bell, cleaned and dried, back to the chamber and dropped it on the floor not far from the old man's outstretched hand. She ran down again and thrust her foot back and forth in all the marks of that other foot that had been beneath the window earlier. She moved feverishly. She returned to the chamber and tried again with brandy and pungent salts to revive the unconscious man. There was a fixed look to the face, not like death. It was a look

she had never seen before, but she was ignorant. She
examined the room.   Could he have fallen, by any
chance, against the edge of that heavy oak table?   It
stood in a position to warrant that suspicion.   She
wished now that she had not cleaned the bell so quickly; she might have put some of that blood on the
table edge.

At this stage in her thoughts she drew herself up
suddenly.   "Oh, what am I doing?"   And again she
spoke aloud, finding a relief in so doing.   She pushed
one of the gold pieces with her naked foot; for she
had been dressed only in a wrapper.   But now she
clothed herself in her usual day garments and hurried back again.   Already it seemed hours since Victor had gone.   It was exactly fourteen minutes.

Olive felt an eating desire to keep at work hiding
what she could, but she dared not do too much lest
she might be questioned, and she did not think that
she could lie—not even for—   Here her mind slid off,
as one might skate away from some dreadful object
that lay, face uppermost, on a field of ice.   She looked
about for the chest of money, but there was none in
sight; and the old man's chosen place in which to
hide his money was not disclosed.

Stooping down once more over Mr. Nawn, Olive saw
on the forefinger of his left hand the same key which
he had been twirling as he talked to her a few hours
before; it was as if he had placed it there, perhaps
after having used it, so that he might have it ready,
or might feel that he knew exactly where it was.

And now the sound of a galloping horse was heard.
Olive thought of Isabel—she would always think of
Isabel at the sound of a galloping horse if she should
live a thousand years.   But this time she was sure that
it was Mr. Jewett's horse.   She ran to the window.
Yes, there was Marcus Jewett, with Victor on behind.
The horse was pulled in long enough for the boy to

slip off, then it went on again, and Victor came running towards the house. He saw her looking through
the glass and he shouted :

"Has gran'pa got well?" She shook her head. She
went down the stairs and had the boy dress himself.
She fastened his clothes with cold, steady fingers. "Is
gran'pa dead?" asked Victor, and again she shook her
head silently. "I heard Mr. Jewett ask somebody if
old man Nawn would have his money put in his coffin.
Will he, mammy?"

"No—no. And I hope he'll get well."

The boy sat down on the floor and began to draw
on one of his shoes. He paused and clasped his
knee. "The honeysuckle was torn down," he said ;
"that best branch, that I've been watching, was pulled
off."

"Victor!" Olive's voice broke forth in a cry. The
boy stared hard. Immediately Olive said, gently, "I
thought I saw you tear the honeysuckle down yourself
when you climbed."

"So I did, some. But not that big top spray ; it
dangled into my eye, so I noticed it."

"It's no matter," was the response.

"But I've been watching it," with the persistence '
of childhood; "Lizzie Fuller 'n' I were looking at it
yesterday ; she said 'twouldn't reach the attic window
this summer, 'n' I said 'twould. And now it's all down,
draggling about. Did the wind blow awful last night,
mammy?"

"No. You'd better tie up your shoe."

Victor stooped over and pulled the lacing together.
"Then I don't see how the vine came down like that.
Lizzie 'll notice it ; she says hers grows faster 'n' ours ;
but it don't. Where'd gran'pa get that bell?"

"It's the old dinner-bell."

"I thought so, but who took it up-stairs?"

"I did. Gran'pa wanted it."

Victor tied the shoestring in a hard knot.   His
mother stood watching him, feeling her eyes burn
into the back of her head.   "If gran'pa dies, shall I
have his money?"

"No, indeed!   Your father 'll have it."

"Mr. Jewett told somebody when he was dressing
himself that it was a mean shame for popper to have
all that money.   I heard him, for the window was wide
open."

"It was wrong for Mr. Jewett to say that."

The boy's face was very serious.   He pulled his
jacket over one arm, then paused with it hanging.   His
eyes, with the deep wonder of youth in them, were
raised towards his mother.   "Ain't my father a good
man?" he asked.

This was the second time he had put this question,
and again an uncontrollable pang went through Olive's
consciousness.   She started forward and drew the jacket over the boy's shoulders.

"You must be dressed by the time the doctor comes,"
she said, precipitately, "for I may need your help."

"Oh yes, mammy," eagerly, "I'll help you all I can."

CHAPTER XLII

In an hour later the doctor had come to Nawn house. Victor and Mr. Jewett followed him into the room where the old man still lay, and where Olive sat beside him. The doctor's eyes darted over the surroundings ; they saw the gold still lying on the floor, and the bell. He did not seem to look at the unconscious man before he said, " Paralysis." He and Mr. Jewett lifted the great, inert bulk, staggering under its weight. They laid it upon the bed and the physician stood gazing down at it. Then he wheeled about and glanced at Olive and remarked :

" It's paralysis, anyway. But he's had a blow." His eyes glanced off towards the table. He stepped forward and ran his finger along the oak edge. " Probably he hit his head there when he fell. And what's all this gold about ? He was counting it over, I suppose." The man bent again over the bed. " It isn't much use. We're helpless, almost, before a thing like this. But we'll try. He may partially rally, but I don't think he'll ever speak again."

The news spread through the hamlet that old man Nawn had had a " stroke," and that he was lying senseless. Miss Rice said she was informed that the old man was found "almost covered with ten-dollar gold pieces." She put on her sunbonnet and went across the bridge to offer to help Olive, but Olive replied that she could get along by herself, with Victor to run of errands.

Miss Rice pushed back her bonnet as she bent forward. "Where's Robert? Have you sent for him?" she inquired. She said that people were asking her where Robert was, and she should like to know what to tell them.

Olive turned her head towards her visitor and met her eyes as she answered, "If they ask you where Robert is, you can tell them that you don't know."

At this moment Esther Rice was simply to Olive like an insect that stung, but that could not be brushed away.

"Good gracious!" aghast. "Don't you know, yourself, where he is, Olive Newcomb?"

"No, I don't."

Miss Rice's vapid face grew more animated. "Oh, the old cat!" she cried. "Is that so? I guess I'll be goin'. I've got to borry some black pepper for dinner; we're goin' to try to have some picked-up fish, 'n' 'tain't good 'thout pepper. I'll come in agin 'fore night; mebby you'll want some help by that time." She stepped to the open door. "If there ain't your mother 'n' Aunt Ruth comin'! Had you sent for 'em?"

"No; but Victor's been there."

The hours passed, somehow. Olive never had any definite memory of the rest of the day, but her mind all her life held tenaciously the picture of those early morning hours. Years after she would dream of watching Victor as he climbed up by the honeysuckle, and she would waken, weak and perspiring.

By noon Mr. Nawn had opened his eyes; but he could not move. There was intelligence—an anguished, helpless intelligence—in those eyes that was dreadful to see. Olive forced nourishment between his teeth. She sat down by his bed and held his old, corded, helpless hand in hers, pressing it closely. She had taken the key from the finger and it lay on the table among the bottles and glasses. When it drew

towards night, Olive, who had been secretly waiting
all day, asked her mother to take her place, as she had
an errand to do.

"Can't you send **Victor?**"

"No; I must go myself. Will **you** sit here?"

The old man's eyes followed his daughter-**in-law as**
she walked from the room, then **they** closed tightly, as
if to shut out the sight of the woman **who** had taken
her place.

Olive did not hesitate. She took her hat from its
hook near the kitchen door, and she walked quickly
over the bridge, her intent face turning once towards
the water below as she hastened along the foot-path.
There was a fear in her mind that she should see **the**
same spectre countenance that had looked up **at her**
from the river. **But the river was clear, of** a pale yellow, and still full from the spring rains.

Olive went as straight and fast as she could to the
Keating place. **If** she **wished** to hesitate when she
passed through the gateway she did not allow herself
to do so, but walked to the door and lifted the knocker.

It was Isabel herself who opened the door. "What,
you?" she cried, stepping back. "Come in."

"**No, I** won't **go in.** I **want** to ask you a question."

"**And** you **won't put** your foot in my house?"

"There **is no** need."

"I will come out, then. Somebody might hear us."

Isabel stepped outside and drew Olive down to the
path. The roses grew along this path, and the air was
sweet with them.

"**Is Robert here?**" asked Olive. She reddened pain-
fully as she spoke, and she compelled herself to look
full in her companion's eyes.

Isabel returned her gaze unblenchingly; but over
the clear darkness **of** her face there spread an ashen
tint. Still, Isabel **was not** thinking so much of the
question which had been asked her as of the fact that

this was Robert's wife who had come to her, the woman who had a right to love him. "Only he isn't worth it," cried Isabel, impulsively, answering the thought in her mind, and not the question which had been asked her. "I don't know why God has made us women so that we should love a man who hasn't the truth in him. Do you know why God does such a thing as that? Tell me, Olive—tell me."

Olive drew back a step. The blush left her face. Her voice was hard as she answered, "We will not discuss Robert, if you please. Is he here?"

"No."

"Are you telling me the truth?"

"The truth."

Olive was turning away, but the other woman caught hold of her skirt.

"What's happened?" she asked, breathlessly.

Olive flashed round upon her, but she controlled herself; she said, calmly, "Haven't you heard?"

"I haven't heard anything. I've been away for three days, and it's not half an hour since I came home. What is it?" Isabel's words came so hurriedly that they tripped over each other.

"Old Mr. Nawn had a paralytic stroke last night. He can neither move nor speak."

Isabel gazed a moment before she asked, "Will he get well?" She was thinking of all his father's death would mean to Robert.

"He can't get well; but he may live a while. If you know where Robert is you should have him come back. People may suspect something if he stays away at such a time."

Again Olive was turning away, and again Isabel delayed her. This time she held fast to the fold of the skirt she had taken.

"Suspect?" she repeated. "What will they suspect? Don't look at me like that. Speak, can't you?"

But Olive was not going to bear any questioning. She forcibly detached her gown from the hold upon it. "No," she answered, "I can't speak. Perhaps I have said too much. It would look well for Robert to be here now. Take my word for that. If you know where he is, make him come back."

Olive walked down the path. The tall rose-bushes brushed their blooms against her as she went. Furtively she put forth her hand and took a rose, crushing it hard in her hand and then dropping it. She heard Isabel's feet hurrying after her, then Isabel, close to her, said, piteously:

"Olive, Olive, I say! I don't know where he is. I can't send for him; I can't make him come back. Olive! Don't look like that!"

The other woman paused long enough to speak; but she looked steadily ahead of her; she did not wish to see Isabel's face again now. She wished that she might never see it again.

"You will hear from him," she said. "You will be sure to hear from him. Make him come back to this neighborhood."

This time she hastened on, and Isabel did not follow her. When Olive returned to her home, she went first to the bedroom that had been hers. She moved without noise, for she hoped her mother would not hear her. She could not speak to any one yet. She locked the door with the big wooden button that Mr. Nawn had whittled out and screwed on when the key was lost. He had said that he wouldn't spend any money for a new key. It seemed to Olive that, at every turn she took in that house, some sordid memory rose and smote her. She had spoiled her life. That was the thought in her mind.

She was sitting on the side of the dismantled bed. Through the open window came the sound of insects humming, and from the direction of the Creeper she heard children's voices. She distinguished Victor's tones, mingled with those of his playmate, Lizzie Fuller. Victor! Why had she named him thus? At this moment she felt that she had been victor over nothing. She rose and walked to the window. The narrow panes blurred before her eyes. She must not linger any longer here. She went with a resolute air up to Mr. Nawn's room.

Her mother started from a doze in the sunlight that came over her as she sat by the bed. "That you, Olive?" she exclaimed, trying to speak animatedly, as if she had not been sleeping. "Mr. Nawn's be'n asleep every minute you've be'n gone. You needn't have hurried. There ain't no change in him, nor ain't likely to be. There, I declare, if he ain't opened his eyes, now you've come! It's the first time, though."

Mrs. Newcomb spoke as if Mr. Nawn were a block of wood concerning which she could make any remarks she pleased.

The old man's eyes, intense, flaming with intelligence, were fixed upon Olive's face. She could not restrain a tremor as she met their gaze. It was as if a countenance carved out of wood had had set in it these vivid eyes—strong, uncanny. She walked to the bed and took the inert hand in her warm clasp. She looked intently down into the eyes, which had retreated still farther under the clifflike brows. Her heart melted with pity.

"Can't I do something for you?" she asked.

The eyelids fell as if with a movement of assent. But what could she do?

"You mean, yes?" she asked. Again the eyelids fell.

She stood holding the hand that could not move. She was silent, thinking. How could his mind reach hers? She bent her head, for she could hardly bear that searching, pleading gaze. How could that mind

"SHE WALKED TO THE BED AND TOOK THE INERT HAND IN HER WARM CLASP"

dwell in that senseless, moveless mass? Couldn't she think of something? She must—she must— Suddenly she remembered Monsieur Noirtier. Her face flushed. Her eyes looked into Mr. Nawn's with quick hopefulness.

"I've thought of something," she exclaimed.

She dropped the hand she had been holding, and left the room. She returned immediately bringing her school dictionary, and paper and pencil. She saw the man's glance go to the book; she held it up so that he could see. A stream of light came from his eyes. Meantime Mrs. Newcomb was gazing absorbedly, but Olive did not notice her. She leaned against the foot of the bed and opened the book.

"It 'll be slow work, but we can do it."

Mr. Nawn's eyes shut and opened rapidly.

"I'll begin with A," Olive explained. "I'll watch you, and when I get to the right letter you must shut your eyes. Do you understand?"

Mr. Nawn closed his eyes emphatically.

"Good land!" cried Mrs. Newcomb. "How'd you happen to think of that? But do you call his mind clear enough?"

"I know it's clear enough. And you mustn't talk so. He understands you perfectly."

"Why, he's just like a log!"

"Don't, mother!"

Mrs. Newcomb sat back in her chair. Olive began with the alphabet and went on to S, when those sharp eyes shut again.

"It's S, is it?" she asked. Yes, it was S.

She was getting more excited. The concentrated intelligence in that gaze was agitating in the extreme. She went on with the letters until she had spelled the sentence, "Send her out." Then Mr. Nawn's eyes turned with startling impressiveness towards Mrs. Newcomb.

"Mother," said Olive, "you must go.   He wishes to say something which you must not hear."   Olive could hardly command her voice.

"Well, I never!" responded Mrs. Newcomb; but she rose and left the two together.

CHAPTER XLIII

"PROMISE"

OLIVE found that her hands were beginning to tremble. She walked slowly, that she might go steadily, to the chair her mother had just left. She sat down in it and leaned forward against the bed.

It is impossible to describe to one who has never seen it the effect of such intelligent eyes looking forth from a dead face, for virtually this man's face was dead, drawn rigid.

"Shall we begin again?" Olive put the inquiry in a whisper. Mr. Nawn's eyelids said yes. "Won't it tire you too much?" The eyelids sprang open widely.

Olive opened the dictionary. She could have accomplished the same thing without this book, but her mind was not calm enough to make the effort to keep the chosen letters in her memory; it even seemed to her that she could not, unaided, recite the alphabet correctly.

Before she began, Olive shut the book once more, looking at Mr. Nawn. "I'm going to try to bear whatever you tell me," she said, her hands clasping over the volume. "Yes, I must bear it. But I'm afraid—I'm afraid."

Her eyes dropped. She could not prevent a shiver from running over her. The face turned towards her was precisely the face she had seen gazing up at her from the Creeper—still, inanimate, with blazing eyes. That she had seen it had been the freak of a disordered, suffering mind, she knew that very well; and the only explanation now possible was on the ground of mere coincidence. She roused herself. How sweet the air was which came in through that open window. She could not bear to inhale that sweetness now. She rose and went to the window to close it. Victor and Lizzie Fuller were running up from the river towards the house. She heard Victor saying as he ran :

"If that branch hadn't been torn down, my honey-suckle would have run higher 'n your's, anyway. Le's look again." Then the boy saw his mother at the window, and he laughed up at her. "Lizzie's caught two horn-pouts," he called out.

Olive nodded ; she shut the sash with a quick hand and walked back to her chair by the bed. "We'll begin," she whispered. She felt as if some one might overhear her.

She ran over the alphabet. It took a long time, or it seemed to do so. She had spelled the words "It was," when she put up her hand. "Wait," she said. But she found that she could not wait while those eyes were consuming her with their unswerving gaze. She commenced—"A, B"—at B she was stopped, and she set down the letter. She knew when she would be stopped again, and she was right ; but she went through the alphabet, and began, once more to have those imperative lids fall at B. That was the end of this sentence. She read it, leaning far forward towards the old man, and whispering, "It was Bob."

Mr. Nawn closed his eyes rapidly three or four times.

Olive sat silent and frozen. She was asking herself stupidly why, since she was frozen, the blood in her burned as it coursed through its channels. And she had known it was Robert, known it with every heart-beat since she had found Mr. Nawn lying on the floor. She started, alert again, impatient at the slowness with which she could talk with Mr. Nawn.

"Don't tell any one else!" she cried, but still in a whisper. But the man held his eyes perfectly still, as if thus to signify that he would not promise. "He struck you with the bell?" asked Olive.

"Yes."

"He wanted your money?"

"Yes."

The imprisoned eyes travelled to the book on Olive's lap. She was calling off the alphabet, when the door opened and Mrs. Newcomb entered, bearing a cup that steamed as she came forward with it.

"It's time the doctor said he must take his nourishment," she explained.

Olive managed to cause some of the strong hot soup and wine to run down her patient's throat. If possible, Mr. Nawn's eyes grew brighter. He looked at Mrs. Newcomb, and her daughter requested her to leave the room again.

When the two were alone Olive asked, "Aren't you too tired to go on now? Oughtn't you to rest?"

"No—no."

Laboriously, painfully, the conversation continued.

"He wanted your money?" repeated Olive. She endeavored strenuously to think of leading questions which might be answered by affirmative or negative. "Did he get it? Did he get the gold you keep here?"

"Yes."

"You were ringing the bell for help—for me?"

"Yes."

"And he took the bell from you and struck you?"

"Yes."

"And besides that blow, perhaps because of it, you have paralysis?"

"Yes."

Olive began to have a feeling that her companion was becoming impatient under this catechism. But wasn't this what he wished to tell her? She became

silent for a moment, watching Mr. Nawn's eyes. She
saw that they dwelt on the book which was lying upon
her lap.

"Shall we go on?"

"Yes."

She spelled out the word "promise." "You wish me
to give you a promise?"

"Yes."

Olive's mind began to arm itself. She warned herself to be careful. If she gave her word she must keep
it ; but not even a dying man should force her to give
her word. The sentence following was spelled.

"Never give any money to Bob. Promise."

"But I'm not likely to have any money."

"Promise."

"It's a foolish promise. I'm a poor woman. You've
always said that Robert naturally inherits your property ; and—and if he marries Isabel he will have her
money."

"Promise." Mr. Nawn reiterated that word with
his eyes. Then he looked at the book, and Olive began the alphabet.

"You're a fool," she spelled.

She sat silent. But in a moment she exclaimed, "I
dare not promise!" She dropped her pencil and twisted her hands together. "It is not in the least likely
that I should give him money, even if I should have it,
and I shall never have it."

Mr. Nawn ordered her to spell again. It was the
same word, "Promise."

She rose to her feet. She was deathly white. "I
cannot—I cannot. If he were suffering—if he begged
of me—could I treat him worse than any beggar?"
Mr. Nawn looked at the door. "Do you mean that I
am to go?" she asked.

"Yes."

"Can't you forgive me for not giving such a prom-

ise as that ? Think how it would bind me !" The old
man kept his eyes fixed on the door. "You send me
away ?"

"Yes."

Olive went out of the room. She met her mother
at the foot of the stairs.

"Is he dead ?" asked the elder woman.

"No ; go and sit with him."

Olive hurried on out-of-doors. She wished to find
Victor. She longed to have his arms about her neck.
She longed to have him press up against her. She was
not able to think clearly now ; but she might be comforted by the child's presence. She left the house and
walked towards the Lombardy poplars. There was
the sound of voices in that direction. There he was,
down on his knees with the little girl, and both were
heaping up gravel into a long ridge.

"Victor !" called his mother. The boy lifted a smear-
ed and perspiring face. "I want you," she said.

"Wait a minute." She stood patiently. Presently
the boy came, rubbing the palms of his hands on the
legs of his trousers. "I can't stay," he said ; "Lizzie
'll be needing me."

Olive made no reply. She stooped and took the
boy's hand closely. The two walked on in silence, but
the woman did not notice which way she was going.
After a few moments Victor said, "Mammy, you
squeeze my hand awful hard."

Without replying in words, Olive relaxed her hold
somewhat. Another moment passed and Victor remarked, hesitating in his walk and looking back, "We
were building a dike—to keep the water out, you know."

"Were you ?" absently.

"Yes. Lizzie's father told her about Holland ; 'n'
we've been living in Holland more'n a week. We've
got to keep the ocean out, somehow."

He tried to pause in his walk, but his mother kept

on, and she still held his hand. They were walking
across a field now. They had climbed a wall without
Olive's knowing that she had done so. The newly
leaved sweet-fern and bayberry bushes crushed under
their feet sent up a pungent fragrance. But Olive
did not perceive it. Her mind was filled with one
thought—that she could not give that promise. It
was a dying man who asked the promise of her, but
she could not give it. Could she promise never to help
Robert, if he were in need? She would not have
money, save as she worked and earned it. When Mr.
Nawn was dead she would find some occupation that
would bring her in wages. She must educate Victor ;
her boy had a bright mind. No woman had ever worked as she would work.

"Mammy, I say, where *are* you going?" Somewhat
querulously from the boy.

They were clambering over the rocks of what was
called "the high pasture." She stopped short and
turned her face towards the valley through which the
little river ran, a June sun shining upon all. The
sense of the great beauty of the scene before her helped to break the hot bonds upon Olive's heart. She
sat down upon one of the rocks ; the tension relaxed,
her eyes filling with tears. She drew Victor within her
arm. "God knows it's wrong for me to think of giving such a promise," she said, aloud.

"What promise?" asked the boy, instantly. He put
up one soiled finger and tracked a tear down his mother's cheek. The action was gentle and solicitous. At
times this boy had very gentle ways with him—winning ways that melted and won you, and that startled
his mother with a fear lest he might have still other
traits like his father. "What promise?" repeated Victor, insisting upon an answer.

"I can't tell you now."

"When will you tell me?"

"I don't know. When you're older. Then I will explain this time to you and ask you if I did right."

This hope, that she could some time ask her son's advice, and lean upon his counsel, was soothing to Olive. Her mind ran forward to the years when her hair would be gray and life would be placid; when Victor would be a good, trustworthy man—as good a man as Israel Newcomb had been. She would be glad then that she had not given such a promise. In some way, as she sat there in the pasture with her arm about the child, the memory of the boy's father seemed blurred to her, and she gave humble thanks that it was so, even for the moment. The sunlight fell warmly on the two, and it comforted Olive, though she would not have expected it to do so. God's sunlight, she called it. She liked to think that God wished the sunlight to comfort her; that He was her Father, and would not try her too much. To a woman, the conviction of the general beneficence and rectitude of the universe is not enough; there must be some sense of the individual, the person, in it all.

Victor nestled a little. "Ain't it queer about Holland?" he asked. "I shouldn't want to live there; should you?"

"No," absently. But though she replied in that manner, the mother was keenly conscious of the help it was to feel Victor near her.

"And you don't know when the dikes 'll give way, you see."

"You can't know," was the response.

"And then the ocean would rush in—rush—rush—and swallow up everything. Just think of it, mammy!" The boy spread out his arms and made a great hissing noise with his tongue set against the roof of his mouth. Then, without any warning of the way his mind jumped about, he exclaimed, "What's a divorce, mammy?" Olive started. The sunlight ceased to be lovely. Victor repeated his question, and then, for a wonder, didn't wait for a reply, but went on quickly. "Tommy Jewett told me my father was going to have one, anyway. Tommy's always saying horrid things, and I know this was horrid by the way he said it. I was mad, 'n' I kicked him. I said popper wasn't going to have one. Now is he?"

"I think he is." Olive was sitting straight now.

"Oh! Well, I'm glad I kicked Tommy. He howled good. When's father going to have it, 'n' what does he do with it?" Victor was gazing with large eyes into his mother's face. He had withdrawn slightly that he might look at her better. Then he drew nearer, with an impulsive movement, and asked, "Don't you want him to have it? Is that what makes you cry; or is it 'cause gran'pa's sick? I shouldn't think anybody 'd cry if gran'pa dies. I sha'n't." The boy pushed the moss at his feet with his copper-toed shoe.

CHAPTER XLIV

DEATH

" Don't talk that way." Feebly from Victor's mother.

" Why not ? I don't love gran'pa any. Do you?" No answer. " Do you?"

" I'm very sorry for him."

" But that ain't loving. What's a divorce ? I asked Lizzie Fuller's mother what 'twas, and she said 'twas a bill. What's a bill ?"

By this time Olive's resolve was taken. She drew Victor nearer to her. " A divorce is a separation made by law between a man and his wife—after that they don't live together any more."

The boy gazed bewildered. " You're popper's wife, ain't you?"

" Yes."

" And he—why, does he want to get rid of you?" with a wide opening of the eyes.

" Yes."

Victor flung himself away from his mother's side. His face turned crimson. He threw out a clinched fist. " I hate my father ! I hate—hate him !" he shrieked.

" Oh, Victor, Victor, hush !" Olive reached out to get hold of the boy, but he evaded her hand.

" You needn't say hush, mammy. I knew 'twas horrid. I'm glad I kicked Tommy. Popper's a mean skunk !"

" Victor, stop !"

" You sha'n't stop me, I say ! And you sha'n't have a bill, if you don't want it. He's a mean skunk. I won't let you have a bill, mammy ! I won't !"

Olive's tears had ceased coming ; her eyes were shining with an excitement that was not all suffering.
"Victor, you mustn't talk so about your father," she
said ; "I will not allow it.   And you can't stop the divorce ; I wouldn't have you, if you could."

"Why, do you want it yourself?"

"If your father wants it, I want it."

Victor's face wrinkled in his confusion.   He was evidently trying to understand, and quite as evidently
failing to do so.   "But it makes you feel bad?"

Olive hesitated ; but, with those clear eyes gazing at
her, she did not think of prevaricating.   "Yes, it makes
me feel bad—or "—with a sudden and bewildering illu-
mination pouring into her soul—"it did make me suffer."   She paused, and then she added, with an air of
finality, "We won't talk of it any more.   And you
needn't speak to anybody about it.   You are too young
to understand.   When you're older, I'll explain everything to you."   She leaned towards the child and held
out her hands, crying, passionately, "Come—come, Victor—come into my arms.   Oh, do I love you too well?
I don't want to love you too well."

Surprised and stilled, almost afraid, Victor moved
into his mother's embrace, where he was held closely
while Olive tried to subdue the sobs that shook her.
Ever since she had lived with the Nawns she had
shrunk more and more from becoming emotional.   She
was repelled by her husband's fits of furious temper ;
more dreadful still, she had begun to feel that his rarer
and rarer seasons of caressing her and of pouring forth
words of love meant only a temperamental outlet that
was as fleeting as it was ardent.   It did not mean love.
Once she had been positive, happily convinced that it
was she alone who awakened such a mood.   But now—
ah, she was in the way of becoming very wise and very
hard, she thought.   Did wisdom always bring hardness?   Perhaps hardness was a good thing.   It would

be well to be like the diamond, that could wound others, but that could not be wounded itself. Has there ever been a sensitive human being who has not had times of thinking thus? No, she must not be emotional.

"Mebby you've got a fever, mammy," whispered Victor, after a few moments. He had remained almost motionless, but now he drew away and gazed at her wistfully. She smiled at him.

"No, I haven't any fever. But I'm tired, Victor. You mustn't mind if I am tired. Now we'll go home, and you can go on with the dike-building."

Hand in hand they went down the pasture. With a very visible pride, Victor helped his mother over a stone-wall, bracing his small body back on his heels to keep himself steady, as he said, "Put your hand on my shoulder." She obeyed him, her eyes growing dim as she did so. But she resolutely put away the soft mood.

When the two reached the house, Olive went directly to the sick man's room. She trod noiselessly, and she found that Mr. Nawn was asleep on his bed, while his watcher slept on her chair.

Mrs. Newcomb rose; she began whispering hoarsely that it "always made her sleepy to set still; and there hadn't be'n nothin' to do, anyway; 'n', for her part, she thought Mr. Nawn was failin' fast. Anybody could see by lookin' at him that he couldn't hold out long."

Olive motioned to her mother to go, while she herself sank into the just vacant chair. She sat gazing at the motionless face on the pillow. The head was upturned slightly, giving a marked prominence to the chin. It was in something such a way that this man had been lying when she had found him senseless on the floor. Yes, her mother had been right when she said that Mr. Nawn was failing. Though that face seemed inanimate and expressionless, there was yet upon it an indescribable look that showed a decrease in strength. The old man was fading away. He had not many more days, perhaps not many more hours, in this world. The time went on swiftly as Olive sat there. Often time has a weird swiftness of motion when you watch by the bed-side of the sick.

The night came on. Mrs. Newcomb brought in a kerosene lamp, lighted. Olive noticed that the wick was high, making an extravagant blaze. She rose quickly and turned it down.

"We must not waste the oil," she said, reprovingly.

The elder woman gave a very audible sniff before she answered, "I guess some folks is past saving kero-sene."

"Hush !"

As Olive said this one word, she turned towards the bed and saw that Mr. Nawn's eyes were open ; he was looking at her with intelligence. Then he glanced at the book which she had put on the table. She took it directly.

"Please leave us," she said to her mother; and when Mrs. Newcomb's petticoats had swished indignantly down the stairs, the daughter bent over the bed.

"You wish to say something ?"

The eyelids fell immediately. She spelled out that one word, "Promise," again.

She dropped the book. She bent over until the young eyes and the old eyes gazed into each other at the distance of only a couple of feet. At first her voice did not obey her summons ; then she said, "Listen to me, Mr. Nawn. I am a poor woman ; I shall be a poor woman all my life, probably ; but, even so, I might be able to help Robert. What if he should need help? What if he should ask me? Could I say no to him? I might save him. I cannot promise—I cannot promise."

Mr. Nawn's eyes closed, and remained closed for a time. Olive took his hand, as she had done before. There was something high and solemn in her face.

She held the hand closely. After a few moments the old man opened his eyes again and directed them to the book. The sentence spelled was, " No matter." A rest, and then, " I sha'n't last till morning."

After that he seemed to sleep. The doctor came, but there was nothing to do, and the doctor said, " He won't last till morning."

When the physician had gone, Olive sent her mother to bed. She told her that she should need no help, but that she would like to have her in the house. Victor came softly and with an awed face to the door, kissed his mother good-night, and went to bed in the next room.

It was only the night, or rather the very early morning, previous that Mr. Nawn had been seized. But it seemed as if days had passed since then. Olive sat by the bed in the dimly lighted room, looking at the large form over which the bedclothes laid straightly, stirred only by the slow, slight heaving of the chest.

At eleven o'clock Mrs. Newcomb came in to stop by her daughter's chair and whisper, in that strident way in which some people speak in a sick-room. " I waked up," she said, " 'n' I thought I'd look in the almanac to see when the tide turned. You know they often go out with the tide. It's jest six minutes to four that it turns. Don't ye want me to spell ye?"

" No, you must sleep." So Mrs. Newcomb went down the stairs again.

At four o'clock the sky was gay with soft, pink clouds; the earth sparkled, the birds sang, the air was sweet. It was at four that Mr. Nawn opened his eyes and looked brilliantly at the watcher by his bed. His face was changed. Olive took the book and paper and pencil. Her cold fingers trembled, but she steadied them. The two spelled this sentence : " You are a good girl." A moment later the eyes had dulled, then rolled upward, the imprisoned jaw dropped heavily, the breast no longer heaved.

CHAPTER XLV

EVERYBODY said first, "I wonder where Robert is !" They said this before old Mr. Nawn was ready for burial, and they continued to say it. Somebody, more daring than the others, wondered if Robert knew anything about who stole that gold from his father. Very likely it was the shock of losing his gold that brought on the stroke.

When this had been said once it was said again, with the addition that young Nawn had got into trouble about money; he had been gambling in stocks with old Drake at the Falls; he was in love with Isabel Keating, everybody knew; and he had just got his divorce. He was in a bad way generally. Well, what could you expect of a fellow who was old Nawn's son, and whose mother's relatives, some of them, had been— well, very queer indeed? Though Robert, to be sure, when he had married Olive Newcomb, had seemed to be well enough. Still, people now remembered that they had thought that Olive, being as nice a girl as ever was, ought to have considered a great while before she married young Nawn. But the two had been in love, if ever a man and woman had been in love. You couldn't tell—you didn't know—how things were coming out.

It was very plain that Robert ought to come home. Here he was, owner of all the property that had been his father's; and he was a free man now; he could marry Isabel any time. What would Robert do with the boy?

Fortunately for Olive's peace of mind, this question about the boy was not put in her hearing. But she knew that the divorce was an accomplished fact. She had been informed officially of the proceedings. She refused to speak on this subject to any one. Even her mother could not make her break this silence. Two or three times Olive had gazed at her mother intently, while a peculiar look came to her eyes; this was when she was thinking that it was her mother who had gone to Robert Nawn and told him that her daughter was dying for him. "And I was dying," sternly, to herself, "and no one ought to have meddled. How can a man or woman dare to meddle?"

The funeral was over; the great house stood in the June sunshine without its old master. The grass and pudding-bags had been trampled in the wide yard by the feet of the horses that had dragged the hearse to the door; the gay orioles flitted in the poplars, and the sweet air rang with their frequent song—the bird-flute that plays the same song for the funeral and for the wedding.

Where was the new master of the house? Already Olive was gathering her belongings together, and pitiably few they were. She would not stay here; she would go to her mother's with Victor, immediately. She would not stay another night in this house, which belonged to Robert Nawn but not to her husband.

She was standing in the great, empty, south front room, where she had brought her things to put them in a trunk that was open there. Her mother had gone on to tell Ruth to have hot biscuit for supper, and to make two pans, and to open a jar of quince preserve. Victor was walking here and there about the house, occasionally coming to his mother to ask a question or make a remark. He had just informed Olive that Tommy Jewett had told him that his, Tommy's, mother had said that Olive and her boy needn't have moved if it hadn't been for that divorce, and that it was a shame.

"Is it the divorce that makes you move, mother?"

"We won't talk of that," had been the answer, with more severity than Olive usually employed in addressing Victor.

"Lizzie 'n' I c'n come up here 'n' finish the dike 'n' play Holland just the same, can't we?" he asked. But before any reply could be given he exclaimed, "Oh, there's Isabel Keating coming across the road. I'm going to meet her; I like her."

A swift hand caught the boy back. Victor looked up frightened into his mother's flashing face.

"Like her—do you?" she cried; then, instantly recovering herself, Olive dropped her hand and said, coldly, "Go, then."

But the boy shrank away bewildered. He had never seen his mother look like that. The next moment he had walked slowly out of the room.

Now Olive heard a step on the grass of the yard; a girl came up to the open window. There was no salutation between the two; they glanced at each other in silence.

"Has he come back?" asked Isabel. She was pale and her eyes were hollow.

"No; but he may have come. How should I know?"

Olive advanced to the window. She stood beside it and leaned one hand heavily against the wall.

"He ought to come," said Isabel; and she added in a whisper, "Do you know what they're saying in the neighborhood?"

"No."

"Folks are wondering if 'twas he that took the old man's gold. They're saying dreadful things about him. Hadn't you heard?"

"No."

"Do you think he could do such a thing?" Isabel

came nearer and her whisper was still lower as she asked this question. There was no answer. Isabel put her hand through the open space beneath the raised sash and touched Olive's arm. Olive moved away from the hand. "Do you think he could do such a thing?" she repeated.

"I don't know," Olive answered, slowly.

"You came to me and told me that Robert ought to come home. I've been thinking a great deal. You needn't be so afraid I shall touch you, Olive Newcomb."

"I'm not afraid."

"Yes, you are. You despise me. You needn't. I thought I was a brave woman and didn't care for any-thing." Isabel peered into the room. "Are you alone in there?" she asked.

"Yes."

There was nothing of Isabel's ordinary, dashing grace of manner in her appearance now.

"I thought I didn't care for anything," she went on, "but something's come over me. Just to think of Robert's— But perhaps he didn't do it." No answer from Olive. "I'm sure you want me to go away," went on the girl, "but I'm not ready to go yet. Did you know the divorce had been granted? Incompati-bility, I believe."

"I knew it had been granted."

"I suppose so. But you didn't know that old Mr. Nawn paid all the expense. And he hated to part with money. Robert told me his father had hurried him about starting the affair." Olive was silent. She was confused, and yet there was a gleam of understand-ing in her mind. Why didn't this girl go away? "I couldn't help coming," said Isabel, almost humbly. "It's so strange for me to feel frightened. You'll see Robert; he'll want to see you. He won't stay away now that all this property is his. And the boy—what about the boy?"

21

"Nothing about him," sternly.

"You know they often give the child to the father; you must know that." Olive stood quiet; Isabel, watching her, felt her own heart contract as she looked at the face before her. "You must have thought of that," she said.

"No," said Olive, speaking thickly, "I hadn't thought of that. No one will ever take Victor from me—no one save God!"

After a silence Isabel exclaimed, "How curious it must be to love a child in that way! I never should."

She turned away, walking slowly, almost as if she were old, out towards the road. She looked up and down the highway, mechanically, and not as if she expected to see any one. As she looked, a horse and buggy came on to the bridge from the farther side. The horse trotted briskly, and the sound of his feet on the planks mingled pleasantly with the babble made by the birds as they flew among the trees and shrubs. Presently Isabel went on along the road and she met this equipage, the horse trotting steadily up the slope. There was only one person in the buggy, a man who, when he saw Isabel, pulled in the lines and lifted his hat as he asked:

"Can you tell me where the old Nawn place is?"

A flush came to Isabel's cheek. She was one of those women who are involuntarily different, more awakened when addressed by a personable man; and this man was tall, well-dressed, with a strong face and strong eyes.

"That's the old Nawn place," answered Isabel. She pointed as she spoke.

"Thank you."

The man drove on, and in a few minutes his horse was standing fetlock-deep in the coarse grass of the Nawn yard. After looking about him, the stranger at last found a place to hitch the animal. He took a

"'CAN YOU TELL ME WHERE THE OLD NAWN PLACE IS?'"

green baize bag from the carriage, and, with it in his hand, he went towards the door.

Olive had been standing just where Isabel had left her. She had not been thinking, she had merely been suffering. She vaguely heard the steps and tried to rouse herself. When the old knocker clanged she walked to the door, which was partially open.

The man took off his hat again. " I was told this is the Nawn place."

"Yes, it is."

Olive did not know that the man's eyes had seen her comprehensively, that they had taken in the noble, unconscious pose of sadness and womanly power, the ripe attractiveness of that face with its pallor and sorrow, that were not at all the pallor and sorrow of a weak woman.

"I have come to see Mrs. Nawn—Mrs. Robert Nawn," said the man. "My name is William Hyland."

"I am Mrs. Robert Nawn," replied Olive ; then she caught at her words—"no, I'm not. I don't know what I am."

Her eyes, large with pain and bewilderment, were raised to the stranger. He extended his hand quickly and took her hand. He led her into the house and to a chair.

"I understand," he said, gently, "and I know you've been suffering. You were Robert Nawn's wife. You were Olive Newcomb."

" Yes."

" You are now divorced. But I suppose you will still choose to be called Mrs. Nawn, on account of the child. I am told that there is a child?" interrogatively.

" Yes," answered Olive, "there is a child." She was sitting motionless, holding fast to the arms of her chair.

"You wish to retain the custody of the child ?"

"I do !" as if she were taking her oath.

"That may be considered later. I came—"

"It need not be considered," in a savage whisper that was yet perfectly quiet, "I shall keep Victor."

Mr. Hyland had not seated himself ; he was standing in front of Olive, one hand resting on the top of a chair. It was a large, well kept hand, very white, and suggesting great muscular power. As its owner continued looking at the woman before him this hand gripped the chair more closely, but the man's face did not change.

"I came," he resumed, "to inform you concerning the late Mr. Nawn's will, and to advise that it be probated at once. I am the junior member of the firm of attorneys, Cabot & Hyland, of the Falls Village. The late Mr. Nawn had very little work for lawyers, but what he had he gave to us."

Olive made an effort to listen, though it was with difficulty that she could detach her mind from the thought that even a suggestion could be made that Victor should be taken from her. "Mr. Nawn did not make a will," she said.

Mr. Hyland smiled. His smile broke up the too resolute expression of his features, and gave a suggestion of something warm and very human. "Pardon me," he returned, "he did make a will."

"But," began Olive, "he always said that he should not do so ; he said he didn't believe in interfering with the prospects of the heir, if a man had an heir." She spoke hurriedly, and there was an expression of confusion on her countenance.

Mr. Hyland smiled again. "It is of no consequence what a man says in comparison with what he does," he responded. "I am aware that the late Mr. Nawn used to talk like that. It's a curious thing that some people are pleased to deceive others ; they chuckle to think what a surprise they will cause some day. I have a copy of the will here. It's as strong a docu-

ment as ever was written. Indeed, the maker of it
threatened us with coming back from his grave to
punish us if there should be a weak spot in it. I flat-
ter myself there isn't a weak spot. With the exception
of one or two little legacies—to speak accurately, two
legacies: one to his son and one to his old house-keeper,
one Barlow—the entire property is yours, Mrs. Nawn ;
yours to do as you please with, absolutely without a
hampering clause. But you are advised not to let
Robert Nawn get any of it—strongly advised. We
counselled the late Mr. Nawn to tie up the whole so
that you couldn't give any to Robert Nawn, but the
testator would not hear of that. He said you should
be a free agent ; he said, excuse me, that he really
believed that you were not the woman to be made a
fool of the second time by the same man. Of course
I don't know what he meant. It isn't necessary that
I should know. Old Mr. Nawn was a richer man, I
fancy, even than he was thought to be. He made
shrewd investments ; he never lost, and he never spent
anything. The entire estate will figure up to something like eight hundred thousand dollars. I am ap-
pointed executor and administrator. I shall probably
be obliged to confer with you frequently until the estate is settled." Mr. Hyland had spoken in a matter-
of-fact tone, watching the face before him as he went
on. "Do you wish to hear the will read, or will you
look it over?"

He took a document from the bag and extended it
towards Olive. But she shook her head. She could not
speak. She was thinking that now she had means to
fight those who should try to take her boy from her.

CHAPTER XLVI

MR. NAWN'S LETTER

At last Olive stirred slightly in her chair. She raised her hand to her head, pressing the palm across her eyes. The stranger was watching her. It was interesting to him to see how a person received the unexpected news of the ownership of great wealth. Usually some phase of innate, long-hidden selfishness cropped out unmistakably.

"Is it true?" Olive had removed her hand from her head and was now leaning forward towards the lawyer.

"Oh yes, quite true," he replied. "Of course it is difficult for you to realize, at first. If you would read the will, the written words would help you to a belief in the fact."

"No, no. I believe it, since you tell me so. But it is strange — strange." Olive's eyes wandered to the window; she looked through it and on to the lush growing grass of the meadows near the Creeper. To be rich—to be rich—that meant everything for Victor. "God help me to help my boy!" she said, aloud, forgetting for the instant that she was not alone. Then she colored deeply, casting down her eyes.

"Amen!" said Mr. Hyland, softly. He drew the chair around and sat down in it. He returned the copy of the will to the bag, but he took out something else, an envelope sealed and addressed. He held this envelope towards Olive, saying, "This is a letter to you. I don't know what is in it. Mr. Nawn, our client, left it with us a few months ago, to be given to you as soon as possible after his death. It may contain instructions, but you understand that no instructions given in that way are any more binding than advice which may be followed or may not be. You should not think it more necessary to obey a request simply because it was made by one who is now dead. It is for the living to decide for the living. But this is not lawyer's counsel, Mrs. Nawn, it is only a friendly suggestion ; and now I will go. I shall directly take the steps necessary to put you in possession. Meanwhile, consult me at any time."

Mr. Hyland rose and looked around for his hat. Olive rose also, but she had a vague expression upon her face. She was plainly trying to adjust herself to the thought of the future that was opening before her. The gentleman walked towards the open door. He found his hat upon the table in the hall. He noted the sordid shabbiness of everything, the desolation. Only that woman standing there, poor as were her clothes, was not shabby. "Good-bye, Mrs. Nawn," he said.

Olive started forward. She extended her hand as if she would place it on his arm, but the hand dropped. "You're a lawyer, Mr.—Mr.—"

"Hyland. Yes, I'm a lawyer."

"Then there's one thing, Mr. Hyland, that I want you to help me to do. I've no one else to ask, no one ; and you're wise, I suppose, and strong."

Here she paused. She had an indistinct feeling that there was too much thrill in her voice. As for the man, he was thinking that he had never heard so sweet a voice. But he waited, without speaking, wishing he might, indeed, be the wisest and strongest in all aid he could give this woman. Olive clasped her hands tightly, then dropped them again. Since her emotion was so strong, she must endeavor to seem cold.

"I hear"—she began in rather a high tone—"that it is possible, since I am divorced, that my child may be

taken from me. I must have him. He shall not be
taken from me. Spend all this money, Mr. Hyland,
but don't let them take him away. I'm his mother "—
she unconsciously raised her hand and put it against
her throat as if she were choking—"he loves me—he
belongs to me. I do fully believe "—solemnly—"that
it will be better for him to be with me. His father
never cared greatly for him, so Victor does not much
love him. Ought I to tell you all this? I don't know,
I am very ignorant. I've lived right here and done
house-work. But, I say, I must keep my boy—at least,
until he is older, and can understand and judge."
Olive took a step forward. Mr. Hyland was perfectly
aware that he was hardly an individual to her, that
he was only something that might possibly help her
keep the boy. "If I know anything," she exclaimed,
with fervid solemnity, "I wish for what is best for
him. He ought not to be with his father. Oh, what
am I saying?"—reddening deeply—"and to you, a
stranger. You can understand that I might be excited by all this."

"She isn't thinking much about the money," were
the words in the lawyer's mind. Aloud he said, in a
simply practical way, "You must remember that you
cannot speak too plainly to your legal adviser, Mrs.
Nawn. He should know absolutely everything that
bears upon the case. You empower me to act for
you, and to give counsel?"

"Yes. And do not forget that there is only one
thing in this world that I really care about—the best
good for my son." The mother spoke these words as
if she had opened a page of her heart, and the man
reverently felt that it was so.

"I shall do all I can," he answered. Then he walked
down the path to his carriage.

At the same moment a door in the rear of the house
opened and shut noisily; thickly shod feet clattered

over bare floors, and Victor flung himself upon his mother.

"The floods have gone over the dike, mammy," he cried; "we're goin' to have an awful time. I wish I had a boat so I could save Lizzie Fuller."

"Hush !" said Olive. "Don't be so rough."

"Who's that man?" in a lower tone.

Mr. Hyland looked at the open door-way and raised his hat in farewell. He saw the tall, pale woman with the anxiously brilliant eyes, holding by the hand a stalwart, sunburnt boy. She bowed in response to his salutation. Then the man drove away.

"Olive ! Olive, I say !" called a voice from somewhere in the back of the house.

"Yes, mother," was the reply. But Olive did not move. She stood holding Victor's hand at the open door. There came the thought that she and Victor were just starting out in a new life.

Mrs. Newcomb came forward into the hall. She had on her best black dress, but the skirt of it was turned up and pinned about her waist, and she wore a long white apron over it.

"I was wonderin' if I should put the bread and pies into that basket, 'n' so take um home to-night," she said.

"No," responded Olive, "you needn't take them. I shall stay here."

"What's that you're saying?" shrilly. "You told me 'fore the funeral that you shouldn't stay here another night."

"Mother," replied Olive, gently, "don't talk about it now. I only know that I'm going to stay here at present. Perhaps"—and here a curious and exhilarating sense of power made itself felt, though dimly—"perhaps I shall make some changes ; and it may be that you and Aunt Ruth will come here to live."

Mrs. Newcomb's eyes became wild. She was afraid her daughter "wa'n't right in her head."

"But this is Robert's house now," she said, "'n' I must say 't I shouldn't think you'd want to stay here one single instant. 'Ain't you got no pride, I sh'd like to know?"

Olive was about to say that it was not Robert's house, but the strangeness of the fact made her hesitate. Could she be mistaken, after all? "I've changed my mind about staying here," was her answer.

She looked back into the front room where she had listened to the startling news. She saw an envelope lying on the table. That was the letter which the lawyer had said Mr. Nawn had left for her. Victor had darted away to his dike and his imaginary flood.

"When I've had time to think, I'll talk with you," Olive now said to her mother.

"I saw a buggy going down the road—has it been here?" inquired Mrs. Newcomb.

"Yes—a man from the Falls on business." Olive had gone into the front room, and now held the letter in her hand.

"You needn't trouble yourself," returned Mrs. Newcomb, testily, "I guess I c'n stan' it 'thout knowing; 'n' if I can't, I sh'll be likely to see Esther Rice 'fore sunset, 'n' if she don't know, I'll jest give it up, that's all."

Mrs. Newcomb passed on into the back of the house again, and could presently be heard clattering dishes indignantly. In the midst of all other feeling, these two women experienced an uncanny sense of freedom, which they enjoyed, though it seemed rather wicked to enjoy it.

Olive went out-of-doors. She held the letter. The superscription was in the close, heavily written hand of the dead man. She paused under a thick pine-tree, but that seemed too near the house. She went on until she stood beneath a great willow, whose branches swept about so broadly that the farther twigs touched

the opposite bank of the Creeper, for this tree grew on
the river's bank. Here was the place in which to read
her letter. This little river was associated intimately
with her life; it was an old friend. She looked down
at the golden-brown sands at the bottom. It occurred
to her that this lawyer—was his name Hyland—had
eyes of the color of this warm-tinted sand on the
Creeper's bed. She did not know that she had noticed
them, and she forgot them directly.

Old Mr. Nawn was buried. He had been buried
four hours now, yes, more than four hours. Why did
she hesitate in regard to the letter? Why do we hesitate at such moments? There seems to be no reasonable reason, but the fact is that we pause at the
edge, and thrust back curiosity and interest. Leaning
against the stem of the willow, Olive opened the letter
that the old man had left for her. It was a thick, long
epistle, and she wondered that it should be so. It began abruptly, and every sentence sounded so like the
writer of it that, as she read, Olive heard Mr. Nawn's
voice as plainly as she had ever heard it:

" It was that business of the butter-mould that first set me thinking.
You'll remember it, fast enough. I was mad with you. I wanted to sell
a bit less than a pound for a pound, and you put a spoke in the whole
affair. Oh yes, I was mad, but when Bob took my side I was madder
with him than I had been with you. I thought it was thundering mean
of him to take up in that way. But Bob is mean, there's no mistake
about that, and he's always been so afraid that he wouldn't get my
property. I shall laugh in my grave when I think of his face when he
finds out. Only I sha'n't think, and so sha'n't laugh. But perhaps I
shall know somehow. I hope I shall. You're a good girl, Olive.
How tremendously sorry I was for you when I found you over there at
the Raymore place when Bob was putting down the carpet ! That is,
I was as sorry as I ever am for anything, save when I lose a dollar
somehow. But that doesn't happen often—I look out for that.

" You see, I knew Bob. I'd known him all his life. He hasn't a
fine thing in him, really. I haven't much, but I do believe I'm a peg
ahead of him. But he's got the face of an angel—no, I mean of that
handsome god—just the kind that women go wild about and endow

the owner with everything noble.   It's unaccountable about women.
Though you're one of 'em, I'll bet you can't explain 'em.   And Bob, when
he was in the mood, had a smile, and such ways—his mother right over
again, only he's a man and she was a woman, and a woman can go
ahead of anything male in that line every time.   You see, I'm writing
helter-skelter, just as I please, and you may read it or not.   But I guess
you'll read it.   I mean you to have this before I've been twenty-four
hours buried.   I shall give it to Hyland, and Hyland 'll do as he says,
though he is a lawyer.

"Yes, it was the butter-mould begun it.   You looked kind of grand
when you said you couldn't use that mould, and you gave me a mighty
strong feeling that you were a right-up-and-down woman, and could be
trusted.   You wanted to do right, too.   There's a lot of talk about
wanting to do right, but who cares about talk?   I gave in about the
butter after Bob had remonstrated with you.   You'd always yield if you
hadn't a principle in the way ; I found that out.   You'd try to eat bran
so as to be saving, if we wanted you to eat bran.   I s'pose you didn't care
so very much if you were hungry.   But when the boy came—why, then
you stood out for nourishing food, if it was plain, for him.   Do you remember that day you wouldn't give the brat skim-milk, though I suggested that you do so, and Bob immediately added that we couldn't afford to drink milk with the cream in it—we ought to make all the butter
we could ?   You repeated that the boy was growing and needed proper
food.   You didn't say it before Victor, though.   He got the fresh milk;
he always had it.

" Don't you think, if I'd chosen to do it, I could have stopped all that?
I'd have put my foot down.   Bob was bewildered because I didn't put
my foot down.   He got off the track, but he didn't know enough to
get on again.   I watched you closer 'n you knew, for when I used to
sit in the kitchen and smoke, I saw every motion you made—I knew
you didn't waste a thing.   The dish-water went into the pig-pail every
time.   I saw how you cooked.   You naturally had rather a lavish hand,
being Israel Newcomb's daughter, but you changed.   As the months
went on, your face changed too.   I tell you, I kept my eye on you.
You knew I watched you, but you didn't guess how closely.   I did
hate to see that line come between your eyes, and that close shutting of
your mouth.   But I couldn't help it.   You'd got Bob hitched to you,
and you'd got to get along as best you could.   If Bob came home and
smiled at you that line faded away.   But finally it didn't make so
much difference whether Bob smiled or not.   And you didn't know
what he was up to—how should you ?   And there was that other girl in
the background.

" Very soon the boy began to be a comfort to you.   Don't love that
boy too well, Olive.   You just mind what I say.   He doesn't look

like his father, or seem like him, but, for all that, he may have a streak in him that 'll spoil the whole lot. Don't set your heart on him. But you will; your experience with your husband won't teach you anything."

Here Olive paused and leaned her head back against the tree, her eyes wandering down the stream. That question and that fear which very rarely left her mind were called into acute life again—would Victor be like his father? She had studied the boy as one studies the most precious thing in the world—hoping and fearing. But who could tell? Sometimes she had moments of resolving that she would not love Victor so much. She would be reasonable in her affection. This resolution was entirely without any result, save that, for a very short period of time, it gave her the sensation that she was defrauding herself. Nevertheless, she was frightened when she stopped to think how she loved the boy. She let her heart pour itself out upon him. This love gave her so deep, so exquisite a happiness that it was as if she were insured against all ills so long as she had Victor. She had felt that so often. She could suffer deeply and keenly, but the very citadel of her heart was safe so long as she had Victor.

As she sat there now, with the old man's letter on her lap, she began to do what she so often found herself doing—reckoning up how many years Victor would still be a child. While he was a child, if God spared him, he would be hers. She was greedy at thought of all the weeks and days. She would hold them, she would give herself a leisurely sense of their dearness and sweetness as they passed; not one of them should slip by without being fully tasted. She would never have to say to herself, "Oh, why didn't I realize?" She would gain that rare art of really living her present.

Then, in upon her other thoughts flashed brilliantly the new knowledge, "I am rich." She humbly asked God to make her able to use her wealth well. She

must make it a blessing instead of a curse. Surely the
Nawn money had never yet been a blessing. How
strange it all was! She shut her eyes and bent her
head. Again she saw that pile of gold on the old
man's table, and the look on the old man's face as he
put his hands in it. And now he had been called away,
and he had left his gold.

She lifted her head. A narrow bar of sunlight came
between the trees full upon the letter in her lap. She
began to read again. Her eyes travelled once more
over the words, "Your experience with your husband
won't teach you anything." "Why should it?" she
asked, aloud. "Victor is a child—he is my own."
Then, with a ferocious accent, "No one in this world
shall separate us! No one! I'm strong for that!
Thank God, I'm strong for that!"

It was some moments before she could command her
attention. The bar of sunlight had travelled a little,
and was now lying across her face. She would not
move to avoid it. A sudden superstition made her
think that it would be a "bad sign" if she were now
to avoid this June sunlight. Why is it that an intense
love of any kind tends to make us superstitious?

With the sunshine in her eyes, Olive yet managed to
read the heavy black writing on the page before her:

"I'm going on with this document at odd times, because I rather like
to do it. I enjoy thinking of your surprise when you find you're a rich
woman. Of course your first thought 'll be of the boy.

"I can tell you the exact minute when the idea of giving you my
money came into my head. It was after I got over being mad about
that butter-mould. And Bob seemed so mean. I was mean; but, by
George! I never could think of half the mean things to do that would
hatch themselves out in his brain. He would gamble in stocks even
while he pinched a cent. I got almighty sick of thinking that he was
going to have my money; but I kept on talking as if I shouldn't make
a will. That was my joke. If there's any life after you're dead, you
may think of me as chuckling over that joke. Bob thinking that I was
living too long, and longing to push me to one side and put his hands

into my gold ! I guess not. I've made the strongest kind of a will, and
I've left him five thousand, and old Barlow five thousand. The rest is
yours. I wouldn't make any restrictions. If I live a few years, you'll
have your eyes opened as to that scamp of a husband of yours, and
you won't give him anything. Mind you don't ! Mind you don't !"

These last words were heavily underscored. Olive
hurried over them, for her eyes had seized upon the
lines following :

"You remember that night the burglar came into my room, and you
ran in and helped me, and the villain got off? You didn't know who
he was, did you ? I never dared to ask."

Olive rose to her feet quickly. The bar of sunlight
had glided on beyond her.

CHAPTER XLVII

INSTEAD of reading any further now, Olive began to fold the sheets of this letter from the dead. She folded them accurately, as if much depended upon the precision of her work. She was not thinking of anything she had been reading, save these words: " You didn't know who he was, did you?" Ah! Hadn't she known? Had not the knowledge dwelt with her as a sort of under-consciousness?

How much does it require to kill a woman's love? Did she love that man now? She began to tremble as she lived over again that moment when she had laid hold of the burglar in Mr. Nawn's room. He had flung her from him, and she had fallen. The instant her hands had touched him, she had recognized him. The very fabric of his coat seemed to send a message through her fingers. She had had no suspicion until that instant. And she had loved him after that. She had carried this knowledge about with her ever since; and she had been able to conceal it from Robert when he came home that early morning. She had let him kiss her; more than that, she had been glad to be in his arms, and to kiss him back again. She made excuses for him in her mind. Perhaps he looked upon his father's money as, in a way, his money; and his father was so very close with him; and poor Robert must have been in a great strait. She had reasoned in that way, and had loved and pitied him.

"I won't read any more now," she thought; "I'm

confused. I have Robert's money—no—I have the money he expected to have. And I'm not his wife— and he will hate me. It is as if I stood between him and what he longs for. Oh, I can't understand it—I'll go back to the house. There are many things for me to do." She began to retrace her steps.

It is true that the love of some women takes a great deal of killing. Their ideal is so entangled with the real that it is almost impossible for them to disentangle it. You draw the real man as well as you can, and the spectator wonders that a woman could have loved such a being. How can her love cling so? But don't forget that it is not the man whom his acquaintances see who is so beloved. Was it the curl of his lip, the turn of his eyebrow, a tone of his voice, that made her invest him with the attributes she could love? Who can tell? When the mysteries of the universe are made clear, perhaps that mystery will be solved. Still, if the man be a good sort of fellow, though not at all the hero she fancied him to be, then her love may subside into a rather comfortable, humdrum friendship, and total shipwreck be averted.

Olive walked slowly, holding the letter shut tightly within her hand. She was surprised that her mind was at liberty to take in the early summer beauty of the country about her. She noted how the brakes had unfolded since she had been on this path the last time, and that the oaks, instead of wearing little rolls of maroon-colored velvet, now had broad, glossy leaves.

She stooped to pick one of the large ferns. When she raised herself, she saw Robert coming along the narrow path towards her. She stopped instantly; she involuntarily looked about to see if there were a tree near, against which she could lean. But there was not; so she stood straight and waited, the letter in one hand, the fern drooping from the other.

Robert came forward quickly. He was evidently

22

going to take her hand, but she made no movement,
and he drew back a little, giving her a questioning
glance. He was pale and worn, but his eyes were brilliant, and he was very handsome, his pallor perhaps
adding to that distinguished appearance which so
markedly characterized him.

"So father is gone," he said, at last.

"Yes." Olive found herself examining the man before her with a new and remote interest, as if she were
some one else, or as if he were some one else.

"I'm sorry it happened that I was away," said Robert. There was no reply to this remark. Olive fancied
that there was a sort of satisfaction mingled with the
real solemnity on the face before her. "I was called
away suddenly," he went on, "and as I might return
immediately, I sent no word to any one." There was
no reply to this, either. Robert put his hands in his
coat - pockets, then took them out again. "It was a
great shock to me," he continued. "I saw the notice
of the death in a Boston paper, and I came home ; but
it was only last night that I happened to look at the
paper. It was sudden, wasn't it ? Father always seemed
so well and strong, though he had aged some. Was the
funeral to-day ?"

"Yes, at eleven this forenoon."

"It was a great shock to me," repeated Robert. Then
he seemed to make an effort, and let his eyes dwell on
Olive's face for an instant. "You needn't be anxious,"
he said, in a constrained voice. "I suppose that father
left property enough, so that I can provide in some
way for you and the boy—that is, if we think it best
for you to have the boy. He'll be an expense to you.
I sh'll do as well as I can, if father left funds enough.
But, of course, you'll have to live in a very small way
—a very small way. You may be able to find something to do to help along a little."

Olive raised the fern she was carrying and examined

it closely ; she actually saw the delicate fronds. But she was hardly thinking of anything—she heard what this man had just said.

Robert looked at the brake, which waved slightly in the wind. He had an impulse to step forward and snatch the thing away, therefore he put his hands in his pockets again. "It was a great shock to me," mechanically reiterating his former words.

Olive raised her eyes. Robert started as he met her glance ; it was cold and clear and contemptuous. He had never seen contempt in those eyes before. "Was it ?" she asked.

"What do you mean ?" quickly. "Of course it was. Father seemed well when I saw him last."

Olive hesitated before she spoke again. Then she dropped the fern ; she clasped her empty hand over the one that held the letter. "Things might better be plain between us," she said.

"Plain ?" he echoed. "Why, yes ; I suppose you've been informed that the divorce has been granted. That's all the affair that I know about. Father approved."

"Yes ; but it wasn't the divorce."

"Not ?" Robert grew yet more pale. But he stood steady and waited.

"Your father told me something before he died."

"But he couldn't stir nor speak, they said. What are you talking about ? I don't know what you're driving at," loudly. "You'd better speak plainly, if you want me to understand."

"Yes, I'll speak plainly. You came to your father's room to take the gold he kept secreted. He tried to defend it—he rang the bell—you took the bell from him and hit him with it—he fell. I know that, besides his fall, he had a 'stroke'—if that is any comfort to you—and you got the gold, save a few pieces that were scattered on the floor. Do I make you understand? Your father spelled out the words from the alphabet to me. He spelled, 'It was Bob.' Don't you think I knew what that meant?" The young man took a step forward, with a gesture as if he would grasp his companion's arm. But she retreated, and held up her empty hand. "Were you going to touch me?" she asked, haughtily. "I have something more to say. I knew you that first time you tried to steal that gold. Good God! I loved you then! What was I that I could love you?—you!"

A crimson so deep that it was almost black rose and covered Robert Nawn's face. It subsided, leaving his face gray. "Did he tell any one else?" he whispered. He glanced about him among the pines and maples. "You spoke so loud. Did he tell any one else? Does any one else know?"

"I believe that I am the only person who knows."

"Why do you speak so loud?" anxiously, glancing about him again.

"My voice is low. I don't wish to publish your crimes."

"That's it — that's it," eagerly. "I'm sure you wouldn't want anybody to know. I couldn't tell whether you suspected or not, that other time; but I was quite sure you'd keep still. And it was just the same as my money, anyway. You know how father was. He wouldn't hear to reason. I wanted to borrow of him. He wouldn't lend; and he told me once that if I ever raised any money on my expectations, he should surely find it out, and he'd make a will. He'd do it, too. I had to have the money—that was the fact; I had to have it. And it was as good as mine, anyway. I s'pose you see, Olive, that it was as good as mine. And father never 'd listen to reason. He always treated me like a child. If he'd treated me more as if I were a man, I shouldn't have had to do some things I've done. You must see that, Olive, don't you?"

But Olive could not speak. It was all she could do to stand there and listen to the words that came quickly from Robert's lips. She wondered, dully, if it were strange that the clearest thought in her mind was the question, "Did I ever love this man?" It was not a shock to her to know that Robert had tried to steal from his father; her mind had become habituated to that fact; but she was shocked, unreasonably so, to see the picture of his inner self that his hurrying words revealed. In spite of a previous knowledge, the moment of clear revelation often delays. It had come now, however, to Olive Nawn.

For a short time she had entirely forgotten about the will; even Robert's reference to his father's words did not recall it to her. She was absorbed in thinking of what Robert really was.

"Of course, Olive, you'll promise not to let any one know from you. People might not understand that the money was as good as mine. You'll give me your word, won't you?" His anxious eyes were on hers. She felt tired and sick. She was trying still to understand herself, struggling with that hopeless problem which confronts us all many times in our lives—the problem of ourselves. "I say, Olive, you'll give me your word, won't you?"

This request at last found entrance into her mind. She withdrew her eyes from their indefinite gaze and fixed them upon her companion. But she waited a little before she spoke. It was a promise that was asked of her.

"I must say," began Robert, his temper rising, "that I should think you'd be just as interested as I am not to have that get out. Folks might not understand about it."

"They might call it burglary—or, perhaps, murder."

She spoke incisively and with apparently perfect self-possession. It was evident that Robert was mak-

ing a great effort to keep control of his temper. Olive
knew his face so well that she could read him as she
read an open book.

"Yes, I should certainly think you'd care as much as
I care to keep it dark about—about my—"

"Robberies."

"Yes ; if you've a mind to call them so."

"That's the name. But you needn't be afraid that I
shall betray you. As you say, I should wish to keep
silent. Have we anything more to say to each other?"

Robert's countenance showed his relief. He could
look at Olive with more discriminating gaze. She was
utterly beyond his reach now. But she was a grand
woman—tall, noble of aspect, in spite of her years of
hard work, and her unhappiness. And was it really
possible that she loved him no longer?—that she loved
him not the least in the world? Robert glanced forward towards the river, which could be heard sliding
along by its banks close to the two. He was uneasy,
he wanted to get away, but he was wondering if there
were anything more that should be said. He did not
mean to see Olive again. He did not wish to be so
uncomfortable as he was now. There was no need,
either. And how large was the smallest sum he could
in decency allow her? There being a boy, of course,
made it different. Perhaps he could better support
Victor by having him with him. That was a matter
which must not be decided in a hurry.

"I shall have to think about some things," he began.
"It's natural that we shouldn't want to see each other
more than is necessary. I shall continue to stay somewhere in the neighborhood until you've arranged to
leave my house. I sha'n't hurry you. I rather think I
shall make some repairs. It 'll take a lot of money,
you know."

Robert became silent, waiting to get the courage to
walk away. Olive was silent, because she was sudden-

ly dreading to say what she must say. He did not
even suspect—but how should he? And how would he
bear the truth?

"You will not need to make repairs," she began,
weakly, and then she reproved herself for her cow-
ardice.

He was gazing at her questioningly. "Why not?"

"Because," raising her head higher, and hesitating,
even now, "because the house is not yours, Robert
Nawn."

The young man involuntarily took a step forward;
then he paused.

"Not mine?"

"Not yours, Robert," in a pitying tone.

"Whose, then? But that's a lie!" fiercely.

"It's truth. It's mine. And I'm not your wife, Robert. Don't forget that. And can't we be reasonable
human beings?" hurriedly. "Listen. Your father
made a will."

"A will? I tell you it's a lie! He always declared
that he wouldn't make a will."

Fury came to the young man's eyes. He had that
futile feeling that if he denied a thing repeatedly, his
denials would somehow have effect.

"He did make a will. I thought I'd tell you."

"Tell me!" with impotent emotion.

Robert set his teeth. He must get some portion of
control of himself. He had a foolish fear that he should
go to pieces. At such moments as these he had a weak
wish that he had been taught self-command. But no
one had taught him anything. Somebody else was to
blame.

CHAPTER XLVIII

"IT'S NOT VICTOR"

OLIVE was sorry for him. She had all her life been sorry for any creature that suffered. "Yes, it's true," she began again, the impulse to comfort Robert getting stronger as she watched his face. "Your father was deceiving you when he used to say that he should not make a will. The lawyer, Mr. William Hyland, has been here. He said he would show me a copy—but I didn't look at it. He said there were only two legacies —to you and Mrs. Barlow—five thousand each. There, now you know, Robert, be a man !"

"Hold your tongue ! Curse the old miser ! I owe more than five thousand now ! I've been unlucky. But who—who—" he stammered into silence, and his eyes besought Olive. Then he cried out, "It's that brat has got it ! It's Victor ! But I'm his natural guardian. Ask your damned lawyers if I'm not."

"It's not Victor."

Olive felt that the whole world was rolling between her and the man opposite. And she was sorry for him, so sorry that her heart ached. That must be because she had once loved him. "Those never loved who say that they loved once." That sentence began to say itself over in her mind as plainly as if she were sitting calmly alone in her room.

"Who, then ? Can't you speak ? What are you holding back ? I'll break the will ! I swear I'll break the will !"

"The property is left to me."

"To you? Oh, that's good! That's first-rate! I like that!" Robert threw his head back and laughed. "But it's odd you joke about it, all the same." He was so pale that he seemed to be going to faint.

Olive had a sensation as if she had done wrong; and it was in vain that she tried to banish that sensation. "It's not a joke. It's the simple truth. Your father has left all his property to me, with the exception of the legacies I have mentioned. Go to Mr. Hyland if you wish to ask other questions. As for me, oh!" with a sudden break in her voice, "I can't stand here and talk any more!"

Olive turned and went in among the trees, hurrying forward, the low-hanging branches flapping against her face as she walked. She came to a branch which held a nest in a fork, and a little gray "chipping-bird" flew up in alarm, making its small cry of distress as it did so.

Olive paused. She recalled that Victor had told her that he and Lizzie Fuller were watching a chip's nest near this path. He had said there were four eggs in it, and she had promised to come and see the nest with him. She stood quite still, gazing down at the bits of eggs, her eyes suddenly becoming wet with blessed tears, and the nest growing vague and misty to her sight. Presently she heard the trample of retreating feet in the direction from which she had just come. That was Robert going away. She hoped that she should never see him again—never. Had he always been so small and mean? Memories came to her which made her whisper "Yes," shudderingly. Her eyes had been opened, that was all. And to have one's eyes opened sometimes brings all the misery one can bear.

When Olive reached the house her mother came to the door to meet her. "Where's Victor?" she asked, eagerly.

"He's washing his face 'n' hands at the sink.   He
came in all covered with dirt.   Ain't you late?   It's
past supper-time, and the toast is dry as a chip.   D' you
see Robert.   He's got home.   I don't see how you can
stay here, Olive, now it's his house—I declare I don't."

"Mother," said Olive, hastily.   "It isn't his house.
It's mine."

"Yours?" aghast.

"Yes.   Mr. Nawn left a will.   I'm a rich woman.
Now, if we talk any more about it to-night, I shall be
crazy.   Please get used to it.   We've got to get used
to it.   I'm going to keep on living here just now, with
Victor ; and I want you and Aunt Ruth to come and
live with me.   Let's have our supper, if it's ready.
And we'll have cream in our tea.   We'll have all the
cream we want ; and I know how you like it, mother."

The three were presently down at the table.   At in-
tervals Mrs. Newcomb laid down her knife and fork
and cried, "I declare !"   Sometimes she added, "I can't
nohow sense it."

"What can't you sense, gran'ma?" inquired Victor.

"That Olive's a rich woman."

The boy stared now.   He also laid down the spoon
with which he was eating bread and milk.   His eyes
grew rounder and bigger.   "Is that true, mammy?"
he asked.   "Are you rich?"

"I suppose so."

He caught up his spoon again and waved it in the
air.   "'Rah ! 'Rah !   Now I'll get Lizzie Fuller a pony,
can't I?   She says she'd rather have a sheltie than anything else in the whole world.   Can't I?"

Olive smiled tearfully.   "Perhaps ; we'll see.   We
must wait till things are settled."

"I can't wait.   I want to get it to-morrow," impera-
tively.

"What do you want for yourself, Victor?" inquired
Mrs. Newcomb, solicitously.

"I know! I know!" again waving his spoon, which this time held a little milk, which sprinkled itself over the table.

"Be gentle, Victor!" from his mother.

"I want a dog—a big, yellow one—big 's Lizzie's pony. I saw one at the Falls when I went with gran'pa. He said I couldn't have it, 'twould cost so much money. Whose money 've you got, mother?"

"Gran'pa's."

The boy looked, with an inquiring, puzzled gaze, from one woman to the other. He swung his feet back and forth under the table. "I thought father was going to have that. I heard him say so."

"Gran'pa gave it to me."

"Then there'll be an awful row."

"Victor!"

"There will; popper 'll make it." Victor slipped down from his chair and walked to his mother's side. He put his arm about her and stood as tall as possible. "Never mind, mammy," he said, protectively, "I'll take care of you."

Olive wished to suppress the joy she felt. Her heart dilated with love and pride, but in it all there was the poison of the fear lest Victor's winning ways should somehow make him like his father. She placed her arm over Victor's shoulders; she restrained herself from drawing him closer yet. She smiled down at his eager, upturned face.

"Perhaps we'll take care of each other," she said. "Don't you think that 'll be a good way?"

"Tip-top. But I can't eat any more supper. I'm going to find Lizzie Fuller. I shall tell her I *think* she can have a pony." And he darted out of the room.

"That's a fact," remarked Mrs. Newcomb, taking up the teapot to pour her third cup. "There will be an awful row. You think Robert 'll stan' it? He's just got rid of you by law, 'n' you've just come into a lot of

money. It must be terrible aggravatin' to him. I c'n
see that. I d' know what 'll become of us all. I can't
git used to it. You rich? I wonder what your father 'd
say. That was jest like him, when Victor, the first
thing, wanted to give away something."

Mrs. Newcomb stirred her tea rapidly; then she
sipped it absently. She pushed her spectacles to the
top of her head, and gave herself up to gazing at her
daughter. Olive was pretending to eat her supper,
and she was not succeeding notably. She supposed
that after a time her mind would clarify.

"There's one thing I do hope," began Mrs. Newcomb,
"and that is, that you won't let Robert Nawn git the
better of you in any kind of a way. Be you going to?"

"Oh, mother, I sh'll do the best I can. I'm confused
now."

"I sh'd think you would be. I sh'd think your head
'd go round like a top. Robert's reckoned on havin'
that money. He'll be ugly. It's in him. I s'pose
there's as much, mebby, as ten thousand dollars, ain't
there?"

"Eight hundred thousand, the lawyer said."

Mrs. Newcomb's cup dropped from her hand and fell
with a crash, breaking on the floor. "Why," she exclaimed at last, "I sh'd think you'd put up a real
han'some monument to Mr. Nawn in the graveyard!
Sha'n't you?"

"I don't know," rather helplessly.

"'N' I sh'd think you'd shingle the roof here; sha'n't
you?"

"Perhaps."

"'N' I certainly would have a man come 'n' dig up
them pud'n'-bag shrubs in the front yard. They're the
lonesomest things I ever did see. They jest about give
me a fit. Sha'n't you?"

"Yes, I think I will," still more helplessly. "Mother,
let's wait until—"

"'N', if I was you, Olive, I believe I'd furnish that north front room. I declare, I can't git it into my head!"

Mrs. Newcomb poured tea into another cup. She had a reckless feeling that she might break cups now, and it was of no consequence.

"Don't talk about it any more, please," from Olive.

"And I would have a dress with fashionable sleeves, Olive," went on the elder woman. "I would have one. You 'ain't looked fittin' with them old-fashioned sleeves."

"Yes, mother, I'll get one."

"'N' I sh'd think you'd—"

"Do stop, please," reiterated Olive. "I've decided upon two things I'll do, and that's as far as I've thought. I'm going to educate Victor, and I'm going to settle some money on you and Aunt Ruth; so that, whatever happens, you'll be comfortable. And you can have the very best tea in the market, mother, even if you do let the old grounds stay in the teapot and spoil the drink anyway."

Having spoken thus, Olive suddenly found it impossible to seem calm a moment longer. She laughed loudly, and then she covered her face with her hands and began to sob.

Seeing her daughter's display of emotion, Mrs. Newcomb immediately joined in with her, but more quietly, and making the remark that, in view of their tears, seemed relevant, "And old man Nawn only jest buried!"

CHAPTER XLIX

ROBERT, when he had left Olive, struck across the pastures towards a wood. The only thought in the tempest of his thoughts which he could clearly make out was the wish to be alone. But when he had gained the wood, he found that he could not stay there. He could not endure to be alone. It was impossible to believe what he had heard. The world was all turning against him. He stood near an oak-tree. He recalled the disdain he had seen in Olive's face. He struck his fist against the trunk of the tree, and he was glad to see the blood drop from his flesh. He struck it again.

"It isn't true!" he shouted. "It can't be true!"

But he knew all the time that it was perfectly true; he knew that it was like his father to do just as he had done. Yes, it was like him. Was the old man laughing somewhere at his deed? Not once had Robert suspected that this thing would happen; but now that it had happened, he knew that it was characteristic. He experienced a horrible desire to get at his father and throttle him.

Robert had come home when he saw that notice of the old man's death in the paper, because he knew immediately that that was the wisest thing to do, even though there might be some risk in it. And he was right in thinking that he was tolerably safe. He must take the risk anyway.

He walked about among the trees, making an effort to stay there by himself. But the horror of being

alone was too great. He hurried down through the
pastures and went, still across fields, to Isabel Keating's house. He hoped to find her in the garden. It
was dusk—a mild, sweet dusk that the young man
hated ; it was atrocious that the nightfall could come
mildly and sweetly.

But Isabel was not in the garden. Robert brushed
among the rose-bushes, and the syringas, and the south-
ernwood. At last he went up to the door. Isabel was
just coming along the hall, and through the screen she
saw Robert. She opened the door, and he entered silently.

The two went to the parlor. There were vines over
some of the windows, and it was almost dark there.
Robert reached forward and took the girl's hand. It
lay cold and still in his.

"You didn't come in time for the funeral," she said.

"No ; I couldn't."

"Folks thought it strange."

"Who cares if they did?"

Isabel did not reply to this. She withdrew her hand
and sat down by a window. The young man gazed at
her as well as he could through the gloom. He wished
that she had felt like greeting him with effusion. It
had begun to seem to him, for some weeks, that Isabel
did not care as much for him as she used to care. He
stood at a little distance, his eyes fixed on the dim outline of her figure. He could see the gleam of her eyes.

"You don't seem very glad to see me," he said, at last.
There was no reply to this remark. Robert felt his face
growing hot. Was she going to fail him just like all
the rest? he asked himself. He could not understand
why the world treated him so. "You know I'm free.
We can marry to-morrow, if we please." As the silence
still continued, Robert came nearer to the girl. He
bent down over her, and constrained himself to speak
gently. "Isabel, what has happened to you?"

"Nothing," with a hint of impatience in her tone.

"You know I'm free now," he repeated; then he added, slowly, "and father's dead."

"I suppose you're rich." She pronounced these words as if she were stating an undoubted fact.

"Of course it isn't known yet how much property father had," he responded.

"You may be sure he had a lot," said the girl; "and he used to say he should let it go where it naturally would go—and that's to you, Robert. Yes, you must be a very rich man."

Robert made no reply. He stooped to take Isabel's hand again, and she let him take it, though it remained cold in his grasp, as it had done a moment before.

"Why shouldn't we be married immediately," he began, with eagerness. "To-morrow. There's nothing to be gained by waiting, is there? We've been wishing for years that we might marry. Say yes to me now, Isabel."

The persuasive, sweet cadence was coming into his voice. He bent down nearer; he kissed her hair, murmuring words of endearment.

She seemed to hesitate; then she rose, walking away from him and leaning against the window-casing, where the faint light fell upon her. "I must think about it," she replied at last.

"Think about it! Haven't we been doing that long enough? Oh, Isabel, do be kind to me now! Do be reasonable!" Isabel was curiously silent and unresponsive. "Can't you speak to me?" he asked, impatiently.

"My mind is full of strange thoughts," she responded. "I don't know why it is, but, now that you are free, now that I may become your wife, I hesitate. I did not think I should hesitate. And you're rich."

"Aren't you glad of that?" Robert's mouth closed tightly after he had asked that question. She did not reply to it.

" Somehow, I'm afraid !" she exclaimed.

Robert restrained himself from stamping his foot.
He became more tender, more impassioned. The fragrant dusk, the half-seen beautiful face, the unaccountable aloofness of this girl, the fear that became every
moment stronger and stronger that, after all, he should
not win her, all inflamed the man's mind and lent him
ardor and impressiveness.

Isabel seemed to waver ; but suddenly she rose, uttering an exclamation. " I've been thinking," she said,
" for a month or two that perhaps, after all, I don't
really love you."

" Isabel !"

" Oh, I know I've had a fancy—a passion I suppose
you'd call it—for a long time for you, and knowing that
you belonged to some one else seemed to keep it alive.
But it hasn't been alive so much lately. Such things
die, you know. They don't have any enduring founda-
tion. I couldn't respect you, of course, Robert, and—
and you couldn't respect me, because I've ..t you love
me, and we planned to marry as soon as we could.
I'll own that since you've really started about the divorce I've felt more and more that I couldn't marry
you. We should be horribly unhappy. I've been in-
fatuated with you—isn't that it?—but I'm getting over
it. Why, two years ago I was ready to run away with
you, and brave everything ; and if I had done it, I
should have killed myself before this, and you'd have
been thankful to me for taking myself off. It isn't
any credit to me that I've been getting tired of you.
I'm just tired of you, that's all. If I were not, don't you
think I'd marry you, now you've got all your father's
money, too ? Not that you'll let much of it go out of
your own clutch, unless you gamble with it," with a
hard laugh. Then, instantly, in a gentler tone, " I've
been wanting to tell you something like this for several months ; but you see it was rather hard to do it."

23

It was Robert who was now silent. A thousand fiery things were flaming up to be spoken, but he could not speak them. His tongue refused. He recalled that he had sometimes fancied that Isabel seemed indifferent, and he had set the fancy aside. But the simple truth was, she had tired of him—as he had tired of Olive. Deadly tired, too, she must be, he thought, to refuse to marry him, believing him to have inherited his father's money. Again he wondered why the world treated him so.

It was of no use to try to say anything. Since words were not things which he could fling murderously, why should he use them? And his tongue refused, too. And a sinking of the heart was coming upon him. After all, Isabel did not love him. He had never thought that she did not love him. Everybody was turning against him.

"Do you really mean it?" he asked, thickly, finding some difficulty in choosing his words. "Do you mean that—what you just said—you know?"

"Yes, I mean it."

Isabel was very sorry for him, and very uncomfortable. But she was also perfectly sure that the excitement and interest of being in love with Robert Nawn were entirely over. If she had had any hope that she could resuscitate that excitement, in view of his supposed wealth, she would have made the effort.

Robert went towards the door. He stumbled against a chair; but it was so dark in the room that any one would be likely to stumble. He reached the path outside. Here he stood still. The memory of his passion for the girl he had just left came back to him piercingly. He turned and hastened into the room. Isabel was standing where he had left her. He went straight to her and took her in his arms. But she slipped away from him.

"Do you think," she cried, in a loud whisper, "that a woman can go on forever loving a man like you?"

He heard her hasten to a door, open and close it behind her. But he did not go immediately. He stood there alone. Finally he made his way, for the second time, out of the house. He walked steadily, and yet with something of the hesitating slowness of a blind man, down into the road and along it, not knowing for some time that he was going in the direction of his old home. It was a light in the kitchen, shining through the windows where the curtains were not drawn, that appealed to his dulled senses and made him say, aloud, "There's Olive—she doesn't care for me, either. And there's the boy—I don't think he cares." He went to the roadside, trampling among the wild rose-bushes and clethra until he reached the fence, upon which he leaned heavily, as one who has not strength to stand. His face was towards that light. Presently he laughed. "Why," he said, "I guess I'm an outcast." He laughed again. He clung more heavily to his support.

After about an hour the moon came up and shone upon the figure of the man clinging to the fence. It was a warm and beautiful summer evening, and when Olive had seen Victor asleep in his bed, she found that she could not sit quietly within doors. Her mother was sitting by the lamp which stood on the kitchen table. She had a newspaper in her hand and spectacles over her eyes; she was attempting to read, but often she looked up from the paper and made exclamations.

"I want to know! I am beat to think Olive's a rich woman!"

Sometimes, if Olive were in the room, she asked her how she could be so calm; as for her, she "couldn't but jest stay in her chair."

When she had remained there as long as she could, Olive rose, saying she would stroll out for a few moments.

" Why don't you go down 'n' meet Ruth? she'll be
comin' soon now.   She was goin' to stay 'n' wait 'n' see
if that man brought the groceries ; he's always awful
late."

"Yes, I will," responded Olive.   She thought that
she would like to walk by Aunt Ruth's side.   She
would tell her aunt about the will, and there would be
no confusing exclamations.   By to-morrow the news
would be all over the neighborhood.   But to-night few
knew it.   She supposed that Victor had told Lizzie
Fuller that his mother was a rich woman ; but that
might be considered a child's way of looking at things.
And to-morrow she would finish reading Mr. Nawn's
letter.

When Olive had stepped out of the house, something
of the calm sweetness of the night made itself felt upon
the attitude of her mind.   All her surprise and per-
turbation left her.   Her pulses beat gently as she paced
along the highway, avoiding the grassy side-path, for
the dew was heavy.   She wished Victor were walking
with her.   She liked to feel his hand in hers, and to
glance down at his tanned, alert face.   But she could
think of him ; she could plan the coming years for him.
Her heart began to beat faster as she did so, but she
smiled to herself as she whispered :

> "I will look out to his future ;
> I will bless it till it shine."

Then she wondered when she should meet Aunt Ruth.
And what a long day it had been !   It already seemed
as if it were days ago since she had seen Mr. Nawn
buried ; and people had continually asked, " Where is
Robert ?"

They had not asked her this question—at least, no
one but Miss Rice had done so ; but she had heard
them, and the answer, from this one and that, had been,
" Sure enough !   Ain't it odd ?"   But Robert had come

now. What would he do about the will? He could effect nothing.

Olive wished to put away from her the thought of the will. She would think of that when she must. Now the reaction from the excitement of the last few days was making itself felt. Just at this moment she was not anxious about anything. As she walked she was resting, listening to the frogs and to the soft-running Creeper. Presently she paused, hesitating, trying to decide whether she should walk down to the bridge, and thinking that she would not do so, lest she might miss Aunt Ruth when she came up the road. She gazed along the highway. The moon rose above a small pine, and its light showed a figure by the fence at a few rods' distance. Olive gazed an instant, then she said, "It's some drunken man."

It was from this direction that Aunt Ruth would come. She would walk to meet her, for Aunt Ruth might be afraid. Olive herself felt some timidity as she went on.

CHAPTER L

A NEW CARE

THE nearest dwelling was the Nawn house. Olive turned towards it for an instant, thinking she would go back. It was a very unusual thing to see a drunken man in the vicinity. If this man were not drunk, his attitude was very strange. But he was too far away, and the moonlight was a sort of glamour. And Aunt Ruth would certainly be afraid. So Olive went on with a show of courage she did not feel. She watched for the appearance of Aunt Ruth far down at the curve in the road among the birches. Perhaps that man would move. How very strangely he stood! And how foolish she was to be afraid of him!

She did not pause in her walk until she came much nearer. She was watching that curve in the road. Then she glanced up at the fence once more. Then she stopped still, gazing as if she would compel the moonlight to reveal more clearly. She meant to go on, but she could only move a few yards, when she stopped again. She forgot that she was expecting Aunt Ruth. Her face was quite white. She would have liked to call out a question, but she found that she could not. Perhaps it was the effect of the moonlight, its weird whiteness. But would the moonlight give that curious resemblance? There was nothing in the attitude that was like Robert; she could not see his face, and she could not recognize his clothes. Why, then, did she think of him? At last she was able to unloose her voice and speak his name; but he did not move and did not reply.

Olive hurried now. She pushed her way through the bushes until she reached his side. "What has happened to you?" she asked. Her voice was as cold as if she had said, "Who are you?" to a stranger.

The man slowly raised his head and turned it towards her. "Nothing." He turned back again; but in a moment he added, "If you don't know what's happened, I'm sure I can't tell you."

Olive was silent. This was Robert. Why wasn't he with Isabel Keating? Why was he standing here comfortless? Was he suffering like this because his father's money wasn't to be his? A rising contempt mingled with her pity, for she did pity him. She could do nothing. She felt like a stone, and it was dreadful to feel that way; it was wicked. She moved towards the road. He lifted his head again.

"I s'pose you're a good woman, ain't you?" he laughed. She made no reply. She stood still. "Yes, you're one of the good kind, I guess. You got 'round father. He used to be mad enough with you, but you got 'round him. You knew how. It's paid you, 'ain't it?"

"Robert, don't!"

"Yes, I will, too. Why shouldn't I? I'm not the kind that bears things dumbly. I'll bear things just as I please. There's Isabel—"

Having said this, Robert became silent. He dropped his head down again on the arms that clung to the fence.

Olive could not go on; something held her there, though her heart was hard and cold. It was a dreadful thing to her to know that she had ever loved this man—this sordid, narrow, mean, ungenerous man. Already that love seemed so far in the past as to appear unreal. What was he going to say about Isabel? Apparently nothing. The silence continued. Olive walked still farther back to the road, the wild-rose thicket which she had penetrated giving out its fragrance, its thorns wounding her.

"Are you going?" more quickly from Robert.

"Yes—since I can do nothing. Good-bye."

"How do you know you can't do anything? You needn't be jealous of Isabel any more." Olive drew herself up haughtily. Her eyes flashed. She would make no reply. She did not care what he meant. "She has sent me adrift. Everybody's cut loose from me. Everybody's down on me."

"I thought Isabel loved you," Olive spoke, in her surprise.

"She's tired of me. She has just told me so. And you've got my money, and you despise me. The world is damned hard to me—that's what it is!"

The speaker's voice had taken on a whimpering quaver. The man let go his hold on the fence and sank down among the bushes. He repeated that the world was damned hard on him, in a still lower voice. Then he was quiet, lying in a heap there.

Olive hurried back to him. She lifted his head so that the moonlight might fall on his face. The jaw hung, and the eyes were half closed. She knelt down and supported him against her shoulder. She would do what she could for him, but her heart was cold and hard. Why was it so hard? She would have said once that it would be impossible that she could become a hard woman. Had she become one? She looked down the road, eager to see Aunt Ruth. She must be coming by this time. Yes, there by the birches the small figure was walking swiftly. Olive waited until it came a little nearer, then she called, loudly, "Aunt Ruth! This way! Come quick!"

Ruth made no answering outcry; she came hurrying on towards the fence, glanced down at the face on Olive's shoulder, and said, in a low voice, "Why, it's Robert!" The next instant she asked, in the same

" ' WHY, IT'S ROBERT ! ' "

tone, "Where shall we take him? Hadn't I better go and get Mr. Jewett to come with his wagon?"

"Yes, yes. But they can't have him at the Jewett's; his wife is sick. Oh, Aunt Ruth, what shall I do? Nobody will want him." Olive's low voice was tremulous. "Perhaps he's dead now."

"No, he isn't dead," was the response from the elder woman, who hesitated perceptibly before she continued—"I don't feel to advise you, Olive. He's made you suffer terribly; but you know best what you ought to do now."

Having spoken thus, Ruth hastened along the road, and Olive watched her as she crossed the patches of moonlight in those spaces where there were no trees. She watched her until she had gone on out of sight. It would be more than a quarter of an hour before any one could come. The moments went on slowly. Olive remained almost motionless, kneeling there in the dampness. Once she heard a carriage cross the bridge—a carriage evidently drawn by two horses, for the rhythmic sound of their trotting feet came plainly on the still air; and from the carriage she heard a woman's voice and laugh. The color rose to her face and her lips compressed, for the voice and laugh were those of Isabel.

When Mr. Jewett came, bringing Aunt Ruth in his "open wagon," Olive assisted in placing that inert figure of a man on the old buffalo-robe on the bottom of the wagon; then she said, "Please drive right to the Nawn house."

Mr. Jewett had his foot on the step and the reins in his hand. He turned abruptly towards Olive and said, "What?" The request was repeated. Mr. Jewett took his foot from the step. "I vow," he began, "I wouldn't do it, Olive. He ain't wuth it. 'N' you're a mighty lucky woman to be red of him. I never seen a feller go on 's he has; 'n' he with such a wife. I vow, you think twicet 'fore you have him carried there. Mebby he's goin' to have a long sickness; you don't know. Lem me take him right to the poor-house. I tell ye, you're well red of him."

"No," with a gentle firmness, "drive to my home."

Mr. Jewett mounted the wagon. "Jes 's you say, of course," he responded, "but I can't help tellin' ye you're makin' a mistake."

So it was that Robert Nawn was laid on the bed in his old room, and the doctor was sent for, and very evidently did not know what was the matter, but felt that he was safe in saying that it was a case of general prostration, and it was uncertain how it would turn out. When the young man opened his eyes he looked stupidly at Olive, who was standing by the doctor's side.

"I suppose you'll give me over to somebody," he said, as soon as he could speak. "Everybody's against me. It paid to get round father, didn't it?" He scowled, and his glance wandered about the familiar place. "Just let me get up again, and I'll break the will." He shut his eyes, but he opened them presently to say, "I guess it's too much to ask you to take care of me, isn't it?"

"I will take care of you," was the answer.

CHAPTER LI

PEACE

OLIVE, having given her word to Robert that she would take care of him, kept it in the letter, and tried faithfully to keep it in the spirit also. She was sorry for him; she would have been sorry for any tramp for whom she was caring. But her heart did not melt with pity. She used to sit by his bed and call herself a hard, cruel woman because it did not melt. She reasoned with herself; she prayed about it. She did everything; she hardly slept, day or night; she was worn to a shadow, and her great eyes looked wildly out from her thin face. She was worn from watching, but still more from the biting remorse that she felt because she could not feel tenderness. It was of no use for her to tell herself that this man had killed all the love and tenderness she had once offered him. Her conscience smote her as she tended him. She did not expect to love him again because he was helpless and dependent, but she thought that she ought to feel a very passion of pity; and she did not. He had trampled everything out of her heart—everything, she believed, but her love for Victor. And she could hardly see Victor now, she was so absorbed. He was mostly cared for by his grandmother. Aunt Ruth helped Olive; a woman from the other side of the bridge was hired to do the housework, and a man did the barn chores.

Once, when Robert was in a heavy sleep, induced by an opiate, Olive brought the letter old Mr. Nawn had left for her, and sat down in the great chair by Rob-

ert's bed. She opened the sheets softly, her eyes running along the lines to find the place where she had
stopped reading.

She found the sentence ; it was this :

" You won't always keep on loving a man like Bob. Some day you'll
wonder if you ever did love him—where that love was there'll be just
ashes—not a live spark. I sh'll do all I can to get him to get a divorce;
he wants one. You ain't saving enough, and he's hankering for that
other woman. He thinks she's more suitable, and so do I. She'll lead
him a life, if she doesn't jilt him. I don't ask any better punishment
for him than to be her husband. He's just like his mother, only he has
a greed for money, without, as I've said a hundred times, knowing much
how to get it or keep it. Don't you give him any of yours. Remember what I say to you, keep that money away from him."

Robert stirred and moaned in his sleep. Olive folded
the paper. How the old man reiterated that his son
shouldn't have his money ! And yet—Olive rose and
walked to the window. The sumptuous summer was
glowing with life outside.

About that money — could she keep it all? She
wished to be just to Robert. When she loved him she
had never thought whether she was just to him or not
—she had given him all. This money was hers, absolutely. And Robert, she supposed, hadn't anything save
his legacy, and he owed that. That morning the doctor
had said he thought his patient " would pull through."
It was this remark of the doctor's that had roused these
thoughts in Olive's mind. She remembered that the
lawyer who had come to tell her about the will had
said that she need not consider herself bound in the
least by any advice the old man had given her. He had
made no conditions in his will. By this time everybody in the country-side knew that Olive was to have
Mr. Nawn's fortune ; and they knew that there was no
end—really no end—to her money And it would all
be Victor's, of course.

Robert fulfilled the doctor's prophecy by beginning

to gain decidedly during the next week ; and he ceased
being delirious. One day, when he lay gazing at Olive,
who was sewing by his bed, he broke the silence by
asking :

"Do you love me any now, Olive?" The woman
dropped her work, but she did not lift her eyes. "Do
you ?"

"No," was the answer.

A silence again, until at last Robert said, "And a
mighty good thing for you, too."

Olive made an effort to resume her sewing, but her
fingers were clumsy. Her patient dropped into a doze.
The next day she did not sit with him so much ; Aunt
Ruth took her place ; and the next day it was the same.
Robert was gaining perceptibly ; he began to be eager
for his food. Sitting bolstered up with pillows, he was
watching the door impatiently, but Olive did not enter.
He heard her talking with Victor in the yard ; the two
were laughing.

"Why doesn't she come in here?" he asked, discon-
tentedly.

"Do you need her for anything?" inquired Ruth's
mild voice.

He moved his head back and forth on his pillow.
"Yes," he answered, "I need her. Tell her to come
here." Ruth rose and went to the door ; she beckoned
to her niece, who came forward, the boy beside her.
She entered the room, and she gently thrust back Victor. Robert saw that movement, and he called out,
"Can't you let my boy come in here?"

"Certainly," replied Olive, and she drew Victor forward. There was always a deadly fear at her heart
when Robert mentioned his son.

Victor stood holding his mother's hand and gazing
at the face on the bed.

"I s'pose they've told you dreadful things about me,
haven't they ?" Robert asked.

The boy flushed, and he lifted his head higher. " No, they haven't, either," he answered. " Lizzie Fuller was going to tell me something once, and mother wouldn't let her."

" Is that so?" faintly from Robert, whose face grew red and then pale. His hands, lying weakly on the coverlid, began to move nervously. He gazed pleading-ly at Olive. "Can't we fix it up some way?" he asked, in a half whisper. " Don't you think we can, Olive?"

Before she spoke, the mother led her boy to the door and told him to "run along." But he hung back, hold-ing her hand and looking up at her. He reached up and pulled her down nearer.

"Mammy," he whispered, his lips touching her cheek, " I won't let him have me—I won't ! Lizzie's father said he'd be sure to try to get me. But he sha'n't ! I'd kill him first !"

" Hush ! No, he sha'n't have you. Now go." Olive returned to the bedside. She was white, and her eyes glittered.

"Victor never cared much for me," said Robert, re-gretfully. There was no reply to this remark. Olive had resumed her seat. "Don't you think you could forgive me?" asked Robert.

" I shall try to forgive you."

" Forgiveness that isn't spontaneous isn't worth much, is it?" he inquired.

" I shall do the best I can."

"Couldn't you love me a little, Olive?" The speaker reached forth a thin, beseeching hand, but his com-panion evaded the touch of it.

" My love is dead," she replied   " I can't help it—I can't help it."

Robert lay silent, his eyes fixed on Olive. This was all there was left for him, and he was trying to grasp it. He was weak, and he thought he was penitent, as perhaps he was.

"I thought women kept on loving," he said. There was no response to this. Olive was wondering if any other woman would feel so hard as she felt now. And yet she was sorry, so sorry for that man lying there. "For the boy's sake," whispered Robert. "He belongs to me, too, you know. For his sake, Olive."

"No—no." She held herself quietly in her chair. It was a terrible thing to distrust. But even if she had believed in Robert, she could never love him again, not if she lived a thousand years. He was utterly gone out of her life, so that she began to think that she had never loved him.

"You're hard," he murmured—"hard as a stone."

"I can't help it," again from Olive. She suddenly leaned forward and rested her hand on the bed. "I want to tell you," she began, speaking hurriedly, "that your father, when he was dying, tried to make me promise that I would not give you any of his money; but I would not promise. He said you should not have it. He seemed to hate you. Don't speak. But I can do as I please—the lawyer says so. There's a lot of it —enough for Victor; and, as for me—oh, it is little that I want, if I have Victor. I am going to make over a sum, a large sum, to you, Robert. I couldn't rest if I did not—I couldn't—"

The man held out both his hands—his hollow eyes sparkled. "You do love me a little, Olive!" he exclaimed.

"No—not in the least," with cold decision; "but I must give you this money or I couldn't rest. I don't know whether I'm right or not; but I've got to do it. Let me tell you now, Robert Nawn, that if you ever try to take my boy from me, I will fight you as no woman ever fought before. Do you understand me?"

"I understand." Into the large, strained eyes of the man came tears that overflowed and ran down to the pillow. "I wouldn't do it, dear—I wouldn't do it," he said, earnestly.

Then Olive leaned over and kissed Robert's forehead solemnly, as if that kiss were the seal of a compact. But, all the same, she knew that she could not trust him, that he could not trust himself.

"Oh, Olive," whispered Robert, with a touch of his old passionate tenderness, "I think I've loved you all the time!" Whereat she smiled, not mockingly, but very sadly.

Olive did not delay. She would not be convinced by Mr. Hyland's arguments and remonstrances. She always replied that she could not rest knowing that Robert was poor. At last Mr. Hyland ceased to argue. He looked at her with unconcealed admiration.

"I don't approve, Mrs. Nawn," he said. "All the same, I was afraid you would allow yourself to be turned."

The lawyer lost no time. Within the week the papers were signed that made over two hundred thousand dollars of old Nawn's beloved money to his unloved son.

Robert was sitting in a large chair by his bed. He took the papers eagerly. "How much was the whole?" he asked; and Olive, as she replied, felt somehow ashamed that she had kept so much, and she knew that Robert was looking curiously at her. Though she knew she was right, she was ashamed.

After that the invalid hurried to get well. He insisted upon going out before the doctor thought he ought. He sent for Mr. Jewett to take him over to the Falls; when the two came back it rained, and Robert was shivering when he went to bed. He had resolved upon returning, although Mr. Jewett expressed surprise. Robert said, gloomily, that nobody wanted him, which, Mr. Jewett remarked afterwards, was true. "And why should they?" he added.

The next day the fever was raging again, worse than before, and on the third day he died. At the last moment he knew Olive, and his dry, cracked lips whispered, huskily, "I do think I loved you all the time."

And now Olive did not smile. But in her heart she knew that Robert had never known anything about love. But, then, it had not been given to him to know.

In the year that followed peace came slowly—a deeper peace and joy every day. And at such times wounds heal in a wonderful manner. Olive repaired and altered the old house. To her great surprise, she found that she loved the place. She could not explain that to herself until she said, one day, suddenly, "Why, it's because Victor was born here!"

She loves to wander about with the boy. They go down to the Creeper often, and she fishes for pout and other such valuable water inhabitants. That is Victor's shriek of laughter that you hear. Olive never sees that face looking up at her from the river. That belonged to the morbid time of suffering.

Often Mr. Hyland rides over on business from the Falls. If you are the owner of several hundred thousand dollars, you will be surprised at the amount of business there is to be done. Mr. Hyland is cantering over the bridge now. At the end of it he can see, through an open space, the front of the house, which is now painted gray, and there are big columns supporting a portico. It is late fall, and a sunset is making everything brilliant.

In the midst of this brilliance, beneath the piazza-roof, stand Olive and Victor. They are both looking at the west, and neither sees Mr. Hyland, whose eyes are fixed on the woman's face.

THE END